PRAISE FOR *HIDDEN* BY CATHERINE MCKENZIE

"[A] delicate, honest exploration of secrets, family, and the varied meanings of true love…"

—*Booklist*

"Sure to please her many fans and appeal to readers who enjoy women's fiction with an element of suspense."

—*Library Journal*

"McKenzie has written a compulsively readable novel about grief and infidelity with great insight and great heart. A truly engaging read."

—HEIDI DURROW, author of *The Girl Who Fell from the Sky*

"Catherine McKenzie's latest book may be her finest. *Hidden* explores the intersecting lives of a man, his wife, and a woman who may or may not be his mistress. Imaginatively constructed, filled with nail-biting tension and gracefully written, *Hidden* is a winner."

—SARAH PEKKANEN, author of *These Girls* and *Skipping a Beat*

"What I love about this deft, intimate novel is that there are no angels or demons here, just adults—husbands, wives, mothers, fathers—leading complex, messy, very human lives. They all struggle to weigh desire against obligation, what they want against what is right. I found myself in the impossible, wonderful position of rooting for all of them—and of missing them when the book was over."

—MARISA DE LOS SANTOS, author of *Belong to Me* and *Love Walked In*

"A compelling novel that kept me turning pages at a breakneck speed. Heartbreakingly honest and real, *Hidden* is a wonderfully relatable tale."

—TRACEY GARVIS GRAVES, author of *On the Island*

"Gripping, smart, beautifully written, Catherine McKenzie's books are always a must read. *Hidden* should be at the top of your list."

—ALLIE LARKIN, author of *Stay* and *Why Can't I Be You*

"Catherine McKenzie breaks your heart in this story of two grief-stricken women mourning the same man. *Hidden*'s complex grace and page-turning sympathy left me satisfied through the very the last page."

—RANDY SUSAN MEYERS, author of *The Murderer's Daughters* and *The Comfort of Lies*

SMOKE

SMOKE

Catherine McKenzie

Published by Lake Union Publishing, Seattle

www.apub.com

Amazon, the Amazon logo, and Lake Union Publishing are trademarks of Amazon.com, Inc., or its affiliates.

ISBN-13: 9781503947214 (hardcover)
ISBN-10: 1503947211 (hardcover)

ISBN-13: 9781503945654 (paperback)
ISBN-10: 1503945650 (paperback)

Cover design by Kimberly Glyder Design

Printed in the United States of America
First edition

For my sister, Carolyn McKenzie Ring,
who goes by Cam now,
but will always be Cammy to me.

Smoke Gets in Your Eyes

Smoke. Everything about it had always meant *away* to her, so now that she was safe at home, it was a smell that didn't track.

But it was smoke she smelled—green campfire smoke—tugging at her consciousness, telling her to *wake up, wake up, wake up!*

Elizabeth's eyes opened. Ben was snoring softly beside her, out like the dead as he always was, and despite everything.

The tang of smoke was both stronger and fainter now that she was half-awake, and she wasn't sure if she'd dreamt it. She knew she should get up to check, but she hesitated, like you do in the middle of the night when you think you might have left the oven on.

I should get up, you think, but maybe it's nothing. I can fall back to sleep, take up my dream where I left off.

But no.

Something was on fire.

Something close, or something big.

Elizabeth's feet hit the cold floor. She shivered through the pajamas she'd put on after she and Ben had finally decided they'd said enough for the night and climbed wearily into bed.

She followed the scent through the house, stopping to check that the smoke detectors were working. They were. They should be; she checked the batteries religiously with the change of season. She felt herself relax and then tense again. The fire wasn't in the house, but it had to be close.

She stopped at the window at the end of the upstairs hall, scanning the horizon of jagged mountains until she saw it: a stack of smoke and heat wavering in the moonlight, racing up into the night, obscuring the stars.

She did a quick mental calculation as to distance and size, a computation she'd performed what felt like a thousand times before, and then went to wake Ben.

"Wake up," she said, shaking his shoulder harder than she needed to. "There's a fire."

DAY ONE

From: Nelson County Emergency Services
Date: Tues, Sept. 2 at 2:32 A.M.
To: Undisclosed recipients
Re: Cooper Basin Fire Advisory

A fast-spreading ground fire has started
at the edge of the Cooper Basin. Housing
structures are threatened. Responding crews
are clearing the area. Nelson County has
issued an evacuation advisory for the entire
Cooper Basin, and the area of West Nelson
bounded by Oxford and Stephen Streets.
Residents are advised to pack important
papers and personal items and be ready to
leave on short notice.

A temporary shelter is being established at
Nelson Elementary. Classes are suspended for
the day, and parents are asked to keep their
children away from the school. Parents will
be contacted directly by the administration
regarding the resumption of studies and their
location.

More information is available at
www.nelsoncountyemergencyservices.com.

Further advisories will be issued as
necessary.

CHAPTER I

Houseguests

Elizabeth

We have a fight—Ben and I—about where to go.

In fact, first we have a fight about whether we have to go anywhere at all.

"You're freaking out for nothing," Ben says when he's shaken the sleep from his brain and understands that the fire isn't in the house but I want to leave anyway.

"We're in the evacuation area."

I show him the e-mail I received from the county's emergency services unit, my phone's glow creating a halo around his face.

He reads it, slowly, meticulously. Doubting me, I can't help but think, even when it's clearly within my area of expertise.

"We're in the evacuation *advisory* area," he says as he hands me back the phone.

He's right, but I know how quickly things can change, particularly in a year like this.

Look at how things have changed between us.

"Right," I say. "As in, you'd be well advised to skedaddle before it's too late."

"It's the middle of the night."

"As if the fire cares what time it is? Please, Ben, will you . . . will you just this once let me have my way?"

"What's that supposed to mean?"

I don't answer him. Instead, I start pulling clothes from the clean laundry basket where they've been sitting for days, neither of us taking responsibility. We've had this kind of standoff about a lot of things lately, communicating through the things not done, the words not said, our inaction as loud and grating as an unfixed faucet's slow drip.

"Elizabeth? Hello?"

I shove the clothes into the backpack I use for my running stuff.

"I'm going. You want to stay? Fine. But I'm going."

"Okay, okay. I'll come. All right? I'm coming."

I add some of his clothes to the bag. It smells faintly of sweat, but that probably isn't the most important thing right now.

Ben shuffles to the dresser and puts on a pair of jeans and a sweatshirt. In the bathroom, he collects our toiletries, grabbing my face cream when I remind him.

We work silently for the next ten minutes, gathering laptops, closing windows, unplugging appliances. It's only when we're standing in the doorway, me balancing the plastic crate where I keep our in-case-of-emergency papers against my hip, that the obvious strikes us.

"Where are we going?" we ask simultaneously, then smile at one another the way we always do when we say the same thing in unison, though that almost never happens anymore.

"My parents' place," Ben answers.

"But—" I stop myself from saying what should be another thing that doesn't have to be said.

We can't go to your parents.

We're getting divorced.

This is what we decided, earlier that night, before we agreed to go to bed because we were too exhausted and too sad to talk about it anymore. Besides, having arrived at the big decision—*divorce*—what did the rest of it matter, really? I didn't care who got what piece of furniture, and though Ben might have had an opinion, he still cared enough about me to acquiesce to my "Enough" and agree that we should both get some sleep if we could.

We are getting divorced.

After ten years of marriage, and six years together before that.

Divorced.

I still can't believe it, even though I was the first to say the word, maybe the first to think it. When I'd allowed myself to ponder it before—during the worst hours of the last few months, in the moments when I'd think, *I can't take this anymore, I can't, I can't*—I was sure that if I finally worked up the courage to say it, to ask for it, I'd feel relieved.

But I don't feel that way. If anything, I feel worse. Like I *really* can't take it anymore, only I'm not sure what it is I can't take.

So we can't go to Ben's parents' house.

We can't.

But we do.

Ben's parents live in a ridiculously large house three miles south of town.

The town of Nelson—regular population: 23,194; tourist population: 100,000, depending on how the economy's going—sits in a bowl surrounded by a series of craggy, snow-covered mountains that form part of the northern Rockies. Before tourism got big, the town's main income came from the vast cattle ranches that filled the valley. These ranches have all but closed down now, and the land's become home to Nelson's wealthiest residents. Ben's parents' house rests on the edge of a thousand acres that used to hold ten thousand head of cattle. Now it's an excuse for my father-in-law, Gordon, to call himself a gentleman rancher.

But that isn't being fair to him, really. Because he is a gentleman, one of the gentlest I've ever met, and I love him, I do. I love Ben's whole family—his reserved mother, Grace; his awkward little sister, Ashley; his uptight, middle-child brother, Kevin. And though they might have more money than is right or fair, life isn't right or fair. If anyone deserves to have this much money, they are those people.

But their house is ridiculously large. It really is.

As we sit in our car, parked in front of the Ridiculously Large House, we have another argument about whether we should use Ben's key to the guest wing and camp out in one of the spare bedrooms until morning, or wake his parents and tell them we're here. Ben wants to let them rest, but I don't think that's right.

"The alarm's probably on," I say, reminding him of something I don't need to, which is something I hate about myself but don't seem to be able to change. "What if we set it off? Do you want your mother to have another heart attack?"

"Of course not. Jesus. Okay, okay, we'll do it your way."

I put my hand on his arm. "I'm sorry. This is really hard for me. I don't know—" I swallow a sob as I look toward the window, focusing on the side-view mirror, the slightly-closer-than-it-appears night.

"I know," Ben says, his own voice tight. "Me too."

"Do you hate me now?"

"No."

"Not even a little bit?"

He takes my hand and folds his fingers into mine. "Not one little drop."

I turn toward him. "I don't see how that's possible. You must at least be angry."

"I'm not."

He gives me a sad smile, and my heart breaks all over again.

"We should go in," he says eventually. "Get some sleep."

We climb out of the car, and I sling the backpack over my shoulders like I used to do in my school days. We stand facing the house, each waiting for the other to make the next move. The high-pitched rasp of grasshoppers fills our silence.

"I'll go in first," Ben says. "Give me a few minutes."

"You're not going to—"

"Tell them? No."

"Promise?"

"I said I wouldn't."

I watch his back as he walks into the circle of light cast by the front porch lamps. A firefly blinks on and off, on and off, along the roofline. The smoke is fainter here, miles away from the fire. It's only one of the night smells keeping me company, along with the aspens and the sagebrush.

Inside the house, lights turn on like dominoes. My stomach clenches, tight with worry. While I mostly believe Ben will keep his word, that he won't bring our bad news into his parents' house, not tonight, I can't be completely sure of what he'll do anymore. Waiting here, counting out the seconds like a child playing hide-and-seek, feeling the weight of the pack on my back, it feels like too many *Mississippi*s have slipped by for Ben to simply be telling them about the fire.

And so, when Ben's mother opens the front door and walks through the dew-laden grass in her bare feet to pull me against her breast in an uncharacteristic gesture of welcome, I do what I almost never do.

I cry.

CHAPTER 2

Ring of Fire

Elizabeth

I wake in the grayish dark from a fitful sleep.

I spent the short night searching for a comfortable position in Ben's childhood bed. It's big enough for two—his parents didn't believe in the traditional twin bed—but I can't get the fire out of my mind. I check my phone (my hand cupped over the screen so its cast-off light doesn't wake Ben) to see if there are any new updates, if the evacuation advisory's been lifted, if my home is going to end up being as lost as my marriage.

Part of me still can't believe it. A fire. *A fire*. Here. In Nelson. Where I came, two years ago, to finally put them behind me.

I worked wildland fires for twelve years, every fire season since I was twenty-four years old. I started out on a hand crew, worked my way up to squad boss, and then became the arson investigator for the regional fire district. From May to September, till the temperatures dropped and the snow flew in the mountains, that's what I did, that's what I was. Even in the off-season, if a fire broke out somewhere and they needed the extra manpower, I'd go where I was asked.

Ben would say: "Anywhere but here."

I caught the fire bug working a summer job as a lookout in the southwest part of Oregon after my sophomore year in college. My friend Susan had been doing it for a couple of summers, and when she had to bail because of a case of appendicitis, I jumped at the chance to replace her. It's funny to think about it now, but several months alone in the wilderness seemed like a good idea then. My best friend had died in a car accident six months before, and I'd broken up with my first serious college boyfriend. I guess I felt like I needed to get away from everything. An obsession with Jack Kerouac—who'd worked as a fire lookout for sixty-three days at Desolation Peak—might've also added fuel to my fire, so to speak.

In the second week of June, I hiked through the woods with enough supplies on my back to keep me fed until a food delivery arrived two weeks later. I took up residence in a tower that gave a breathtaking 360-degree view of the most beautiful forest I'd ever been in. I stayed there for sixty-five days (take that, Kerouac), and I watched. I waited. I cried and I read and I laughed, and when the summer was over, I felt whole again. I signed up for another summer and, though I'd met Ben by then, another after that. At the end of my third summer, I realized I wanted to be closer to the action—not just spot the trail of smoke from a distance but get to know it, feel its heat, fight it, conquer it.

So I trained and studied and got strong. When I was ready, I went where the fires were. I spent a lot of time away from Ben. Eventually, it felt as if I'd spent most of my life waiting. Waiting to get back to him. Waiting to start the family we'd always wanted, to have a job I loved *and* a marriage. Waiting till the air warmed up and the snowmelt ran into the creek beds. Waiting for that first bolt of lightning or careless cigarette to set off a telltale white plume above the horizon.

Waiting for a fire to spark.

I was so sick of waiting.

But now all I can do is wait for morning to come.

I slip out of bed quietly at daybreak. I put on a pair of jeans and a warm fleece as armor against the morning chill. It's only September 2, the day after Labor Day, and it feels like winter is going to show up early, a welcome relief from our kiln-baked summer.

In the bathroom, I run a brush through the tangles of my shoulder-length red hair, noticing the dark smudges a sleepless night always leaves under my pale-green eyes. The makeup lights around the mirror glint off the gray hairs I haven't bothered to cover up yet.

Back in the bedroom, I write Ben a quick note on a piece of paper I find on his desk and leave it on the indentation my head made in my pillow. He's breathing easy as I close the door gently behind me.

I leave by a side door, careful to unman the alarm first, and then I'm behind the wheel of my car, a beat-up blue Subaru Outback, driving toward what anyone in their right mind would drive away from.

As I bump along the dirt road, I run into the smoke that's already started to spread out and settle into the valley. The acrid tang stings my nose, making it itch.

In town, there's a ghostly quiet along Main Street that I haven't seen in the longest time, maybe ever. Certainly not in the summer, when the tourists stomp along the wood-plank sidewalks and linger in the overpriced art stores and T-shirt shops. The town's pretty without all the people in it. I used to know that. How could I forget?

I take the ring road around the base of Nelson Peak, and a mile north of town, I'm stopped as I approach the perimeter that's been set up by the fire crews. It's made up of fire trucks, utility vehicles, and the first of what I know will be an eventual forest of white trailers if they don't get this thing under control soon.

I flash my badge at one of the patrollers from the sheriff's office. I should've given it back when I retired, but I held on to it. One of many things I should've let go, but couldn't quite bring myself to.

"Just want to get a look and do an assessment," I say to the uniform. He nods and pulls the tape aside.

As I drive past him, the hairs on the back of my neck stand up in protest. Coming out here was a bad idea. In fact, keeping any ties with the life I was trying to leave behind was a mistake. If I'd cut the cord entirely, maybe I wouldn't be here, two years later, no baby, almost no marriage, driving backward in time.

A cliché. A fucking cliché. Maybe that's everyone's life; I can't tell. But I'm starting to feel as if my old life followed me here, like it missed me and couldn't stay away.

I park my car with its nose pointed toward the fire and watch the beehive of activity. The yellow hoses heavy with water and fire retardant. The flash of axes and the whirring chain saws. A hand crew is working to keep the fire that's still licking at the husk of what was once a house from spreading to its neighbors. The crew boss is barking orders into his radio. I can almost hear what he's saying through the helmet I'm not wearing.

Someone taps the glass next to me. I unwind my window, letting the past roll in.

"Hey, Beth," Andy says, his face crinkling with pleasure despite the circumstances. "You here to work the fire?"

Nelson Elementary is where we would've sent our kids.

I try not to think about that as I pull into the school's half-full parking lot an hour later. Thinking like that is beating myself up. And though I feel like I deserve a beating sometimes—a metaphorical one, anyway—I need to stop administering them to myself.

I've never been inside the building before, but it feels like my own elementary school did, only smaller. As if I'm Alice in Wonderland

and I've taken the pill that makes you grow larger. Even my feet feel too big as they slap against the tiled floor.

I follow the hastily made paper signs to the principal's office, where the incident commander has set up the command center. Like an air traffic controller, the IC's the hub through which commands and information flow to the field operations. Doesn't matter how good your crews are or whether you have the latest equipment, if your IC doesn't cut it, the fire isn't going to be contained.

Her right-hand man, the operations center dispatcher, is sitting in front of a bank of computer screens. I don't recognize the OCD, but the IC's an old friend.

Kara Panjabi gave me my first crew job, and she's been watching out for me ever since. Fifty-five, her perpetual smiles have creased deep lines into her light-brown face. She might seem soft on the outside, but she can out-bench-press many of the men on her crews, a feat she's often asked to demonstrate at camp events, in the down moments.

' We may have had some words when I told her I was leaving, but that doesn't mean she isn't happy to see me now.

"Elizabeth! I wondered when you would arrive."

We hug. She smells like balsa wood and citronella and, always underneath that, smoke. It's a fragrance that works its way into your skin, your hair, and even now, two years away from it, I still catch its scent clinging to me every once in a while, like a lover who doesn't want to let go.

She releases me. "You do not call, you do not write."

"I've been . . . busy," I say, ducking away.

"You've been out to the site?"

"Before I came here."

"Andy is there, yes?"

Andy's the one who told me where to find Kara.

"Stop it."

"Stop what, exactly?"

"Using your creepy ESP skills on me."

Kara comes from a long line of fortune-telling mystics. She claims not to believe in "all that nonsense," but that doesn't mean she isn't above using the keen powers of observation she learned at her *dadi*'s knee.

"You say that because you are envious."

"Probably."

We grin at each other. Then Kara's eyes do a quick up and down, landing on my stomach. I cover it reflexively.

"I'm not . . ."

"No? I'm sorry to hear that."

I turn toward the computer monitors. They're showing the live feed from the cameras that were already set up in the area, as well as from the crew's helmet cams.

"The helmet cams are new," I say, after I figure out what the unfamiliar view must be.

"Something we're trying out. I'm not sure about them yet."

My eyes go from screen to screen. Black-and-white images of flames and smoke and crew. "It's jumpy. Hard to follow."

"Agreed."

"What's your take?"

"Why don't you tell me?"

I look to the map of the area that's been tacked to the wall above the monitors. There's a red *X* marking the spot where the fire began, on the plain at the northeastern base of Nelson Peak where the Cooper Basin housing development is. Nelson Peak's south side faces the town proper and contains the town ski hill. In the summer, there are trails to hike, run, and bike on. Tourists ride horses up the winding paths, and the town rec center sits at its base. My own house is on its western slope. Nelson Peak is literally the heart of this town, and from what I'm seeing, it's a heart that's going to need a triple bypass to survive.

"It's going to spread quickly after the summer we've had," I say. "And the terrain's going to be tough when you push it into the hillside."

"We've got to push it there, though."

"Yes. Structures first."

"Structures first."

Kara goes to speak to the dispatcher, transmitting orders to the crews to start directing the fire away from the houses and up the backside of the mountain if it can't be contained. Her next call will be to bring in additional crews, those better equipped to fight on hard terrain. The ultimate goal will be to build a line that can contain the fire so it can be suppressed, but a lot of fuel is going to be eaten up before that happens. And dollars too.

A squat woman enters the room holding a megaphone under her arm. She has a tweedy look about her, like she should be out calling the hounds before a hunt.

"Ms. Punjab," she says through her teeth.

"It's Panjabi," I say. "Who are you?"

She doesn't acknowledge me. "I have a school to run," she says to Kara. "When will I be getting my office back?"

"Impossible to say, Ms. Fletcher. My best estimate at this point is a week."

"A week! But the fire's barely spread."

Kara taps her finger on the top of one of the computer screens. It's showing a weather map, which I can read like a book after so many years of practice—days and days of hot, dry, and windy weather are on the way.

"Bad fire weather coming."

"What does that mean?"

Kara purses her lips. "Things are going to get a lot worse before they get better."

COOPER BASIN FIRE
Local Resident Loses Everything in Minutes

POSTED: Tuesday, September 2, 8:02 AM
By: Joshua Wicks, *Nelson Daily*

A fast-moving ground fire started on the western edge of the Cooper Basin housing development around 1:30 a.m. Tuesday morning. It is still burning. First responders were called to the scene after a resident smelled smoke and called 911.

An evacuation advisory is in effect for the Cooper Basin and the area of West Nelson bounded by Oxford and Stephen Streets. A map of the evacuation area can be found on the *Daily*'s website, www.nelsondaily .com.

Nelson County Emergency Services advise residents to collect their important papers and any portable valuables and be ready to evacuate. While the fire is spreading rapidly, the town of Nelson proper and residents who live outside the evacuation area "have nothing to worry about," said Sheriff Dwayne Thompson. "We've got the best people working on getting the fire under control, and we have every confidence that it will be contained soon."

Although firefighters arrived within minutes of the 911 call, it was too late to save the home of John Phillips, 67.

"I've lost everything," Phillips said. "I didn't even have time to take my clothes or photos or nothing."

Phillips was unaware of the fire until woken by the smoke filling his house.

"My bedroom's on the second floor," Phillips said while being treated for minor smoke inhalation by an EMT. "I knew right away it was bad and lit out the window."

Phillips, whose wife died two years ago, said he was lucky his window was open and that "it gives out above the front porch. I kind of hung off the trellis and let go. Never been so scared in all my life."

It's too early to say what started the fire, Sheriff Thompson said, but there was no lightning in the area last night so a human cause is likely.

"We've handed over responsibility for the fire to the county services, and we'll be conducting our own investigation as well to determine whether it was arson or human carelessness," he said. "Due to the dry conditions we experienced this summer, well-publicized fire warnings have been in place for months. If anyone is found to have committed a violation, they will be prosecuted to the full extent of the law."

Authorities are encouraging residents to sign up for emergency service alerts via text or e-mail if they have not done so already. More information can be found at www.nelsoncountyemergencyservices.com.

CHAPTER 3

Rise and Shine

Mindy

Living on the far east side of town, Mindy Mitchell didn't hear about the fire until pretty late in the day, all things considered.

It wasn't her fault, wasn't that she didn't care about such things (of course she did), but she was finding it harder and harder to keep up with the world these days. The world outside her family, that is.

It was almost funny, really. She always thought that when her kids were older (Angus was sixteen now, and as tall as his father; Carrie fourteen, with the graceful poise of a dancer, the only trace of her traumatic, hole-in-the-heart beginning being a thin scar along her breastbone), she'd have time for herself again. For her interests, whatever those were these days. But instead, her kids' lives seemed to take up more space now than when they were helpless infants.

Writing club, ballet class, the annual food drive—all of that was on today's list of things Mindy was supposed to help make happen. Time to put her feet up, or to read a book, or for anything else, for that matter, never seemed to make it onto the list.

Her husband, Peter, didn't seem to have this problem. There he was, sitting across from her at the breakfast table, popping fruit into his mouth while he flicked through the *New York Times* on his iPad. Of course, he *was* an involved father. At least compared with some of her friends' husbands, who referred to looking after their own children as "babysitting" and who called in their mothers the moment their wives were out of the house. Peter knew the names of their kids' friends. He made it to at least half of their various sports activities. When they were sick, he was sometimes the one who stayed home with them (back when he and Mindy were both working). But he'd been made a manager at the bank, and she'd lost her job at the high school science lab when its budget got slashed, and so, now, her domain was entirely domestic.

She never thought she'd end up like this, one of those women who stayed home, who fretted over the caloric content of her kids' meals, who planned menus weeks in advance. *Not that there was anything wrong with that.* (Mindy was always quick to amend her thoughts, as if the women who were perfectly content doing these things might hear them and feel judged.) She'd just had other plans. She spent eight years studying cell biology in what felt like another lifetime. She was supposed to be curing cancer by now.

Instead, she found herself helicoptering over her kids, as if her constant attention could keep them safe, although she already knew it couldn't.

Mornings were spent making sure Angus and Carrie ate something, put their plates in the dishwasher, were wearing acceptable clothing, had their homework and the right sports equipment, and got into Peter's SUV so he could drop them at school on time. That morning, like too many lately, had also involved prying Angus out of bed and almost physically pushing him into the shower. She didn't like to think about what the lingering smell in his room meant, telling herself that she too had experimented in high school.

And so, it was almost nine when she opened her e-mail and saw the alert from the county's emergency services unit.

Seeing it there in her inbox, nestled innocently between an e-mail from her sister and some spam that had gotten past her junk mail settings, made her heart speed up until rationality kicked in. Surely if there were any *real* danger, the town would have done more than send an e-mail.

And yes, the home page of the local paper, the *Nelson Daily*, confirmed it; the fire was spreading up the north side of the Peak, eating through the timber like it was firewood, but the town itself was safe. For now. Residents should, however, remain on "high alert."

Mindy felt as if she'd spent the last fourteen years on high alert, ever since Carrie had suddenly turned blue at eight weeks, and it was only because they lived next door to an EMT that she'd come through it without permanent brain damage, or at all. Mindy hated this feeling, but she'd also gotten used to it. Most of the time, it simply felt like a part of her, one she didn't know how to amend or remove.

Mindy shook these thoughts away and leaned toward her screen. She wasn't wearing those new glasses her doctor had prescribed, the ones whose very name made her feel old, and the images were blurry. She moved forward and back until the words came into focus. The picture above the feature was of a man in his late sixties sitting on the lip of an ambulance, a red blanket around his shoulders, gazing at the smoking ruins of his house.

"Local Resident Loses Everything in Minutes," read the headline.

And already an idea was forming in Mindy's mind.

As Mindy struggled through her spin class an hour later, her thoughts were fixed on that image. John Phillips, the paper said his name was. Wife dead two years ago. Lost everything he had.

"And up!" screamed the instructor, Lindsay, who taught the class as if she was training the thirty- to fortysomething women who attended it for armed combat.

Forty-four-year-old Mindy raised her butt from the saddle. Rivers of sweat were running down her face, which she knew was the point, but she always wished she didn't look as if she were about to have a heart attack every time she exercised.

She was pretty sure she'd never seen John Phillips before, despite living in Nelson for over a decade. She was always surprised by how, in a place that had fewer than twenty-five thousand people in it, she would come across folks she'd never even heard of all the time. And not only people who'd just moved there. No, people like John, who'd lived in Nelson all their lives. How could he not at least look somewhat familiar?

But that was probably because there were so many towns nestled into Nelson, like those Russian dolls that lived one inside the other. On the outside were the "real" Nelsoners, who could trace their families back two generations at least. Then came the rich, both old money and new—though that created divides too. And then the Sportiva Crowd, as her friend Kate called them—young men and women who were attracted to the place because of the great outdoors, and who all looked like they'd stepped out of some Nike+ ad—tall, taut, and clear-eyed.

There was a middle class too of course; she and Peter were part of it. But it always felt to Mindy like they were rubbing up against something, as if the two halves of their doll hadn't been machined properly and could never quite match up.

"Sit two minutes!" Lindsay screamed.

She didn't seem to be sweating, Mindy noticed, which really wasn't fair.

"Did you read about that guy who lost his house in the fire?" Kate Bourne asked Mindy, talking out of the side of her mouth so Lindsay wouldn't see.

Talking was strictly forbidden in class, and even Kate was a little scared of Lindsay, who'd actually tossed a few offenders from the class permanently a few weeks back.

"I was just thinking about that," Mindy panted back as she pushed the strands of dirty-blonde hair that had escaped her pony-tail away from her eyes.

She had been coming to this class for a year now, when Kate first invited her, but it never seemed to get any easier. Nor had she experienced the benefits Kate had promised (toned thighs, a butt that didn't sag so much, losing the fifteen pounds she never lost after Angus, and the other ten she never lost after Carrie). But Mindy knew better than to complain about that to Kate. "If you really worked at it, you'd see the benefits," she'd say, and Mindy would feel worse about herself than she already did.

"It's so sad," Kate said, pedaling smoothly to the beat of the salsa music Lindsay played to motivate them.

Kate didn't seem to be sweating much either, Mindy noted. But, then again, Kate was one of those women who always seemed to look put together, no matter what the circumstances.

"It is," Mindy said. "I was thinking—"

"How many times do I have to say it? NO TALKING!" Lindsay's voice sounded as if it had been amplified by a megaphone.

Mindy looked at the ground, wondering if it was possible for her face to get any redder. Or whether there was any way she could quit spinning class without it causing a crisis with Kate. After coming to the conclusion that neither was possible, she spent the rest of the hour focusing on her pale legs as they pushed the pedals up and down.

Her feet kept spinning, but she couldn't get John out of her mind.

"So what were you saying in there?" Kate asked as they peeled their wet clothes from their bodies. Kate's black hair was pulled back in a perfect ponytail, the ends perfectly even, and the slight redness in her cheeks made her green eyes glow bright like a cat's.

Mindy looked away. Maybe it was because she had twenty pounds on Kate (at least), but she never felt comfortable stripping naked in front of other women. There was something about it that reminded her of the humiliation she'd endured in her high school locker room. If she was being honest, that's how she still felt. Like her body was something that had to be hidden away, a secret she had to keep.

"About Mr. Phillips?"

"You mean Fire Guy?"

Mindy bit the inside of her cheek. Kate was always doing this, classifying people by a defining characteristic. On one level, it made it easier for her to talk about people openly. (Who but Kate's closest friends would know that Bad Hair Mom was really the mayor's wife, who did, admittedly, have bad hair?) But Mindy couldn't help but wonder what Kate's name for *her* was, when she wasn't around. Hole-in-the-Heart Mom, probably, though most of her would rather not know.

"Yes," Mindy said. "That's his name. John Phillips. His wife died two years ago."

"Right. I read the article."

"Anyway, I was thinking, maybe we could do a fund-raiser or something? You know, like the Fall Fling, only it would be for him? So he could buy a new house?"

And there was another thing—when Mindy was around Kate, she lost the ability to speak in declarative sentences. She was just one big question.

Kate let her towel drop to the floor as she stepped into her barely-there underwear. Mindy could never tell whether Kate just didn't care or was showing off her fit and tanned body.

"Mmm. What do you think, Bit?"

Bit—Betsy—Loman was another member of the Spinners' Club, as Kate called them, a subset of the Coffee Boosters, the group of twenty or so women that Kate ran herd over. Mindy had known most of them for years, mainly through her kids, but had only started hanging out with them regularly about a year ago, after The Falling Out, as Kate would call it.

"I think it's a . . . great idea?" Bit said as she watched Kate's face to register her reaction.

Bit always wanted to please everyone. Even Mindy felt full of self-esteem when she was around Bit.

Kate nodded. "In fact, we should just turn the Fall Fling into a fund-raiser for Fire Guy. It's not like the hockey club really needs the support."

Bit colored and went silent.

"Maybe we could split the money?" Mindy said, worriedly. "Didn't we raise a hundred thousand dollars last year?"

"Don't be silly, Min. What's a hundred thousand going to buy you in this town?"

CHAPTER 4

Private Eye

Elizabeth

The first time Ben brought me to Nelson, I couldn't stop staring at the view. It was everywhere, that heart-stopping beauty of snow-covered hills and bluebird skies. Even though it was winter, and terribly cold, I felt the damp bone chill of my native Ottawa lift. *This is what winter is supposed to be like*, I remember thinking. *This is a place where I could live.*

And that's exactly what Ben asked me to do four days later, after we'd skinned our way up one of the smaller peaks and were resting on a sunny rock before taking our powder run down. Live with him. In this town. Be his forever.

It had, up to that point, been a rocky four days. Though I knew Ben came from money, and I'd met his parents in other settings, it was an adjustment seeing that money up close.

Being inside the money.

It wasn't just his parents' Ridiculously Large House. Or the fact that his sister, Ashley, actually wore pink Polo shirts and kneesocks, like something out of *The Official Preppy Handbook*, which had been a joke in my high school, something to consult at Halloween. I hadn't grown up in a hovel, and I knew which fork to use with which course, but everything around me seemed so antiseptic.

Every corner tucked, every meal restaurant quality and prepared by the staff—the *staff!* If *Downton Abbey* had existed then, I would've felt like I was caught in one of its episodes, that I was the crass Canadian visiting my very proper relatives, and it was only a matter of time before I—gasp!—served myself from the wrong side of the platter.

The only place that felt anything like home was Ben's room. It had been professionally decorated, sure, but Ben had covered over the handprinted wallpaper with posters of his favorite book and album covers: *Nineteen Eighty-Four, The Dark Side of the Moon, The Outsiders.* The posters themselves were kind of magical—they looked more like paintings—and when I got up close to them, I realized that's exactly what they were.

"Where did you get these?" I asked.

"Oh, I, um . . . I did those."

"You paint?"

Ben ducked his head, looking for something in one of his desk drawers.

"I used to."

"Why'd you give it up?"

"Because I'm not any good."

"Have you looked at these? They're perfect."

He turned toward me with something hidden behind his back.

"I can copy. If you know of any art-theft rings that need a good forger, I'm your man."

"But surely if you can do this, you can paint other things?"

"If I'm not working from someone else's piece, I might as well be drawing stick figures."

"That's . . ."

"Pathetic?"

"No, of course not."

He grinned. "Don't worry. I'm over it. Besides, Grace and Gordon would freak if I told them I was going the starving-artist route."

"Have you told them you've decided to go the starving-teacher's route instead?"

"I thought I'd leave that till the last minute."

"Mmm. Say, what've you got behind your back, there?"

"Oh, this?" He pulled his hand out in a magician's now-you-see-it-now-you-don't move to reveal a baggie half-full of hash. "You think this stuff's still good?"

"Only one way to find out."

So we went out to the back of the property and got stoned while sitting in a snowbank, then giggled our way through another proper dinner like teenagers. Three days later, when we were resting on that mountaintop, breathing in the thin air, our hearts racing from the altitude and effort, and Ben put his hand behind his back again, I laughed.

"Is this really the place?"

"I thought it might be the perfect place, actually."

I was about to protest, to say that we still had a tricky descent to do, and there was the risk of avalanche—

Then Ben was on one knee in the snow, and the hand behind his back held a small velvet box. He told me that he knew he wasn't going to be able to offer me all that his parents had, but he loved me with his whole heart.

"Will you be my wife?" he asked.

And every part of me shouted *yes*.

Between my fire-site diversion and my reunion with Kara, I end up getting to the office way late, which is sure to piss off my boss, Rich Parker, the town's prosecuting attorney. He was elected to the position three years ago, after serving as deputy to the previous prosecutor for most of his career. Rich's latest deputy—a kid fresh out of law school who'd read *To Kill a Mockingbird* one too many times—quit a few weeks ago, so it's just me and Rich and Rich's assistant, Judy, in the office.

We work in a small building across the town square from the courthouse. I'm Rich's private investigator. I'd taken an investigator course years ago as part of my arson training, and when I quit fighting fires, it seemed like a natural fit, though I didn't have any real idea what the job would entail. I guess I had vague notions of unraveling mysteries—corporate frauds or missing-persons cases, with maybe a murder thrown in there every once in a while to keep things interesting. Not that there'd been a murder in Nelson in twenty-five years, which was obviously a good thing.

"We mostly get domestics here," Rich had said, propping his cowboy boots up on his desk, his chair at a precarious angle. Those boots were his only concession to his good-ol'-boy upbringing. From the knees up, he cultivated a bigger-city look: pinstriped three-piece suits, mostly, whatever the weather, with conservative ties knotted with a full Windsor.

"Domestics?" I'd said, nervously wondering if the summer dress I'd chosen for the interview was a misstep. My usual work clothes were fire retardant. The dress was the closest thing I had to office attire.

He looked at me like he was pretty sure I was one of the stupider people he'd met. He had a few wisps of gray hair he combed across his head; the rest of it was a close-cut monk's cowl. His eyes were an indiscriminate brown.

"Domestic violence. You *did* say you were trained, yes?"

"Yes, of course. I wasn't thinking. Sorry."

He rested his head back on his chair like he wished he had a ten-gallon hat to tip back.

"Domestics, drunks, a couple meth labs. That's the usual."

"And what would I be doing?"

"Evidence gathering, mostly."

"Isn't that the police's job?"

"You'd think. But no. There are fifteen guys in the whole department, and only one of them is detective grade besides the chief, and he's too busy running the place. The deputies do the basic legwork, but if we end up taking something to trial, we need more than they can provide." He swung his legs forward and leaned toward me. "I like to win. Do you like to win, Elizabeth?"

"Of course. Who doesn't like to win?"

He took me on, mostly, I think, because there weren't any other candidates. The work was usually pretty basic: skip-traces and property searches and canvassing witnesses for the way-too-many "domestics" that happened in this town, especially on Friday nights. There had been one murder since I'd arrived—I couldn't help wondering whether my morbid assumption about the job was to blame—but the guy confessed tearfully within minutes of being picked up.

Another domestic, gone terribly wrong.

I ended up liking the routine more than I thought I would. It wasn't just an office job. But it could be damn depressing too, especially when the women wouldn't press charges, despite the cuts and bruises evident on their faces. Two years in, I was still trying to decide if it was going to be a long-term gig, but given the other turmoil in my life, I'd put off thinking about that for the time being.

Thankfully, Rich isn't in when I get there. Maybe he's late getting back from his Labor Day weekend fishing trip with his buddies. He was planning on going to Nelson Lake, where he maintains a rustic cabin I'm always slightly fearful he'll invite me to.

I ask Judy where he is. There's a fifty-fifty chance she'll tell him I was late out of boredom. I know from past experience that my dustups with Rich are one of the things that "keep it interesting 'round here," according to her.

Me, not so much.

"He's at court," Judy says between cracks of gum. She's fifty, and it's a habit she should have given up long ago, like the cigarettes that have stained her fingers yellow, but I guess it's really none of my business. "They're arraigning the robber."

"Oh, right."

The town's first bank robbery in years was all anyone was talking about last week. The man had been caught on Friday, three counties over, and hauled back to town. I wonder if he's willing to confess after spending a weekend in the town jail, which is 99 percent drunk tank, especially on a long weekend.

"Where you been?" Judy asks. I notice she's switched to her fall look, an ill-fitting suit and a mock turtleneck in a berry color. Her steel-gray hair is in an elaborate topknot. "You need to dress for where you want to be in life," she often says. "An extra in a movie?" I was once unwise enough to ask.

"Thought I'd take a look at the fire," I say.

"That's not likely to be our jurisdiction."

"I know some of the people working it."

She shrugs and turns back to the game of Scrabble she's playing online. Her score is 455 to her opponent's 212. She's kicked my ass every time I've played her, so much so that she won't play me anymore. "Too boring," is her assessment, and I can't help but agree.

I grab a cup of coffee from the teensy kitchen, and go to the nook I call my office. It's really just a large broom closet that was cleared out when I arrived. The only other real office is reserved for the deputy, and Rich refused to let me move in there, even temporarily. It might give a candidate the "wrong impression," apparently, to know that he'd be working in a space that used to be occupied by the likes of me.

The floor and shelves are littered with case files and banker's boxes, mostly to do with closed cases. We don't have a budget for filing cabinets. I've almost spent my own money to buy a couple, but I make so little that Ben talked me out of it. I did splurge and buy a small metal plaque for my door, so my shiny name, ELIZABETH MARTIN, greets me like a brass band each morning.

I open my e-mail to check for new fire advisories and find a message from Ben.

Thanks for leaving a note, it says.

Two years ago, I'd know exactly how to take this e-mail, and the note I'd left would have said something funny, maybe something suggestive. Terrible stick-figure drawings of what I'd do to him in bed later had been a staple between us, for instance.

And back then, the e-mail reply from Ben might have contained a further suggestion. Or a link to a related video. Fun. Lighthearted. An example of the reason he was still the person I most wanted to talk to in a room full of others.

But now, *now*, I read his words, and I don't know what to think. My note was neutral. *Couldn't sleep, off to work.* This e-mail might be too. Or it might be veiled sarcasm, simmering anger, a passive-aggressive *fuck you*. We are both so full of sarcasm and anger and aggression these days, always so ready to take anything that could be read two ways in the worst direction. Just reading this e-mail makes me feel drained, like I'm a tubful of stale water whose stopper's been pulled.

Sorry, I write back eventually, my go-to response, one that should never give offense but still manages to. *Sorry*. An apology, a state, an expression of sympathy. I'm all of these things and none of them. And if I keep thinking this way, Judy will be in here cracking her gum at me while I cry into my desk's enameled surface.

Instead, I check the rest of my e-mail (no new fire advisories) and read the town newspaper (big spread on the fire filled with pathos, which is the paper's bread and butter). Then I spend an hour poking around the online property register, which, as a killer of feelings, is about as good as you can get without a prescription.

I'm looking at the property register because Rich has this "feeling" someone's manipulating the real estate tax system by putting false property values into the deeds of sale. He gets these feelings every couple of weeks, mostly when he's worried about his poll numbers.

He's up for reelection next year, and because the conviction rate hasn't gone up under his watch (to be fair to him, the rate was already crazy high, so going down a percentage point would be a disappointment), he needs a "major takedown" to keep his seat. Of course his "poll numbers" are just the scuttlebutt he hears at the local coffee shop, and there isn't anyone running against him, but "constant vigilance" is apparently needed.

I make a list of potentially suspicious transactions as I go, and then sit staring at my computer screen, refreshing the Cooper Basin fire page on ForestFires.com every five minutes like a rat in one of those Skinner boxes hoping for her next hit.

Ben doesn't answer my e-mail.

"Late again, Liz?" Rich says, appearing behind my computer screen. He's wearing his it-didn't-go-well face, and I'm guessing the robber got bail.

"Elizabeth."

"Pardon?"

"I've told you a million times. I don't answer to Liz."

I should probably just let him call me Beth, but that name's reserved for people I like.

"Fine. Elizabeth. Whatever." He frowns at me, rocking back on his cowboy boot heels. "What's got your goat this morning?"

I turn my computer screen so he can see the map. "I'm in the evacuation area."

"The what?"

"Of the fire? The Cooper Basin fire?"

"Oh, right."

"We're okay for now, but—"

"I'm sure it'll be fine. These things always get close, but we haven't had a fire in town since, what, 1954?"

He says this like it is both vividly clear in his memory and a million years ago.

"I'm not sure, but—"

"Speaking of the fire, we got the call from the sheriff. They're going to need your services."

"My services? For what?"

"You used to be an arson investigator, yes? Or was that just something you put on your CV to impress me?"

I ignore the insult. "They think it's arson?"

"They've got to rule it out, you know that. Besides, there have been fire warnings in place all summer. Even if someone was simply careless, we'll have to prosecute."

"Seems harsh."

"Tell that to the State. This thing's already going to cost half a mil, I heard."

Given that he's been at the courthouse all morning, I have no idea where he's "heard" all this information, unless . . .

"How did the bail hearing go?" I ask.

He lets out a *humpf*. "His parents hired some fancy lawyer. Old judge Otis didn't know what to do with himself. Gave the kid bail on a five-thousand-dollar bond after listening to him for only five minutes. Can you believe that?"

"Ridiculous."

"Damn right. Anywho, the fire is all anyone's talking about at Joanie's. That robbery is yesterday's news."

Joanie's is his coffee shop. Gossip central.

"So, you'd better snap to it," he says. "Deputy Clark's waiting for you."

"I'm not really sure that's a good—"

He waves his hand impatiently. "Get to the sheriff's office. Fire's a wasting."

CHAPTER 5

You Take Sugar with That?

Mindy

After spin class, Mindy followed Kate and Bit to the Nelson Perk, the town's trendy coffee bar, which, in a move that Mindy can only think of as ironic, recently decided to start selling decaffeinated coffee exclusively. This was, to Mindy, the perfect equivalent of the cupcake shop that opened up a few weeks ago selling only "healthy" cupcakes.

If you're going to go cupcake, what's the point of going healthy?

Mindy would rather have gone to Joanie's, where she used to hang out—the homey diner full of old-timers and their gentle gossip (*Did you hear, Fred? They's talking about putting in a new culvert under the river come spring*)—but the one time she'd suggested it, Kate looked at her like Mindy had used her lipstick to color in her eyebrows, and then started cackling.

"You are *so funny*," Kate said, her go-to phrase when Mindy did something she couldn't process. Like if Kate pretended it was on-purpose humor, she could continue to ignore the fact that Mindy didn't really fit in.

Mindy wasn't quite sure how she'd ended up in this position—questioning, uncertain, feeling like she almost hated her friends half the time. She knew she should quit them, but the thought of having *no* friends, of being back where she was a year ago . . .

Well, no, she couldn't go there. They might be inadequate rebound friends, but at least they were talking to her.

In the parking lot, Mindy quickly checked the fire's progress on her phone after a furtive glance over her shoulder. She didn't know why she was acting like someone who was having an illicit e-mail affair, but something about the fire felt personal.

The cause of the fire was unknown, she read. It started on the edge of the Cooper Basin, in steep and rocky terrain heavy with downed fuels and low-moisture brush and tinder. While the quick response of local fire crews contained the northern edge of the fire, it was spreading up Nelson Peak and was already five hundred acres in size.

Was the fact that it was 10 percent contained a good thing? How long did it take to contain a fire? There hadn't been a fire this close in the whole time she'd lived in Nelson, but Mindy was still distressed by her ignorance. More evidence that her world had become too small, too insular.

Mindy stowed her phone and hurried to catch up with Kate.

The rest of the Coffee Boosters were already sitting at the best table, of course, the one with the perfect view of the street so they could watch the passersby without, you know, actually seeming to watch them. Honor Wells and Keffie Bristol and Caramel Homer, women who didn't attend spin class, but who dressed like they'd just come from there. Mindy wasn't sure when workout wear became acceptable casual attire for women who put their makeup on before they brushed their teeth, but maybe it was the price of the goods ($150 for a pair of yoga pants!) that made it all right.

The Perk was half-full. A few other groups of women, stealing envious glances at the Boosters; a couple of college students surfing the Internet; Earnest Writer Guy, as Kate called him, frowning at his laptop. He was always using some writing program that was supposed to make him write a certain number of words each day. Judging by the panicked look on his face, he wasn't going to be making that day's quota.

"Mindy has an *idea*," Kate announced when Honor et al. had made a space for her on the faux-leather bench, and she'd placed her order with their usual server for "a tall white *café* with *no whip*." Which was just a latte with a shot of espresso, sans caffeine, but sounded so much more authentic when Kate ordered it with a dash of the remnants of her high school French.

"Ooh," Caramel said in a cooing tone that was so like her ten-year-old daughter's that Mindy had to keep herself from saying, "Oh, grow up" whenever she heard it.

If Mindy put her finger on the one reason she needed to break free from this group of women, it was that. Her brain, and how catty it became around them. How critical.

She usually reserved such judgments for herself.

"Do tell," Caramel said.

Kate looked at Mindy expectantly.

"Well, you know the fire?" Mindy said, feeling like the question was justified this time, since it was entirely possible that none of the Coffee Boosters had heard about it yet.

"Of course!" Honor and Caramel said in unison.

"Right, well, um . . ."

"Go on," Kate said, darting her tongue at the foam on her just-arrived small white whatever.

"Well, I was thinking. I mean, *we* were thinking, that instead of using the Fall Fling money for the hockey team, we'd use it to help out the fire victims."

"*Are* there fire victims?" Keffie asked.

"There's at least one. His name is John Phillips." Mindy stopped, gulping for air and getting a mouthful of faux-coffee fumes for her trouble. "His wife died two years ago, and he's lost everything."

"Ooh," Caramel said again, like John's tragedy was something tasty she knew she shouldn't eat but probably would after everyone had gone to bed. "That's *so sad*."

"Totally," Kate agreed. "But we're going to fix it."

"But," Caramel said, working it over in her mind, "we only raised, like, a hundred thousand last year, right? That's not enough for a house. And what if there are other victims? Shouldn't we—"

"Not a house like *ours*," Kate said. "I'm thinking more of an apartment, or a condo or something. He's alone. How much space does one person need?"

Asks the woman whose house is at least ten thousand square feet, Mindy thought, and then felt herself blushing even though she was almost certain no one, not even Kate, could read her mind.

"But still—" Caramel said, before she caught a glance from Kate and swallowed her words.

"We're doing it," Kate said. "Plus, people will give way more this year if that's the reason."

"But what about the hockey team?" Keffie protested. "They have to rent ice time and buy equipment, and it's an important cause too." Keffie had three boys, all in hockey, and her husband's real estate business wasn't doing so well despite the average house price in Nelson being three times the national average. "Should we really be putting in all this time to help one person?"

"Maybe she's right," Mindy said, feeling guilty for suggesting it, even though Kate had insisted. "I could always organize something separate? Maybe in a couple of months?"

"No," Kate said. "What's wrong with you guys? This is a chance to do some *real* charity, not just some bullshit excuse for a party. You want a party? Come to my house on Friday. This. Is. What. We're. Doing."

Bit and Caramel looked down at their coffee cups, like penitents. But, for once, Mindy didn't have a sarcastic thought in her mind.

No, at that moment, she was proud that Kate was her maybe, sort of, almost friend.

CHAPTER 6

Point of Origin

Elizabeth

I glance at the squad car's clock as I drive with Deputy Clark back to the fire. It's twelve fifteen. Ben will be on his lunch break at the high school and might be reachable. I pull my phone out of my pocket, telling the deputy I need to make a quick call.

Ben answers on the second ring. I can hear the din of conversation behind him, a burst of laughter fairly close by. The usual sounds of the staff lunchroom—not that different from the regular lunchroom, if memory serves.

"Hey," I say. "How's your day going?"

"All right, considering."

I search his tone for any trace of the sarcasm I felt in his e-mail this morning, but there's nothing. Maybe it was all in my head. Or maybe he doesn't want to let the people around him know what's going on with us. The fact that I can't tell anymore is a weight on my shoulders.

"Kids happy to be back at school?"

"You know it."

"Right. Um, I was thinking . . . maybe we should go check on the house later? Pick up a few more things. Looks like this is probably going to turn serious."

"You mean the fire?"

I glance at the deputy. He's clearly listening in, but since I'm only a bucket seat away, I can't blame him.

"Yes," I say. "The fire."

"Can you meet me after Write Club?"

"What time does it finish again?"

"Four forty-five. Like it always has."

Another thread of a fight. I should know his schedule by heart a long time by now.

"I might be tied up."

"With what? You're the one—"

"I know. I'm sorry. I'm just . . . I'd like to check on the house."

"You're not making any sense, Beth."

"Probably not."

"Where are you, anyway?"

I look out the window. Up ahead, two bison have their noses in the stream that runs next to the road.

"Bison jam," I say to Deputy Clark. "Careful."

He slows down to match the other traffic crawling by the scene like it's a car accident.

"What?" Ben says. "You're where?"

Something tells me that the fact I've been drafted to investigate the fire is the last thing Ben wants to hear right now.

"I'm out on a case."

"Well, then, why don't *you* call *me* when you're free?"

"I'm sorry," I say again.

God, I'm so sick of apologizing.

He doesn't say anything. I listen to the mechanical silence as the deputy and I edge past the cars full of people snapping pictures on their cell phones. I imagine Ben sitting in the staff room, his hand cupped around his phone to create a zone of privacy, the edge of his shirt collar between his teeth to keep him from saying something he'll regret.

"I should go," I say eventually. "Love you."

Ben pauses long enough to remind me that this isn't something we should be saying to each other anymore as a casual good-bye, even if it's true.

"Talk soon," he says, and the line goes dead.

I put my phone on my lap, hoping he'll text me in a moment to say the words back, like he used to do when we fought on the phone and calling back seemed too dramatic, but my phone stays mute.

Deputy Clark picks up his radio and calls in the traffic slowdown. Our eyes meet, and despite the weight tugging at my heart, we share a conspiratorial smile. *People*, our look says. *What can you do?*

"Your house in the line of fire, ma'am?" Deputy Clark asks as he steps on the gas. He speaks deliberately, almost as if there's punctuation between his words. Commas mostly and an occasional period. He's twenty-five, and his campaign hat is tipped back far enough to reveal a rash of acne across his forehead.

"Yes, unfortunately."

And don't call me ma'am, I want to say. *Jesus.*

Instead, I tell him where our house is. How the smoke woke me in the night. I leave out the rest of it, though a small part of me wishes I could confide in him. They way you do sometimes with complete strangers on a long plane ride, the thorough knowledge that you'll never see each other again an erasure of reticence.

"This must be weird for you, then," he says. "Investigating this."

"All part of the job, right?"

"Yes, ma'am, I guess it is."

Another version of Write Club is where Ben and I met in our last year of college.

As a science major headed—I thought—to med school, it had been strongly suggested to me as a way to round out my CV. Not

Write Club, necessarily, but something, anything, other than the excessive lab time I'd been putting in alone with my assays. I'm not sure what drew me to that particular club. I wasn't a writer, never felt the desire to put what was going on in my head down on the page. I read a lot, still do, but I never thought up my own stories. But I had a friend who'd joined the year before, and I was 100 percent certain that my ex, Jason, wouldn't be there, which would be a welcome change from the 24/7 interaction we were still forced to endure as a result of being in the same program.

This guy named Morris, who was a teaching assistant in the MFA program, ran it. He had this terrible, affected air about him. Now I'd say he was a hipster before there were hipsters—he wore oversize glasses and sweaters with strategic holes, and seemed to feel that bathing was optional—but back then, my friend Cecily and I just thought he needed to invest in some good deodorant.

It was the second meeting I'd attended, and I was still on the fence about whether I was going to keep going. Cecily was late, and before I could get my "I'm saving this seat for a friend" out, Ben sat down next to me.

"Has he pulled out The Story yet?" Ben asked, nodding to Morris.

Most clubs I knew were more democratic, but Morris ran it like it was just another class he was TA-ing. Morris was talking about the importance of his *process* while fairly obviously focusing his attention on three freshman girls who were looking at him with wide-eyed adoration.

Yuck.

"Um, what?"

"You haven't heard about it?" Ben smiled. He had a natural white smile, straight black hair, and sage-green eyes. Five eleven. Broad shoulders. Pretty much the opposite of Jason, in a good way.

"No. Should I have?"

"Uh-uh. But you probably will."

"Dude, what the hell? Who are you?"

"I'm Ben Jansen. And you're Elizabeth Martin."

Before I could ask how he knew my name, he leaned forward conspiratorially. He smelled like sleep even though the class was at four in the afternoon. I'd learn later that Ben was a big fan of the restorative afternoon nap.

"It's this piece he wrote—the *only* thing he's written as far as I can tell—some semiconfessional thing about his sister's death that he uses to get whoever catches his fancy each semester into bed."

"And women fall for this?"

"They do."

I looked closely at Morris. His hair was wiry and about to turn into natural dreadlocks. His glasses were round and too small for his face. He seemed incapable of talking in anything but a lecture voice.

How good would a short story have to be to make me remotely interested in sleeping with him? I admit I was slightly tempted to find out.

"Idiots," I said to Ben.

"How so?"

I motioned to the girls watching Morris, taking notes, *eager*.

"Women. Like falling for ugly rock stars because they write about feelings in sappy ballads."

"Is *that* why that happens?"

"Yup. We pretty much go in for whatever makes us think men understand us."

"Ha! That's what you should write about."

"No way."

He smiled again and shook his head. "You'd be doing a service to mankind."

"I bet I would. Say, why are you telling me about this anyway?"

"Oh . . . I . . . just have a feeling you might be this semester's pick."

He looked down at the notepad in front of him. He'd written my name in block letters, tracing it over as we spoke.

"You'd be mine, anyway," he said quietly.

And like the girl that I was, my heart started to fall.

No one I recognize is manning the fire's perimeter when we get to John Phillips's house. The guys I know, those with the most experience, like Andy, are likely on the backside of Nelson Peak, fighting the upper edge of the fire, trying to get fuel out of the way so they can contain the blaze and keep it from spreading over the ridge, where it will slide down the hill like a ski racer into town.

It used to be that all forest fires received this treatment. If it burned, it needed to be put out, regardless of the cost. But public policy has changed over the years. A century of suppression taught us that fire makes forests healthy, and that one in every ten years is less devastating than one in a hundred. Now, if the fire's naturally occurring and it isn't threatening a populated area, we let it burn, because smaller fires prevent bigger ones in the end. "Fire Use Fire," the policy's called.

The most ridiculous term ever invented.

Of course, regardless of my findings, this fire will need to be suppressed, because although it might be good for the forests that surround Nelson to have it consume the downed trees and underbrush that have accumulated over the past fifty years, it clearly wouldn't be in the town's interest.

Or in mine.

Deputy Clark escorts me past the trucks, equipment caches, and people milling about till we get a couple hundred yards from the scorched shell of John Phillips's house.

We take a lap around the property, keeping our distance. It's still too dangerous to go inside the blackened structure, but I have a pretty good idea from the burn patterns in the grass that the fire didn't start inside, anyway.

When we've done the perimeter sweep, we climb into a full kit of firefighters' gear: boots, gaiters, jacket, gloves, a helmet with a mask and a breathing apparatus. The fire is a thousand yards away, but better safe than sorry. It takes a moment to adjust to the unfamiliar weight of the equipment—a wildland firefighting kit is much lighter—and the brief moment of claustrophobia having a mask over my face always produces.

My nostrils fill with the chemical smell of the suit as I walk slowly, notebook in hand, eyes on the ground, searching for the fire's source.

"So," I hear Deputy Clark say through the radio that connects our helmets. There's a quality to the sound that always reminds me of astronauts doing a spacewalk. "How does this work? Is it like processing a regular crime scene?"

"You could look at it that way. Officially, there are four potential causes of a fire: natural, accidental, incendiary, and undetermined. We need to figure out which box this fire fits into."

"Undetermined doesn't sound like a cause."

"You're right. We don't usually check that box."

It was a point of pride among arson investigators. Undetermined was like a failing grade, one you gave yourself.

"How do you figure out which to check?"

I pull up my visor and push aside my breathing apparatus. I take a deep breath. My nose is flooded with the scent of charred wood and burned grass. I search for undertones of something that shouldn't be there. Gasoline. Kerosene. Some other accelerant. But there's nothing. So far, the only chemical I can smell is the all-too-familiar one found in the standard retardant that's been dumped liberally in the area. What I really need is a hydrocarbon sniffer—a handheld device that can detect the presence of ignitable liquid residues in the air—but the department isn't equipped with one.

"There are lots of ways to figure out what causes a fire," I say, pulling my visor back down and readjusting my mask. "They have signals, fingerprints they leave behind, like any criminal."

When I started my arson training, I realized I'd been learning these signals for years. That as I fought fires, I was also absorbing their grammar. So when I took the specialized courses in fire chemistry, dynamics, and how to read a scene, it all seemed obvious and natural. As if the fire wanted me to know what started it, if I was patient enough to listen.

If only I were as good at reading the hints left by those around me.

I continue. "The first step is to establish where it began, which is called the area of origin. Here, that's pretty simple."

I make a sweeping motion that encompasses the smoking house and the path of singed grass leading to the back of the property and into the woods.

"Even if the neighbor hadn't called it in before it left the lot, it would be clear that this is where the fire started."

"Does that mean it's a human cause, then? There wasn't any lightning in the area last night. I checked."

"We'll see. Once you've established your area of origin, you need to look for the point of origin, the source of the fire. Again, the fire helps us do that."

I point to the streaks in the house's backyard. The entire half acre of lawn is black and sodden with a mixture of water and retardant, and there's a distinct pattern that makes it obvious—to me, at least—that the fire moved *toward* the house, not away from it.

"You see that pattern? That's telling us where the fire came from. So now we just need to follow its path."

We step across the seared ground. The protective suit and boots stop the heat from burning our feet, but I've already started sweating.

The burn pattern leads me back to the edge of the property, where the grass goes from short to long to woods.

And there's my likely culprit: a fire pit.

"Once you have your point of origin," I say, "then you need to find out what sparked it. Out in the woods, it might be something as innocent as a piece of glass, or as dramatic as a lightning strike.

Near people, it's generally going to be a human source. A campfire left lit. Garbage burned carelessly in a barrel."

Deputy Clark points to the stone pit. "That's where it started, isn't it?"

I bend down and hold my gloved hand above the white ash. It's still radiating heat. It contains a few pieces of charred wood, the remnants of some paper, and two burned-out beer cans.

"Get me a paint bucket," I say. "And a shovel."

CHAPTER 7

The Blame Game

Elizabeth

As we drive back to the elementary school, I'm starting to feel like a yo-yo. Our house to Ben's parents' house. Their house to the fire. The fire to the elementary school. The school to work. Work to the fire. The fire to the school.

Each time I settle on a direction, *snap!* I'm pulled in another.

We're driving back to Nelson Elementary because that's where John Phillips was taken after the EMTs treated him for minor smoke inhalation. I actually need to interview him *and* his neighbors, but the latter have scattered like the four winds. He's the only one we have a fixed location on.

At the school I check in briefly with a harried Kara, then follow the signs for the gym. It's already been set up to shelter as many as possible, with rows and rows of empty camp cots and piles of army-surplus blankets and lumpy off-white pillows. I wonder where all the kids are, then remember they've been given a "fire day," much to their delight, I'm sure. What will be done with them if the fire isn't contained and this place starts to teem with refugees is something that hasn't been worked out yet.

I ask the lead volunteer where Mr. Phillips is as the gym doors clang shut behind us.

"He's over there," a woman I know slightly named Honor Wells says, pointing to a lump of blankets in the far left corner in a condescending voice. "Sleeping, I think."

He might have been earlier, despite the penetrating fluorescent lights, but he isn't when we get to him. He's just lying on his back, staring at the ceiling tiles, his arms folded behind his head, which is resting on his palms.

"Mr. Phillips?"

"Kristy?"

"No, Mr. Phillips. I'm Elizabeth Martin. And this is Deputy Clark. We're from the police department, and we have a few questions for you."

"You can call me John."

He sits up slowly, blinking his brown eyes like we've just turned on the lights. His hair is snow white and close-cropped, and his face has the deep tan of someone who works outdoors. He's snagged three blankets and two pillows. The bed he's on is in the corner farthest away from the doors.

A man with a plan, it seems. Or good instincts, at least.

John places his bare feet squarely on the shiny wood floor. He's wearing a pair of blue hospital scrubs and smells like industrial soap, presumably from the school showers.

I begin by asking him some basic questions about his background. He answers me in a rambling way, his mind flitting back and forth between the present and the past like they hold equal weight.

For instance, he tells me that he picked this bed because he was in the army over forty years ago, and he still remembers how hard it was to sleep in a room full of snoring men. And that was when he was in basic training and so tired that he should've been able to sleep through a bombardment, let alone the little kind of noises that shook him awake now.

"It's the days I have trouble staying awake through," he says, his gaze fixed on a far-off place. "Like earlier. I just put my head on the pillow, thinking I'd rest for a moment, and who knows how long I slept for."

"You've had a shock," I say. "It's the way the body copes."

"I beg your pardon?"

"Going through something like you have, you can feel very tired afterward. For days even. It's a normal reaction, but if you keep feeling poorly, you should see a doctor."

"That doctor in the ambulance said I was okay after the . . . fire."

His eyes go vacant, then snap back to attention.

"You're fine, John. Safe," I say to him, placing my hand on his shoulder gently.

"I've lost everything."

"I'm so very sorry. You can stay here for now, and I'm sure that . . ."

I stop myself, because what am I sure about? That it will all be okay? That there will be people and money to help him? That when they shut this shelter down, he'll have somewhere to go? How can I say anything like that to him, when I don't even know it for myself?

If he notices my trailing thoughts, he doesn't acknowledge it. He simply blinks slowly as he looks around him.

"This is Nelson Elementary, ain't it?"

I confirm it is, and he goes off on another tangent. This isn't the elementary school he went to. Well, it has the same name, of course, but this building was built twenty years ago. The one *he'd* attended was torn down when it was found to be full of asbestos and the school district was sued for two cases of lung cancer. He liked that building, which was new when he attended it. Back then, everyone in town was pretty much like him; cattle ranchers' sons and dairy farmers' daughters. School cleared out at harvest and calving times. Reading, writing, and arithmetic made up most of the curriculum—it was all anyone who grew up in Nelson needed.

Things are different now, of course, he says. He knows that. But it doesn't mean he has to like it.

He stops, his eyes going blank again.

I can tell that Deputy Clark is growing impatient, but when he makes a move to say something, I signal him to let John talk. The talking is also part of the shock. I've found over the years that I get more out of someone if I just let them flow. People abhor the vacuum of silence in a crowd. It's a natural instinct to fill it with whatever is foremost in your thoughts. If I were in his place, I'm sure I'd be babbling about Ben and what was going on between us and how it wasn't my fault, it wasn't his fault, these things just happen sometimes. As it is, I know John will work his way back around to the fire, and if I'm lucky, put this case to bed before Ben even has to know I was working on it.

So I let the silence rest until John continues. "We never had any kids, me and Kristy. Kristy, that's my wife. You sounded like her for a second. Anyway, Kristy couldn't or I couldn't or we both couldn't. We never really bothered to find out. No money for the doctor, and besides, we both knew that if it was one or the other's fault, we'd start to blaming, and resentment would grow until there was nothing else between us."

He looks surprised at what he just said. I'm holding my breath, my heart thumping in my chest.

Out of the mouths of scared old men.

"You have any kids?" he asks me.

"No."

"I bet you'd be good at it. You talk to people like they're real, not like . . ." He nods over to where Honor is folding blankets. He lowers his voice. "She talks in that way people do to folks past a certain age. You know that way?"

I know what he means. Honor's the kind of person who speaks to seniors like they're hard of understanding. As if they already had one foot on the other side.

"I do," I say. "So you've lived in Nelson your whole life?"

That's right, he says, his whole life and his daddy's life before that. And he worked construction, used to anyway, and he's lonely now, without his wife. He doesn't know what's going to happen, and he feels like he might be to blame.

"To blame?" I say. "Do you mean for the fire?"

Deputy Clark leans forward, notebook in hand, looking as if he's getting ready to take a statement.

"I was asleep," John says. "Why I'd be to blame for the fire?"

"You might've noticed it sooner," Deputy Clark says. I shake my head, but he presses on. "Or maybe . . . Were you using your fire pit last night, sir?"

"The . . . Is that where the fire started?"

"Likely."

"It's too soon to say that for sure," I correct the deputy, trying to keep the anger out of my voice. He's given up a piece of information he shouldn't have, and we can't get it back. John Phillips was a blank slate before, but now he's marred. If he knew where the fire started, it could have been proof of something. Now it's only proof of Deputy Clark's lack of training.

John stares off into space again, and I can't tell whether he's trying to be careful about his answer or whether his brain's simply on a skip-track. I let my own eyes travel around the room as a way to distract myself from pressing too hard, and that's when I see her: Mindy Mitchell is standing at the gym's entrance, talking to Honor.

What's she doing here?

Volunteering, probably. A sliver of an uncharitable thought forms, but then I dismiss it. I'm still furious with her, and I can feel it in me like a shot of adrenaline. But it would be completely irrational to be irritated by her altruistic instincts. Ben would say everything that happened between us was irrational, but it's one thing to hear about a fight and another to be in it.

I turn my back to the door, hoping Mindy doesn't notice me. I've spent a year successfully avoiding her in this small town. One more day seems possible.

"Is there anything else you can think of?" I ask John. "Even if it doesn't seem like it might be connected, you never know."

His hands travel to his shoulders and down his body to his knees, as if he's trying to press out the wrinkles in his clothes.

"They tell you about those kids?" he says slowly.

"What kids?"

"The kids I've been complaining about all summer. I phoned it in a couple times to your office, Deputy. You check." He turns his body and leans back against his pillows. "They come at night and sit around that fire pit and drink beer. Wait till I'm asleep. Think I don't know they're trespassing."

"These kids ever started a fire in your pit, you know of?"

"Sure enough. That's one of the reasons why I called the police. Kids foolish enough to start a fire in these conditions . . . Well, they could burn the whole town down."

"Do you know their names?"

"No, ma'am. But I'd recognize them if I saw them."

CHAPTER 8

Winner, Winner, Chicken Dinner

Mindy

After dropping off food and clothing donations at the elementary school, checking with the administration that Angus would be allowed back into Write Club, and taking Carrie to her intensive ballet class, Mindy spent several hours doing the kinds of chores that were slowly driving her insane. Picking up the dry cleaning, taking her car to the car wash because it had been six months and the inside was starting to get embarrassing, and, finally, driving to three grocery stores to get everything on her list because no one store had everything she needed. One-stop shopping was not a concept that had made its way to Nelson. And even if it did, what did it matter? Because what else would she be doing with her time, anyway?

That was an awful thought, wasn't it, to think she had nothing better to do with her time. Not that taking care of her family wasn't something worthwhile. But for years now, ever since the kids were old enough to feed and dress themselves, and even she had come to accept that Carrie was finally out of danger, she'd had this nagging feeling she should be doing *more*. For a while, her part-time work at the high school had kept the worst of it at bay. But then she'd been laid off and the days stretched before her. So she joined committees and volunteered at the school and her days were full—yet she still had time to go to three grocery stores in one day.

Maybe that's why she was already obsessing over John Phillips. Why she was making a mental list of all the things the Coffee Boosters would need to do to change the focus of the Fall Fling from earning money for the hockey team to getting him a new home. The event was only five days away, and she could already imagine the disappointed expressions of the rest of the organizing committee when the new focus was announced (by Kate, she fervently hoped). But they were doing the right thing, they *were*, so for once she wasn't going to worry about gaining acceptance or pissing people off or any of the things she normally worried about.

She just wasn't.

Besides, if Kate didn't care, why should she?

Mindy bought the chicken she was going to serve for dinner at her last stop, because she'd seen enough warnings about chicken and how you needed to make sure to get it right home and into the fridge. And she'd cook it properly this time, with no pink juices flowing out of it. She was ashamed to admit that despite years of effort, she still hadn't perfected cooking a chicken. It was such a basic thing—she thought it should be, anyway—and the fact that she was often hurrying it back to the oven after Peter's carving knife had revealed that, once again, it wasn't cooked through, was an embarrassment.

But it was Peter's favorite, roast chicken with spices on top and a lemon inside, served with garlic rosemary potatoes and a tossed salad, and she liked doing things to make Peter happy. Even after all these years, she made sure that Angus and Carrie didn't completely divert her attention from the person, the reason, she was living this life in the first place.

Angus. She had barely thought about him all day, she realized with a start. For once, the focus of her worry had been pulled away from her sixteen-year-old son. She'd spent so much time fretting about Angus this year, a constant slice of pain, like a deep paper cut, that his absence from her thoughts brought a kind of sting too. Because something was off about Angus, though she didn't know what.

It hadn't been any one thing, just a series of small incidents. He wasn't off in the way Carrie had been, not in need of medical attention. And not in the building-bombs-in-the-basement kind of way (please, God, no). He'd simply moved out of her orbit and into a place she couldn't quite understand. Was it depression like her brother suffered from? Was he struggling with his sexuality? Was he being bullied at school? No matter how many times she'd asked and poked and even snooped, she couldn't figure out what it was.

Only that there *was* something.

Take this morning. Mindy had a feeling he'd been sneaking out at night, going off to smoke pot or whatever kids were smoking these days, and the way his clothes were strewn on the floor, that lingering scent, his complete lethargy, all seemed to confirm it. But as hard as she and Peter tried, they could never catch him. Room searches came up empty. The alarm on the house was never disabled. And teenagers like to sleep a lot and experiment and . . .

So, so, *so*.

Peter always said she shouldn't worry so much, though she knew he was concerned too. He kept trying to get Angus to do the things they used to do together: throwing a ball around, going for long bike rides, rock climbing. But Angus wasn't interested in those pastimes anymore. Not in doing them with his dad, anyway. And Peter's quickly hidden hurt broke Mindy's heart each time she saw it.

At least Carrie seemed to be skimming on top of whatever was dragging her brother under. As if being born with a hole in her heart had given her extra buoyancy. That might be a problem later on, Mindy knew, but for now it seemed to keep her safe from the worst of what many of her friends' teenage girls were going through.

But Angus. They really did have to do something about him. Soon.

Mindy's mind skipped to how strange it had been to see Elizabeth at the elementary school, even if it was only a glimpse across the room. That's all she'd had of her since The Falling Out. And what was she doing talking to John Phillips? Mindy guessed it was about the fire, but it felt odd to see two people who had dominated her thoughts for completely different reasons talking together.

Was it the emotional loss she felt when she and Elizabeth stopped speaking that made her suddenly attuned to Angus? She wondered about that, knowing that when she was down she tended to amplify other people's feelings. As if she was a magnifier of other people's anguish. And that probably explained her obsession with John Phillips too. At least this time, it was going to lead to something good.

As she pulled into her driveway, Mindy resolved to put these thoughts of her head. And it worked, after a fashion. Peter arrived home while she was checking the chicken for the eighth time, using the meat thermometer he got her, not for her birthday or their anniversary or anything crass like that, but just because he knew she stressed about it and he wanted to help in the small way he could.

"You should just set that and forget it," he said. He was wearing one of the suits he'd bought when he got his promotion at the bank, a dark-blue one, with a white dress shirt and a striped tie the kids gave him for Christmas. His sandy hair was still thick, but it was starting to contain shots of gray, particularly where it met his neck.

"Oh, sure, Ron Popeil, that's easy for you to say."

He held up his hands in mock surrender. He had long, tapered fingers that went with his six-foot-four height. "I know you don't think highly of sales," he said. "But Ron Popeil? Sheesh. That's low."

Before Peter started at the bank, he worked in the sales department of the hospital. As Mindy had explained to him more than once, she didn't have a problem with selling *per se*. It was the idea of selling medical services, that patients were treated as sales units, something to measured, counted, *budgeted for* that disturbed her. Not that working at the bank put him in a better moral position. Certainly not when the houses of family after family were being repossessed. Problems Kate and the Coffee Boosters never had to face, or even really understood.

"Who says I don't think highly of sales? Plus, Popeil made a shit-ton of money. I could get behind that," Mindy said.

"Don't let the kids hear you talk like that."

"I'm sure they say a lot worse out of our hearing."

He cocked his head to the side. "Hello, who do we have here?"

"Pardon?"

"I mean, where's my wife and what have you done with her? The Mindy I know and love would never be so blasé about our progeny's potty mouths."

"Oh, I know. I'm in a funny mood."

She was in a funny mood. Like her brain was stuck on fast-forward, whirring, whirring, whirring.

"It's that spin class, I tell you." Peter took her in his arms and pulled her close. His hands traveled down to her backside and cupped her butt, which did feel, for once, slightly more toned. "You're always riled up after that class. Not that I mind—"

"PDA alert!" Carrie yelled from the other side of the room, where she was sitting at the kitchen table, doing her math homework. She was still wearing her ballet clothes, tights, a black leotard, and a pink shrug, her corn-colored hair pulled into a perfect bun.

"Now, honey," Peter said. "You want your parents to love each other, don't you?"

"Not, like, in front of me."

"How do you think you were created, huh?"

"Oh, Peter, hush," Mindy said, but she was laughing.

Peter's hands, she noticed, hadn't moved from her backside. Maybe she could put all this energy to use later, after the kids were in bed.

"Angus! Mom and Dad are being disgusting," Carrie called.

Angus was sitting, zombielike, in front of the kids' computer, which Mindy still insisted on being in full public view. No private porn searches for her son. Not in her house.

"Oh, grow up, Carrie," Angus said, his eyes never leaving the screen. "Maybe if you actually kissed one of those guys in your ballet class instead of—"

"Dinner!" Mindy said, right before she landed a smack on Peter's lips.

CHAPTER 9

How a House Became a Home

Elizabeth

The interview with John Phillips leaves me worn out. I don't know if it's the sadness that seeped from him in a way you could almost touch, or how he sat there, alone on a cot in a room crowded with them ready to take in a townful of people who hadn't shown up yet. Ready to take in Ben and me if we didn't have somewhere else to go.

Deputy Clark drops me off at the office, and we part with few words. At my desk, I type up my notes from the fire and the interview with John, making a list of things to follow up on tomorrow: get a copy of the police reports he mentioned, see if any other neighbors were having trouble with kids loitering on their property, try to track down the group of kids who might've started a fire that's still blazing, growing. Up to six hundred acres now, according to the latest alert, with crews coming in from all over and low containment.

I check the weather forecast again and, as Kara said, it's bad. Starting tomorrow, there'll be wind and heat and not a drop of moisture in sight for days. I say a small prayer that the weather guys are as off as they normally are, but I've noticed they never seem to get it wrong when it counts. That late May snowstorm that ruins Memorial Day weekend, or that torrential rain on the Fourth of July? Those always seem to happen. But the cooler, cloudy day needed after a heat wave? That occurs by fluke—unexpected, almost unbidden.

"Well, folks, we're not sure what happened exactly, but that beautiful day we predicted just didn't seem to materialize. Instead, a high ridge of . . ."

And what's with the singsong voices they deliver the weather in, anyway?

But, yeah, it's looking bad. No matter which way you shake it.

I close down my computer and text Ben: *Meet me at the house now?*

His answer comes a moment later: *I'm on my way.*

Located in the western foothills of Nelson Peak, our house isn't something a wildland firefighter and a teacher could have afforded but for Grace and Gordon's generosity.

We never planned on owing money to them, or to anyone for that matter. It was something we both hated, debt, being in debt, owing things to other people. We had that in common. But our house, well, we both fell in love with it the first time we saw it.

And love makes you do funny things sometimes.

We'd been looking at much smaller places on the valley floor. Small houses, on shady streets, that looked like they hadn't been properly winterized. I'd go into one of them, and all I could see were the problems: the bathrooms that needed to be redone, the kitchens that required ripping out, not because I was so picky, but because it was a question of basic sanitation. A town where a third of the population is transient is hard on the real estate. And the thought of scrubbing off years' worth of ski-bum grime defeated me.

But we were near to closing on one of the better-than-the-others houses because we needed somewhere to live—our current place, a rental, was being repo-ed by the bank, and they didn't want a tenant—when I saw an ad in the *Nelson Daily*. A newly finished A-frame with a view of the mountains, surrounded by large aspens. I could imagine the break they'd bring from the summer heat, and the shimmering gold they'd turn in the fall.

Ben looked skeptical when I showed him the listing, but I could see a light in his eyes. And it was shining out of both of us as we walked around the sun-filled house and breathed in the smell of freshly sawn lumber.

We could have a family here, I thought. *It's perfect.*

The real estate agent was blathering on about square footage and how it was a hot property market and we'd better scoop up the house while we could. But when I saw the asking price—and we'd better come in at asking, the agent told us—my heart sank.

"We can't afford this," I whispered to Ben while we were pretending to check out the pantry off the kitchen.

"I know, but . . . I think there's a way. If we can both swallow our pride."

I knew what he meant. Go to his parents, do the one thing we'd promised never to do, which was ask them for anything.

But this house. This house with its picture windows that seem to lay the whole town out at our feet, and the big stone fireplace in the great room that keeps it cheery all winter long, and the evergreens that make the air feel freshly scrubbed even though the day is hot and muggy, *this house* was worth the sacrifice of our principles.

"I can do it if you can," I said.

We squeezed hands to seal the deal, our wedding bands clinking against one another as if they had sought each other out to make a toast.

Ben is waiting for me on our wraparound porch, sitting in the wood swing we spent one sweaty weekend putting together a few years ago.

We always seem to get into fights when we try a joint home-improvement project, and so we've found it easier, over the years, to split up the tasks. I rolled paint on the walls in the winter months, in my haphazard way where it might take a week to get a room done. He'd start and complete a project in a blitz, working almost frenetically to finish the bookshelves that lined one side of the great room, or installing a new dishwasher as soon as the old one broke.

But this swing, this lovers' swing, was something that took two sets of hands, and so we worked together, and fought, and right before it was done, I sliced my finger on the sharp edge of the packing crate it came in.

"Sit right there," Ben had said as a red stain bloomed on my hand. "Keep it elevated."

While he rushed off to find our first-aid kit—*It's above the sink!* I almost called after him, then bit my tongue—I peeled off my sweaty shirt and wrapped it tightly around my finger. I sat on the swing wearing my taupe-colored bra, holding my throbbing hand to my chest and pushing at the ground with my feet, wondering how I could be so careless.

Ben returned a moment later with the tackle box I'd converted into a first-aid kit. Even though I was the one with the EMT training, he moved efficiently, quickly, finding the right size bandage and antibacterial cream without my having to tell him what to do. He removed my shirt from my finger gently, then wiped the blood away with a stinging cloth. He held my hand with care while he bandaged me up.

"All better now?" he asked, kissing my forehead.

I nodded, and he sat down next to me. I leaned my head against his shoulder and laughed.

"What?"

"At least we didn't get into a fight."

He started to laugh too, and we sat there for a while, chuckling and admiring the view.

Ben is not laughing now.

"Where do you want to start?" he asks, all business.

"Maybe we could go room to room and take the easy stuff? Photographs, bills, DVDs. I still have a couple of those plastic containers in the pantry. And the fridge, we should clean out the fridge."

He nods and stands. He follows me inside, and the smell of smoke seems stronger in here than under the sheltering pines. Already the house feels like it's been abandoned.

"I'll take the kitchen," Ben says. "And I need to get my writing stuff."

This surprises me. While Ben mostly writes on a laptop these days, he has notebooks full of poems, short stories, and half-finished novels going back to his teens. I'd just assumed he took those with him when we left last night. I would have. But Ben's writing, or Ben not writing, that's just one of the things we don't talk about anymore.

"I thought—"

"What?" he says, with an edge to his voice.

"Nothing, forget it. I'll get the other stuff."

He grunts and walks toward the kitchen. I follow him to get a plastic container. The muscles in his neck are taut. Ben is angry, I realize. Not just annoyed, like he might have been this morning or definitely this afternoon, but honest-to-goodness angry. The anger I asked about when we were parked outside his parents' house, which he denied.

The anger he said he could never feel about me.

But yet, here it is, taking up residence in the house we've deserted.

When we get back to Ben's parents' house, the backs of our cars filled with plastic containers full of food and memories, it's thankfully past dinnertime. There is no casual dining in that house, and I don't think I can stand a whole dinner of keeping up appearances.

Gordon and Grace are on their way out for the evening. Gordon in his dinner jacket, Grace in an ice-blue sheath dress covered in crystals. The symphony is coming to Nelson for the night, an event I've often meant to go to but somehow always end up skipping.

Grace eyes the stacks of crates that Ben is building in the entranceway. She wears her thick white hair in a blunt cut, and Ben's green eyes are the only color in her face.

"Stay as long as you like," she says, kissing the air near my cheek.

"Thank you. It shouldn't be too long."

She nods her head, her eyes full of sympathy, and it's a good thing they leave then because otherwise I might be crying into her shoulder again. As far as mother figures go, I'm much closer to her than my own mother, who left me with my dad when I was eight after they split up. It's not as bad as it sounds—I saw her on weekends and holidays, typical "dad days"—but I could make it seem that way if I wanted to without trying too hard.

After they leave, Ben and I go into the kitchen. It's full of endless white marble counters and dark wood cabinetry, pretty much the opposite of our battered oak cabinets and laminate countertops, but I'd take ours in a heartbeat. Our kitchen the way it used to be, anyway, where we'd build meals together and laugh at the sometimes disastrous results.

Ben pulls food from the Sub-Zero fridge.

"Chicken double-decker?" he asks.

"Please."

He starts assembling the makings of his famous-in-our-house sandwich: toasted bread, chicken, lettuce, tomato, bacon, mayonnaise, repeat. It's like two club sandwiches stacked one on top of the other, so big it takes work to get your mouth around, which is part of its appeal. We have never, not once, eaten these sandwiches and not ended up giggling our asses off as we watch each other try to navigate them. It's a standoff to see who crumbles first. Eventually, you give in to the fact that the only way you can eat the sandwich is by picking it apart with your hands and using a knife and fork.

"How was school today?" I ask.

Ben works at one of the two town high schools. There's the public one, which is much like the one I attended—large classes, kids from all walks of life, teachers who are underpaid and overworked. And then there's Ben's school, a private one that costs forty thousand dollars a year to attend. It's called Voyages, which always makes me think it should be taking place onboard a ship rather than in the sparkling facility that sprawls over several acres on the far east side of town.

It's where Ben went and where some of his old friends send their kids now. He hadn't wanted to teach there—he really would've preferred to be in the public school system, or so he used to say—but there wasn't a job open when he passed his qualifications, and he wanted very much to stay in Nelson, so he gave in. "I'll teach them to be little liberals when their parents aren't looking," he said ruefully when he told me about his decision. "Work on the inside."

"How was Write Club?" I say now.

"The first rule of Write Club is that you don't talk about Write Club."

"Ha."

"It was fine. Same group of kids, mostly."

"That Tucker kid and his friends too?"

"Looks like it. Apparently, every budding sociopath likes to share his dark fantasies with his classmates."

Ben finishes building my sandwich and pushes it across the counter to me.

"Do you think that's what it is?"

"Who knows? I hate how I have to wonder half the time whether I should be reporting kids to the principal because of the zero-tolerance policy on violence."

Last year Ben had no choice but to turn one of Tucker's stories over to the principal because it went into detail about how he wanted to practice cutting up his sister by starting with her ballet outfits. He'd initially been suspended for three days, but when it turned out his sister didn't even take ballet, he was let back in and the principal (and Ben) had to apologize to the family while Tucker looked on with an evil smirk. The next week, Ben found a cut-up ballet leotard in his staffroom mail cubby, but when they couldn't prove who'd left it there because the camera feed was down, that had been the end of it.

"You don't have to run the club," I say.

"Hardly seems fair to the other kids if I don't. Besides, maybe I can be a good influence."

"I'm sure you can," I say gently.

Ben watches me as I pick up my sandwich and try to get a corner of it into my mouth.

"So," he says. "Who'd they send?"

"*Mmmfff?*"

"To command. The fire?"

I put it down in defeat. "Kara."

"I like her."

"I know. Will you pass me a knife and fork?"

"Ha! Victory is mine."

He walks to the utensil drawer, doing a little dance along the way, and removes a knife and fork. Then he takes out a second set.

"Wait," I say. "You didn't even *try*. You totally defaulted."

He shrugs instead of giving me the laugh I expected.

"How do you know Kara's in command?" he asks.

I feel like I've walked into a trap. Like Ben already knows the answer, and he's waiting to see if I'm going to tell the truth.

"The sheriff's department asked Rich for my help with the investigation."

Ben just looks at me, waiting. I feel a stab of sympathy for John Phillips because this is how I made him feel earlier. Like there was a silence that needed to be filled.

"It makes sense, right?" I say, speaking quickly. "They have to figure it out. All those fire warnings and how much money it's going to cost and . . . Anyway, it looks like it started in this guy's fire pit."

Ben starts slowly cutting into his sandwich. He takes a bite and chews it thoughtfully while I resist every impulse I have to say something more.

"Someone was stupid enough to make a fire outside after this summer?" he says eventually.

"He said there's been high school kids hanging out there at night, drinking beers, burning stuff."

"Did he know who they were?"

"Just general descriptions. Sixteen or so. White. Rowdy."

"Sounds like half my class."

"Right. Actually, did you hear anything at school today?"

"Such as?"

"Rumors? Kids acting weird? Don't the teachers usually know what's going on?"

"I don't patrol the halls looking for the telltale heart."

"Yeah, well, I'm probably going to have to go to the school. And to Nelson High. Start asking questions. See if there's any connection."

"That's going to make you popular."

I cut off a corner of the sandwich and chew it. The mayonnaise and bacon feel overwhelming in their normalcy and goodness.

"Miss Popular. That's me."

Ben smiles as my phone flashes next to me with an incoming text. It's from Andy Thomas, and the part that's visible to both of us on the screen reads, *Talk?*

Ben's smile runs away and is replaced by the hard, angry look he was wearing earlier.

"You better answer that," he says, then stalks out of the room.

DAY TWO

From: Nelson County Emergency Services
Date: Wed, Sept. 3 at 12:01 A.M.
To: Undisclosed recipients
Re: Cooper Basin Fire Advisory

The Cooper Basin fire continues to spread rapidly and has now consumed more than 800 acres of brush and timber. Because of the direction of the fire's path, the evacuation advisory for the West Nelson area bounded by Oxford and Stephen Streets has been lifted, though an advisory remains in effect for the Cooper Basin. There will be emergency vehicles and heavy machinery working in those areas overnight. Residents can expect the activity to be disruptive. There is a possibility that the West Nelson evacuation advisory will be put back in place should circumstances change.

More information is available at www.nelsoncountyemergencyservices.com.

Further advisories will be issued as necessary.

CHAPTER 10

To-Do

Elizabeth

I wake on Wednesday morning with the first streaks of sun coming up over the horizon. Ben's bedroom has never had proper curtains, and unless I'm in total darkness, my body always rises with the sun, like a switch has been flipped in my brain.

I reach under my pillow for my phone and see the e-mail from the county's emergency services floating on the screen. I'd put my phone on vibrate, sure I'd wake if it buzzed in the night, but the e-mail came in just after midnight, and I'd heard nothing.

I read it and think about what it says, how it means that we can return home now, if we want to. Then I check the weather map again, and I visualize all the downed timber I saw on the backside of the Peak on my trail runs. That's what the fire is rushing toward, where Kara and her crews are pushing it, hoping to contain it, stop it.

We're better off staying where we are.

Besides, do we even really have a home to go back to?

I turn on my side, away from Ben, and come face-to-face with the photo sitting on the nightstand. It's from our wedding day, taken on top of Nelson Peak. I look at our smiling faces, our full-toothed grins. We'd eaten our canary, and we were *proud*.

It was a glorious June day ten years ago—typical Nelson summer weather, all skyscraper skies and dry warmth. It wasn't a big ceremony, not according to Grace and Gordon, anyway, just our college friends, immediate family, my fire crew, and some old friends of Ben's. Despite that, the planning of it all felt like more than I could manage. If it hadn't been for Grace's generous offer of a wedding planner, it never would have gotten done. I couldn't focus on the details or make decisions that should have been easy. Maybe it was the timing that was getting to me—I could be called away to a fire, theoretically, at any moment—but as the ceremony grew closer, my anxiety rose to a steep peak.

It wasn't that I didn't want to marry Ben. Of course I did. But there was my own parents' divorce. And the fact that I hadn't lived in one place since college. And Ben was hinting that he wanted to start a family soon. And . . .

"We can cancel if you want to," Ben had said, finding me hiding out in his boyhood tree house in the small woods on his parents' property, my knees tucked under my chin, my arms wrapped around my legs. I wanted to small myself up, maybe disappear if I could manage it.

I looked at him, wondering how he knew what was in my head, what I'd never said out loud, even to myself. And then I was so relieved that he did, I almost broke down completely.

"I don't want to do that," I said in a wavering voice.

"You sure?"

He copied how I was sitting so our arms were touching. I could hear the snowmelt rushing in the brook just out of view.

"Could've fooled me," he said.

"I'm sorry."

"I don't want to make a mistake this big, Beth. If you don't want to do it, then just say."

I dropped my arms and turned to him. I wanted to crawl into his lap like a child. I wanted it to be just the two of us getting married right there in the tree house with only the birds as witnesses, the wind in the new grass our wedding song.

"I'm not ready."

"I figured."

"No, I'm ready to get married. It's all the other stuff."

"What stuff?"

"A house and babies and quitting my job and—"

"What are you talking about? We don't have to do any of that."

"We don't?"

He lifted my chin with his hands. Our faces were inches apart.

"Of course not. Who says we do?"

"Your mother, for one."

"Ignore her."

"I think you want those things too."

"I do want some of them. But only if *you* want them. When you want them."

I searched his face, feeling my heart speed up, maybe in relief, maybe in happiness.

"But I can't be responsible for all those decisions," I said. "If you want those things . . ."

He placed a finger on my lips. "I want you. And I'm not making you responsible. We'll decide together. When the time is right."

"But how will we know when the time is right?"

"We just will. Okay?"

I kissed him for an answer, and four weeks later, after a sleepless night on my part, we assembled at the base of the mountain and rode a rusted yellow ski chair up to the summit. I was worried I'd lose a shoe or that the light chiffon of my dress would get torn on the rough metal seats. But Ben had arranged for blankets to cover the chairs, and he held my shoes in his hand until we got to the top, keeping me distracted by finally revealing how his parents had reacted when he'd announced our intended marriage location.

The ceremony took place on the wood-slatted lookout that gave a view of the town and the spiked, snow-covered mountains behind it. The columbine was out in droves that year, and a white raft of flowers circled the platform, their gentle perfume better than any hothouse blooms. As the wind whipped around us, we said the old, solemn words.

In sickness and in health.

In good times and in bad.

Till death do us part.

I felt them weave around us, binding us together.

When we were man and wife, Ben took me in his arms, kissed my trembling lips, and said, "You're stuck with me now."

He lifted me up and carried me, bride-style, into the old ski lodge, and we sat down to the formal dinner Ben's parents had insisted on. I could only imagine how much money they'd spent transforming the 1960s decor into what I was seeing: walls draped in soft silk panels; pink and blue lighting; tables set with the finest linen. I caught my father's eye, and he raised his eyebrows twice, our signal for *Nicely done, kid*. I shrugged and shook my head, hoping he'd find a way to enjoy himself even though he was seated with my mom and her new husband.

And as we sat there, drinking champagne and cutting into thick slabs of beef, looking out over this town that was to be my home, all the worry leading up to the ceremony seeped away.

It was done, and we were one, and I knew the strength of our love could carry us through anything.

I roll back toward Ben to find him awake.

"Hey," I say. "You still angry?"

"I wasn't angry."

After he saw the text from Andy on my phone, we spent the next thirty minutes hissing at each other like snakes, arguing as quietly as we could, even though his parents were out for the evening. Like if we shouted, the volume of our words might stain the walls, creating evidence of our discord for his parents to find when they returned. And then they would know, and then . . . Neither of us knew what happened then.

"You told me you weren't speaking anymore," he said at one point.

"We're not. Today was the first time I've talked to him in a year."

"Don't lie to me, Beth. Okay? Just don't."

"Why don't you believe me?"

"You know why."

"I've apologized for that over and over. What more can I do?"

And so on.

Oh, we are good at fighting, Ben and I.

We've had so much practice.

"I don't want to argue anymore," I say to Ben now as we lie facing each other, bound together by circumstance, our pasts, and, somewhere underneath it all, the love that sometimes feels erased by everything that's happened.

"I never wanted to," he says.

"Ben."

"I'm joking, okay? It's just a joke."

Not funny, I think. But, "Okay," I say.

"Can I ask you one thing?"

"Of course."

"Did you at least try not to be involved in this fire?"

"Yes. Of course. But Rich—"

"No, that's fine. That's enough."

"Ben," I say again.

He closes his eyes. "Let's not right now, okay?"

"Okay."

"And just . . . don't see him again, all right? Andy."

"I won't," I say, although it's already on its way to being a lie.

Ben's eyes stay shut, and after a few moments I know he's fallen back asleep. Maybe he isn't really that angry, if he can just slip into slumber. Then again, falling asleep has always been as easy for him as closing his eyes.

I watch him as he breathes in and out. The dark rough of his beard along his jaw. His full lips that still, all these years later, surprise me with their softness. The perfect length of his nose. Is he really sleeping, or has he just retreated behind its facade to turn the page on us? Does he still dream about me the way he used to, waking up with my name on his lips and his intentions hard against my back? He agreed to the divorce, but does he want it? Did he just give up on us because I was insisting, or is it what he wanted too?

I could drive myself crazy with these questions.

I've spent months doing that very thing.

I shove them away, rise, and take a quick shower. As I lather my hair with shampoo, a waft of smoke emanates from it, like I've spent too much time roasting marshmallows on a mosquitoed summer night. It reminds me that the fire can still find us, even out here.

When I walk into the kitchen, it's a few minutes after six. Despite the early hour, Gordon is sitting at the island working his way through his morning grapefruit. He's wearing a pressed white shirt and dark slacks—all he needs is a tie and blazer to complete his Captain of Industry look.

"Good morning, my dear," he says, lowering his *Wall Street Journal*. "What would you like for breakfast this morning?"

He's asking me, but he's really addressing Rosalia, their live-in maid, who's the daughter of the woman who mostly raised Ben and his siblings. Rosalia is standing discreetly at the stove in a blue smock uniform, making an egg-white omelet, Gordon's second course every morning after his perfect half a grapefruit. Nearly six feet, Gordon is still as trim as he was when he married Grace forty years ago, something she's fond of mentioning. The same applies to her, come to think of it, but that's not the kind of thing you say about yourself. At least, not when you're Grace.

I know better by now than to protest Gordon's offer of Rosalia's services, so I put in an order for a poached egg and toast and push down my middle-class resistance. I might as well enjoy the amenities while I can. There's surely a time limit on this hospitality. It surprises me, in a way, that I'll miss this place. Though I've mocked it and never felt quite comfortable with its rhythms, there's comfort in knowing a set of parents—whole, intact, loving—were available and welcoming.

"Grace asked me to remind you about your appointment for your fitting tomorrow," he says when I've taken a seat across from him.

Grace is a late riser, and she often uses Gordon as a kind of verbal e-mail service. She's never used actual e-mail. Too impersonal, she says, though I suspect computers make her nervous.

"Fitting?"

My phone buzzes with an incoming message, and I pull it from my pocket to check for what I'm sure is a fire update. But it's not about the fire. It's an automatic reminder from one of the town's two divorce lawyers about an appointment I scheduled a couple of weeks ago as a way of making myself tell Ben that I wanted to separate. I'd meant to cancel it. I only wanted to put a clock on bringing it up, not on getting it done. I shove the phone into my pocket, hoping Gordon doesn't notice my shaking hand.

"Surely you haven't forgotten about the Fall Fling?" he says, amused, over his half-lowered paper. "I believe the theme this year is a very original 'black and white.'"

Gordon's ambivalence about all the socializing he has to do is one of the things I like about him. Between the cocktail parties and the art events, he could be in his tux every other week. Many of his friends are. But Gordon prefers the comforts of home over glad-handing. He and Grace have some sort of arrangement, some calculus about how much of it he needs to do to keep his standing. But the Fall Fling is the height of the social season, an event we've often been dragged to. And Grace knows I'm hopeless at picking the right attire, not because I can't choose a pretty dress but because I'm simply likely to forget to do so until it's too late. She took me to my first fitting two weeks ago when the dresses she ordered came in. Tomorrow's appointment is for final adjustments.

"Oh, right, of course," I say. "I've been a bit distracted by . . . the fire. It's Saturday, yes?"

"I believe so."

"Still being held at the base of the Peak?"

"I'd imagine."

"They might have to cancel it. If the fire worsens."

"Oh?" he says, not bothering to lower the paper this time. "That would be a blow to the whole town, I'm sure."

I suppress a laugh. "Either way, it might turn out to be a front-row seat to watching half the town being burned to a crisp."

"Surely not," he says, and the subject is closed.

"So Deputy Clark should do some interviews at the high school and at Voyages too," I tell Rich when he gets into work and I've filled him in on what we've learned so far from a forensic perspective. Likely source: fire pit. Likely cause: human.

"Based on what?" Rich asks.

"Our interview with John Phillips."

I hand him a copy of the report I typed up in the still morning. I've had a productive couple of hours. I feel strangely proud that Judy will have nothing to complain about with respect to my arrival time today. I was in the office, ensconced in my closet, long before she came in.

As Rich scans my pages, I look out his window. Like so much of the town, it has a view of Nelson Peak. The smoke behind it is thicker today, and a haze has enveloped the mountain, so from where I'm standing, it looks out of focus. It's hard to imagine anything marring it, worse still our house.

Rich puts the report down and leans his chair back, resting his boots on the desk.

"Seems pretty obvious what happened here, even if Phillips won't admit it. Why not just bring him in for formal questioning? Then we can decide if we'll lay charges."

"But he says there have been kids hanging out on his property. Teenagers. Drinking, using his fire pit, that sort of stuff. He says they were there that night."

"At one in the morning? On a Monday night?"

I feel a prickle of unease.

"He *has* made complaints about them before. I found these in the system."

I pass a second set of papers to him—the police reports of the complaints Phillips made to the sheriff's department. A pack of rowdy teenagers had been using his backyard as their personal playground all summer, drinking, setting off firecrackers, leaving things on his porch for him to trip over when he came roaring out into the night to drive them away. A sort of Chinese water torture of harassment, for God only knows what reason.

"If these check out, I think it's our most likely avenue of investigation," I say. "Guys like Phillips know better than to burn anything in these conditions. Besides, same logic applies, right? Why would he be out there at one in the morning?"

"I've found," Rich says, his chair precariously close to tipping over, "that logic rarely applies in these kinds of situations."

CHAPTER 11

Root Causes

Mindy

Angus's birth had been so easy that Mindy thought her friends had been lying to her about the trauma of childbirth. Rationally, she knew this wasn't true, that she was simply lucky the mind-blowing pain they'd described to her, in detail, hadn't been part of her equation, that she'd barely had to push because Angus seemed so eager to get out in the world he left without a moment's hesitation.

He'd been an easy baby too. Sleeping through the night at six weeks, happy to amuse himself with his blocks, and simple to leave at the half-day day care she'd enrolled him in so she could finish writing her PhD thesis and apply for postdoc positions without any sense of guilt. After all, she'd been in day care from an early age, as had Peter, and they'd turned out fine. *Fine.* Angus leaped so easily into the arms of strangers, he'd surely be fine too.

So there wasn't any reason to think things would be different with Carrie, and in the beginning, they hadn't been. Her birth had been a bit more of a labor, but Mindy felt like this was her due. And despite their worry that he'd be jealous of his new sister, Angus simply seemed fascinated, hanging over her crib for hours making faces and babbling to her in his particular brand of baby talk.

Eight weeks, they'd had. Eight weeks as a normal family of four, adjusting, laughing, trying to catch naps when they could. Eight weeks of thinking that her life was on one track when it was really on another.

Then Mindy found Carrie blue and gasping in her crib when she went to wake her for a feed on a beautiful afternoon. Mindy's scream reached out through the open window and brought her neighbor, the EMT, running. He'd performed the CPR that saved Carrie's life while Mindy frantically found the phone, dialed 911 and then Peter, convinced that Carrie was already lost. On the blurred ride to the hospital with Angus clinging to her, crying uncharacteristically, Mindy couldn't help but feel that she should have known something like this would happen. That it was happening because she hadn't been 100 percent caught up in the well-being of her children. That in keeping some space for herself, she'd been selfish, and this was her punishment.

What was wrong with Carrie turned out to probably be genetic, one of those anomalies that takes two flawed genes, one from each parent, to produce. If that was the case, then both she and Peter created the problem at the moment of conception, and in total ignorance. It was called ventricular septal defect, which meant there was a hole in her baby's heart. Though most cases were diagnosed soon after birth and treated easily, somehow the large hole in Carrie's heart had been missed. That happened sometimes, the doctors reassured her. Peter was convinced that they were just worried they'd be sued.

Mindy couldn't think about that. Who cared about lawyers and money and pointing fingers when there was a chunk of her daughter's heart missing? Two open-heart surgeries later, Mindy still felt like she was in shock—shivering, cold, unable to focus. Although Carrie's prognosis was good—there shouldn't be any lifelong problems so long as she had good dental hygiene, of all things, because there was still a risk of bacteria getting into her blood and hiding in the rough areas that remained in her heart—Mindy felt permanently changed by the experience. Gone was the nonchalance, the ease of motherhood she'd experienced before. In came the Mindy she was now, the one with no confidence, the hypochondriac who made constant vigilance her motto.

That Mindy agreed to move to Nelson without a passing thought. She would never run a lab now—how could she leave her kids in the hands of strangers? It didn't matter where she lived, so long as it was safe for Carrie, safe for Angus. And Nelson was beautiful, the air was clean, everyone looked so healthy, perhaps they could recover there. Perhaps *she* could recover there.

In a sense, she did. Years passed, and nothing happened. Carrie grew and fell in love with ballet and found a focus Mindy felt was almost frightening sometimes. Angus turned into a funny little boy who lived to make his mother laugh. Days would go by when Mindy wouldn't think the worst, then weeks. She started working part-time, not at anything complicated, just the chemistry lab at the high school while the kids were in school, which left her available when they needed her.

She realized now, though, that when she thought she was manning the fort, what she'd really been doing was letting her guard down. She'd been lulled back into happiness, and that had made her lax. Left her in some halfway house between the old Mindy and the new.

But today she woke with the fear firmly back.

And the name on her lips was Angus.

"Angus! Get over here and eat your breakfast."

An hour after the terrifying beginning to her day, Mindy sighed. She hated how often she had to raise her voice these days. No, more than that. Actually *yell* at her children to get them to do anything she asked. She'd always flinched around people bellowing at their children before she had kids, as if those parents' words were a whip that might catch her by accident. But it seemed to be the only way to get her kids' attention now, as if they knew the hollering was so against her nature that it was like a slap she'd never administer.

But still, Angus didn't move. She walked over to the computer where he was zoned in to his Ask.fm feed—though not too zoned in to minimize it before she could focus on the words.

"How many times do I have to tell you? No computer before school unless it's—"

"*For* school. I know, Mom."

"Then what are you doing?"

"It's just . . . these guys are being mean to Willow, and I wanted to check if she was okay."

He ducked his head as he'd done his whole life when he was saying something that was leaving out an essential detail. Willow Koning was, well, in Mindy's day, Willow would've been Angus's girlfriend. These days, Mindy didn't know what they were, only that Angus's usual brashness and confidence slipped when it came to her.

"I'm sure she's fine. Plus, you'll see her in half an hour. Come eat."

He closed the browser without opening his page again. She knew from experience that he'd changed the computer's settings so that if she reopened it later, his password would be deleted automatically. She kept meaning to ask Peter to change the settings so she could . . . not snoop exactly, but be a parent like you needed to be these days in the world of cyberbullying and Ask.fm and "No one's on Facebook anymore, Mom. That's for *parents*."

"Listen to your mother," Peter said from the table when Angus was already halfway there.

Something in Peter's tone made Mindy look at him carefully for the first time that day. He had dark circles under his eyes, and his lips dragged downward like they did when he hadn't been sleeping properly. She chastised herself for not noticing. She wasn't one of those women who'd replaced their husband with their children. Peter was usually front and center on her radar, right there along with them.

As she watched him slice a banana, she wondered whether his sleeplessness might also have something to do with Angus. Not that slightly off feeling they'd both had the last year, but the twang of panic that was still lodged in her chest. She should mention it to Peter, she knew, but she didn't want him to dismiss it.

"Everything okay?" she asked instead.

He looked up, dazed, unfocused. "Just a potential situation at work. I can't really talk about it."

Another worry joined Mindy's list. There'd been a lot of layoffs at the bank. Well, a lot by Nelson standards. Two, to be exact. Peter losing his job would be a real crisis, though they were conservative savers by nature. With college coming up and health insurance and . . . Mindy shuddered. What was wrong with her today?

"Should I be concerned? I can try looking for work. It's been a while since I—"

"No, no. It's nothing like that. I might have to get the police involved in something, that's all."

Mindy felt a measure of relief, which was immediately replaced by guilt. Ever since the economy tanked, Peter had to repossess more houses than he could count. Sometimes, people did things— ripped out fixtures, took appliances, or worse—as an act of revenge against what they saw as unfairness. Peter didn't condone that kind of behavior, but that didn't make it easier to get those people in more trouble than they were in already.

"Repossession gone wrong?"

"Something like that."

She reached over and rubbed his knuckles. His skin was rough, dried out.

"I know you hate those kinds of cases."

"I'll survive. What's on your plate today?"

Mindy turned to watch Angus as he slowly ate a piece of pancake toast that had gotten cold waiting for him (it was French toast, really, but the name they'd given it when the kids were little had stuck). She felt too nervous to eat. Whether it was because of the way she woke up that morning or what was coming up later in the day, she wasn't sure.

"Oh, me? I'm going into the lion's den."

CHAPTER 12

Threads

Elizabeth

I decide to walk the six blocks to the sheriff's office for my meeting
with Detective Donaldson, who filled out the police reports lodged
by John Phillips. To the extent the sheriff's department looked into
his complaints, which seems to be not really, Donaldson would
know what isn't in the reports.

"If there's anything that isn't in the reports," I can hear Rich's
skeptical voice.

I shut Rich out as I walk along Sullivan Street and turn right on
Main. A haze fills the streets, making my eyes water. The sound my
feet make as they hit the slatted sidewalk boards feels crushed, like
it's weighted down and can't rise to announce my presence like it
normally would. It's an eerie feeling; it makes the town seem der-
elict, though it's the thick of the workday.

The sheriff's office is in the old post office, a nondescript stone
building from the sixties. There's another sheriff's office on the west
side of the town square, a tourist version with a covered wagon over
the entrance, where little kids get gold stars to wear on their lapels,
and a mock shootout occurs every day at two o'clock—the apocry-
phal time the only shooting that ever happened in town occurred,
a hundred and twenty years ago.

Detective Donaldson has one of the two enclosed offices in the Main Street building; Sheriff Thompson has the other. Everybody else shares desks in the bullpen, which is full right now at the shift change. Deputy Clark is talking to another officer by the coffee machine. He tips his hat at me when I catch his eye.

Donaldson's office is in the back corner. He's on the phone. He waves me in, holding his thumb and index finger a half inch apart to indicate he won't be long.

He hangs up a moment later, and we go through the usual pleasantries, or what passes for them these days. No new news about the fire. Yes, I think it might get bad. No, I wasn't so sure the case was that open-and-shut.

"Clark tells me the fire pit at the back of Phillips's house was the point of origin. So I'm thinking it's time to bring him in for a talk," he says. About forty, he has the confidence I've come to associate with detectives through the reality of television, because everyone knows they're the smart ones. Of course, that includes me too, so I should shut the hell up.

"But what about the kids he mentioned?" I say. "The reports checked out, right?"

He runs his hand over his receding hairline. His head is almost shaved, but the just-visible W pattern on his forehead gives him away.

"Those kids weren't starting fires, they were harassing him. Throwing crap at his house. Stringing toilet paper between the trees."

"But if they were in his yard that night . . . they *had* been back there before, yes?"

"Sure enough. Drinking beer. Smoking pot and God knows what else."

"You ever figure out who they were?"

"My best guess was one of the gangs from Spanish Town, but I could never get anyone to talk to me. They don't talk to gringos."

"Didn't Phillips say the kids were white?"

"It was dark out. He saw kids running away. What does he know?"

I grit my teeth. Donaldson doesn't want to think it could be "ordinary" kids, as he calls them, white kids with rich parents who don't live in the one poor area in town. Kids with parents who'll hire lawyers and make his life difficult. I've seen this kind of thinking from him before, the few times we've worked together. His first port of call is always Spanish Town; I heard he'd even gone looking for the bank robber there, though the bank's video footage clearly showed a head of blond hair under the bandanna the robber wore across his face. It's also probably why he—and Rich—are fixated on Phillips. No one will come to his defense.

"So," I say, "what's your theory? John Phillips burned his house down on purpose by lighting a few pieces of paper in the fire pit two hundred yards from the building?"

"Maybe he laid a trail of fire-starter from there to the house, knowing the evidence would be burned away?"

"But it wouldn't be. And nothing's been found in the wreckage. Where'd he put the can, for instance?"

Donaldson shrugs. Details. Details.

"And why'd he do it?" I can't help but add. "Everything he owned was in that house."

"All right, all right, calm down, calm down." He leaves out the *little lady*, though it's clearly implied. "I wasn't saying he did it on purpose. Accidents happen, you know."

Four and a half years ago, I worked an out-of-state fire that turned out to have been started by a child who'd gotten hold of his father's barbecue starter and wanted to imitate the way his dad lit the fire for marshmallows on their camping trips. It was the end of a very dry spring, and fires were blazing up everywhere. Though I was supposed to be investigating the fire, we were shorthanded, and I ended up working on the site, which I was more than happy to do because I was having trouble shaking off the devastation this strik-ing little boy had caused. I couldn't wait for the beautiful oblivion of sleep that would come after twelve hours of grueling work.

But exhausting myself physically and mentally wasn't enough to drive away the last conversation I'd had with his mother. The fire had killed two people at that point—the grandchildren of an older couple who hadn't checked the batteries in their smoke detectors—and emotions were running high. When I went to see her in their tiny apartment, Karen—or Carol, how awful that I can't remember—had been up all night soothing her son's nightmares. Their phone was ringing off the hook. I asked her why she didn't unplug it.

"I don't want to miss their call," she said. She was young, not even twenty-five, but she looked at once childlike and older than I was. Her clothes didn't fit properly, and the house had an ingrained messiness to it, something much more permanent than could have occurred over the past few days.

"Whose call?"

"The parents. Of those kids. When they call . . . I want to be here."

"I don't think—"

"They'll call. I would if I were them."

The phone rang shrilly, and she leaped toward it. I could hear the deep rumble of an angry male voice spilling forth from the receiver. She listened for a moment, then hung up. It wasn't them.

She sat back on her listing dining chair, folding herself into it like it was a capsule that might catapult her out of there and into outer space. She cracked the knuckles of her fingers rhythmically, a practice that's always set my teeth on edge. She had an odd pattern of bruises on her arms. It took me a moment to figure out they were caused by fingers. A set of large hands had pressed into her forearms long and hard enough to tattoo the skin. The owner of those hands was nowhere to be seen. One of the guys on the crew said her husband had been down in the local pub since the news broke. I guess he had enough time to leave his mark before he went.

"Are they really going to arrest Timmy?" she asked. "Can you even arrest a seven-year-old?"

"I don't think that's going to happen. He's too young."

"When we went to the police station, he thought it was a field trip. He kept wondering where the rest of his class was."

She broke down. I sat there, trying to keep myself from crying, wondering what the protocol was. I hadn't received training for this. I'd already done what I was supposed to—determine the cause of the fire—and it was only a sense of guilt that had brought me to her apartment. I felt, somehow, that I had set this in motion and should find a way to stop it, though there wasn't one.

I heard a door creak, and Timmy was in the room. He was small for his age, wearing stained footy pajamas, with a thatch of white-blond hair that stood straight up. He padded up to us and put a protective hand on his mom's shoulder.

"You're making my mommy cry," he said, and I wasn't sure if he was asking or telling.

"Yes, I'm sorry."

"I don't like it when she cries."

I had no hesitation about what I wanted to do in that instant. Take him in my arms and hold him close. Protect him from the outside world that was calling him a pyromaniac in the making, a sociopath. So I did. I scooped him into my lap and held his slack body against mine while he looked up at me with wide blue eyes. He smelled of milk and Johnson's shampoo, baby smells even though he wasn't a baby anymore. He sucked on two of his fingers, self-soothing. We sat like that until his mother gathered herself, and then I let myself out of their broken home. I left quickly, because if I hesitated I had this wild feeling I'd simply tuck Timmy onto my hip and never look back. I could save this kid. Not in the abstract way we all saved people every day, working out of sight, unacknowledged. In a concrete way, like taking in a stray cat and feeding it properly, gentling it, teaching it that not everything in life had to be as bad as it thought.

When I got back to camp an hour later, I waited in the long line for the outdoor showers and spent my allotted time scrubbing my body with rough soap as if I could erase the terrible day. I went through the food line mechanically and took my plate of spaghetti and garlic bread to a picnic table where there was a group of firefighters I didn't know. I didn't want to talk to anyone. I just wanted that feeling of being alone-but-not-alone that you can get in a crowd all working toward the same thing.

But one of the men didn't leave me alone.

"You're the arson investigator, right? Elizabeth Martin?" a man who was about my age—middle thirties—asked. He had dirty-blond hair that curled close to his head and dark-brown eyes. His face was tanned and lined, but handsome.

"How did you know that?"

"I'm Andy Thomas. I saw you being interviewed last night about that kid. Poor fucker. He's screwed for life, isn't he?"

"What about the people who died? They're really screwed for life." I colored at the force of my anger.

He ducked his head and took a long drink from his water bottle. "You're right, of course. But I still feel for the kid."

"Why?"

"How's he going to live with that? Knowing he killed two people, maybe more? All because his dad left a barbecue starter where he could get at it. Like we all do every day."

I ate a few bites of my food. "Most would disagree with you. There's basically a lynch mob outside his apartment building."

"Sick fucks. They should be raising money for the lifelong ther-apy he's going to need. I just wish he didn't have to know. You think his parents are smart enough not to tell him?"

I thought about the low-level poverty he was living in, his young mother, his drunk-since-the-incident father. Maybe I should have told her not to say anything. Maybe I should have walked that child right out of that house.

"He'd find out eventually, though, wouldn't he? All he has to do is Google himself."

"Yeah, I guess. Goddamn Internet."

I turned toward him. His hair was wet and he smelled fresh from a shower, but he still had streaks of dirt and ash across the bridge of his nose and imbedded under his fingernails.

"Why are you telling me this, anyway?" I asked.

"That's a long story. And maybe I'll tell you someday if we be-come friends."

"Sure, no problem, I get it."

I bent my head toward my plate, certain my face was turning bright red.

He laughed. "Dude. Seriously. I'm not that mysterious. I became a firefighter because when I was on a camping trip when *I* was a kid, we had a campfire when we shouldn't have and ended up burning down a thousand acres. No one died or anything, but I've always wondered what it'd be like if someone had. What *I* would be like."

His face was so open and guileless that I felt instantly attracted to him. It wasn't a sexual thing, though it could've been. It was more the ease with which he gave access to his emotions. The simplicity of his personality. He wasn't a puzzle to be pieced together. There wasn't any trick. I could tell right then I wouldn't have to work to know what he liked, what he wanted, what made him tick. And if for some reason I couldn't figure it out, he'd just tell me, if I asked.

"So you've clearly had a crappy day," he said. "Want to tell me about it?"

And I found to my surprise that I did.

When I get out to the fire-site, the white trailers have multiplied overnight. There are more than two hundred people working the fire now, and there's already a sense of permanence setting in, a mobile community. Large yellow tractors, backhoes, and earthmovers dot the hillside. The green- and yellow-suited firefighters move among them like so many worker bees.

Containment, containment, today's watchword is containment.

I find Kara in one of the trailers. Her mobile command center has arrived, but she'll keep the one at the elementary school, anyway, she tells me, "just in case." I suspect she's really keeping it to drive the tweedy principal batty. I think that, and then Kara smiles at me and says, "There's that too."

"So what are your visions telling you?" I ask as I watch the crews working on the hill with the precision and grace of years together.

"You're aware that I do not actually have visions."

"Tell that to Andy and the rest of them. Tell that to me, for that matter."

It's not that I believe Kara really has ESP or visions or whatever it was her grandmother was famous for. But she does have an intuition about people, events, and the things around her, like being tuned in to a different frequency that lets her hear what people are thinking, which way the wind is blowing.

Where the fire will go.

"Andy and the rest of them?" she says, smirking.

"I don't know what you're talking about."

She turns back to her computer screen. "You found the point of origin?"

I fill her in on the details.

"Any reason why Phillips might want to burn his house down—or part of the town for that matter?"

"Don't think so."

"Just sloppiness, then?"

"Not sure about that either."

She looks at me for a moment, then nods. "You like this man."

"I feel sorry for him, sure, but . . . Assigning blame isn't really my responsibility. I need to pinpoint what started it and leave the consequences to others."

"I doubt you'll be able to separate the origin and the consequences in this instance."

"That's what I'm afraid of."

Kara turns back to the monitors. The one she's looking at captures a hotshot crew returning from their shift. A familiar bunch of old friends, including Andy.

"He's doing well," she says. "Since you left."

"Why are you telling me that?"

"I thought you'd like to know."

"I saw him yesterday. Here, in fact."

"Did you now?"

"Which you obviously know. Don't you have a fire to manage?"

She smirks again, this time at herself. "I do."

"Ben says hi."

Her smirk drops. "I *am* sorry about you two."

Does she mean the divorce? The lack of a baby? Better not to ask.

"Me too."

"I assume you have some purpose in coming out here? Besides checking up on me, of course."

"You're all about button-pushing today, I see."

She pulls me into a hug. "Oh, my darling, I'm sorry. I have a bad feeling about this fire, and I'm taking it out on those around me."

I pull away and look her in the eye. The usual twinkle is missing. "How bad?"

"Quite bad."

"The town?"

My house?

"Not that bad, I hope, but . . . it's going to be a close one. Too close to call right now."

I look out the smudged window of her camper and wonder, not for the first time, how the life and death of a town can be in the hands of a few hundred men and women no one will ever know. Strangers who are putting their own lives on the line while the town they're trying to save is probably just complaining about the smoke, and how they're never going to get the smell out of their drapes. Most of me wants these people to stay ignorant, of course. But a small part of me would like reality to hit them, just for long enough to wake them up, see the world outside them for the place it really is.

"It might be kids that did this," I say to Kara.

"Young children?"

"Teenagers. They'd been harassing Mr. Phillips. Drunken stupidity, probably."

"Do you think they know?"

"Perhaps. Think they care?"

"Cynical, cynical."

I wrap my arms around myself. "Sorry, I'm kind of irritable lately."

"That is understandable."

We say good-bye, and I walk out into the camp, wandering through the trailers, listening to the banter. I'm delaying, I know, but when I see Andy emerge from the showers with a towel wrapped around his waist, I realize I was also looking for something.

Him.

Ben's request from this morning comes back to me, but it's already too late.

"Beth," he says. "You're back."

"Just visiting. You got a minute?"

"Let me get changed, and I'll be right out."

I sit at the picnic table outside his tent, wondering at myself. If Ben knew I was waiting to talk to Andy, that might really be the last straw. And yet, part of me feels like knowing I'm not at fault entitles me to this. To this person who understands what I've been through, am going through, and with whom I've never had an awkward silence or a misunderstanding. I need the kind of comfort he provides, and maybe I'm being selfish for looking for it, but here I am.

Andy emerges from his tent in an old pair of jeans I recognize and a sweatshirt I don't. His feet are bare except for a pair of flimsy flip-flops. He prefers to go barefoot when he can; he likes his feet to be "free" when they aren't encased in the heavy boots that are a necessity for our work. I admire, as I always do, the compact power he exudes.

"What's up?" he asks, sitting next to me on the bench. Another thing I've always liked about Andy—he's never too self-conscious to sit next to what he wants, instead of across from it.

"It feels like it's happening again," I say. "Like four years ago."

"The Miller case? A kid started this fire?"

"Kids. Teenagers. I think so, anyway."

"I'm sorry, Beth."

I lace my hands together like I would if I was seated in front of a priest. And perhaps that's what this is, a confession of sorts.

"I'm not sure I can do it."

"You're not doing anything."

I take a ragged breath, but all I get is smoke for my troubles.

"Aren't I, though? Everyone wants to blame the homeowner. I could leave it at that. I *should* leave it at that."

"But you don't think it's him?"

"It might be, but maybe not."

"You have to do what's right."

"Do I?"

He looks at me, and for the first time since we met, I'm not exactly sure what he's thinking.

"You always do what's right. That's who you are."

"What if I don't want to be that person anymore?"

"You can't run away from yourself. I'd have thought you knew that by now."

CHAPTER 13

There's Going to Be a Change of Plans

Mindy

Before Mindy could face the Coffee Boosters and the rest of the Fall Fling organizing committee, she needed reinforcements. Caffeine and calories, not the empty substitutes found at the *Perk*, but the real thing.

So she went to Joanie's. She hadn't been there since that last, terrible day with Elizabeth, and the caffeine and grease that coated her senses before she'd even walked in the door smelled like memories.

This used to be their place, hers and Elizabeth's. They'd come here and spend hours together after whatever mutual activity they'd signed up for that month. Particularly in the winter months, when Elizabeth wasn't working and after Mindy got laid off, they'd drink bottomless cups of coffee and eat half of whatever treat the other ordered. Mindy hadn't had a friend like that since college. She'd moved to San Diego for her master's degree, where she didn't know anyone, and the women—and men, for that matter—in the lab where she worked were an insular, prickly bunch. It got easier when she met Peter at a party she'd forced herself to go to, but then they moved and had the kids, and then Carrie got sick and they moved again. And while she had acquaintances in Nelson, mostly the other moms she met on her endless circuit of child-related chores, Elizabeth had been the only close connection she'd made outside her family.

Elizabeth was the one who suggested that she take an EMT class. Elizabeth needed to re-up her qualifications, and having heard all about Carrie and the years of restless concern that followed, she thought it would be good for Mindy. Peter had been surprised at her interest, but that twelve-week course had been some of the best time Mindy had spent in years. Learning how to assess and treat basic medical emergencies. Staying in the barracks outside of town with the much younger participants for the last intensive weekend. The thrilling stress of taking the final exam and passing it with flying colors. She'd felt almost high with the exhilaration of it for weeks.

Then Carrie had come down with a bad flu, and Angus had failed two math tests in a row, and Elizabeth had left for the summer, and Mindy settled back into her life with a thud.

Now, as she made her way through the 1950s-style diner, she found herself hoping Elizabeth would be there, sitting at the chipped Formica counter, maybe, or getting a nondescript to-go cup. Instead, the closest thing to Elizabeth was her boss, Rich, holding court in his usual Naugahyde booth with the triumvirate of men who ran Nelson: the sheriff, the mayor, and the head of the tourism board.

Mindy sighed and took a seat in the booth behind Rich and the others. She gave her order for a coffee, black, to the pleasant waitress who still knew her name. And wasn't it nice that she could just say, "Coffee, black," that she didn't have to remember some complicated set of words to get what she wanted. She felt so light-hearted she added an order for one of the cinnamon Danishes she fantasized about when she was in spin class.

Spin class. Mindy had forgotten all about it. Guilt and dread descended in equal measure. Kate would be disappointed. Heck, she was disappointed with herself, but what could she do to fix that now, or erase the bites of Danish that had already slipped so easily down her throat? She felt at sea, and this place was an anchor. Her panicked awakening still clung to her, and she was worried about Peter, and oh, she didn't know. If only she could pick a direction and stick to it. If only she wasn't so apt to be carried along in the trail of whomever it was she was closest to at the moment, like they had a bigger gravitational pull than she did, and she was only a satellite in their orbit.

It was a hard place to be, up there in her head, so she tuned in to the conversation behind her. They were talking about the fire, and she was glad that at least some people in the town seemed as consumed by it as she was. They weren't saying anything unusual at first, but then Rich was talking about Elizabeth, about how she had this ridiculous theory, that she didn't want to accept the obvious. But he didn't say what the obvious was, and Mindy couldn't follow his intimation.

"And of course, old lady Fletcher's got her bun in a knot," Rich said in his usual pontificating style. Oh, the fun she and Elizabeth used to have imitating how he talked. "You'd think she was running a hotel out there."

"Not that surprising she's unhappy about having the shelter in her school. Kids need education and all," the mayor said. He was a tall, wiry man in his sixties who'd had a lock on the position for at least twenty years. "My office is fielding thirty calls a day from irate parents."

"Unhappy was yesterday," Rich said. "Today it's all, 'I've got this whole room of beds and food and only three guests.'"

"Guests? That's a good one."

"What's she calling you for?" the head of tourism asked Rich. "Housing's my department."

"That's what I told her. But she thinks that because my girl is investigating the fire, I somehow have control over the rest of it."

Mindy cringed. If Elizabeth knew Rich was referring to her as "my girl," she'd be livid.

"Phillips been brought in for questioning yet?" the mayor asked.

"Nah, not yet," Sheriff Thompson said. "Thought I'd let him stew for a couple days. Get him in the right frame of mind before we tackle him."

"You're a sadistic bastard, aren't you?" the mayor said.

"How else you gonna keep this town in order?"

Rich pulled out his ringing phone and made a face. "Just make sure you're not digging your own grave come election time."

Sheriff Thompson laughed. "I wouldn't start planning any funerals just yet."

"She didn't want no funeral," John told Mindy an hour later.

They were sitting at a folding table in the gym at Nelson Elementary, where they'd been for the last twenty minutes. The cup of coffee one of the volunteers had brought him was sitting untouched on the table. He wore a camp blanket around his shoulders like a cape, tied at the neck above the V of his hospital scrubs.

"Your wife?" Mindy asked, feeling slightly disoriented.

After she'd finished her coffee and Danish, she had another two hours to kill before the Fall Fling meeting, and she found herself driving to the elementary school. She wanted to meet John Phillips, she decided. Newspaper articles and overheard conversations weren't enough to propel her through the fight she knew was coming. Besides, it seemed kind of odd to be advocating for someone when you weren't even on a first-name basis.

After a brief hesitation on his part, now they were. It hadn't taken long for Mindy to get an introduction to John's peculiar, circular way of talking. He seemed to have no filter, and there were moments when she wasn't sure if he was talking to her or to his dead wife, Kristy. As far as Mindy could tell, John hadn't had anyone to talk to in a long while, and now that he'd gotten started, he didn't quite know how to stop.

For instance, when she asked him how he was doing, he told her that he'd woken up that morning feeling confused and lost. It wasn't that he didn't know where he was, he said. He felt like he didn't know *who* he was. It was likely something he'd never known. But to the extent that he had, well, all that knowledge, that accumulated life, had been burned to dust, to earth, broken back into its original elements, like Kristy was at her insistence.

And that's how they'd gotten to talking about funerals.

"'Don't you be wasting our money on funerals and caskets and nonsense,' Kristy had said when the doctors made it clear that the cancer was going to take her," John said, delivering his wife's words in a high-pitched wheezy voice that made Kristy come to life. "'You need to act sensible and take the cheapest option. Don't let those funeral people push you around neither. They's worse than used-car salesmen, I tell you. You listening to me?'

"She never thought I was listening to her. But I always was. Course I used to talk more, when we were first together. But she didn't really like what I had to say, and it got so it was easier to keep myself to myself, if you know what I mean."

Mindy did know. She'd often felt that it was easier to stay silent, to agree, to express herself only when she absolutely had to. Mindy told him it was a natural way to feel.

John gave a deep grunt and continued.

He'd been sitting by Kristy's bedside at the hospital, wondering how they were ever going to pay for the treatments he was sure the doctor was going to say were necessary. When they'd talked about it earlier, Kristy thought the army would pay for everything. She said it was "his due," but that was because she thought, since he never corrected her, that he'd done something in the army worth a damn. He hadn't known how to tell her, all those years later, that what had really happened was that, just shy of his second year in, when he heard he was being sent *back* to Vietnam, he'd tried to escape ("desertion" it was called), and it was only because he'd tripped and fallen down a hole some sadistic CO had made one of the other privates dig that he'd been allowed to leave for "medical reasons," rather than be thrown in the stockade.

Mindy thought about intervening then, telling him he didn't have to confess these things to her. But she stopped herself. She was supposed to be making him feel better, after all. And if this helped, well, who was she to judge or censure?

She made a sympathetic noise, which was all the encouragement he needed to continue.

After Kristy died a few pain-filled weeks later, John said he'd done what she wanted. He hadn't listened to that slick man in a suit who talked about payment plans and how to give Kristy an "appropriate" send-off. He'd used their small savings to pay for her to be cremated and poured her remains from the plastic bag they'd given him into an old ceramic pot she liked.

Then he'd put her up on the kitchen shelf and gone back to work.

"I'm so sorry," Mindy said, reaching out for his coarse hand. "Were her . . . were her ashes lost in the fire?"

John got a far-off look in his eyes, like he was trying to remember exactly where he put something. "I guess they were. Jesum. I never thought of that."

"I shouldn't have brought it up."

"That's all right, miss. Aren't nothing you can do about it. What did you say you were here for again?"

"I, uh, wanted to ask you something." She took a deep breath and sprang ahead. "Do you know the Fall Fling? No, well, it's this big fund-raiser some of us throw every year. Usually we raise money for the hockey team or something like that. But this year, I thought, *we* thought, we'd rather do something different. And I wanted to ask your permission first, to make sure you were okay with it."

"What do you need my permission for?"

"We'd like to put the money we raise toward buying you a new house."

"Oh, no, I couldn't possibly—"

"Nothing fancy or anything—goodness, we don't raise that much money—but enough to buy you a condo, maybe, or at least let you rent something decent while your insurance and everything gets sorted out."

"Don't have no insurance."

"Well, something more permanent, then."

He turned his eyes toward her. They were wet with tears and reminded her of the basset hound her family owned when she was a kid.

"Why'd you do something like that for someone like me?"

"Everyone deserves someplace to live," Mindy said.

He bent his head, and Mindy couldn't tell whether the sobs that escaped through his hands were sounds of gratitude or grief.

CHAPTER 14

Accusations

Elizabeth

After talking to Andy, I decide to try to find some of the other Cooper Basin residents to see if they saw anything that night. Everyone in the immediate vicinity should have evacuated, but having seen human fire nature up close, I'm sure I'll find at least someone hanging around. Unfortunately, the one neighbor I'm able to track down—a nosy parker in her midseventies who's standing at the fire perimeter watching the hive of activity like it's an episode of *The Real Housewives of Nelson County*—doesn't "know nothing." John Phillips kept to himself, apparently, and *she'd* never had any problems with the kids who were causing him trouble.

"So you've seen them?" I ask. "Around his house?"

"Not seen them, exactly. Heard them, more like. They find themselves awful funny, and that's a fact. Remember that? When you thought whatever you were doing was so important you could be as loud as you liked? When you didn't even think about whether it was disturbing others?"

I did remember. I might have even been the loudest of my high school friends, and I still feel embarrassed for my fourteen-year-old self tramping through the snow in full living color.

Oh, but we could *laugh*, though.

"And Monday?" I ask. "Right before the fire? Did you hear anything that night?"

"I might have. Memory's not the same as it was. Age, you know. It happens to everyone."

I take down her name and information so I can pass it on to Deputy Clark, and then I decide that my only real option at this point, other than going to the high schools and seeing what I can dig up there, is to go to the shelter. Surely John Phillips isn't the only person who's using the gym.

I'm not entirely sure why I'm so reluctant to go poking around the schools. Part of me feels out of my depth. Ben has such an intuitive understanding of what makes teenagers tick. I used to tease him that it was because he was still a teenager himself, back when we used to tease each other without it leading to an argument.

I seem to be missing that skill. It isn't that I've forgotten what it was like to be a teenager. I can still torture myself with all-too-accurate recollections of the stupid things I blurted out in class, or the way my heart felt when my first love decided I wasn't worth the effort. But all those years spent in the wilderness unplugged me from popular culture. I didn't listen to the music or watch the TV shows that connect this generation, if anything does. Whenever Ben tells me about something teenagers are using to torture one another these days—things like Ask.fm or Snapchat—I shudder. The record in my head of my youthful transgressions is enough. Who needs something that the entire world can see forever?

My decision to go to the elementary school turns out to be fruitful when Honor Wells assures me that, yes, several of John Phillips's neighbors *are* staying there. But my relief is immediately tempered when I see Mindy standing up, inexplicably, from a table where John is sitting.

Two sightings in two days. I feel like the universe is calling me out. *Here's someone you should do better by*, it's saying. *Something else you need to fix.*

Mindy seems just as surprised to see me, and we stand there, on opposite sides of the cavernous gym, staring at each other as if we've both seen ghosts.

Then Mindy raises her hand in a half wave, and I wave back, and she hustles out the back door like something's chasing her.

Mindy and I were in the same "Welcome to Nelson" class that I took soon after I moved to Nelson.

It sounds stupid, like something for elementary-school students rather than adults. But I was encouraged to join by Ben's mother, and she was right. Nelson is a small town, but it has so many aspects to it, so many activities and nooks and crannies, that it's helpful to have a guide.

It was also nice to meet others in the same boat. Most of the people in the class were women, young ones at that, and even Mindy and I weren't that old at twenty-eight (me) and thirty-four (her). But we both felt older, somehow. She, because of all the crap she'd been through with her daughter, and me because of everything I'd seen in my job. I'm sure there are some people who can watch generations of houses and wildlife destroyed repeatedly and keep a sense of joie de vivre; I am not one of those people.

Mindy and I wouldn't have been friends in other circumstances. That much was clear from the beginning. She was afraid of her own shadow; I got a thrill from running into deadly situations with a rebel yell. But beneath the surface differences, there was enough to hold us together. We were both new. We both felt like outsiders. We had husbands who fit right in to the town like they were putting on a pair of comfortable slippers.

We each had trouble making friends.

I think we both also felt like we had something to learn from the other. Me, to be less heedless, more mindful, and to transform into the person I'd need to be, to be a mother to the children we were going to have, of course, just as soon as we were ready. And Mindy, well, I'm not sure if she'd put it quite like this, but I always thought Mindy saw something of herself in me. Not how she was when I met her, but maybe how she used to be. Sometimes I'd get these glimpses, in a quip or an inappropriate laugh, that hinted at the person she might've been if life had dealt her a different hand.

Despite our differences, we got close pretty quickly that first winter. It was a quiet fire season, and I didn't get called away. It was also particularly cold and snowless, a combination that had the whole town going stir-crazy. We took a pottery class together, just for something to do, and in between the off-kilter cups and bowls we fashioned with our hands, we ended up as confidantes.

Life moved on after that. Spring came, and I went away. She had her family to care for, but we stayed in touch. We'd grab lunch when I was in town, and Ben and I would have her and Peter and the kids over for dinner. I always liked that, especially once Ben and I had moved into our house. The way the kids' shouts and laughter echoed off the high beams in the great room, that was going to be the sound of our house all the time soon, soon, *soon*.

Spending time with Mindy was one of the things I was look-ing forward to when I moved back home full-time. But instead, our friendship turned out to be the first of the things I ended up shedding.

The first in a line that ended with Ben.

We'd been trying to get pregnant for several years before I quit my job. When I first saw Ben after coming home from the fire started by little Timmy, I knew. Knew that all my hesitation and waiting for the time to be right was the wrong way to go about it. That if I didn't plunge in without overthinking every potential aspect, I'd never do it.

I threw away my birth control pills and told Ben I wanted to get pregnant. The smile that lit up his face strengthened the beat of my biological clock. And we two, to whom nothing bad had ever happened, to whom life had come easy, were so certain that this decision, once taken, would be no different. That my want, and Ben's want, and the chemical reaction we always produced when we hadn't seen each other in a couple of months would be enough. *Pow!* The miracle of life. Easy peasy.

It hadn't worked out that way. The months turned to years, and I never even had a close call. Being away from each other half the year didn't help. I began to read about infertility obsessively online. I became convinced that one of the factors keeping us from getting pregnant was the stress related to my job. And then I learned that there were physical impediments, and it felt obvious to me that if we really wanted it, I would need to make trying to get pregnant my full-time gig. Ben insisted that I didn't need to give up my job. Maybe it wasn't meant to be for us, and that was okay. But I knew some things he didn't, and a hard reality set in: I wasn't going to have it all if I didn't make a change. Maybe not even then. And though I loved what I did, I loved Ben too. I wanted to be a mom. In that moment, that felt like the thing I wanted most of all. I could find another job. There would always be another fire I could go back to. I couldn't say the same about the family I now desperately wanted.

So I quit. I came home. We had a sex schedule we stuck to rigorously. I ate all the right foods and exercised and kept my stress to a minimum. Only I still didn't get pregnant. I got crazy. So damn crazy that being around kids started to feel like punishment. Every month where the line didn't turn blue added another layer of resentment. Toward Ben, myself, the choices I'd made years ago that were coming home to roost.

And being around my best friend, with her two perfect children and her better-than-average husband and her overwhelming fears that it would all be taken away, became a form of torture. But I couldn't tell her that because what kind of person did that make me? Ungrateful. Awful. Being around Mindy was making me start to feel awful.

Then Mindy had a pregnancy scare. She was forty-three, and she and Peter had sex irregularly, I knew. Like not even weekly, sometimes not even monthly, and yet, there she was with a missing period. Feeling that feeling she always had when she was pregnant, she said. But how could she have a baby? How could she go back to all those sleepless nights, and then there was the genetic risk the baby would end up just like Carrie had, only worse.

We were sitting in Joanie's when she leaned in close and whispered, "I'm thinking of . . . not keeping it."

My coffee cup slipped from my hand and cracked in its saucer.

"You're what?"

"Shhh, people are staring."

I looked down at my ruined cup. My hands were trembling.

"I know I'll probably have to go out of state," Mindy continued. "But . . . would you come with me? I'll never get Peter to agree."

I felt like the blood was draining from my body. I was—am—100 percent pro-choice, but that she could be making that choice in the face of what she knew I was going through, that she could be asking me to participate in it . . .

"You've got to be fucking kidding me," I said, trying to keep myself from throwing the two halves of the cup against the wall above her head. "You're asking me that? *Me?*"

"Oh, Beth, I'm terrible. I wasn't thinking."

"How could you be so goddamn selfish?"

"Now, hold on—"

"After everything Ben and I have been going through, and you just want to . . . throw it all away? Because it might be a bit inconvenient? Because it isn't on your wall chart of activities?"

"That's not what I said at all."

"Isn't it, though?"

Mindy's face was bright pink. "I'm a mess. I don't know what to do. I guess I shouldn't have talked to you about it, but who else am I supposed to go to?"

"You *guess* you shouldn't have talked about it to me?"

"Don't do that. Don't talk to me like that."

"Like what?"

"Like you're the only one who's had bad things happen in their life. Carrie was born with a huge hole in her heart. She almost *died*. It's genetic. It would be totally irresponsible to have this baby."

And so then it wasn't just a possibility, it was already a baby. A baby she could have that I couldn't.

"I'm so fucking sick of hearing you talk about that," I said. "Get over it already."

"Excuse me?"

"It's your excuse for everything. 'I had to give up my career because of Carrie.' 'I had to move here because of Carrie.' 'I can't do anything I want because of my kids.' Blah, blah, blah. You chose all that, Mindy. Other people have kids who were sick, and they don't make their whole life about it. And she's fine, *fine*. She's been fine for years. You just cling to your kids because you don't know what to do with your own life."

"And you're so different?"

"I'm nothing like you."

"Right. That's why you gave up the job you love because it might help you get pregnant. And now you're angry at Ben, even though he didn't ask you to do that. You keep making bad decisions, Beth. That's the whole reason you can't get pregnant."

"I can't believe you're bringing that up. I told you that in confidence, not so you could use it against me."

"I don't even know what's happening here. How did this become about you? Why is everything about you?"

Mindy stood up then, her arms trying to fit into her coat.

"This is what happens, right?" she said. "This is when you see whether your friends are really your friends. Pottery and hikes—that's the easy stuff. But this right here . . . I guess I should've known better."

"So this is all my fault?"

"Just forget it, okay? Forget I even exist. I'm sure that won't be too hard to do."

She gave up trying to put on her coat and left the diner to the stares of those around us. And I just sat there, fuming, full of righteous rage because goddamn it, my fundamental point still applied, didn't it?

Oh, I'm such an amazing person.

No wonder Ben was so quick to agree to a divorce.

When I shake off my brief non-encounter with Mindy, I talk to two couples who lived near John Phillips to see if they saw anyone or anything around his house. It feels strange to be doing this with John himself in the room. He's at the other end of it, past the sentry of beds, but I can feel his eyes on me, like something pressing gently into the space between my shoulders. I have a constant urge to turn around, as if I'll find him standing right behind me in some kind of *aha* moment. But of course that's all in my head, like so much of my life, and so I keep my eyes facing front as I try to focus on what his neighbors are telling me.

The upshot of which is, "We saw and heard nothing."

Both of the couples I talk to—young, exhausted, grieving for the potential loss of their homes, their things—ask me the same thing: Is it his fault? They want to know who put them here, who might have taken away everything they have, and whether the old man hunched on his camp bed had something to do with it. I give them the same response—I don't know what happened yet, that's what I'm trying to figure out. They shouldn't jump to conclusions, though, and remember, he's already lost everything.

But the way they steal looks over my shoulder at John, well, those looks are much stronger than the one gently prodding at my back. If the fire claims their homes, John Phillips might need to be moved to another location for his own safety.

When I'm done, I circle around the gym, feeling the pull of another conversation with John. When I finally stop in front of him, he seems to be expecting me.

"They's blaming me, yet?" he asks. He's wearing the same hospital scrubs from yesterday, and there's two days' worth of beard growing gray on his chin.

"No one's blaming you, Mr. Phillips. Should they be?"

A patch of sunlight falls across his face, and he blinks into it. He shudders, then sits up straighter, his back making a popping sound.

"Have you seen the bathrooms here?" he asks.

"No, I haven't. They awful?"

He leans forward and starts to tell me about his bladder being another casualty of his age. How he often feels like he did when he was a little boy, when the urge to go would take him by surprise and he'd stop playing and rush toward the nearest tree yelling to anyone that would listen, "I gotta pee!"

He pauses for a moment, rubbing at the fabric of his hospital scrubs. He likes their soft give, he says, the way they make him feel cared for, even if only temporarily.

"You were talking about the bathroom?" I prompt.

"Ayuh. That's right." The, well, the urinal wasn't the same as the one in *his* Nelson Elementary. That one was this round, tiled thing in the middle of the room that the kids would stand around. When they were done, they'd press a lever on the floor with their foot, and the water would whoosh down and away.

"*Whoosh*," he says. "*Whoosh*."

Whoever designed that bathroom had clearly forgotten what it was like to be a boy, John was certain, or at least, was never the target of other boys. They call it bullying now, but back then his father just called it "toughening up," and John, apparently, needed a lot of it. That was the only explanation for how much time he spent with his head in the urinal, or shoved into a locker, or at the mercy of his father's fists when he was stupid enough to complain about something that happened at school.

Sometimes Kristy had been a bully too—he could admit that now. She didn't get physical, but she sure could push him around with her words. He wondered if there was something about him that drew those kinds of people into his life. Did he give off some kind of weakness tone only some could hear? Was it like a dog whistle's high-pitched call?

Maybe that was it. Maybe that's what explained those *boys*.

My attention sharpens. "The boys who were bothering you?"

They first showed up about a year ago, he says. Last summer that was, when he was doing his final stint of carpentry work, though he didn't know that then.

He was lying in his lumpy bed on a muggy summer night and had just gotten to sleep when a sound rang out like a shot. *Bang!* He got up and ran to the window, but he couldn't see anything except the backs of a few slim shapes running off into the dark. He'd gone downstairs and found the first of many presents they'd leave him over the next year: a cow patty with a firecracker in it. It still had a wisp of smoke coming out of it, and the explosion left a smelly mess that blocked the front door. He'd left the back way and scraped off his front porch with a shovel, then gone round to the back of the property to get the hose and to see if they'd done any other damage. That's when he found the beer cans and smelled that acrid citrusy smell that always reminded him of stinkweed.

"Drinking and getting high on my property. Making a fool of me night after night. Making it so I couldn't sleep, and I made mistakes at work and ended up getting fired. After thirty-two years! A man makes a couple of mistakes, and that's all the chance they give him. That's the only job I've ever known how to do."

"What about the police?" I ask. "How come you didn't go to them sooner?"

"Ha!" he says. "The police? The police are worthless." Even though Kristy had said to tell them (well, he'd imagined she'd said it, he knew that, but he knew her well enough to know that's what she would have told him to do), the police, when he finally went to them, had shaken their heads and written in their notepads and done nothing to stop any of it.

John's words cease suddenly, and his eyes get round like a cartoon character's.

"What is it?" I ask.

He opens his mouth to speak, but nothing comes out. He just makes a *mwamp, mwamp, mwamp* sound, like a guppy out of water.

He raises a shaking hand and points to the other side of the gym.

I turn to follow his finger. Honor is standing at the volunteer table unloading several Tupperware containers from a large carrier bag. There's a slouching teenager standing next to her who looks vaguely familiar.

"Him," John finally manages to get out. "It's him."

From: Nelson County Emergency Services
Date: Wed, Sept. 3 at 4:17 P.M.
To: Undisclosed recipients
Re: Cooper Basin Fire Advisory

Weather has become a factor in the Cooper Basin fire, as the forecast for the next several days is for windy, dry, and unseasonably warm temperatures. The fire's rate of growth has doubled, and the blaze has now consumed more than 1,700 acres of brush and timber. Total personnel on-site exceeds 250 and is expected to climb to 500 by the end of the day tomorrow.

The evacuation advisory for the area of West Nelson bounded by Oxford and Stephen Streets has been reinstated and expanded to include Broadview and Northway. A map of the area is attached. Residents are advised to pack important papers and personal items, and be ready to leave on short notice.

More information is available at www.nelsoncountyemergencyservices.com.

Because of the current unstable nature of the fire, advisories will be issued hourly until the situation has improved.

CHAPTER 15

Packed

Elizabeth

When I walk outside the elementary school, I notice the change in the weather immediately. The system I've been tracking since yesterday has swept into the valley; it's now abnormally hot, dry, and windy. My hair whips around my face as I pull out my phone. And there's the fire advisory I was dreading. The relatively slow nature of the burn has accelerated. Despite the all-hands-on-deck approach, the fire is having its way with the hillside up the back of Nelson Peak and is spreading to the west. I do a quick calculation; at this rate of progress, it will be at my front door in forty-eight hours.

Goddamn it! Why is there only an advisory in place and not an evacuation order? What is Kara playing at? I feel a rush of anger, though I know it's irrational. Kara's the best in the business. If she can't get this fire under control, no one can. My stomach flips with anxiety, a ripple of nausea trailing through my gut. We aren't going to beat this one. Something deep inside of me is sure of it. And that means we're going to lose everything. Our house. Our things. The life we built there under the aspens.

It's not lost on me that two days ago, I set something in motion that would likely result in me losing all that anyway. And in that moment, I thought I didn't care enough about any of it, that I could leave everything behind, including Ben, and start over somewhere else.

Well, ha. Ha, ha, *ha*.

What an idiot I am. I care. I care about the photographs that are still scattered throughout our house. I care about the Counting Crows T-shirt I stole from Ben back in college that I've slept in so many times it's caught my scent. I care about the cache of love letters Ben wrote me when we were apart.

I care about the clothes I shouldn't own tucked away in a room we've never used.

And Ben. *Ben*. All I want right now is Ben.

I tap out a text to him with shaking fingers: *I'd really like to talk*. I almost write the word *please*, but something stops me. Too desperate, perhaps. Too needy.

I hold my phone and wait, but he doesn't answer. I check the time. Classes have ended; there's no reason for his silence other than the fact that he doesn't want to talk to me. I dial his number, and the phone rings and rings and rings, but he doesn't pick up. He hates voice mail, so I don't even have the satisfaction of hearing his voice. Ben always answers his texts. Ben always answers his phone.

Ben does not want to talk to me.

My stomach turns again, and I rush to the side of the building. I don't have time to find a trash can, so I fall to my knees next to the bushes and throw up with a foul familiarity. My body often betrays me in this way, particularly in moments of personal distress, like it's trying to hurl the bad parts out of me along with the contents of whatever I last ate.

The energy bar I'd grabbed from the glove box in my car doesn't taste any better the wrong way around.

And as I hold my own hair to keep it out of my body's vengeful path, I can't help but wonder, *Will I have anything left to lose by morning?*

When I pull myself together, I know I should go back to work. I should take the information I've gleaned from John Phillips, the ID he gave me of the leader of the kids who've been harassing him, and involve Deputy Clark in formalizing it. But instead, all I do is tuck the paper containing the name—one I'm all too familiar with—into my pocket and point my car in another direction: home.

When I pull up in front of our house, there's a cloud of smoke swirling around it like it's sitting in the middle of a set for a 1980s music video. But there's a surprise too. Ben's car is tucked into the carport, the engine still buzzing from having just been turned off.

I enter the house through the unlocked front door, a trail of smoke following me in and mingling with our house smell, that particular mix of the inhabitants that seeps into any house and becomes unnoticeable until you've been away for a while.

"Ben?"

"Upstairs," he says, his voice coming from a surprising direction. I thought he might be here to collect the rest of his writing things—what he'd once referred to as the detritus of his dreams, but couldn't bring himself to throw out.

The books Ben could never finish. The baby we could never produce.

Our life was full of things we couldn't achieve together, or apart.

I take a left at the top of the stairs. At the end of the hall is the smallest bedroom in the house, the one the real estate agent told us would be "just perfect for a nursery." We'd beamed at her then, convinced that this piece of the puzzle—a real house for us and our family—would fortify our recently made decision. On the day we got the keys to the house, we made love in that room, on the floor, all tender passion, and Ben said, "Shall we tell her where we made her?" as we lay curled together, the cool air marbling our skin.

Ben's on the floor now, sitting in front of a large plastic carton that's half-full of baby clothes, folded in neat piles. Next to him are the rest of the closet's contents, a whole year's worth of gender-neutral clothes for baby's first year, arranged by size.

That closet is my secret shame, though it began innocently enough. Mindy was getting rid of some of her baby things, giving them to Goodwill, and I was helping her go through them when I came across the most exquisite little dress. It was Carrie's christening dress, she explained, bigger than it should've been because they hadn't been able to christen her until she was two. Or maybe they could've done it before, Mindy said with a blush, but it seemed like bad luck.

"How so?"

"It's not even like I really believe in all that smells and bells and . . . it's just the idea, you know? Christening. It's supposed to wash away your original sin. My mother always told me that babies who died before they were christened couldn't get into heaven, and . . . this is so stupid, right, but I felt like if we did it before we knew she was out of danger, we were preparing her to go there. To heaven."

She laughed at herself, but I hugged her, impulsively. She rested her head on my shoulder for a moment and sighed.

"Well," she said, pulling back, "look at me. Someday this stuff isn't going to bother me so much."

"Why don't you keep the dress? Save it for when Carrie has a girl."

"Yes, maybe. But you should take some of this . . . Look at all of it. I can't believe how much there is."

I protested but ended up leaving with a bundle of onesies. I snuck them into the house feeling like they were contraband. As if I too was touched with the reverse magical thinking Mindy described. If I planned for the baby, the baby might never come. But when I hung the little outfits in the closet, they looked so very *right* there, like they were coming home. It wasn't long before I found myself surfing Baby Gap on the Internet late at night and ordering sale items to my post office box.

I always thought the contents of that closet were my little secret.

"What are you doing?" I ask Ben now.

He turns his head to the side so I can see his profile.

"It didn't seem right to leave these. Not the way the wind is blowing."

I sit next to him on the hard floor, the pile of clothes between us, and start removing them from hangers, dividing them into his already started piles. He watches me for a moment, then joins in. We make short work of it.

There isn't so much to it, after all.

When the last piece is folded, Ben snaps the plastic cover on the bin.

"All this stuff, it's probably going to smell like smoke," he says.

"We'll wash it, then."

"We should probably get the rest of our clothes. As much as we can."

"Yes," I say, but neither of us makes any attempt to move. Instead, I reach out my hand until it covers his. He flinches, briefly, but then his muscles relax and he turns his palm over so it's flat against mine.

"How long have you known about this?" I ask.

"The clothes? Always?"

"Are you mad?"

"No, of course not."

"Do you understand?"

"I do. I always did, you know."

I bow my head like it might keep the tears from coming, but all it does is drop them onto my lap when they start.

"Hey, now, hush," Ben says. "It's okay."

He wraps his arm around my shoulder and pulls me to him. I turn my head before it reaches his chest, and my lips come up against his chin.

I kiss it reflexively, and then Ben's lips are on mine and we're clinging to each other and his mouth is everywhere—my face, my neck, my breasts when we get my shirt off. Then the bin full of baby clothes is pushed aside and we are fused together on the floor, my legs tight against his back as he pushes as deeply inside me as he can, and for a few minutes, everything between us is forgotten.

We lie there, afterward, in the quiet room, filling it with the sounds of our breathing. The wind rattles the window in its frame, and I feel that same prickle of gooseflesh I did the last time we did this here.

I wonder which of us is going to speak first, what either of us is going to say. I don't know how I feel about this or how he does or even, really, why it happened. Does it mean we regret our decision? Are we both trying to cling to the one thing that always remained good between us, no matter how vicious our words got? Is this just an excuse to feel something, anything, other than loss?

I don't get a chance to find out, because right when I feel like one of us, maybe me, is going to speak, say something important even, my phone starts buzzing insistently in the pocket of the pants we flung aside in our haste. I let it go to voice mail, but then the buzzing starts again, and I haul myself up, feeling bruised by the floor, and slip Ben's T-shirt over my head while I reach for the phone.

"Liz?" Rich says. "Where are you? All hell's breaking loose here."

"What? I—"

"What did I hire you for if this kind of shit was going to happen?"

I sense Ben standing next to me, climbing slowly back into his clothes. He must be able to hear Rich's angry tone coming out of the phone.

"I don't know what you're talking about. What's going on? What's happened?"

"I told you Phillips was responsible for this."

"But I really don't think he is. I saw him today, and he was able to tell me who the ringleader of that gang of kids is, and—"

"You're not listening to me. He did it."

"Why are you so sure all of a sudden?"

"Because his house was about to be repossessed."

DAY THREE

CHAPTER 16

Take Cover

Mindy

When the roar of low-flying planes started at three in the morning, Mindy was fully awake.

She'd been tossing and turning all night, never able to catch even a moment of sleep. She knew this because every time she finally closed her eyes and opened them again, sure it must be at least an hour later, less than five minutes had gone by. It was enough to drive anyone insane, especially since Mindy felt like she was halfway there already.

It had started with the e-mails. Well, one e-mail, to be precise, her own. She and Kate had written it together, but Kate had insisted Mindy be the one to send it because it was "her idea, after all."

Her idea.

She was starting to feel as if it had been a bad one.

Take how the organizing committee had reacted to the news.

"Will everybody calm down and let Mindy speak!" Kate had said to them in a stagey voice. She'd studied theater in college, and the voice-projection training came in handy sometimes.

They were gathered in one of the meeting rooms at the Nelson Arts Center. Tablecloths, votives, and long strings of fake fall-colored maple leaves were scattered around the tables waiting at the edges. Twenty irate-looking women sat in the kinds of plastic chairs the elementary school used, too low to the ground and too narrow for a grown-up backside. Mindy was up front with Kate, and she'd just finished dropping the news that they were going to shift the focus of the event.

"I mean it," Kate said. "Shut it. All of you."

She looked around the room sternly, and Mindy had that sense again that she was glad Kate was her friend. So what if she was catty and domineering and sometimes made Mindy feel like she was a twelve-year-old girl? When it came down to it, Kate did the right thing.

"I just don't get it," one of the women said. "Why does it have to be now? Why does it have to be him?"

"I'll let Mindy answer that," Kate said. "She's taken a shine to Fire Guy."

Mindy looked down at her feet as if the tops of her sensible shoes might somehow hold the words she needed to say. All she saw were blank floor tiles, so she raised her head and looked out at the women. They really did seem vulnerable sitting in those tiny chairs. But not as vulnerable as John Phillips, shivering under his blanket.

"I'm guessing that none of you have ever met John Phillips," she said with a cracking voice. "I hadn't either. But then I went to see him this morning. Right now, this man has nothing. Those chairs you're sitting in? He has one of those next to his bed. Only his bed is not a bed, it's a cot. He's got a pair of hospital scrubs, and someone gave him a book from the school library. A Harry Potter book, which he told me he found mighty interesting, all things considered. His wife died two years ago. He has no kids. No insurance. Like I said, he has nothing. Can you imagine that? Well, I can't. So you asked why we should do this, Susan. Why him? Seems pretty obvious to me."

Mindy sat down with her legs shaking and misjudged the distance to the minuscule seat beneath her. She almost teetered off and onto the floor, but Kate's strong hand caught her at the last moment and righted her.

"Anybody else have questions?" Kate asked, still holding Mindy firmly in her grip. "No? Then let's get to work."

After the meeting, Mindy and Kate took their time writing the e-mail that would be sent to the Fall Fling mailing list to advise them of the change in plan. After the reaction from the committee, they knew they had to set the tone just right or there'd be no end to the complaining. And on some level, Mindy could understand why people might be upset. The tickets were all prepurchased, and they'd been sold on the promise the money would go to the hockey team. Only the thing was, even if the fire and John Phillips hadn't happened, the money wasn't really going to the hockey team. That was something only she, Kate, and Bit knew about.

The hockey team was overfunded. That's what Kate explained to her yesterday afternoon while they were sitting at Kate's kitchen banquette, as she called it, enunciating the *tt*'s strangely.

Mindy always felt as if she'd made bad life choices in Kate's ultra-modern and pristine house. It wasn't that it was somewhere she wanted to live—it didn't feel like a home to her—or because of how much it cost. She wasn't a materialistic person so long as her kids were taken care of. No, it was how clean it was. Not that Mindy's home was dirty, it was just, well, a house with kids and busy people living in it and no help but her to pick up after them all. On the rare occasions when Mindy and Pete had people over for dinner, Mindy spent half the afternoon trying to figure out where to hide the kids' sports equipment and the winter coats that never seemed to get put away, even when winter was long over.

But, yes, Kate had said nonchalantly. The hockey team hadn't really needed any money for years. And because of this, Kate was secretly funneling the money they raised every year into a fund to renovate the town library, which was barely able to stay open. Kate had three hundred thousand saved, and this fall she was going to get the rest of what they needed by having a library renovation fund put on the special projects initiatives list that got voted on once a year.

"Three hundred thousand dollars?" Mindy had asked incredulously. "Didn't anybody notice it was missing?"

Kate shrugged as she pulled her ultrathin silver laptop from the drawer where it lived in the kitchen. Kate had a drawer or a cabinet for everything. "Even for condoms," Bit had whispered to her once behind a cupped hand, flushed with her boldness.

"Clearly not," Kate said.

"But how is that possible?"

"Oh, honey. You can hide anything in this town if you plan hard enough."

Mindy had sent the e-mail around 4:30 p.m., then turned off the computer and got tied up in dinner preparations. Angus and Carrie arrived home just as she was starting to cut up vegetables for the stir-fry she was going to make, and she asked them to help with the prep.

For once, amazingly, Angus hadn't protested. He'd picked a knife out of the chopping block, testing the blade's sharpness as Peter had taught him to do, and asked what she wanted him to cut. She set him on the broccoli and cauliflower, and stood watching him for a minute like she was seeing a ghost. And maybe she was. The ghost of Angus past.

Cooking together had been their thing. Mindy loved trying new recipes or seeing if she could replicate a dish she'd enjoyed in a restaurant, and mostly, she was pretty good at it. Except for roasted chicken, of course. But that night she felt in her element. And it was so nice to be working with Angus and chatting about his day that she forgot about the e-mail altogether.

"How's Willow doing?" she'd asked him from across the kitchen island, certain she'd get something snappy back in reply.

But instead, Angus had said, "She's all right. Some of those guys . . . well, you know kids are mean, right, Mom?"

"Yeah, I remember."

He stopped chopping and looked at her. Mindy wasn't sure whether he was more surprised she could relate to what he was saying or that she remembered what it was like to be a teenager.

"Right," he said after a moment. "Well, like, there's these guys, and they've kind of decided Willow's the problem, but she's not the problem, you know?"

"I think so. Sometimes adults do that too."

Angus cut the head of cauliflower in two with a big *thump*.

"Tucker's the fracking problem."

"Angus. Language."

"What?"

He gave her his innocent face. Years ago, he'd been into *Battlestar Galactica*, and that's how they swore on the show. Fracking this and fracking that. Mindy found it intensely annoying, but Angus had picked it up with gusto. The problem was, when he said the word in public, it sounded enough like the word it wasn't to make people snap their heads around and mentally put her on their Bad Mother list. So he'd long been forbidden from using it, and then, of course, he naturally stopped using it when *Battlestar Galactica* became a "stupid kid thing and *never* tell *anyone* I watched it, okay, Mom?" about a year ago when he'd started hanging out with Tucker and company.

"Nothing," Mindy said. "So, what's going on? What is Willow supposed to be the cause of?"

"You wouldn't get it."

"Try me."

"It's just Tucker being Tucker. He always needs to have all the toys."

Mindy almost laughed. That was a classic Peter line right there, and it was funny to hear it come out of Angus's half-Peter voice. But she stopped herself because she sensed the fragile ground they were on and didn't want to do anything to disturb it.

"Well, someone should've taught him to share," she said.

Angus rolled his eyes, and Mindy knew their moment had skipped away.

He finished up the vegetables soon after and drifted back to the computer. Mindy watched him frowning at the screen, scrolling through his news feed. She wished, not for the first time, that she had some way of seeing directly into his mind, believing that if his thoughts could be projected on a wall, she might be able to understand and fix whatever had gone wrong.

So with dinner and Angus and cleaning up, she'd forgotten all about the e-mail and the impact it might have until an hour after dinner, when she'd gone to look something up on the Internet she and Peter were debating (something silly about how old an actress in the TV show they were watching was) and she'd seen her inbox.

Forty-seven new messages.

At first, she thought she'd been spammed or hacked or whatever it was called when you suddenly got a million "investment opportunity" e-mails at once. Then she noticed they all had the same subject line as her Fall Fling e-mail, and she clicked open the first one nervously. It ended up being pretty typical.

I must say I was quite shocked/perturbed/disturbed/surprised/taken aback by your e-mail. While I applaud/support/encourage/back acts of charity, this is really neither the time nor the place for this type of action. Surely the town/state/federal government/Red Cross will be taking care of the victims. I suggest/strongly encourage/expect/insist you rectify this situation immediately as I understand that everyone is very upset/angry/furious/calling for your resignation at your unilateral action.

Four more versions of this missive came in while she was reading the first one, and another thirty before she went to bed. Not that all of them were negative (positive e-mails were running one to three), but it was clearly a major problem for most. She tried to phone Kate, but as the call went to voice mail, she remembered that Kate and Stuart were out on their monthly "date night," for which she insisted both of them leave their phones at home. Mindy wrote Kate an e-mail telling her she could call whenever, and then she took her phone with her to bed.

She had to hide the phone from Peter and put it on silent because he'd insisted that she put it away, but after he started snoring, she pulled it out of her dresser drawer and found another twenty messages waiting for her.

So she was awake when the air bombardment started, and it was what finally drove her from bed. Peter slept through it all, as did her teenage children, who seemed to be able to sleep through anything.

She crept downstairs quietly, anyway, and went and sat at the computer, thinking that maybe a casual browsing of the sale section of the J. Crew website might calm her nerves.

And that's how she found Angus's messages.

COOPER BASIN FIRE
Witness to Investigators:
Local Teen Should Be Interviewed

POSTED: Thursday, September 4, 6:45 AM
By: Joshua Wicks, *Nelson Daily*

The *Nelson Daily* has learned that a witness has identified a possible suspect in the Cooper Basin fire. Yesterday, the witness told fire investigators the name of a local teen who may have started a fire in the fire pit behind John Phillips's house. It is that small fire that has turned into the large one that is now burning out of control on the north side of Nelson Peak.

The fire was started around 1:30 a.m. on Tuesday morning. Phillips's house is the only one so far to be lost in the fire, which has now claimed over 3,000 acres of brush and timber. More than 250 fire personnel from around the state have been called in, and that number is expected to double by the end of today.

So far, crews have managed to direct the fire away from the Cooper Basin housing development by pushing it toward the Peak. However, the current hot, dry, and windy weather is predicted to remain in place for the next several days and exacerbate an already precarious situation created by this summer's lower-than-average rainfall. It is becoming more likely by the day that the Cooper Basin fire will be the worst in Nelson County in a century.

Authorities have said that given the fire warnings that have been in place since June, the person or persons responsible for starting the blaze will be prosecuted and held liable for the costs, which are now estimated at one million dollars, and will likely reach much higher than that.

The *Daily* has learned that the suspect is part of a group of teens known to loiter around Phillips's property. The suspect is a student at Nelson's exclusive Voyages high school.

The evacuation advisory has been reinstated and expanded. Maps of the evacuation area are available on www.nelsondaily.com, at all county offices, and through the Nelson Emergency Services website. Residents should collect their important papers and any portable valuables, and be ready to evacuate. They are encouraged to sign up for emergency service alerts via text or e-mail if they have not done so already. More information can be found at www.nelsoncountyemergencyservices.com.

CHAPTER 17

Bombed

Elizabeth

I wake up in the middle of an air raid as the low buzz of a fixed-wing plane rattles the house.

The windows shake.

An engine revs.

My heart pounds in my chest.

It takes me an instant to connect the dots. The fire's being water-bombed. Big, heavy planes and helicopters equipped with tanks carrying water and fire retardant are releasing their cargo on Nelson Peak to try to do what the human crews couldn't.

Mimic God. Make it rain. Stop the fire.

The plane's engine revs again, followed by that distinct rippling sound a water bomber makes when it releases its cargo. I imagine the clouds of bright pink liquid fanning out from the plane, speeding down toward the dancing red flames. I listen to the plane as it banks away, lighter now, circling back to get another load. The whine of its engine is joined by another, and another behind that.

I listen for a few moments until it occurs to me that it's fully light out. It feels late, later than it should be. I check the time; it's just after seven. Both of us have overslept.

"Ben," I say, shaking him slightly, amazed that he can sleep through this. "Ben."

He grunts and turns on his side so he's facing me. A short lock of hair is standing straight up. He'd say he needs a haircut, but I've always liked his hair longer.

"What time is it?"

"Seven twelve."

"Shit," he says, but he makes no move to get up. His green eyes are caked with sleep like I'm sure they used to be when he was a boy. "Are we under attack?"

I smile. "By water."

"Ah. That makes more sense."

"Than?"

"The dream I was having about Robert Duvall. I think we were in *Heart of Darkness*."

"You mean *Apocalypse Now*," I say, doing that thing I do again, but smiling anyway, because Ben always does this too. Confuses some piece of basic social knowledge in a way that makes sense but is slightly off. I've often thought he did it on purpose, but I could never get him to admit it.

He yawns. "Whatever. You knew what I meant."

"I did."

"So?"

"What did you—"

His phone buzzes on the nightstand. Once, then twice, then twice again in rapid succession.

"That can't be good," he says.

He rolls over and picks it up. His screen is cluttered with e-mail notifications. He swipes at the first one and sighs deeply as he reads it.

"Is it about the fire?" I ask, my stomach back in its nervous knot.

"Not directly. Oh, hell. Did you know about this?"

"Know about what?"

Ben's jumped out of bed, his eyes glued to his phone. "Jesus."

"What's going on?"

"Read the *Daily*," he says, pulling a shirt out of the suitcase we brought back to his parents' house last night. "Goddamn it. This is all wrinkled. I can't go to work like this."

This is not how Ben reacts to things. He's not fussy. He usually couldn't care less what his shirts look like as long as he meets a certain standard for work. Whatever the *Daily*'s published, it must be pretty bad.

"Just give me a minute," I say. "I'll iron it for you."

"You don't have to do that."

"It's fine. I want to."

I get up, grabbing my phone off the nightstand as I go, and head to the bathroom. I read the newspaper article Ben was referring to while I empty my bladder. Someone's leaked the fact that Phillips has identified one of his teenage harassers. Rich is going to lose it.

When I got to the office last night after Rich's almost coitus interruptus call, he was mad, but also gloating. Rich loves knowing things others don't, and since my wrong direction (in his mind) with John Phillips had cost him only a day of investigator's time, he wasn't that stressed about it.

John Phillips had a motive. His house was about to be repossessed and so obviously he'd burned it to the ground. An "open-and-shut case," Rich called it. One more for the win column to keep his stats headed in the right direction.

The problem was, as I pointed out to Rich probably too smugly, my investigation made it nearly certain that the house hadn't been burned down on purpose. The fact that a smallish fire had gotten this out of control was pure chance. And, as I'd explained to Detective Donaldson, it made no sense for someone who wanted to burn their house down to start a fire in a pit two hundred yards away and hope it would somehow make it to the house. Especially given how little fuel there had been in the fire pit and the fact that there were no accelerants anywhere. As far as I was concerned, the fact that his house was about to be repossessed and that he'd been served the papers a few days before was just a coincidence.

"There are no coincidences," Rich said.

I sighed. Next he was probably going to tell me that everything happens for a reason.

"This might make it easier to investigate," I said. "If everyone thinks we already have our man, it'll be easier for me to talk to them."

"Talk to who, exactly?"

"The kids who've been harassing John Phillips. He identified one of them at the shelter. I should at least look into it."

"Why am I just hearing this now?"

"I . . . I was about to come tell you when you called."

"Who is it?"

"A kid who goes to Voyages. So I should check that out. Follow procedure."

I skidded over this quickly, hoping Rich wouldn't ask for the kid's name. Because even though I knew keeping things from him was a bad idea, telling him this particular kid's name was almost certainly worse. Especially before I was sure of anything.

He worked his jaw. "Why are you so all-out convinced that it wasn't John Phillips who started the fire?"

Happy he'd changed the subject, I explained, as patiently as I could, about my conversations with John Phillips. How I saw the effects of the harassment he endured up close. How scared he was when he saw his tormentor at the shelter.

"No one's that good an actor," I said. "Certainly not him. And I'm 99 percent certain it was an accident either way. We can wrap this up if that's what you want."

"Are you kidding? You know how much this fire's costing? I've already gotten a call from the governor's office telling me in no uncertain terms that we'll be pressing charges and taking a civil suit to recoup the costs."

"Phillips doesn't have any money. That's a waste of resources."

"Don't be so naive. The governor's up for reelection, same as me."

"So, someone's life is going to be destroyed because it's an election year?"

"It's about following the chain of command. Which is a life lesson you don't seem to have absorbed."

I grit my teeth. "What would you like me to do, boss?"

"Get Phillips down to the sheriff's office for questioning tomorrow. And then we'll see."

Phillips is going to be questioned today, at nine. I'm going to have to hustle to avoid being late. But I said I'd help Ben, and that feels just as important in this moment.

I open the linen cupboard in the cavernous bathroom next to Ben's room and pull out the ironing board and iron I remembered seeing stashed there. I carry them awkwardly into the room and set it up. Ben's on the phone, standing there in bare feet and his pants. His shirt is draped over the end of the bed.

"No," he says. "That's a bad idea."

I hear mumbling from the other end of the line. It sounds like the voice of the school's vice principal, Janet Kores. She's been at Voyages for ten years, and she and Ben get along well. They have the same philosophy, part of which involves un-teaching the lessons the kids' parents have taught them about what's right and wrong. Not that they're that direct about it. They would've lost their jobs a long time ago if they were.

Given what's in the *Nelson Daily*, I'm not surprised Ben's phone is blowing up. I'm surprised my own isn't as well. Rich and Detective Donaldson must be livid that the *Daily* got wind of John Phillips's ID of the kid. Especially since they both seem hell-bent on not pursuing any course of investigation that doesn't involve John Phillips. I wonder how Joshua Wicks found out about it? Maybe someone in the department's leaking information? But if that's the case, then how come he doesn't know about the foreclosure on John Phillips's house?

I wait for the iron to heat up while Ben finishes his phone call. He's pacing back and forth like a lion in a cage, giving largely monosyllabic answers. "Yeah." "You may be right." "No, I haven't heard anything." "She's right here. I'll ask her."

He ends the call as I snap his shirt onto the ironing board. I place the iron on the fabric. It spurts out steam.

"Ask me what?" I say.

"If you're going to be conducting interviews at the school today."

"Where'd you hear that?"

"Stands to reason if the police think one of our kids did it. Shit. Did John Phillips really ID one of them?"

"He did."

"Who is it?"

I look at the shirt carefully, making sure I'm doing it right. Ironing's not usually my department.

"You know I can't tell you that."

"That's what I told Janet."

He sighs as he sits on the edge of the bed. "Today is going to be such a shit show."

"I'm sorry."

"Not your fault," he says, then gives me a rueful look when he realizes that, in a way, it is.

"Look," I say, "you didn't hear it from me, okay, but yes. John Phillips has identified a kid from Voyages as one of the teens who's been hanging out on his property. But he didn't see anyone that night, which makes it all speculation at this point. And I don't know if there's going to be interviews at the school today. Rich and Detective Donaldson think John Phillips did it."

"Careful," Ben says, pointing to the iron. I've let it rest in one place too long. Thankfully it hasn't left a mark. "Well, that's good, then. Janet will be relieved."

"Only you can't tell her."

"Right, I know."

"Seriously, Ben, I mean it. I could lose my job."

"I said I wouldn't, okay? I won't."

I look down at the shirt again. I know this place. This teetering tone we take with each other, which could tip into a fight if we don't take care but probably won't if we do.

We haven't been taking care. Not for a long time.

But I'm so sick of fighting, and I can still feel the pressure of Ben's lips on mine from yesterday.

So.

"I know you won't," I say. "Here's your shirt. Ready for the day."

He starts to put it on. I stand in front of him like the traditional wife I've never been and take over doing up the buttons. When I get to the top, I smooth it out and give him a light kiss on the mouth.

"There you go, all set."

He smiles at me, amused and momentarily distracted from his phone, which is still pinging every few seconds. My own phone starts to vibrate in the pocket of my robe, but I ignore it.

"About yesterday," he says.

"I'm glad it happened."

"You are?"

"Aren't you?"

"I thought, you know, because of . . ." The divorce, he's going to say but doesn't. Saying that word once was enough. "This is confusing."

"It is."

"We should . . . try to figure this out."

"We should." My hands are resting on his shoulders. He's tall enough that I have to crane my neck back a bit to look directly into his eyes. "I didn't think it would be this complicated." *I didn't think it would be this hard.* "Maybe . . . Why don't we see this as an opportunity."

"How so?"

"Like a vacation or something," I say. "Maybe we can put all that stuff to the side for right now and concentrate on what's in front of us."

"That doesn't sound like you."

"But that's the problem, isn't it? Me? Us?"

"Where are you going with this?" Ben asks. "You're the one who wanted . . ."

"You know I'm not any good at this sort of thing."

He looks me straight in the eye for a moment, holding my gaze in a way he hasn't in a while. Then there's a low thrumming sound outside that builds and builds until another plane empties the contents of its reservoir, and the moment, if it was a moment, is lost.

CHAPTER 18

I Know What You Did

Mindy

Outside of family matters, one of the things Mindy regretted most in her life was saying those few simple words to Elizabeth: *I think I may be pregnant again.* Oh, what a stupid, stupid thing to say to a friend who she knew longed to have a child and had been trying so hard to do so. And then to compound it by revealing that she was thinking of not keeping it . . . Mindy had no idea what she was thinking. Of course, she wasn't thinking, she was panicking. Panicking at the thought that she might have another baby whose heart was missing a central piece growing inside her. Panicking at the thought that this one might not make it. Knowing full well she couldn't survive going through that again.

But it was stupid and thoughtless just the same, and when Elizabeth had thrown her words back in her face and stormed out of the dinner, Mindy laid her head down on the greasy Formica and wept.

When she'd gotten her period the next day, she'd e-mailed Elizabeth to let her know. She felt like she owed her that much, at least. But she wasn't going to apologize. Elizabeth had revealed what she really thought of Mindy, and there wasn't any going back from that. Of course, they had both said cruel things, so cruel

Mindy surprised herself. How long had it been since she'd argued with someone like that? When had she ever done so? But she wasn't going to apologize, just the same. Especially after Elizabeth didn't even write back to acknowledge that the thing that had sent them spiraling out of friendship had never even existed at all.

Mindy was still frozen in front of the computer when the rest of her family finally stirred to life.

She had spent hours reading through what she found and still didn't feel like she could process it. Angus had said that kids could be "mean." Mindy knew mean. This wasn't mean, it was cruel. Manipulative. Deliberate. In fact, the more Mindy thought about it, the more the word *sociopath* skittered through her mind. Or was it *psychopath*? She could never remember the difference. Regardless of the terminology, the important thing was that, for the better part of a year now, the kids Angus was hanging out with, who Mindy thought were his friends, were using him as a whipping post.

The fact that she'd missed what was going on filled Mindy with shame. Even though she'd known there was something wrong with Angus, she hadn't pushed. She hadn't made it her business to get to the bottom of it, even though it was supposed to be her occupation. Her children. Their happiness. That was her going concern. And now Mindy had that same feeling she'd had all those years ago when she found out about Carrie's illness. As if she were the cause. That some flaw in her mothering had left her son vulnerable, had made it so he would not only be the target but keep it to himself.

Oh, Angus, she thought. *Why didn't you say anything?*

But Mindy knew the answer to that question. It was all over the pages she was reading. Angus had clearly decided that keeping the lowest profile possible was the only way to survive. That going along with it all, being the toe kick of his little gang of thugs, was preferable to the alternative.

Angus was, quite simply, afraid.

It rang through in his tentative exchanges with Tucker and the others, and in the difference in tone when he wrote to Willow, whose interest he'd been sure for months was some ruse. Mindy had cried when she read the exchanges between them when Angus had finally decided to trust Willow and open up about what was going on. She cried and then she stopped reading because those messages were innocent and belonged to her son.

But that certainly wasn't true about the others, the ones from those boys.

As her family moved around upstairs and the planes droned constantly outside, Mindy's whole body quivered with rage as she read through the last exchange, the one that started Tuesday morning on Ask.fm, their current instrument of torture.

The way it was set up (a simple ask-one-of-your-friends-a-question mechanism) seemed to Mindy to be the perfect device for bullying with plausible deniability. Because if it's phrased as a question, you're not actually saying something happened, you're just asking. Just asking! Just asking things like, *Is it true that Willow hooked up with Tucker last night? Is it true you were watching? Did Angus start the fire at John Phillips's house?*

That last question made absolutely no sense to Mindy until her e-mail pinged with an alert about the latest article in the *Daily*. The headline said it all, really. "Local Teen Should Be Interviewed."

Mindy scanned the article, her eyes stopping on the word "Voyages." She felt sick to her stomach. So many possibilities skittered through her mind. Tucker was an awful child, and he could be using the mystery around the fire as one more arrow in his quiver of abuse. Or he could be trying to cast blame on Angus for something he himself had done. Or . . . But Mindy's mind couldn't take her any further.

Because she couldn't help thinking that maybe, just maybe, what Tucker was asking was true.

Mindy was bumped from her thoughts by the reality of Peter and Carrie coming downstairs in all their usual noise for breakfast.

"There you are," Peter said, looking relieved. "Have you been up all night?"

Mindy finished shutting off the computer. She wasn't sure what error in the system allowed her to get past Angus's defenses and see into his account; she only prayed that rebooting the computer would hide her tracks and that Angus couldn't tell that she'd taken screen shots of the messages and forwarded them to her own e-mail account. Even though she knew she'd have to confront him with what she'd found soon, she needed some time to think about the implications.

"The planes woke me up," she said as another one shook the house for emphasis. "How did you sleep through it?"

"If years of crying babies didn't get through . . ."

"Oh, right. How'd I let you get away with that again?"

"Beats me," Peter said, kissing her on the cheek. "But why don't I make it up to you by taking care of the monsters this morning while you go back to bed?"

"Like one sugar-cereal breakfast is going to make up for years of sleepless nights."

"A man can dream, can't he?"

Mindy kissed him back with a pounding heart. Why hadn't she told Peter? Right then, in the kitchen, while Angus was still in the shower?

Mindy went upstairs determined to print the messages in the office nook in their bedroom so she could show them to Peter after he'd taken the kids to school. She'd go to his office and they'd talk this through like they did everything. And then they'd come up with a plan.

Mindy felt calmer once she decided this. Another plane passed by. Mindy pressed her face to the window that faced Nelson Peak to see if she could observe it dumping its load. There was too much smoke to see that far, but not too much to see that someone was hanging out by their trash cans, looking hesitant.

Mindy hurried down the stairs and shoved her feet into the first pair of sneakers she could find. She was still in her nightgown, but she wasn't worried about that at the moment. A teenage girl was standing by the garbage cans, shifting her feet nervously as she looked up at Angus's window.

"Willow?" Mindy said. "What are you doing here?"

Willow started like a doe. She looked ready to run away on her thin legs, encased in those ankle boots Mindy couldn't understand the appeal of. Her thin, almost white-blonde hair was straight as a pin and covered half of her angular face.

"Willow?" Mindy said again.

"I thought I'd . . . wait for Angus. He said he might want to walk today."

"Does your mother know you're here?"

Mindy was close enough to her now to feel Willow's trembling.

"Noooo. You won't tell her, will you?"

Willow's mother was notoriously strict even in the best of circumstances, and these were anything but—though, of course, Mindy wasn't supposed to know that.

"You're not doing anything wrong, are you?"

Willow shook her head emphatically.

"Then I see no reason for your mother to know you want to speak to Angus. But, Willow, if there *is* something, well, I wish you would tell me."

"You're so nice, Mrs. Mitchell."

"Perhaps you could tell Angus that."

"Oh, but I do. You know, like, all the time."

Willow was putting on an act, Mindy knew. Acting like she thought a grown-up would expect a kid to act in this kind of conversation. She wasn't going to tell Mindy anything. There weren't going to be any confidences. But this girl had been kind to Angus, so much kinder than Mindy had known, and she wanted to return the favor. If she was being completely honest with herself, she needed Willow on her side if she had any chance of figuring out what kind of trouble Angus was really in.

"We're running a bit behind this morning, Willow. So why don't you run and get your bus and you'll see Angus at school, all right? Unless you wanted a lift?"

Willow chewed on the edge of a lock of hair. "No, I'd better not."

"I'll tell Angus you were here."

Willow started to leave. Mindy watched her take a few tentative steps before she turned around.

"Angus is a good kid, Mrs. Mitchell."

"Why are you telling me that?"

She shrugged. "People don't say that sort of thing enough, you know?"

CHAPTER 19

The Box

Elizabeth

There's no proper interrogation room at the sheriff's office, so the questioning of John Phillips takes place in one of the jail cells in the basement.

I've wondered before, and I wonder again today, whether this was actually a deliberate tactic of whoever designed the station. If you're already in jail, so to speak, when you're only being questioned, does that speed things up? Are people more likely to spill the beans in that environment or less? Nobody's ever been able to give me an answer, and I don't think they allow those kinds of psychological experiments anymore, but it would be interesting, I bet.

Someone has found John Phillips some clothes, not ones that fit, mind, but it's still better than the hospital scrubs that somehow had the opposite effect on him than they did on doctors. Like they robbed him of his authority, rather than gave it to him. Not that the clothes he's wearing now are much better. His brown pants are two inches too short, and there's a stain above the breast pocket of the shirt that takes a bit of imagining to explain how it got there.

But his eyes are clearer today, focused, and the hints of intelligence I've heard during his rambles are there in the silences and shorter answers he's giving to the detective's questions than he did to mine.

Good for you, I can't help thinking. *Don't let the bastards intimidate you.*

"So," says Detective Donaldson as he takes a seat on a metal chair he's brought into the cell with him. John Phillips is sitting on the bed, his hands on his knees, his back ramrod straight. "You didn't think it was relevant to tell us that the bank was foreclosing on your house?"

"Nobody asked me anything about that."

"Well, sir, that's not such a nice attitude to take now, is it?"

John looks at Donaldson without blinking.

"Mr. Phillips?"

"Did you want me to answer that?"

I can feel Donaldson's flash of rage from across the room. I'm standing in the hallway, leaning against the adjacent cell. The bars are digging into my back, but I have a feeling this won't go on too long.

Donaldson closes his eyes briefly. When he opens them he's got a big grin on his face.

"Mr. Phillips, I think we got off on the wrong foot."

"If you say so, Detective Donaldson."

"I do." He opens his palms wide. Nothing to hide here. Now watch me pull a rabbit out of my hat. "I'm sure you can see it from my position, right? I'm trying to figure out how all this got started and obviously, as one of the people affected, I'm sure you want the same thing. Am I right?"

"Ayuh."

"Good, good. And the more information I have, the easier it is to determine what's important and what's not. Makes sense, right?"

"Sure."

"Excellent. And Ms. Martin over there, you know what she does, yes? Yes. Good. Well, she tells me the fire started in your backyard, and naturally, I'm sure you'd think the same thing I'm thinking if you learned the owner of the house whose backyard it had started in was about to lose his house to the bank, wouldn't you?"

"I can see that."

"Of course you can. You're a rational fellow, I can tell. So, naturally, when we found that out, and you hadn't told us about it, it made us . . ."

"Suspicious?" John asks.

"Precisely."

John rubs his hands across his chin and looks at me between the bars. "You think that fire was set on purpose?"

"She can't answer your questions," Donaldson says, as much to Phillips as to me.

"So's I got to tell you whatever I know, and you don't have to do the same?"

"That's how this works."

"Doesn't seem fair."

"I can see how you'd feel that way. But we all have to live by the rules, don't we?"

John nods.

"That must've been real upsetting to receive those papers, wasn't it?"

John chews on his lip for a minute, getting that vacant look in his eye. "It was pretty upsetting, I'll admit. But it weren't no surprise or nothing. Hadn't been paying the mortgage for months. Knew it was only a matter of time."

"That must be right stressful. Wondering all the time whether you were going to lose your home."

"That's the way life works sometimes."

"You're a better man than me. I'd be hopping mad. Paying the bank all those years and them raising the rate on you like that? Making it so it was impossible to make the payments. And then your work drying up. Terrible, just terrible."

John blinks rapidly a few times, like he might be holding back tears.

"Did you say something, Mr. Phillips?"

"You talked to that kid yet?"

"Now, what kid would that be?"

"I told her," he says, pointing at me. "We saw him at the shelter. Tucker, I heard his mom calling him."

The thing I miss the most about living in Nelson is water. More specifically, the ocean. Not that my native Ottawa was on the ocean; far from it. But every summer, when my parents were still together, I would be packed into the back of a four-door sedan along with everything else the car could hold, and we'd be off on some epic car ride to the ocean. Maine. Cape Cod. New Hampshire. Nova Scotia. Prince Edward Island. I don't know how my parents stood it in the days before iPads and DVD players, but they did.

When we'd finally arrive at the end of whatever road they'd chosen, there'd be the ocean, its saltiness filling up our senses, making even the texture of your skin feel different after a few days.

I had this ritual. I'd walk down the beach in my bare feet and stride right into the water up to my knees. I'd stand there and stare out at the vastness, feeling the pull of current sucking at the sand between my toes as I exhaled in and out, in and out, letting myself become one with the tide.

There are pictures of me like that going back to when I was two. Always from behind, my body changing and growing throughout the years, but the core always the same. This was my happy place, my center, me.

It's not that there isn't water in Nelson. There are beautiful lakes within an easy driving distance, and being on their rocky shores and cutting through their black surfaces with my body is also essential to my well-being. But there's really nothing like the ocean for restoring me to myself.

That's what I'm thinking about now, as I receive yet another dressing-down from Rich about my shoddy investigative skills and how I'm skating on thin ice and if he has to use one more metaphor I'm out on my keister.

If I could plant my feet in shifting sand, everything would be all right.

"Let me get this straight," Rich says to me in his office after he's been filled in by Detective Donaldson on what took place during John Phillips's interrogation. "You've known since yesterday that my nephew was potentially involved in all of this, and you decided to keep that information from me?"

Because that's the reason I kept the name John Phillips gave to me to myself: Tucker Wells, son of Honor, is also Rich's nephew. A nephew I'm fairly certain he's helped out of a jam or two along the way, and a nephew who—if he somehow *is* responsible for the fire—would pretty much ruin Rich's chance for reelection.

"Yes, but—"

"Does that sentence end with an explanation of why I shouldn't fire you right now?"

"I was trying to spare you."

"Spare me?"

"If it was nothing. If it turned out that John Phillips was responsible, after all, I didn't think it was worth upsetting you."

"But yet you stood in this very office not twenty-four hours ago and tried to convince me to let you interview him."

"Because it was the right thing to do."

"Because you thought that if I knew who it was, I wouldn't let you?"

"I'm not quite sure how to answer that."

Rich sits down in his desk chair heavily. I'm certain all he really wants to do is file this information away in a drawer and forget it ever happened. But it's too late for that now.

"I want to know how Wicks got hold of this story," Rich says. "Or maybe it was you who told him?"

"What? No, of course not. Why would I do that?"

"To draw attention away from Phillips."

"I don't have any vested interest in Phillips."

"You think he's innocent."

"I do. We need to go out to the school and interview those kids."

"I don't think that's called for. Perhaps a quiet conversation with Tucker on the side, but—"

"That's exactly what we can't do. Not with the newspaper sniffing around. What if his name gets out? That's going to look like favoritism, like you have something to hide."

Rich tips his chair back slowly. He's quiet for a full minute, maybe more.

"Do you have a strategy? For what you would do at the school?" he asks.

"Tucker has a gang of friends. I'd start with them and see what that turns up."

"All right, I guess we don't have any choice. I'll call the administration and tell them you're coming. Take Deputy Clark with you. And the parents will have to be alerted and present during the interviews. And you had better tread lightly. If I hear that you've been making unfounded accusations against anyone . . ."

"Of course, I understand."

I pass Judy on the way back to my closet. She's playing online Scrabble with someone and has just gotten a ten-letter triple word score.

"Nice one," I say. "Do you have Joshua Wicks's number?"

She doesn't look up. "It's on the website."

"You know it isn't."

"What do you need it for?"

"I have something I need to ask him about."

"Tucker Wells?"

"How do you know about that?"

"I have ears, don't I?"

"Do you have the number, Judy?"

"I'll e-mail it to you."

"Thank you. That wasn't so hard now, was it?"

She ignores me, intent on her game.

I sit behind my desk as my phone flashes with a text. It's from Ben.

Call me, it says simply.

I feel my heart speed up in a way it hasn't in years.

I remember the first text I got from Ben; it was something suggestive, and then he sent another one patting himself on the back for taking to texting so quickly. But that was a long time ago. Too often lately, our texts have become just another way to communicate household chores—could I bring home some milk, did he remember to take out the trash—or to continue whatever argument we were having in a passive-aggressive way that did credit to neither of us.

Now he wants me to call. He must be on break, because he wouldn't have me call him in class, but I can't be certain. Ben is right; I don't know his schedule anymore. Another detail I've let slide, another thing to beat myself up for.

My body feels full of self-inflicted bruises.

Ben picks up on the third ring.

"What's going on?" he asks without preamble. "All the blinds are down. In administration."

I know from experience that this act is reserved for when things are at their worst. Like some cheap venetian blinds will give the administration the superpowers they need to solve whatever crisis drove the blinds down in the first place.

"Ugh. And they're saying nothing?"

"They never say anything. We get more info from the students. They always seem to know what's going on before we do."

"Wasn't I saying that the other day?"

I wish I could catch the words as they tumble out of my mouth, roll them back up into my brain.

Thankfully, Ben doesn't take it badly. "You were."

"Are you hearing anything from that quarter?"

"You're kidding, right?"

"What?"

"You wouldn't tell me anything this morning, and now you expect—"

"That's not the same thing and you know it."

"Do I?"

I turn my desk chair around so I'm looking out my meager window. I should've known this would happen. That whatever thin veneer we'd coated ourselves in these last twenty-four hours wouldn't last. It hasn't had time to harden.

"Elizabeth? You still there?"

"Still here."

"Why did you call?"

"Because you asked me to."

"No, I meant . . . Forget it."

"I wanted to talk to you," I say.

"You did?"

"Don't act so surprised."

"Everything surprises me, these days."

"Me too, whether you believe it or not."

"If you say so."

"Look, I am coming to the school, okay? We're going to be doing some interviews."

"No wonder the blinds are down."

"Yeah."

"I'm having trouble believing that one of these kids could be the cause of all this."

"That's because you see the good in everyone."

"You really think that?"

"Yeah," I say. "I do."

We fall silent again, but somehow it's better this time.

"You have that thing with my mother today, right?" Ben says. "That fitting thing?"

"I think so. At four thirty."

"Maybe we could go to dinner after?"

"Thai Thai?" I say, hopefully.

"That sounds good."

"It's a date."

My mouth stumbles over the words, but maybe this is what we need. A date. A beginning. A foothold.

Or maybe I should stop overthinking everything for once and let it just be dinner. Sustenance.

"I'll meet you there at six," I say.

"Will do. And don't be too tough on Tucker. We don't know if he did anything yet."

"How did . . ."

"You're not the only one who can keep secrets."

CHAPTER 20

Back to School

Mindy

Before turning up at the school, Mindy had the presence of mind to call ahead (she couldn't show up during class hours these days and expect to be admitted), and so Ben was there waiting for her by the side door, as he said he would be.

As with Elizabeth, she hadn't interacted with Ben since The Falling Out. She'd seen him around town and in the distance at school events, but they hadn't spoken. It was strange to Mindy that she hadn't realized it until now, but she'd missed Ben too. Even though it was Elizabeth she'd been closest with, they were all friends separately. It was one of the things she'd loved about them, about her and Peter and them. When the couples had dinner, they didn't split along gender lines; they all talked together. Or she'd talk to Ben while Beth talked to Peter. Ben knew as much about Mindy's life as anyone (well, almost, anyway), and when someone like that goes away, they take a piece of you with them. But it made perfect sense that they hadn't spoken. Elizabeth was the one who'd brought them together, and the fight had torn them all apart.

"You want to come in?" Ben asked. He looked older than the last time Mindy saw him up close, more mature somehow. As if the last traces of childhood were erased by what had gone on in his life since she knew him. Which seemed an odd thing to happen in a year, until Mindy thought about the last twenty-four hours of her life. If she'd taken a picture of her own self three days ago and compared it with how she looked this morning, she was certain she could tell the difference.

"Is there somewhere we could go outside?" Mindy asked.

"I've only got thirty minutes till my next class. But hold on a sec."

Ben disappeared back into the building while Mindy shivered inside her anorak, though it was more than adequate protection against this ridiculous weather. It was hot without any chance of rain. The slate sky was indistinguishable from the layer of smoke between it and the ground. She'd only worn it out of habit.

The fire. In the chaos of the morning, Mindy had forgotten to check for the latest update. She pulled out her phone and tapped on the saved link in her browser. It was still growing. Officials were hopeful that the water drops, which had stopped an hour ago, would do the trick. But just in case, crews would begin preparing structures closest to the fire's path. Cutting down trees and removing undergrowth. Bringing in hoses and equipment to be ready at a moment's notice. One of the areas where that work was under way included Ben and Elizabeth's house, she saw when she opened the map. She couldn't imagine what that must be like. Yet there she was, burdening Ben with her own troubles.

She was about to leave when Ben reappeared wearing an anorak similar to Mindy's. It was part of the town uniform, one for every season. Perhaps they both wished that if they dressed normal-weather appropriate, they might bring it to pass.

"Follow me," he said.

They walked in silence to the edge of the school grounds. Voyages occupied a ten-acre campus near the river that snaked through the southern edge of the valley. Though it was one of the older schools in the district, several substantial endowments from alumni meant that the low collage of buildings looked freshly built. The classrooms were sunny and large, the class sizes small, and the facilities incomparable.

Peter and Mindy were able to send Carrie and Angus there only because her father had set up a trust that got funded by his insurance when he died. There was enough for private high school and college for both kids, so they fulfilled her father's wish despite their fear that the kids might feel out of place surrounded by children from much wealthier families.

Was that the reason all this was happening? Mindy wondered. Was Angus being singled out because his parents lived on one of the "flat" streets, where the houses were built in the last twenty years on a relatively modest scale? Because they didn't have a ski chalet in Vail and were perfectly content with their bargain-priced passes to the aging Peak?

Ben came to rest at a picnic table that overlooked the river. He stooped to pick up a cigarette butt.

"The kids are lucky that portable DNA test never got approved," he said.

At first Mindy thought he was joking, but then on second thought, he probably wasn't.

"What's up?" he asked as he folded himself into the table.

Mindy sat opposite him. Normally she would have hemmed and hawed, but the mixture of anger and terror coursing through her made her direct.

"I'm worried Angus is mixed up in the fire."

"Because of the story in the paper this morning?"

"That, and other things."

"The suspect can't be Angus. If Phillips identified him, surely you'd know about it?"

Mindy's fears ebbed and then grew. Sensible Ben should be right. Only he didn't know what she knew. And he wasn't looking her directly in the eye.

"You know who it is, don't you?" she asked.

"No, no. Elizabeth couldn't tell me."

"Elizabeth? What does she have to do with this?"

"She's been investigating the fire. You didn't know?"

"No. I . . . You know we're not talking, right?"

"Yes, of course. I just thought that everyone knew she was . . . Forget it. Why do you think Angus might be involved?"

She explained about the messages she'd found, how she'd been able to get into Angus's Ask.fm account. She showed him the printout of the most recent exchanges she found between him and his "friends."

Ben's eyes narrowed as he read them, two red spots appearing high on his cheeks.

"That little . . . This is not good."

"That's why I brought it to you."

"Why me? Why not take this directly to the principal?"

"You've always been nice to Angus. And, honestly, you probably know as much about him as I do these days."

"Why do you say that?"

She motioned toward the pages. "That's just the tip of the iceberg. It's been going on all year. The . . . bullying, I guess you'd call it. And I had no idea. We had no idea."

Tears splashed down her face onto her anorak.

"Hey, now, don't cry. That's what teenagers do, right? Keep things from their parents."

"But I knew something was wrong with him. I knew and I didn't do anything. Have you noticed him acting strangely in any way? Is he . . . Do you think he could have started the fire?"

"Whoa. Wait a minute. Back up. Those messages are just Tucker stirring the pot. There's nothing here that shows that Angus did anything. Was he even out of the house that night?"

Mindy hung her head, looking at the tips of her shoes between the slats on the picnic table. One of the most basic things she always thought she'd know about her son was his precise location at all times. But she couldn't turn away from the truth of her answer.

"I don't know."

CHAPTER 21

The Good Son

Elizabeth

Deputy Clark and I drive out to Voyages after lunch. I call Joshua Wicks on the way, using the cell number Judy tracked down for me after she vanquished her latest Scrabble opponent.

"Wicks," he says in a deep baritone. Though it almost sounds fake, this is his natural speaking voice, one more likely to belong to Andre the Giant than an eager, small-town reporter.

"This is Elizabeth Martin from the prosecutor's office. I'd like to—"

"I remember you. And I can't reveal my sources."

"I didn't ask you to do that."

"But you were about to."

"Mr. Wicks, you must know that writing a story like that is going to raise questions."

"That's exactly why I wrote it."

"But how did you know to write it? What makes you so sure it's true?"

"Are you questioning my journalistic integrity?"

I want to remove the phone from my ear and smash it into the dashboard.

"I'm simply trying to figure out what's going on. This is a delicate investigation, and if someone's giving you information they shouldn't be—"

"Here's a tip. Free of charge. If you want to keep things secret in this town, don't conduct interviews in full view of numerous witnesses."

He slams down the phone, but it's a satisfying noise. So it's not such a big mystery, after all. He spoke to someone at the shelter—surely not Honor Wells—and learned that John Phillips had pointed the finger at Tucker. Then he assumed that armed with that information, we'd do the right thing and question the kids who might be involved.

And here we are about to do that very thing.

Does one ever know if they're the chicken or the egg?

When we arrive, the vice principal, Janet Kores, is there to greet us at the front entrance. Ben has class right now, and it's not like we'd let a teacher sit in on the questioning. We had to let their parents know, of course, a process I was sure was going to derail the whole thing because of the flood of angry calls to Rich. But he must've put his foot down with his sister, Honor. Doing this all quietly is in everyone's best interest, for now.

Janet's nearing fifty. She's tall and wiry; she and her partner, Helen, recently went to Maine to get, as she put it, "legally married." Five years ago, that would've cost Janet her job; this year, she got a nice gift from the senior class and a small write-up in the *Daily*. Sometimes progress really does happen.

The fact that Ben's not there and Janet is, the nervous look on her face, the stares and whispers and turned heads in the hall—none of this surprises me. What does surprise me is who they've decided we should interview first: Angus Mitchell.

"What's he doing here?" I ask Janet when I catch a glimpse of a miserable-looking Angus sitting between his parents through the glass panel in the classroom door. He's grown almost as tall as his dad, and he's wearing his dark-red hair cropped short. Angus's hair color is one of the things that Mindy and I used to laugh about because it was so much closer to my own than hers or Peter's. Sometimes when we were together, people thought he was my son.

"Some information has come to light . . . His mother approached us, actually."

"Mindy?"

"You know that kid?" Deputy Clark asks me.

I watch Mindy and Peter through the glass. Mindy's face is so red she looks sunburned, a sure sign she's in distress. Peter is harder to read. When I knew him, he was always a happy guy, but now there are deep lines burrowed into his forehead.

"I used to be friends with his parents," I say.

"That going to be a problem?"

"No, it's fine." I turn back to Janet. "What did Mindy tell you?"

"I think it's best if you hear that directly from Angus."

I rub my hands over my face. I am in no way ready for this.

"Shall we go in?" Deputy Clark asks.

All three of them startle at the squeak of the door. I introduce Deputy Clark as we take a seat in front of them, and I'm hoping the formality of the process will cover the awkwardness of our first conversation in a year being under these circumstances. Mindy speaks to me in clipped sentences. Peter is slightly warmer.

Deputy Clark pulls out a mini-recorder and sets it on the desk.

Mindy eyes it nervously. "Is that . . . necessary?"

"Well, ma'am, it's standard procedure."

He lets that information sit there, waiting for an objection. Right now they're talking to us willingly. They could stop this interview, say no to it being taped, whatever they want to do. But there's the power of authority—and a million TV cop shows—working against them. They'll agree to the tape for the same reason they'll answer our questions: because they believe that if they tell us their story, things will work out.

After enough time has passed for them to register an objection, Deputy Clark starts in with the preliminaries: name, location, time, those present.

"Now, son," he says to Angus. If this wasn't all so serious I'd laugh at this guy, who's all of nine years older than Angus, referring to him as if he could be his progeny. "We hear you might know something about how the fire got set. That true?"

"I don't know anything."

Peter's face clouds with anger. "Angus, we've talked about this."

Mindy puts a protective hand on his back. "Come on, honey. Tell them about the messages."

Angus stays silent.

Peter blows out an exasperated breath. "This is ridiculous. The kid you really need to be talking to is Tucker Wells." He holds his hand out, and Mindy puts a set of folded papers in it. "Look at this. He's been harassing my son about the fire, not to mention bullying him all year. He's clearly trying to cast blame on someone else for his own actions."

He thrust the papers at me. I read through them. They're from a messaging service I don't recognize and contain a list of questions and replies between Tucker Wells, Angus, and a third person ending on Tuesday morning about an hour after, if I remember correctly, the first article appeared in the *Daily* about the fire. *Did Angus start the fire at John Phillips's house?* reads a question posed at 9:23 a.m. by mothertucker. *Suck it, Tucker!* said willowmaker21 soon after. *You'll regret that,* wrote mangledangus a few minutes later. The earlier messages went back through the weekend, and mainly involved Tucker taunting Angus about a girl named Willow—Angus's girlfriend, presumably.

"We'll be speaking to Tucker later today," I say. "But tell us, Angus, have you ever been to Mr. Phillips's property?"

He nods slowly.

"With Tucker?"

Another nod.

"Anyone else?"

"Just some other guys."

"Angus!" Peter says. "This is not the time to be protecting anyone."

Angus turns his head toward Peter as he mumbles something.

"What?"

"I said, they're my friends."

"They most certainly are not your friends. Is that what you really think friendship is? Is this?" Peter takes the pages from me and waves them under Angus's nose. Never in all the years I've known him have I ever seen Peter close to this kind of angry.

"I get it," I say, holding up a finger to Peter as I pull my chair closer to Angus's to make the conversation between us. "You don't want to feel like you're snitching. But nobody's going to get in trouble if they didn't do anything. I promise."

"Yeah, right."

"Hey, Angus," I say, putting two fingers under his chin and bringing his face up so we can make eye contact. "Remember those cake pops I used to make?"

Most of his face is a blank, but I catch a blink of a smile.

Cake pops.

Years ago, Mindy went through a no-white-sugar phase with the kids, and I made the mistake of bringing fully white sugar cake pops (like a lollipop, only cake) to their house for one of the kids' birthdays. Angus was so upset when Mindy put her foot down and said he couldn't eat it, I'd found a no-sugar version of the recipe online and brought a bunch over the next day. He must've been about eight or nine, and they kind of became our thing. Whenever he had a birthday or some special event, that's what he wanted, and that's what I made him.

"Angus?"

"Yeah, course."

"Remember what I told you about them?"

He nods and there's that blink of a smile again. Here and gone. Here and gone.

The thing was, the no-sugar versions kind of sucked. So I reverted to the original recipe without telling Mindy, figuring a bit of white sugar couldn't hurt the kids twice a year. And once, when Angus was about eleven, I had him over to make them and he found out about the switch. He'd giggled and said, in this supersolemn voice, "I can keep a secret."

"I can keep a secret," I say now. "Forget everyone else. Just tell me. Were you and Tucker and the others at John Phillips's house that night?"

His eyes dart back and forth like he's checking for the exits, but after a moment he leans forward and whispers in my ear, "I already told you. I don't know *anything*."

Deputy Clark and I spend the next two hours in fruitless conversations with sixteen-year-olds, accompanied by their parents. At the end of it, what we can piece together is that: (a) Tucker and his friends did regularly hang out in John Phillips's backyard. Tucker had a "hard-on" for Phillips, as one of the chattier boys told us, but nobody really knew why; (b) Angus Mitchell was sometimes with them and sometimes not, and nobody really understood why he hung around with those jerks because Angus was a nice kid and they treated him like crap; (c) Tucker had a thing for Willow and was angry she seemed to prefer Angus over him, but that (d) there was a rumor she'd finally made out with Tucker on Monday night, and maybe Angus had been there too, though that was unconfirmed.

Before tackling Tucker, our last interview of the day, I suggest a break to Deputy Clark, and I go seek out Ben.

I find him in the teacher's lounge, grading papers. He has a steaming mug of tea by his right elbow, and a smudge of pen on the bridge of his nose. I want to wet my finger and rub it off, but Ben always hates it when I do that sort of thing, especially in public.

"Hey," I say, sitting across from him. "I need your help."

"Oh?"

"Could you stop that for a second?"

He puts his pen down. "I thought I couldn't be involved."

"Not in the interviews, but . . . Look, we've got Tucker up next and we've hit a roadblock."

"What do you need me for?"

"I was wondering if there's maybe something I could use that would give me an edge. Make him feel like I know something about him I shouldn't."

The door opens and closes behind us. A teacher I don't know walks in, gives Ben a wave, and then retreats to the corner where the mail cubbies are.

"What kind of thing?"

"Has he ever said anything to you about Angus? Or about hanging out on John Phillips's property? Maybe something that seemed innocent at the time?"

He rubs the bridge of his nose, and the pen mark gets worse.

"Nothing comes to mind. Maybe you should just ask Tucker what you want to know. Maybe he'll surprise you."

"You think that's likely?"

"No. I do not."

There's a coughing sound near us, and I look up. The teacher who came in—twenty-five, fresh-faced, blonde hair in a bouncing ponytail—is standing at the end of our table.

"Hi," she says, holding out her hand. "You must be Elizabeth."

Her hand is slim and delicate in mine, which is still calloused and rough from my years working with heavy equipment.

"I am. And you are?"

"Stephanie. I teach English."

I don't look at Ben. I've never heard him mention anyone named Stephanie.

"How long have you been teaching here?"

She cocks her head to the side. "Three years now? Yeah, this is my third year."

"And you teach with Ben?"

"Sure do. He's been great at showing me the ropes."

"Has he?"

"Couldn't have made it without him. Say, were you two talking about Tucker Wells? Sorry, couldn't help overhearing."

"We were. Why?"

"Well . . . you're the one investigating the fire, right?"

"That's me."

"This might interest you."

She walks back to the cubby wall. Each teacher has a mail square and a deep drawer below. I watch her while she rummages around her drawer, then I turn to Ben. He's lowered his head back to his papers.

I badly want to ask him what the hell is going on, who this Stephanie person is and why he's never mentioned her, but now is not the time.

"Ah! Here it is."

Stephanie walks a paper back to me. I can't help but notice how her pencil skirt shows off her slim but curvy legs, and how the sweater she's wearing makes her eyes stand out. Half the teenage boys must be in love with her. Does that go for my boy too?

She hands it to me. "This is something Tucker wrote in my class last spring after he switched out of Ben's section after the . . . you know. Anyway, he never picks his work up, the little bugger, but this was actually quite good, though slightly gruesome."

I look at the title. *Fire Starter*.

"From what I remember," she says, "it's about a kid who finds out he has an affinity for fire kind of accidentally—camping with his dad or something—and then he keeps building fires until one day, he goes too far and sets a town on fire. I might be getting some of the details wrong, but it's definitely something like that." She cocks her head to the side again, her ponytail swinging. "Funny," she says. "I forgot all about it till just now."

Tucker is sitting in the classroom when I get back, and his mother, Honor, is by his side. I know her vaguely, the way you do in this town. Like how I know that Mindy's been hanging out with her this last year, along with Kate Bourne, a woman who dislikes me intensely because I tried to convince her to press charges against her husband for an incident she's done a remarkable job of keeping quiet.

"Are we waiting for Mr. Wells?" I ask as I take my seat.

"He's out of town on business," Honor says, her voice tight. "Let's get this over with, shall we?"

I nod to Deputy Clark. He goes through his usual preliminaries with the tape, then starts the questioning.

"Do you know a man named John Phillips?" he asks.

Tucker gives him a haughty look from beneath the fringe of blond hair that half-covers his left eye. "Everyone knows who he is. Because of the fire."

"What about before the fire?" Deputy Clark asks. "Did you know him then?"

"I'd seen him around."

"Around where, exactly?"

"Maybe I've been on his property once or twice."

"Maybe?"

He shrugs. "Yeah, okay, so me and my boys have hung out there a couple times. So what?"

"What did this hanging out on someone's private property entail?"

"Entail? Jeez, dude. Dictionary much?"

"Tucker!" Honor admonishes.

He slinks down in his seat. "Sorry, man. Just messing with you. Stuff, you know, hanging out. Talking . . . about things. *You* know."

"Drinking? Smoking? Playing pranks on Mr. Phillips? That sort of stuff?"

"Nah, man. That's where you got it wrong. We never did any of that."

"So when Mr. Phillips reported to the police that you'd harassed him on numerous occasions, he was making it up?"

"Maybe some other crew was hanging there. I just know it wasn't me or my boys. We don't do stuff like that."

"Of course you don't, honey," Honor says, patting his back.

He shoots her a look. *I'm handling this, Mother.*

"So," I say, "that whole cutting up a ballet outfit and leaving it in Mr. Jansen's cubby, that was just a one-off?"

"You can't pin that on me."

"I'm not hearing a denial."

"We have already addressed this with the faculty, as I'm sure you know," Honor says. "And I'd appreciate you not bringing it up again."

"Right, sure. Well, how about this, then?" I pass Tucker's story over to his mother. She sucks in her breath as she reads the title. "You fantasize about starting fires, Tucker? Maybe put that fantasy into action? Things get out of hand the other night?"

"That's just fiction. You know, imagination. Jeesh. What is it with you people? You write one little story, and suddenly everyone thinks it's about you. Like, is that what everyone thinks about Stephen King? He writes all kinds of crazy shit, and I don't see him getting arrested."

"Tucker!"

"You know it's true, Mom. This place has it out for me."

"We're only trying to get to the truth," I say. "No one has it out for anyone."

"Then why are you even talking to me? Everyone knows who did it."

"Who did what?"

"Who started that fire." He crosses his arms across his chest. "It's no big secret."

"This is no laughing matter, young man," Deputy Clark says with a sternness that takes me by surprise. "Property has been destroyed. People's lives are at risk. If you know who's behind this, stop playing games and tell us."

"Or what?"

"Or we'll have to charge you with obstruction of justice."

"What?" Honor says. "That's the most ridiculous . . ." She reaches into her purse for her phone. "When my brother hears about this—"

"Oh, relax, Mom. Honestly. Fine. Whatever." He gives that shrug again. "I don't believe in snitching, but seeing as you're leaving me no choice . . . It was Angus Mitchell. He told me so himself."

CHAPTER 22

Trust Issues

Mindy

Though it was only midafternoon when she and Peter were driving Angus home from school, it felt like the end of a very long day.

As if Angus's stony refusals during the first interview weren't enough, all three of them had been hauled back into the room with Elizabeth and Deputy Clark to be told that Tucker had pointed the finger at Angus. He'd said that Angus had confessed to him that he'd started the fire. Angus denied it, clearly and repeatedly, and then returned to his clammed silence about anything else. Mindy wasn't sure what worried her more: the fact that Angus had friends who might set him up for something he didn't do, or that the possibility that he *had* done it was taking root in her heart.

"Don't worry," Elizabeth said after Angus was allowed to leave to use the bathroom. "We don't believe Tucker."

"Why are you so sure?" Peter asked.

"I read through those messages. Even if Angus had something to do with this, the last person he'd confess to would be Tucker."

"Does that mean Tucker did it, then?"

"I don't have any evidence of that either."

"So where does that leave us?"

"Back where we started, I'm afraid. Angus knows more than he's telling us. I need you to try to find out what that is, okay?"

Mindy had stared at Elizabeth for a minute, trying to see past her professional exterior to the friend she thought she'd known so well. She'd caught a glimpse of her in the classroom, when Elizabeth had reminded Angus of his cake pop days, even though Mindy knew she was using it to try to get information out of him.

After that, although school was still in session, Mindy and Peter decided Angus had had enough for the day.

Mindy certainly had.

Her phone rang demandingly when they were stopped at the moose crossing near the game preserve. No matter how many times she saw these slim-legged creatures and the menacing palmate antlers of the males, she never ceased to be impressed.

Peter shot her a look when she reached into her purse. He hated when people talked on cell phones in the car. But when she saw Kate's name on the call display, she knew she had to answer it.

"It's Kate," she said by way of explanation.

She swiped to accept the call, but Kate already seemed to be talking to someone.

"I said, put that down. Put that down now or there will be consequences!"

"Kate? Hello?"

Mindy had never heard Kate so frazzled. Had she already heard about Angus?

"Mindy?"

"I'm here."

"Oh, thank goodness. I've been trying you for *ages*."

"I had my phone off."

"Have you seen the e-mails?"

Mindy's first thought was that Kate was referring to Angus's messages, but then reason kicked in. Kate was calling about the Fall

Fling fall-out, of course, which must still be going on despite how far Mindy felt from it.

"I saw some of them last night . . . have there been more?"

"I've spent the whole day on the phone, but I think I've finally got it all sorted."

Mindy looked back at Angus. He had his earbuds in and was listening to something angry, loudly enough that Mindy could hear it.

"Does this mean we're going back to the original plan?" Mindy asked.

"We most certainly *are not*. We gave our word to that poor man, and we're not going back on it. So what if a few people won't show up? The tickets are nonrefundable."

"That's great, Kate, thank you."

"You sound distracted."

"I'm in the car. I really should go."

"Did you know Honor had to go into school today because the police wanted to interview Tucker?"

Mindy felt sick to her stomach. "Yes, I heard that."

"Isn't that just too much? As if he had anything to do with it."

"I really have to go, Kate. I'll call you later, okay?"

Mindy didn't wait for Kate's permission; she just hung up and stowed the phone in her purse.

"Sorry," she said to Peter.

"What was that all about?"

"The Fall Fling. Everyone's pissed off we're using it to raise money for John Phillips's new house instead of the hockey rink—"

The car lurched forward, then back, as Peter applied the brakes sharply. Mindy felt her body snap against her seatbelt, followed by her head hitting the headrest.

Peter threw his arm out across her breast to hold her steady.

"You okay?" he asked.

"I think so," Mindy said, bringing her hand up to her neck. She turned in her seat to check on Angus. He was still looking out the window, his head bouncing to the beat as if nothing had happened. "Did you see a moose?"

"What? No, I . . . You're using the Fall Fling to raise money for John Phillips?"

"I didn't tell you?"

Peter dropped his arm, gripped the steering wheel, and put his foot on the gas.

"No."

"Goodness. I could've sworn I did. It's all this stuff. The fire. The Fling." She nodded over her shoulder toward Angus. "There's too much going on in my head."

"Did you know his house was being foreclosed on?"

"You mean, by the bank?"

"I shouldn't be telling you this, but . . . yes. It's one of my files, the one I mentioned to you the other day."

"You mean the one you had to call the sheriff about? You called the sheriff on John Phillips?"

"His house was about to be repossessed, and it burns down in a fire? You're damn right I did."

"But he didn't do anything wrong. I mean, if the police thought he had, they wouldn't have been doing those interviews at the school today, right?"

Peter's hands gripped the steering wheel so hard his knuckles showed white.

"We have no idea what happened that night, Mindy. *No idea.*"

Mindy wanted to say something to contradict him, but she stopped herself. Because what could she say, really? That she was halfway convinced Angus had something to do with burning down that poor man's house? That knowing this was a possibility made it all the more important for Mindy to make sure John Phillips was taken care of?

How do you say something like that out loud about your son, even if it's to your husband?

How do you even think it?

When they arrived home, Peter sent Angus to his room to "think about his refusal to cooperate," though Mindy doubted it would have any effect. They went into the kitchen, but as soon as they sat down, Peter was up and pacing.

"Can you stop that, please?" Mindy asked. "It's driving me nuts."

Peter sat back at the kitchen table, staring at his hands as they flexed and unflexed on its surface. The depth of his silence made Mindy feel afraid. Not afraid for her safety or anything like that, but afraid for Peter. Afraid for her family. It was a feeling she was used to, of course. Sometimes she thought she felt more comfortable afraid than not, but this had a different tinge to it.

"What's going on, Peter? Talk to me."

"What else aren't you telling me?"

"What do you mean?"

"The Fall Fling. The messages. Going to talk to Ben this morning. You've never kept things like that from me before. We don't keep secrets. At least, I thought we didn't."

Mindy knew what he meant, but she also knew it wasn't really true. She and Peter were truthful with each other, yes. They shared the big things, the important things. But everything that had been in her head for the last twenty years? No. Peter only saw the tip of that iceberg, and that's the way it was going to stay. That's the way it had to stay.

"I didn't know what to do," Mindy said.

"Why didn't you tell me?"

"You've been so preoccupied with work, and I didn't know if there was anything really happening and—"

"No. Stop. You found out our son was being bullied, that he might be getting set up for causing this fire, that he might actually be involved in it, and you don't tell me? Do you know how that makes me feel? Do you realize how serious this is? If he was involved, we could lose everything, Mindy. Everything."

"What do you mean?"

"Haven't you been reading the papers? Whoever's responsible for this fire is going to get prosecuted. Held liable for the costs. Do you have any idea what that would do to us?"

"I didn't know," Mindy said. "I didn't realize . . ."

Peter rose and came to her side. He took her in his arms and held her to his chest.

"We have to talk to each other, Min. We're in this together, right?"

Mindy nodded into his chest. "Of course we are."

"No more secrets, okay? Angus didn't do this. We're going to prove it."

Mindy nodded once again, but this time she stayed silent.

Because Angus was out of the house that night, of that she was almost certain.

CHAPTER 23

The Fitting Room

Elizabeth

About a year after we started trying to get pregnant, I suggested to Ben that we get tested to find out if there was a reason it wasn't happening.

Ben said no.

At first, I couldn't get a straight answer about why. If there was something wrong with one of us, or both of us, maybe we could fix it. And if there wasn't anything, it might help us to know that too. Take the pressure off. Relieve the stress building between us that was making sex a chore rather than a pleasure.

But, no, Ben said. No.

I should've left it there. I should've let him have his choice. But I couldn't. I could never leave anything alone, a fatal flaw of mine, no surprise, but this, this I really couldn't let be.

So I prodded and pushed and inquired and made a downright nag of myself until he finally told me what was bothering him: What if it was him?

That's what he was worried about. I wanted this so badly, he felt, so what would happen if he was the reason we couldn't conceive? What would be the consequence of knowing that information?

Would I leave? Would I choose to find my happiness with someone else to achieve what I so obviously wanted?

And oh, how ironic that the tables were turned in this way. That I, who had once been so full of doubts, was now so single-minded about wanting a family. That scared him too.

No, no, no, I told him. No. I would never do that. *We* were the most important thing. Forever, always. I meant those words. I repeated them and repeated them, but I couldn't change his mind. He didn't want to know, he said. Couldn't I just leave it be?

And then *I* began to wonder.

He was the one who worked with kids, who taught them and understood them and would make such a great dad one day— better, I feared, than the mom I'd be. And didn't people often accuse others of what they themselves were most afraid of? What if that's what he was *really* concerned about? That if I were the one with the problem, *he* wouldn't stay?

These thoughts worked and worked their way through my brain until the only rational thing I could think to do was get myself tested.

I'd find out if it was me. If it wasn't, that wouldn't mean it was him, but at least I'd be in the clear. And if it was me, well, I'd decide what to do when I got that information.

So even though I knew it wasn't what Ben wanted, even though I knew it might cause the very problem I was most worried about, I went for the tests.

I didn't take them in Nelson. Medical confidentiality is only a paper concept when there are only three gynecologists in town. Instead, I waited until I was called away to a fire out of state, and on a rest day I drove six hours to a city surrounded by green rolling hills. I paid cash for my appointment so it wouldn't show up as an insurance claim. I gave blood and urine and suffered the indignity of a vaginal ultrasound being administered by a young technician who looked at me as if I was contemplating something wrong, and persuaded the doctor to give me the results over the phone since I wouldn't be able to come back to get them in person.

And amazingly, after the tests were done, I kind of forgot about it. It was out of my hands now, like letting go of a helium balloon. My worry rose gently and then disappeared from view.

Six weeks later, an e-mail from Dr. Korn popped into my inbox. I took my phone with me into the bathroom like I was receiving texts from a lover. As I called the number provided, my hands were shaking.

The receptionist put me through to the doctor as I braced myself against the tub. He was sorry, but the news wasn't good. I had "scarring on my fallopian tubes," likely the result of an undetected case of chlamydia, which was all too common these days, he hastened to assure me, and "nothing to be ashamed of." But my chances of conceiving naturally were "extremely low." Surgery might correct the problem, but it might not. There was always IVF.

For a moment, my mind focused on my ex-boyfriend, Jason. He was the one who'd given me the STD that had caused this, discovered months after we'd broken up during a routine checkup. Had my doctor said something then about the potential consequences? Had I blocked it out because who really hears that kind of information when you're twenty-one?

What was I supposed to do now? Tell Ben? Not tell Ben? He didn't want to know this. He'd told me so over and over, and I'd ignored him. But if I didn't tell, if I kept it to myself, then I'd be living with this enormous secret, going through the motions of trying to get pregnant when I knew it would be wasted effort. Ben knew me too well. He'd know something was wrong. And that would fester between us.

Round and round and round I went until I felt that familiar wave in my stomach, and I found myself hovering over the toilet reliving that day's lunch. Ben found me like that—who knows how long I'd been there—and he rubbed my back and got me a wet cloth and asked if there was anything else he could do.

And then he said something about maybe there was a reason I was sick. He looked so shy and nervous and waiting to be happy as he said this, that I knew what I had to do.

I had to keep this to myself.

And that's what I did.

When the interviews are done, I find Ben waiting for me in the hall. The last bell has rung, and the building's emptied out like there was a fire drill, which maybe there will be if the latest fire report has anything to say about it.

Is it ironic that investigating the fire that might burn down my house in 1.7 days has made me forget there's a fire that might burn down my house in 1.7 days?

I'll have to ask Ben.

"They want to put some equipment around the house," he says, waving his phone at me.

I take it. It's an e-mail to the ten families that live in our cul-de-sac. They'll be bringing in equipment overnight, and tomorrow they'll start felling trees and laying hoses. Kara's last stand against the fire if it makes it over the ridge.

I hand the phone back to Ben.

"This is bad," he says, "right?"

"It's bad."

"You get anything useful in there?"

"I can't . . ."

"You can't talk about it, I know."

"That's not what I was going to say. I just need to process everything. I feel like the answer's staring at me in the face, but I can't see it."

"Like me. I'm staring at you in the face."

I smile. "You are. Does that mean you set the fire?"

"Nuh-uh. You're my alibi, remember?"

We grin and then drop our grins quickly as we remember why we're each other's alibis—because we were discussing the end of our marriage when the fire was set.

"Don't you have that dress fitting with my mother?" Ben says.

"Oh, God. I forgot all about that. What time is it? Shit. Is it too late to cancel?"

Ben frowns. Cancelling on his mother is not acceptable. I should know. I've done it too many times before.

"No, right, of course not." I check the time on my phone. "I should be able to make it. It was at 4:30, right? She said 4:30?" I sound hysterical, even to myself. "Sorry. I'm not sure what's gotten into me. You still haven't told your mother anything?"

"You asked me not to."

"Okay, thank you. I should run."

I lean forward and give him a peck on the cheek. Two students walk by, and one of them gives a low whistle.

"All right, Mr. Jansen!"

It's so good to see that high school hasn't changed one iota.

I arrive at the dress shop ten minutes late, despite driving faster than I should through the backstreet shortcut Ben showed me years ago. Grace is waiting for me on a velvet-covered settee, immaculately turned out in perfectly pressed slacks and a Chanel jacket she has in what seems like every shade. We hug briefly, and I catch her scent—Shalimar and expensive soap. Hugging her is like coming out of a spa treatment. But today even she is tinged with a bit of smoke. It's taken up residence in every nook and cranny in town, and when I look out the window at the Peak, the plume rising up behind it seems darker, ominous, alive.

Caroline's Dress Shop is a quirky place, an odd mix of designer clothes for the discerning set, and tight jeans and spangly T-shirts for their daughters. Caroline's a former ski bum who married a biker bum she met a few years after she moved here. She opened the shop like so many do in this town when they realize they need a permanent source of income. It's not her life's dream, but living in this town is, so she makes the best of it. Until she opened this place, women had to travel to the next state to buy a decent dress.

The dresses Grace has picked out for us this year are Vera Wang. Not wedding dresses, of course, but from her regular collection, more affordable but still an expense I protested when Grace first showed me what she wanted us to wear. She likes our dresses to complement each other, and so she often insists we order from the same collection. Grace waved my worry away with the ease of someone who doesn't have to think about money, saying the dresses would be on them.

"How are things, dear?" she asks. "You're looking a bit tired."

I haven't seen her since early Tuesday morning—what already feels like a lifetime ago. Is it really only Thursday?

"Ben told you I've been working on trying to solve what started the fire?"

"Yes, he mentioned something about that."

Grace and Gordon have never approved of what I used to spend my time doing. I think they both admired it, but they didn't understand it, especially Grace. How I could work a job that took me away from my husband for such long stretches? Grace was particularly happy when I quit and came home, though I couldn't tell her, or Ben, the real reason. Hours of Internet research had convinced me there was still a possibility I could get pregnant naturally, but each month I was away from Ben diminished it. I owed it to him to give us our best chance since I was the reason we needed it in the first place.

Mindy was the only one I told. She'd repaid my confidence by throwing it back in my face during out fight. And when Grace and Gordon find out about the divorce, I'm sure it will be a sad confirmation of what they always suspected: that I wasn't as committed to Ben as I ought to have been.

Caroline comes out from the back. She's tall and blonde and athletic in a way that so many in this town are. She's wearing similar clothes to me—skinny jeans and a cashmere sweater Grace gave me for Christmas—but with an elegance I can never pull off.

"You ladies ready?"

"Lead us through," Grace says.

She takes us into the fitting area. Caroline was smart enough to have two installed, one for the "older ladies," a group I realize with a sinking heart that I now firmly belong to, and one for the teenage set. "Our" fitting room is dressed like a funky, expensive boutique in Greenwich Village. There's even champagne available if you need to drink while you shop.

Our complementary ivory-cream ball gowns are hanging outside of two of the fitting rooms. The other two cubicles' curtains are closed, but rustling, occupied.

"Busy time of year," Caroline says. "With the Fling coming up."

"Quite," Grace says.

We go into our respective rooms. The woman next to me starts talking to her friend in the next cubicle over. I listen casually as I strip off my clothes, avoiding looking at myself in the mirror. Years of fighting fires has left its scars, and it isn't something I feel like being reminded of today.

"I can't believe people are being such B-I-T-C-Hs about all of this," says a voice I recognize but can't immediately place. "I mean, it's charity. Hello!"

"I'm not surprised at all," says another, stronger voice which this time I know. Kate Bourne, Queen Bee of the crowd Mindy runs around in now. "Ugh, I hate white dresses."

"But you picked the theme," says her friend, who must be that one with the weird name. Bitty, Boopsy? I can never remember.

"What does that have to with anything?" Kate says.

I pull my own dress from its wrapper. It unzips in the back, and I step into it, noticing the pattern my socks have left around my ankles.

"They've been harassing poor Mindy. And then," Kate lowers her voice, "you know they questioned Angus at school today. *The police.*"

I reach behind me to try to zip up the dress, but I'm having trouble. I can't quite get a proper grip on the zipper. It seems stuck in the wispy fabric.

"Angus is such a nice boy. That Tucker, though . . ."

"I've told Honor more than once that he's a little devil. Why, he's been trying to lead my Chris astray for years, but he stands up to him."

I want to laugh. Chris Bourne has a juvenile record that's going to have to get expunged when he turns eighteen if he ever wants to get a decent job. Like father, like son.

"Elizabeth Martin was the one that questioned him," Kate says. "Honestly, after the way she treated Mindy, I could just spit I'm that mad."

Grace coughs in the stall next to me. "You all set, dear?"

"I'm having trouble with the zipper."

"Come on out," Caroline says. "I'll help you."

I step out, a bit self-conscious about the way the dress is gaping open at the back like a hospital gown. Caroline leads me over to the pedestal in front of the mirrors. Grace walks out to see. Her dress fits her perfectly.

Caroline stands behind me, tugging gently at the fabric to dislodge it from the zipper. It comes free, and she starts to pull it up.

"You look just the same as on your wedding day, dear," Grace says.

I look at myself. I feel like I can see each of the last ten years etched into my face, layered over the girl I still was then.

"That's sweet of you to say."

"It's true."

Kate and Bit walk out of their dressing rooms. I make eye contact with Kate in the mirror. We're wearing the same dress—or ones so similar it's hard to tell the difference. She looks momentarily confused, but then her face falls back into its usual repose of hard certainty.

Caroline tugs on the zipper as the fabric tightens around my rib cage.

"I'm having a bit of trouble here, Elizabeth," Caroline says. "I'm not sure what happened. It fit so beautifully before."

I hear the slight censure in her voice. Have I gained weight recently? I couldn't tell you. Eating has felt mechanical for weeks. But the dress is certainly tighter than it was the last time. It's hurting my breasts as she works the zipper up.

"Are you . . ." Caroline lowers her voice. "Having your period right now?"

Her words fly around my brain as ten puzzle pieces snap together. How tired I've been. Throwing up yesterday. That I can't remember the last time I had my period. How emotional I've been feeling . . . Oh my God.

Oh my God.

My hand goes to my stomach as I catch the delight on Grace's face in the mirror.

"Don't tell Ben," I say without thinking.

DAY FOUR

From: Nelson County Emergency Services
Date: Friday, Sept. 5, at 7:33 A.M.
To: Undisclosed recipients
Re: Cooper Basin Fire Advisory

There has been no improvement in the weather outlook for the Cooper Basin fire, which continues to spread. It is currently only 10 percent contained, and has now consumed more than 4,000 acres of brush and timber. It is only 1,000 yards away from the north ridge of Nelson Peak, where fire personnel have been working for the past two days to build a substantial firebreak to keep the flames from spreading down the south side of the Peak and into town.

Total fire personnel on-site now exceeds 750. Air bombardments continue on an hourly basis. The Witches' Pool of the Nelson River is being used as the main fill site for water tanks, and a road detour has been set up to keep traffic from interfering with operations. A second water-fill site is being established at Nelson Lake. The Nelson Lake road will be closed until further notice.

The evacuation advisory has been converted to an evacuation order. All residents of the Cooper Basin and West Nelson have been ordered to evacuate their homes. Fire personnel are continuing to install hoses and other protective measures around housing structures. It is important that this process not be interfered with. State troopers will be in place to keep people out of the area.

There will be a town meeting tonight at Nelson Elementary at 8:00 p.m., where the fire incident commander will give an update on the forecast for the next 48 hours. All residents, especially those living in the evacuation area, are encouraged to attend.

A map of the evacuation area is attached to this message.

More information is available at www.nelsoncountyemergencyservices.com.

Because of the current unstable nature of the fire, advisories will be issued hourly until the situation has improved.

CHAPTER 24

Flash in the Pan

Elizabeth

There's this video on YouTube that I watch all the time. It's from a camera that was left in the woods to catch the path of a fire. Superimposed over the image is a bar graph that shows the rising temperature. A time-lapse clock keeps pace in the corner.

The first seconds of the video are peaceful. The woods are quiet, the trees straight poles that reach up through the undergrowth toward the high-above sun. If you look toward the rear of the frame, there's a clearing filled with sunlight. Something should be hopping through at any minute. A rabbit, maybe, or a deer.

Then the leaves start to shake, and the sky darkens. Is a rainstorm coming? White flakes flutter through the flame. Is that snow? No. Everything is green, and there's that temperature gauge, rising slightly. The explanation hits you as the first hint of orange glow tinges the left-hand side of the frame.

It's ash.

Things happen quickly after that. The trees let off what looks like exhaust as their sap and moisture heat to the boiling point and escape. The screen is filled with smoke and bright orange light. Flames wick through the grass and brush like they're a conduit. The trees—so alive a minute before—go up like candles as the temperature hits four hundred degrees. Now all you can see are flames, only they're flames like you've never seen them. Not campfire flames, or woodstove flames, or even burning a brush pile.

The air is flame.

The screen is one burst of flickering orange. There is nothing else to see.

When the temperature hits nine hundred degrees, the trees reappear. Only now, they're black, glowing sticks, like the sparklers we used to have on birthday cakes or wave around on national holidays. The fire is already retreating, whipping around the base of the trees it destroyed, creating its own atmosphere, making sure it eats everything there is before it moves on.

The temperature gauge starts the downward slope of the bell curve. As it descends, all that's left are black poles and dirt. The flames are starving, dying. They were too greedy. If there's nothing for them to move on to, they will die.

At five hundred degrees, a patch of sunlight flits through the frame. The smoke has dissipated enough to let the world back in.

The fire goes as quickly as it came, leaving nothing behind but ash and wisps of smoke.

And when you look at the time, you realize the whole thing happened in a minute.

I wake up sick. Sick to my stomach. Sick in my soul. I feel trapped and scared and unsure of what to do about it.

The obvious thing is to tell Ben. Shake his sleeping shoulder and confess. But somehow—is that really such a surprise to me?—I can't bring myself to do it. I don't know what it means yet, the fact that I'm *pregnant*, so how can I talk about it with him, this man who, four days ago, *four days ago*, I asked for a divorce?

How am I supposed to think here? Here, in this house that isn't mine. In this room that has nothing to do with my life. I've never been good at thinking; I just know how to *do*.

So I do: I get up and get dressed, and I go fight the fire.

It's so early I need to turn my headlights on, but even if the sun was higher in the sky, there's so much smoke everywhere I need to use my fog lamps. Smoke ghosts trail across the road and close in on my car. It's almost claustrophobic, and I'm happy when the wind picks up and swirls them out of my path. Then I think about what the wind means for the fire, and all happiness drains away.

My phone beeps to remind me I have voice mail. The message was left last night when Ben and I were at dinner, when I'd shoved my phone in my car's glove compartment, determined not to check on the fire every minute, to be present in my life for once.

It's a message from Ben's mother. I listen to it when I'm stopped at a red light.

"Hi, dear. I'm calling to see if everything is all right. You left the store so fast you forgot your dress. Christine says she can let it out so it will be fine for Saturday. I . . . I hope we'll all have something to celebrate together, soon."

I'm flooded with guilt. After my blurted response to figuring out I was probably pregnant, I convinced Grace not to say anything because I hadn't taken a pregnancy test yet, and I didn't want to create any false hope. She agreed, reluctantly, but I knew there was a clock on my telling Ben and that I'd raised all kinds of red flags by looking more petrified than joyous. And who knows how much of the conversation Kate Bourne and her acolyte heard? Maybe it was all going to turn up in the *Daily* this morning.

And yet, here I am, driving away from my problems.

Again.

Only this time, I'm bringing a small part of them with me. The baby. *The baby.* What am I doing thinking of that prospect as a problem? Better question: What am I doing bringing her, him, the future of us, into the fire? I should turn back. I should . . . No. It's fine. I need this. I'll be safe.

We'll be safe.

When I get to the site, I use my old badge to get through security and then go find Andy. He's assembling his crew to go on shift, and I tell him only that I'd like to help. I know he wants to ask me what this is all about, but I will him not to with a look, one he knows me well enough to understand. He leads me to the equipment closet, and gets me kitted out. A pair of green Nomex pants and a yellow Nomex shirt. Leather gloves. Steel-toed boots. A helmet with a roll-up face shield. Protective glasses. A backpack, weather kit, and water bottle. An ax.

I heft its familiar weight in my gloved hand and go through my mental checks. I'm ready for this; I have to be.

When I emerge from the curtained-off changing area, Andy pulls a handkerchief out of his pocket and ties it around my neck. He chuffs me on the chin and gives me a wink. I feel small and weak and strong and ready. I don't think I've ever felt so many things at once, all pulling in different directions. I need something to draw my focus in, make it steady on something other than me.

When Andy is satisfied that I'm ready, I tell him he's making me feel like a kid, and he says he does it to all his crew. Then we leave the trailer and join the line of men waiting for him. Andy consults a map, and we follow the path they've made over the past few days, slow and winding at first, then straight up.

Together, determined, our boots keeping time against the earth, we walk into the fire.

Two hours after I've climbed into the hot zone, I'm exhausted, my lungs are smoke-filled, and I'm full of a feeling that's become so alien to me it takes me a minute to figure it out.

I'm happy.

Not happy about my life, or this mess I seem to have gotten myself into. But happy in this moment, with a hoe in my hand and the whir of chain saws in my ears. I feel . . . safe. I know that

sounds impossible, but, yes, safe—in my bubble of smoke and effort and sweat.

We're building a firebreak along the top of the ridge, a strip of
land from which we'll remove all the fuel. The trees are cut down,
and the earth is turned up—our Maginot Line against the destruc-
tion we passed on the way up. No farther, no farther.

On the other side of the ridge, maybe a mile away, is my house.
They're cutting down trees there too. Laying hose and spraying
roofs with water to replace the rain that will not come. I've been in
many neighborhoods, too many, that have had this treatment, so I
can picture my house, roped off and surrounded by equipment like
it's a crime scene, as if I've seen it with my own eyes, which Ben and
I decided last night we wouldn't.

"Let's not go there," he had said at dinner. "It would be . . . too
much."

We were at our favorite Thai place, Thai Thai, sitting at a table
next to the window. The name of the place always cracks us up,
and its owner has become a friend. When I worked up the courage
to ask, years ago, why *that* name, Sammy shrugged and said, "I'm
Thai, it's Thai."

This made us laugh all the harder.

Despite my seesaw of nerves, we had a good time. I pushed past
the voice in my head saying, *Tell him, tell him, tell him,* and focused
on our five-star hot pad thai and the lettuce-wrapped *larb* I'd ordered on a whim.

When Sammy slapped our food on the table, he'd winked at us
and said, "Date night, yeah? You know you my favorite couple."

I gave Ben a nervous smile. I could tell Sammy had outdone
himself on the spice front by the sweat that was already breaking
out on Ben's forehead, three bites in. A positive side effect: the
spices were so strong that the restaurant was the only place I'd been
in two days that didn't smell like it was on fire.

"Am I going to regret eating this?" I asked, my fork hovering above my food.

"Probably," Ben said.

"Good."

He was wearing a sweater I'd given him years ago in the exact shade of slate green as his eyes. It felt good to see his whole face smile.

"Same old Elizabeth."

"Is that a bad thing?"

"No. It's one of the things I like about you."

"Just one, huh?"

"There are others."

"That's good."

He flashed me a grin and set back to his food. I ate a few tentative bites. It was extremely hot, and something about it tasted off. Was this a pregnancy effect? I'd read somewhere that the hormones did that, made food taste different than usual.

Tell him, tell him, tell him.

I shoved the thought away. I hadn't even taken a test yet. I had a box of them at the house, bought in bulk in another town back when we were trying so the news wouldn't spread through Nelson like . . . wildfire.

It always came back to that, didn't it?

"I'm guessing Tucker didn't confess?" Ben said, taking a swig from his beer, then a long drink of water for good measure.

"Uh, no."

"You think he did it?"

I knew he didn't actually expect me to answer, but *fuck it*, I thought. I couldn't keep one more thing to myself.

"He's hiding something, that's for sure."

Ben's eyes were tearing. "What about Angus?"

"Him too."

"Hard to imagine that Mr. Cake Pop had anything to do with this."

"I know. Did . . . What did Mindy say when you spoke to her?"

He signaled to Sammy for another beer. Mine lay untouched in front of me, but I didn't want to call attention to that fact by offering it to him. Would it be awful if I had a few sips so it wasn't obvious I wasn't drinking?

Tell him, tell him, tell him.

"You should call her," Ben said. "She's really worried. No surprise. Those messages are upsetting."

"Kids are so mean."

"People are mean."

I took a small bite of noodles. My mouth lit up. "I just meant . . . Remember what you were like then?"

"Sometimes it feels like yesterday."

"Right? I feel like I walked around with the volume turned up all the time back then. You know?"

He shrugged. The sweat was rolling off his brow, but he kept on eating, determined not to let the food defeat him.

"Has Angus changed?" I asked. "Since he's been hanging out with Tucker and those other boys?"

"He's certainly been quieter the last year or so. Remember how much he used to talk?"

When Angus was a kid, he was like a wind-up toy. Just start him talking about something, anything, and away he went, and went, and went.

"I'd forgotten," I said. "It makes me feel sick to know he's been going through all that and nobody knew. And now . . . Oh, hell. Tucker pointed the finger at him. He said Angus did it."

Ben put down his fork. "That little fucker."

"But what if it's true? This will *destroy* Mindy." I looked down at my plate, my eyes suddenly filling with tears. "I really don't want it to be Angus."

He lifted my bowed head, so we were looking each other in the eyes. "This is not on you. You're only doing your job."

"I know, I just . . . Ugh, let's stop talking about this, okay?"

"Of course."

He pushed his plate away and used his napkin to wipe his brow. I put my hand on his arm. It felt like he had a fever.

"You going to admit defeat?" I said.

"Never surrender."

I laughed. "Oh my God, Corey Hart."

"What now?"

"Corey Hart. The 'Sunglasses at Night' guy? We've talked about this before."

"Stop speaking Canadian and eat your food."

"It's too hot."

"Nothing's too hot for you. Isn't that what you always said?"

"I did," I said. "I do."

Tell him, tell him, tell him.

"I'm glad we're doing this," I said.

"Me too."

"You want to tell me about it?" Andy asks. When I check the clock, I see that it's not even ten yet. I've lost all sense of time. But that's exactly why I came up here, and why I did this for so long. I've never found anything else that was as easy to get lost in.

We're taking a break to "water up," as Andy put it. We're sitting across from each other on two recently cut-down trees. The bark digs into my backside. My throat is scratchy, and my tongue feels like I've eaten a package of sour candies. The top layer of skin is going to peel off at any moment.

"Tell you what?" I say.

"Come on, Elizabeth."

His face is filled with soot, as my own must be, and the whites of his eyes look almost bleached in the middle of all that black.

"I can't talk about this with you."

"Fair enough," he says, true to form. I have a flash of what things might've been like if I'd given into temptation, let something happen between us. Would it all be so easy if we were actually together? Then again, wasn't it easy between Ben and me for the longest time?

Life works on easy, smooths it down and wears it away until there's only the grit left between you.

I swish the lukewarm water around in my mouth and look down the hill. The fire's closer than it was when we got up here. It feels like it's racing up to meet us, to test the trench, our resolve, our will. I try not to think about the fact that if I turn around and walk for ten minutes, I'll be able to see my house.

I stand up quickly. My stomach does a double axel, and my ears fill with a buzzing sound.

"Elizabeth?"

There's a hand on my arm, then the loamy earth beneath me.

"Come on now, deep breaths."

I try to follow his stern command, but I can't get any air into my lungs.

I hear footsteps, murmurs, voices. There are more tall, strong men standing over me, casting shadows and worry.

"What's wrong with her?"

"Should we call the EMTs?"

"No, I've got her."

Now I'm being lifted up, and like the baby who might be inside me, I curl into a fetal position. I can hear the thud of someone's heart, most likely my own. My eyes are closed, and I have no sense of direction, like a pilot who can't tell which way is up.

All I know, after a while, is that we're descending.

The lower we go, the smokier it is, but the only way out is down.

CHAPTER 25

Fight Fire with Fire

Elizabeth

Ben found out about the tests I took.

I'd never hidden anything from him before, so I had no procedure for secret keeping. I deleted the email from the doctor's office, and paid the doctor in cash, but I had to fill up my car on the way there and buy some lunch, and I paid for both of those things with our joint credit card. And Ben, who isn't suspicious but is oddly finicky about paperwork, saw the charges and asked what I was doing so far from where I said I'd been. I stammered and hemmed, and then I completely folded. It's one thing to keep a secret when nobody asks about it, I learned. A whole other thing to actively lie in the face of your trusting husband.

So I told Ben. He was angry. Very angry. Not that I'd taken the test, but that I'd kept the fact that I was doing it, and the results, from him. He said he hadn't meant to make me think I couldn't get tested myself. That wasn't his choice to make; of course, it wasn't. Just because he didn't want to know if it was *him* didn't mean . . . But that was exactly the impression he'd conveyed, I couldn't help myself from saying, combative when I should've been contrite. And so we fought and fought, and then there was silence. An awful enduring silence that was a kind of noise in and of itself, like a background hum you can't block out once you've tuned in to it.

When I broke it the next day, Ben assured me that the results didn't change anything, but this was why he didn't want to know in the first place. Because he knew I'd think it would change something. And how could I not trust him, how could I be so wrong about his reaction after all these years? How could I not give him the benefit of the doubt?

"I don't know. I don't know. I don't know," I repeated like a yogic chant, as if it might bring us peace or balance or restore our universe. But that sort of thing never does—it isn't any kind of answer, and so I brought about what I was trying to avoid. Ben was angry and hurt, and as I came to realize in the next few weeks, I'd shattered the elemental trust that had always existed between us.

That's where Andy came in. Oh, not in the way you'd think. I wasn't sleeping with him, or even worried I might do so. We truly were friends—Andy knew that, I knew that, and I thought Ben knew that too. Only he didn't anymore.

It's hard to pinpoint what it was that made Ben start to distrust that friendship. I was so nervous in those days and weeks following the revelation of my lie, I'd chatter away, saying anything to fill the space between us. And, clearly, I said too much about Andy. I missed the signs. Those warnings that I'd done enough and said enough and . . . *Would I just stop talking about Andy? Why was I talking about him so much, anyway?*

As those words came exploding out of Ben's mouth one night at supper when I'd been talking long enough I could feel my throat getting dry, I knew all at once where this was going. Ben no longer took that he knew me for granted. People had affairs. People who spent long months away from their spouses in the company of others had affairs. God knows I'd regaled him with enough stories of that very thing happening all around me over the years. We'd even joked about who he'd sleep with in his faculty. What about the physics teacher with the stick brown hair and no makeup who hadn't aged since Ben had taken classes with her? Or the dolled-up office assistant who had a crush on him?

Ha. Ha. Ha.

If I'd known about the existence of Stephanie, I might not have laughed so hard. But we were so arrogant, so confident that nothing like that could ever come between us. And when it did, when that suspicion crept in when we weren't taking enough care to keep it at bay, it knocked the wind right out of us. Nothing had even happened—not that Ben believed me—but it didn't matter. The act of losing trust was enough. Enough to make him question everything I did, every trip I took, to make him sleep as far away from me as possible without actually moving to another bed. Enough to eventually drive me to the bathroom floor in the middle of the night with my forehead pressed to the cold tiles thinking, *I can't take this anymore, I can't take this anymore, I can't.*

"Elizabeth, you need to talk to me now."

The hand on my face is soft and callused. The voice has a familiar lilt to it. I'm lying on something soft, but the blanket covering me is scratchy. I can't place myself in time, and I feel nauseous and weak. Have I become a time-traveler?

I try to open my eyes, but I can only make them flutter.

"Kara?" I say weakly.

"I think she's coming around," says another voice that snaps me into myself. *Fainted, pregnant, Andy.*

Oh, God, no. No, no, no.

"Ben?"

I force my eyes open, and it is Ben who's standing over me, of course it is. I glance swiftly around the room, looking for Andy, but he's not here. Relief. Relief, followed by guilt. Why do I keep repeating the same mistakes over and over? Why?

Ben crouches down in front of me. He's dressed in his teacher clothes—khakis and a button-down shirt. He strokes the side of my face, pushing my hair away from my eyes. He looks so worried, my guilty heart fills with sorrow.

"You okay, Bethie?"

"You never call me that anymore."

Our eyes lock, and I'm halfway between a sob and a laugh. *You never* . . . How many times had we promised *we'd* never say something like that to each other? And how many times in the last year have we done so?

"I'm sorry," Ben says.

"It's fine. I'm fine . . . I don't. What happened?"

"You lost consciousness," Kara says. "Up on the ridge. The men brought you down."

I look up at her. Her normally smiling face is lined with concern, but also with something else. Censure.

She knows. She knows everything.

Please don't say anything, I plead silently, knowing somehow that she'll hear me but not that she'll obey.

She hesitates, then gives me the briefest of nods.

"What were you doing up there?" Ben asks.

"I woke up this morning and I saw the fire report and I wanted to do something to save . . . to save us. That sounds so stupid."

Ben squeezes my hand. "No, I get it."

"I feel like an idiot."

"No, Beth. You just gave us a scare."

I push myself into his arms, lay my head against his chest, breathe in the scent of him. How could I want anything but this, him, us? Why was I never willing to fight as hard for that as I was to protect other people's property? Why do I question, question, question and never do anything about it, when I do something about everything else?

What is wrong with me?

"Am I okay?" I ask Kara over Ben's shoulder.

"I think you will be."

CHAPTER 26

Alarm Bells

Mindy

That morning in spin class, Mindy didn't feel like talking. As Lindsay barked orders at them to *get their asses up!,* she lifted herself off the seat and worked through the exercises with a newfound focus. Sweat ran down her face, and her muscles ached, and she still hated every moment of it, but she seemed to have found another gear.

Clearly, fear was a great motivator.

Because Mindy was afraid.

Afraid for her son, afraid for her family, afraid for her marriage even.

They wouldn't survive this, she knew with an odd certainty. If Angus had done this thing, even accidentally, something would be torn in her house that couldn't be repaired. The deep-down mistrust she had of their son, this she knew would be unforgivable to Peter.

"Sit!" Lindsay screamed.

Mindy rested on the uncomfortable seat. Kate and Bit were here today, but they hadn't taken their usual places next to her. For all Kate's professed support, Mindy knew it was a temporary thing. Kate couldn't be seen to back down, so she'd defend Mindy publicly right up until she didn't have to anymore, and that would be it.

Mindy couldn't summon the energy to care. Elizabeth was the person she needed now. Elizabeth, who'd looked so tired and drawn yesterday. But so determined too. So certain.

That's what she needed, Mindy realized. Not Elizabeth herself, but Elizabeth's resolve. Elizabeth's confidence. She needed to find her way toward those things, or back to when she had those things, and when she did that, she knew, she'd be able to fix what was broken.

But for right this minute, all she knew how to do was keep her feet moving.

And so that is what she did.

Her phone was ringing from her locker when she got to the dressing room. She fumbled with her key to get to it before it went to voice mail. When she finally found it in the bottom of her purse, she didn't recognize the number, and she had three missed messages. It stopped ringing, then began again immediately.

"Hello?"

"Mrs. Mitchell?" a woman with a flat voice asked. Her age seemed indiscriminate, like Mindy might as well have been talking to a robot.

"Yes?"

"This is Nelson Alarm calling. There's been a breach of your system."

One of the women from her class walked by and gave her a disapproving look. Cell phones were strictly forbidden on the premises, as they interfered with the Zenlike atmosphere the health center was striving to achieve. Mindy turned so she was facing her locker. She would've climbed in there if she could.

"What does that mean? Is someone robbing my house?"

"None of the perimeter alarms have been set off, but it appears that someone has been tampering with the alarm system."

"Did you call my husband? Did you send the police?"

"Yes, ma'am. We couldn't reach your husband, but we did send the police. They couldn't find anyone on the property, and everything seemed secure."

"Is it possible that this was just some sort of glitch?"

The woman/robot on the other end of the line gave a polite cough. "No, ma'am. We're quite confident the trouble is on your end."

Mindy sighed. There most definitely *was* trouble on her end.

"Can you send a technician to see what the issue is?"

The woman tapped a few keys. "We have someone in your area now. Will you be home in an hour?"

"I can be, yes."

"We'll tell him to swing by."

Mindy hung up, puzzled. But that feeling wasn't anything new. She hadn't had all the clues to her own life for a while now. What was one more missing piece?

"What was that all about?" Kate asked, startling her.

Oh, so you're talking to me now? The thought was so loud in Mindy's mind she wasn't sure if she'd said it out loud. But Kate's face was still curious, so she guessed not.

"Nothing. Just some trouble with my alarm."

Kate was standing topless with her towel over her shoulders, covering each breast. Her hands hung on the ends of the towel like she was a character from a movie set in a football locker room. Bit was hovering behind her, shifting from foot to foot, her hair a wild mess from the class.

"I'm still getting a ton of e-mails about the Fling," Kate said. "And about Fire Guy."

"I stopped reading them."

"That must be why they're e-mailing me, then."

"Or maybe it's because you're the organizer?"

Wow. She had said that one out loud. At least, she was almost certain she had, since there was a blush of anger rushing up the sides of Kate's face.

"The police interrogated Angus yesterday?" Kate said.

Mindy turned back toward her locker and started pulling off her clothes.

"It wasn't an interrogation. They kept that for Tucker."

Again, out loud. What had gotten into her?

"I heard all about that from Honor. Only she told me that it was *your* son that did it."

Mindy turned around so fast she surprised herself.

"Angus didn't do *anything*. And if I hear you've been telling anyone that, you'll regret it, Kate, I mean it."

Kate laughed. "Oh, Mindy, you should see yourself right now."

She walked away. Bit was left standing there, her mouth hanging open slightly.

"Better run along, Bit," Mindy said. "You wouldn't want to leave Kate waiting."

And as Bit scurried away after Kate, Mindy smiled.

Because she thought she could see a path to herself now.

At last, finally.

"This is a pretty easy system to bypass," said the twenty-one-year-old technician the alarm company sent to Mindy's house. He had four earrings in his left ear and a full sleeve of tattoos of dragons and other fantastical beasts. Mindy felt even more suburban than usual standing next to him.

He had the alarm panel open and connected to his computer with a collection of flat green cables. His rapid eye movement over his computer screen contained a level of focus that reminded Mindy of herself when she was studying the rats she used in her experiments.

Her phone rang. It was Peter calling.

"Where are you?" he said, a note of panic in his voice.

"I'm at home. Everything's fine."

"Thank God. I came out of a meeting, and I had four voice-mail messages from the alarm company. I thought . . ."

"I had the same reaction when they caught me at the gym. There's something wrong with the alarm. The technician's here now."

"So no one broke in?"

"I checked everything. Nothing seems to be missing."

"Do you need me there?"

"No, it's fine. I'll see you tonight."

"I thought we'd go to the town meeting."

Mindy walked away from the technician. She looked out the window in her living room. Her street was midday quiet, all perfectly normal except for the haze of smoke.

"How come? We don't usually."

"Have you read the recent fire reports?"

"No, but I can see smoke out the window."

"It's looking really bad, Min. And I want to hear what's going on from the horse's mouth."

"How about we all go? I don't want to leave Carrie and Angus at home alone right now."

"Agreed."

They said good-bye, and Mindy walked back to the technician. He was typing furiously as code darted by on his screen.

"Was it a power surge?" she asked.

"Nope. Someone was definitely tinkering in here."

A new litany of worries ran through her mind. Why would anyone be tinkering with her alarm system and then not take anything? Maybe something scared them off? Maybe they'd be back?

"How did they do it?"

"There's lots of ways to bypass these kinds of systems," he said. The badge on his uniform said his name was Mic. Could that really be his full name? Or was it Mica? Michael? Did his mother actually look at his glistening, squalling form and think, *I should name my child after a microphone*? "You know how your door and window sensors work?"

"Not really. Are they not secure?"

"Depends. For instance, if you put a strong enough magnetic field next to them, they trip."

"Trip as is in stop working?"

"Yup."

"Is that hard to do? Create a strong magnetic field?"

Mindy felt like she should know the answer to this question.

"There are instructions on how to do it all over the Internet. Pretty basic stuff."

Of course there were. Just like you could learn how to build a bomb or buy guns or . . . Wasn't the government supposed to be reading everyone's e-mails precisely so they could prevent that sort of thing?

"What about the motion detectors? They're a backup, right? If someone gets in, then those would go off, wouldn't they?"

He gave her a flat look. Mindy felt terribly naive.

"They work on infrared signals that detect changes in the room's temperature. All you have to do is use something to block the signal. Usually a large piece of Styrofoam will do. Or with some systems, you can point certain kinds of lights at the sensors, and that fools them for enough time to get past them."

"I'm not sure I really want to know this."

"Better to be warned than unarmed."

"Are you talking guns?"

Mic shut his laptop. "I'm talking about someone who's smart enough to get into the panel and erase the in/out information it stores even if the alarm's disabled."

"What do you mean?"

"This keypad sends a signal to the alarm center, right?"

"I thought that was just if it was tripped."

"Nope. Every time someone enables or disables the alarm there's a record. We don't keep them for that long, just a month or it'd take up too much room on our servers. But this system's kind of old, and you can fool it by getting it to send a signal to your own base station—basically a small box attached to a cell tower—so the alarm center never gets the signal."

"Is that what triggered the alarm? Someone did that?"

"No, this person's cleverer than that. Well, almost, anyway. They hacked directly into our servers to try to erase the call information, and that triggered an internal alarm in our firewall, which is why you got the call."

"But I don't understand. How would that help someone break into the house?"

"It didn't. As far as I can tell, they were trying to erase an exit and entrance from another day."

"You mean, it was done from inside the house?"

"Likely."

"What day?"

"Early Tuesday morning. Any idea why anyone would want to do that?"

CHAPTER 27

You Can Bank on It

Elizabeth

Two hours after I wake up in Kara's office, I'm at the bank, waiting to talk to Peter Mitchell.

After I convinced Ben I didn't need any more medical attention and that he should get back to class, I took a shower at the camp and climbed back into my own clothes. I kept expecting Andy to show up and explain how he knew to disappear once he'd gotten me to safety. Because if Ben learned I'd been up on the ridge with him that would be the end of us, even if I am pregnant. So it's another secret I'm going to have to keep, and it's one I need him to keep too.

But Andy was nowhere to be seen. And if I've learned anything at all in this last little while, which is doubtful, it's to leave well enough alone.

I found my marching orders from Rich on my phone when I checked it. Stay away from Tucker, get that Mitchell kid. Those aren't the exact words he used, but they're close enough. But I don't want to do that. I don't want to accept the consequences of what that will mean if by some miracle Tucker's actually telling the truth. Or be a party to what might occur if everyone decides to believe him even if it isn't true.

So now I need to eliminate all the other possibilities. I need to do what I should've done all along—investigate John Phillips, make sure the fire wasn't his doing, instead of just going on instinct like I have been. Because going on instinct, which is pretty much how I've lived my life since that first summer at the fire lookout in Oregon, has brought me to this broken place.

Peter, in his banker's suit, looks hollow-cheeked and nervous to see me. What can I be here about but Angus?

"I'm not here about Angus," I say as soon as he's closed his office door behind us.

"You're not?"

"No. Don't worry."

He sits heavily in his chair. "How can I not?"

I glance at the picture of Peter and Angus and Carrie and Mindy that sits on the corner of Peter's desk. It's from a couple of years ago, taken out at the lake. We were all there that day, basking in the sun, splashing one another in the water. One of our last good days together.

"I'm worried too," I say. "But there might be another explanation."

"What do you need from me?"

"You were the loan officer on John Phillips's mortgage, right?"

"I was. Why?"

"What made you call the police about it?"

"When a house that's about to be repossessed burns down, it seems obvious the homeowner might've had something to do with it."

"But he knew that for a while, didn't he?"

"Theoretically, I guess, but he was only served the papers that day."

"On Labor Day?"

"It was supposed to happen the week before, but the process server kept missing him. He had to get an order permitting him to leave the papers at Phillips's house without him being there. It came through late Friday, but he thought he'd give the guy the weekend, so he says. Probably had plans. Anyway, he went over there midday on Monday, and then, what, like six hours later this guy's house burns down? Does that make sense to you?"

"No, it doesn't."

"Right, so . . ." He shrugs. "That's why I called. Didn't that deputy tell you all this?"

"He left that part out. Clearly."

"Seems like kind of an important detail."

"He's new. No detective training."

"My son's freedom is on the line here, Elizabeth. What the hell?"

"It's my fault. I should have spoken to you earlier."

"But it doesn't prove anything, does it?"

"It might." I stand to go. "Thanks for your time."

He sits there, looking miserable.

"What is it, Peter?"

"Mindy thinks he did it."

"What?"

"Angus. Mindy thinks Angus did it."

"Why?"

"She won't tell me, but I know there's something. You know Mindy, she's terrible at keeping things to herself."

"But you guys always talk about everything."

"I thought so," he says.

"You must be wrong. If Mindy knows something, she'd tell you."

"You don't know what she's been like this last year. Or Angus either."

"Ouch."

"It's true, though."

Is it possible that Mindy's changed so much in a year that the ten years before that are no longer an indicator of her personality?

Am I an idiot to be asking that question? Of course it is. It's more than enough time.

"You should talk to her," Peter says.

"I think I'm the last person she wants to talk to. Or confide in."

"You broke her heart, you know."

A lump forms in my throat. "I didn't mean to."

"In my experience, intention doesn't often have much to do with result."

I ask Deputy Clark to meet me at Joanie's for coffee. We sit in what used to be Mindy's and my booth, me on my usual side where there's a tear in the Naugahyde I always have to force myself not to make bigger, him on the side that faces the door, though he doesn't seem to be all that interested in the foot traffic.

I thought it was better to bring him here than to do some formal dressing-down at the station or to get his boss involved. I also want to get a sense of what Detective Donaldson's doing with the Tucker-blaming-Angus situation.

He takes the scolding well, such as it is, and tells me that Donaldson's bringing Angus and Tucker in for formal questioning in an hour. My heart goes out to Mindy and Peter. I can only imagine the panic Mindy must be in. But then again, maybe not. Maybe I don't know her anymore, like Peter said, and I should just let go of thinking I do.

Deputy Clark pushes an envelope across the table.

"What's this?"

"The lab results from the fire pit. You know, the debris we found?"

I rip it open and scan the report. Beer cans. Paper. Wood. Gas chromatography and mass spectrometry are negative for IRLs.

"What's an IRL?" Deputy Clark asks, reading the report upside down.

"Ignitable liquid residue. If an accelerant was used, it sometimes leaves a chemical trace. Has the house been searched for things like kerosene or Coleman fuel or acetone?"

"Acetone?"

"Nail polish remover."

"They didn't find nothing like that, far as I know."

"Look again. And sweep the woods around his property. What about his car?"

"What about it?"

"Check the gas tank. Gasoline's the most commonly used accelerant. He could have siphoned off his tank and used that."

"But I thought you said the tests came back negative?"

"They did, but I didn't take complete soil samples. And there isn't always a residue."

"Couldn't we take more soil samples now?"

"No point. The area's been exposed to the air for too long."

"How come you didn't take those samples the first time we were out there?"

"Because I didn't detect any pour patterns or localized burning that would indicate they were used."

"Sorry for asking."

I moderate my tone. "It's fine. Also, Phillips said he didn't have any insurance on his house. Make sure that's true." I slump down in my seat. I'm not sure my brain was built for this. "This is such a mess."

"What are you going to do?"

"Honestly? I haven't got a bloody clue."

CHAPTER 28

Interrogation Two

Elizabeth

Another day, another interrogation.

When did this become my life? I should be at my house, peeing on a stick to confirm what I accept by now is true. And then I should go somewhere nice and peaceful with my husband to tell him the wonderful news. Instead, my house is off-limits, I'm basically hiding from Ben, and I'm sitting in a police station watching two boys twitch nervously on wooden benches.

This is not good.

Honor is sitting at the far edge of the bench she's sharing with Tucker like she wishes she could be somewhere else. It doesn't take a psychology major to figure out that a part of her knows her son could be behind all this and she doesn't want to have anything to do with him. In contrast, Mindy, Peter, and Angus are shoulder to shoulder to shoulder on their bench. This time it's Angus who looks like he wishes he could detach from them. And this starts my mind swinging back to him as a possible source of the fire, what-iffing and what-iffing till I want to flee.

I make eye contact with Mindy and beckon her to me. She's reluctant, but she comes over anyway.

"Yes?"

Her tone surprises me. It's both more forceful and more wary than it's ever been before, but what should I expect? I broke her heart—I broke her heart!—and I may have something to do with her family's ruin. I wouldn't talk to me if I were her.

"I'm sorry, Mindy."

"Uh-huh."

"Truly."

"Is that why you called me over?"

"No, I . . . Peter thought you may know something. About Angus's involvement in all this. He thought I should ask you."

"Peter thought? You've been talking to Peter?"

You talked to Ben! the six-year-old inside wants to scream.

"I had to interview him at the bank today for something else. Anyway, that's not the point. Do you know something?"

Mindy folds into herself, gathering strength or maybe tucking something away.

"No."

"Are you sure? Even something small might mean more than you think."

"Yes, I'm sure. Give me some credit, Elizabeth."

I knew this conversation was a mistake, that it wouldn't lead anywhere. But I need to start repairing the things I've torn down, and Mindy seems like a good place to start. The Mindy I knew, anyway. This fierce creature? I don't even know where to begin with her.

"I'm sorry."

She folds her arms across her chest. "You already said that. Is there anything else?"

"No, I—"

"Good. Can we get this over with so I can take my son home?"

"I'll talk to Detective Donaldson."

She returns to Angus's side. I watch her wrap her arm around his reluctant shoulders, then I go looking for Donaldson. Before I make it to his office, I'm stopped by the sound of Mindy's voice.

"You quit that! You quit that right now."

I spin on a dime and hurry toward them.

"What's going on?"

"That boy," she says, pointing at Tucker, who's slouched and smirking in the way only a sixteen-year-old kid who's never wanted for anything can, "was trying to intimidate Angus."

"Now, Mindy," Honor says, "I know we're all under a lot of pressure, but there's no reason to start accusing anyone."

Honor closes her mouth quickly, realizing a moment too late how out of place her comment is, given the situation.

"I heard him," Mindy says. "I heard him tell Angus he better fess up. Or else."

"I never said that," Tucker says.

"Angus?" I ask. "Has Tucker been saying things to you?"

He mumbles something I can't hear.

"Speak up, Angus. Defend yourself," Mindy says.

"He didn't say anything," Angus says.

Mindy's mouth sets in a line, and she stands up and marches toward Detective Donaldson's office, beckoning me to follow her this time. Peter and I make eye contact briefly before I tail her into the office.

"That boy out there," she says, not even bothering with niceties, "is trying to scare my son into confessing to something he didn't do. Why are they even near each other? Isn't that a breach of protocol?"

Donaldson looks unfazed. "Mrs. Mitchell, we can't watch them all the time. If Tucker's doing that, and mind, I'm not saying he is, then I'll talk to him. But it would be best for all of us if you convinced your son to tell the truth."

"Why are you so sure he isn't?"

"I can't get into that with you right now, Mrs. Mitchell. But he knows more than he's saying, that's for sure. Tucker too. Things are not going to turn out well if they don't do the right thing."

"What would be the right thing here, according to you? My son confesses to setting the town on fire? What would happen to him if he did that?"

"Well, now, I don't rightly know. Those decisions are above my pay grade. But no one wants to see someone go to jail over a mistake, least of all a child. And I can tell you this, if there's a deal to be made, it's now. If those boys confess, they'll likely take it easy on them. Otherwise, I can't guarantee anything."

"Just leave it, Mom, okay?"

Angus is standing in the doorway looking pale and upset.

"What are you doing here, Angus? I told you to stay where you were."

"I'm so sick of people talking about me like I'm not there."

"Oh, honey," Mindy tries to embrace him, but he shoves her off.

"You going to ask me questions or what?" he says to Detective Donaldson.

"You have something you want to tell me?"

"Maybe," Angus says, and Mindy's hand flies to her mouth.

Before Angus sits down to talk to Detective Donaldson, he asks to go to the bathroom. When he comes back out, something's clearly changed. Whatever he was going to tell us is now bottled back up inside. His answers are monosyllabic, he gives even less information than he did during his original interview, and Donaldson looks more and more unhappy as the meeting goes on. He finally releases him after an hour with a stern lecture about "behaving like a man should." Mindy and Peter leave the station with Angus sandwiched between them, and I don't know what to think anymore.

The interview with Tucker goes no better. He sticks to his story that Angus did it, but he has no evidence to offer.

After Tucker leaves, I ask Detective Donaldson about what he said to Mindy earlier, whether he really does know something that he's been keeping back.

"I might, yes," he says.

"You going to let me in on it?"

He sucks on his bottom lip. "When the time's right."

"I thought I was leading this investigation?"

"And how's that been working out?"

"Take me off the case, then."

"You still have your uses."

"What does that mean?"

He opens a folder on his desk and pretends to start reading the document inside.

"How'd you know I was questioning those boys today?" he asks casually.

"Deputy Clark mentioned it. I would've thought you'd tell me yourself."

"You been talking to Joshua Wicks? The reporter for the *Nelson Daily*."

"I know who he is. Why do you ask?"

"That story in the paper yesterday. We have a leak in this investigation. So I'm locking this ship up tight."

"And what, I'm in the lifeboat?"

"At least you're not drowning."

The stick turns blue.

The stick turns blue.

The stick turns blue.

I've used up my cache of pregnancy tests. They're all blue, all positive.

I'm pregnant.

I'm in my evacuated house, sitting in my evacuated bathroom, in the middle of my evacuated life, and I'm pregnant.

I. Am. Pregnant.

I've imagined this moment so many times I thought I'd know exactly how I'd feel when it finally came. Joy, happiness, relief. The run, squeal, and jump into Ben's arms. His delighted smile. The joyous calls to our parents, our friends. How I'd look to ease that information into every conversation for months on end, damn telling people too early. How all the sacrifice and time would be worth it because sometimes you have to give something up to get what you want, and this is what I wanted more than anything.

This is what I want.

Isn't it?

But now, here, with the smoke wafting past the windows, and the fire just over the ridge, and the yellow hoses surrounding my house like it's a crime scene, and the lies I had to tell to get past the security gate, and this secret I've been keeping from my husband—I never imagined it like this. How could I?

Ben. Ben. Ben.

I need to tell him. Come what may.

I pick up my phone to call him, but it's already buzzing.

Where are you? says his text. *I'm at the town meeting, and everyone's asking for you.*

I arrive at the school with only a few minutes to spare. I should have timed all this better. I should have timed my life better, come to that, but that isn't something I can fix right now. All I can focus on is whether there's a way I can slip into the room without anyone noticing my lateness, which I know is a faint hope given the role I'm supposed to play, and the phone call from Ben that dragged me from the bathroom floor to get me here.

The bathroom floor. I've spent way too much time making life decisions on a few square feet of tile. It's time to get up off the floor and face things.

I'm not sure where I'm supposed to find the strength to do that, though.

I circle the building, searching for a side entrance. I find what I'm looking for and something else too: John Phillips, leaning against the door frame, gazing off at the sun setting over the mountains. The view is breathtaking, the way it always seems to be when the fire is at its worst. The way the sky turns the same orange as the flames. The dark mists of smoke being lit from within. It never ceases to take my breath away.

John Phillips is wearing a new set of ill-fitting clothes that must've come from the bottom of a charity barrel. Maybe he'll be better off after tomorrow night. If the mavens of the Fall Fling are really going to give him the proceeds from the event, he can at least buy pants that come down past his ankles.

"Are you going to the meeting, Mr. Phillips?"

"Meeting?"

"The town meeting? To discuss the fire? It's in the auditorium tonight. Supposed to start in a few minutes."

"You think it's a good idea for me to go?"

"No one's blaming you for the fire, Mr. Phillips," I say with a flash of guilt.

"Is that so?" He tries to kick at the dirt, but the floppy canvas shoes he's wearing don't produce the desired effect. "You might try telling that to the families they got in here with me now."

"Have they been bothering you?"

"They won't let me alone. Always whispering, staring. I can never sleep."

"Let me talk to—"

"Don't matter, anyhow. I expect I'll be moving on from here soon."

"We don't know how long you'll have to stay, actually, I'm sorry to say, so if there's an issue with some of the other . . . residents, you really should speak up."

He gives me a smile that makes me feel every second of our age difference.

"You're a good person, Ms. Elizabeth."

"Oh, I . . ."

"Didn't you say that meeting was about to start?"

"Will you come in with me?"

His eyes glide away. "I think I'll watch the sunset for a while."

"Don't stay out here too long by yourself."

"My dear girl. I am always by myself."

CHAPTER 29

Pressure Cooker

Mindy

Mindy was so exhausted when they left the police station, the last thing she wanted to do was attend the town meeting, but Peter was strangely insistent. So they picked Carrie up from her ballet class and drove to the town's Mexican restaurant for an early dinner. Carrie and Angus both had their headphones on in the backseat. Carrie was likely listening to some classical piece judging by the graceful arm movements she was making. Angus was listening to something harsher, angrier—music she could never understand or get the appeal of.

At the restaurant, Jose brought them to their usual table, the one by the window where they'd had countless family celebrations, moments, ordinary dinners. He confirmed that they wanted their favorites (fajitas for Mindy, double beef tacos for Peter and Angus, a Mexican salad for Carrie), and they tried to act like a normal, happy family. That was impossible, of course, something Peter seemed to recognize with his last minute add-on: a double margarita.

That they had been just that—happy—less than a week ago was something Mindy couldn't quite wrap her head around even though she'd lived through it, and was living right in the middle of the change in circumstance now. Maybe they hadn't been happy?

Maybe the undertow they'd felt from Angus, or his angst in the first place, was a symptom they ignored, a flaw they hadn't picked up on like the doctors with Carrie's heart?

Mindy looked around the restaurant to distract herself. It seemed like the whole town was there, doing the same thing as they were. Or maybe it was because so many people had been evacuated from their homes, the elementary school couldn't feed them all. To Mindy, it felt like a roomful of people waiting for bad news.

Were they really still going to hold the Fall Fling tomorrow night? It all seemed so banal now, so useless. Of course she still wanted Mr. Phillips to end up somewhere better than where he was, but beyond that, she was so far removed from the obsessed woman she'd been two days ago, she couldn't even understand her. When she thought back, it was like she was watching a home movie of the life of someone she resembled physically. Recognizable, but different enough to be disconcerting, like hearing your voice on an answering machine.

All that mattered now was Angus. Keeping him safe. Keeping what she'd learned that afternoon out of Detective Donaldson's hands. To do that, to keep her family intact, she was willing to do anything, come what may, even lie to Peter.

Not that he asked her anything throughout dinner other than to pass the salsa. He just gave her meaningful looks over the rim of his margarita glass as if they could communicate telepathically. But the only signal she was receiving was that he was pissed off. That one was coming in loud and clear.

Finally, their food was half-eaten and Peter's drink was down to the divot in his glass, and it was time to go. Back in the car, head-phones in place, they drove.

The town meeting was being held in the auditorium at the elementary school. It was renovated several years ago to make it multifunctional. A stage was installed with set pieces that could be adapted to almost any plan. The seating was that soft, flipped-chair kind you find in movie theaters.

It was a familiar place to Mindy and Peter. They'd attended concert after concert there over the years. Angus squeaking away bravely on his clarinet when he was eight. Carrie doing that surprisingly heartbreaking solo contemporary ballet performance in the flowing green dress they could barely afford when she was ten. And before heading off to middle school, first Angus and then Carrie had walked across the stage in little miniature caps and gowns to receive their "diplomas." They'd forgotten lines in plays and been embarrassed when Mindy had been roped into participating in a group "health" class, and oh, oh, oh . . . Mindy's *life* had rolled across that stage. So many pieces of it.

But at that moment, a strong, small woman, who Mindy figured must be the Kara she'd always heard Elizabeth talking about, was standing on a box before a lectern. Her dark brown hair was tied back in a neat bun that reminded Mindy of the way Carrie wore her hair, only it had a thick, glossy texture to it no child of hers was ever going to achieve. She had that same erect posture too, the slight turn out of her feet, and a burnished balsa-wood complexion. Something about her quiet assurance made it easy to see how she marshaled the respect of the thousands she sometimes had at her command.

As they found a set of seats together, Mindy realized that the room felt electric. She'd never understood what that saying had meant before, not really, but it actually was as if a current were swirling through the auditorium, like that game she'd played as a child where you all held hands and someone touched a battery. Everyone looked strained, even Kate Bourne, who was sitting with Bit across the room. The room buzzed with nervous chatter, like the din of a funeral reception in its second hour.

Kara stood there calmly surveying them. Behind her stood four burly men, almost at attention. Sunburned faces, wild sun-stained hair, untrimmed beards. They looked tired and grim, these "area commanders" who Kara introduced to the audience at precisely one minute after eight, identifying first herself, and then the men one by one.

It was only when Kara said the last man's name, Andy Thomas, that Mindy thought to look for Elizabeth.

She found her just off the stage where Ben was standing too, scowling at Andy. Elizabeth had always said that nothing happened between her and Andy, but Mindy wondered, not for the first time since their fight, whether Elizabeth had been entirely truthful.

Kara asked for silence several times. By the time she'd gotten it, Elizabeth had found her place on the side of the stage.

Kara gave her a curt nod, then proceeded with her talk.

"Thank you for coming tonight. I know the last couple of days have been an extremely stressful time for all of you. Many of you have had to leave your homes. Many of you are scared. Many of you have questions. This is why I've assembled my team here for you tonight. We'll give you a brief overview of the situation as it stands now and then open the floor for questions.

"We'll be here as long as we need to be. There are no wrong questions, nothing too small, nothing you should keep to yourself. But first let me assure you of this: we are doing everything we can to protect this beautiful town. This is a tough fire. A tenacious fire. The weather is not helping. We're up against a formidable foe. But we believe we have the measures in place to contain it. Please believe me that there's nothing that is more important to my crew and me in this moment than achieving that goal. We will give our all to bring it about."

Kara stepped back. Andy replaced her to explain where the fire was and what they expected it to do. There was a screen set up next to him, projecting a PowerPoint presentation. He used the statistics they'd been reading all week: the acres consumed, the weather report, the number of crew and equipment on-site. But there was something in the way he explained it all that made it understandable. Not just words on a page, but images too. This is what an acre of land looks like, this is five thousand acres. This is where the line has been drawn, this is why we draw that line, this is what we hope to achieve. This is our greatest enemy: the weather, the weather, the damned unrelenting fire weather. If the weather didn't turn . . . Well, that was the cold, hard reality he hoped they had no chance of facing. But he'd been looking and looking at the maps with their weather specialist, and he thought he saw a glimmer of hope. Tomorrow, maybe, or the next day, if the stars aligned, there'd be a break in the heat, the wind, even a hint of rain.

"But if that doesn't happen, are we totally screwed?" asked a twenty-something man who had the broad shoulders and skinny hips of a rock climber. "Like, shouldn't we be evacuating the whole town?"

There were murmurs of assent around the auditorium.

"No," Andy said. "That's not necessary. We've placed fire breaks all down the south and west sides of the mountain." Images flashed onto the screen next to him. Elizabeth's street. Elizabeth's neighbor's house. Elizabeth's home. "We've done all we could to fortify these areas. Even if the fire gets over the ridge—and that's still a big if—we're continuing to make sure that there's nothing for it to consume. It's a simple equation: fire needs fuel to survive."

"But what about those houses? That looks like fuel to me."

Andy spoke patiently. "The houses have been heavily watered, and we've installed a complete set of hoses around them if anything blazes up. We've also been cutting down trees between the houses so the fire doesn't have anything to catch on and spread. No structure is completely safe in this kind of situation, but we're doing our best."

"When can we go home?" asked another man, whom Mindy recognized as a father of two who lived one block over from Elizabeth. "We've been sleeping on our friends' floor for four nights. My children are scared. We couldn't find our cat before we left and . . ."

Ben walked over to him and put a hand on his shoulder. He leaned in and whispered something while the man buried his face in his hands. Ben led him away from the microphone and back to his family.

"This is one of the hardest things to deal with in these situations," Andy said. "Not just the possibility of losing our things, but the displacement. Anyone who needs a bed will have one provided. We're also serving meals twice a day. And, most importantly, there are counselors on hand. Please, don't be prideful. This is one of the most stressful things someone can go through. We want you all to come through safe and sound, both mentally and physically."

A woman in her late fifties approached the stage looking determined and angry. She stooped slightly with the beginning of osteoporosis but seemed formidable, nevertheless.

"What about how this fire started? Look at what we're all going through and that man," she lifted her finger and pointed it toward John Phillips, who was standing near the left stage door in a shadow he must've thought protected him from view. "That man is the reason all of this is happening and he's getting fed and a roof over his head and . . ."

Elizabeth stepped forward. "We're working diligently to establish what caused the fire. Please have some patience with the process. We do not yet know exactly what happened. Let me repeat that. *We do not know what happened.* And until we do, I'd ask you all to please remain calm and rational. Rumors aren't proof of anything."

"You mean the rumor that a bunch of kids started it?" someone yelled.

"I heard you guys know exactly who did it," said another voice, younger.

"That's not true," Elizabeth said. "That's exactly what I'm talking about. I'm not sure what you've heard, but there is an ongoing and confidential police investigation. Just because something is printed in the newspaper or you hear it from a friend does not make it fact—"

"What about this, then?" asked that same young voice, holding his phone aloft. "Seems like this video makes it all pretty clear."

In the chaos that followed, Mindy leaned her head over Peter's phone as she tried to keep her body from being overtaken by the shakes.

After the kid shouted out about the video, people began pulling their phones from their pockets. When she checked, Mindy hadn't received the video link in her e-mail, but Peter had. It came from an anonymous address. Kara called for order, but no one was listening.

Mindy turned to Angus, but he was just sitting there, staring straight ahead with his jaw rigid. Carrie was on the other side of Peter, craning in for a view.

When she turned back to the phone, Mindy saw that the footage was from the town-square cam. It had been installed years ago and streamed live on the *Nelson Daily*'s website, along with a few other strategically placed cameras around town. If you wanted to, you could spend the whole day watching the world go by on those cameras. Tourists posing for pictures. Locals scurrying from one place to another. And for the last couple of days, smoke swirling through the abandoned square.

The footage was time-stamped from late Monday night. As it neared midnight, a group of kids—four boys and one girl—walked through the square. They were all wearing puffy vests and hooded sweatshirts with the hoods up, and Mindy remembered how cold it was that night. It was impossible to tell who they were. Their heads were down, and they were moving quickly.

The video sped up. Whoever edited it had put it on fast-forward. One minute, two, ten. Then another teenager walked through the square. He was wearing the same uniform as the others, and the same posture too. Hands shoved into his pockets to keep out the cold. A knit hat pulled down tightly over his ears. Another anonymous kid.

He left the frame and the assembly room held its collective breath as the frames sped up again, and minutes, then an hour, flashed by. When it slowed down, the original four boys weren't strolling through the square; they were running as fast as their feet could take them. The girl was missing, and the fifth boy was also nowhere to be seen.

The time stamp on the footage was 1:22 a.m.—approximately ten minutes before the fire started.

The tape sped up again. Now it was 1:42 a.m. The fifth boy and the girl appeared, walking slowly, hand in hand. It would've been a touching scene except for what had come before, what the whole room knew was happening elsewhere. In his free hand, the boy was holding something that kept emitting a weird flash. *On/off. On/off.* The couple stopped next to a bench, kissed, then gave each other a quick hug. The boy watched the girl walk away, absentmindedly bringing his left hand closer to his face. *Flash, flash.* He was flicking a lighter on and off, and when it got close enough, it illuminated his face clearly.

It was Angus.

DAY FIVE

COOPER BASIN FIRE
New Evidence Links Local Teen to Fire

POSTED: Saturday, September 6, 7:08 AM
By: Joshua Wicks, *Nelson Daily*

There was a dramatic ending to the town meeting last night when video footage from the town square camera came to light that appears to link a local teen to the setting of the Cooper Basin fire, which has been raging on Nelson Peak and threatening the town since early Tuesday morning.

The fire began at approximately 1:30 a.m. on Tuesday. Local authorities have been investigating its origin since then. As this paper previously reported, a local teen was suspected to have been involved in starting it. Last night, as a town meeting with fire officials was taking place, footage from one of the town's surveillance cameras was posted online anonymously and appears to implicate at least one teenager with the origin of the fire.

It is not yet known who released the surveillance video. While the identity of the teens in the video cannot be revealed since they are underage, the *Daily* has confirmed that a sixteen-year-old male was taken into custody last night and is now the prime suspect. If he is found guilty of either negligently or deliberately setting the fire, he could face jail time, substantial fines, and civil suits against both the minor and his parents. The current estimated cost of fighting the fire is at three million dollars and climbing daily.

To date, over 500 homes have been evacuated. Approximately 7,000 acres of brush and timber have been consumed, and the fire is nearing the break that firefighters have been working on all week just below the north ridge of Nelson Peak. If it continues at its current pace of advancement, the fire is expected to reach the top of the Peak this evening.

The local weather outlook remains an issue, with the current unseasonable temperatures and high winds expected to continue.

Neither the sheriff's office nor the investigator in charge returned the *Daily's* calls. The paper received an official response by e-mail from the sheriff's office just before going to press advising that "this is an ongoing investigation and details will be made public when appropriate."

Maps of the evacuation area are available on this website, at all county offices, and through the Nelson County Emergency Services website. All residents should collect their important papers and any portable valuables, and be ready to evacuate. Residents are encouraged to sign up for emergency service alerts via text or e-mail if they have not done so already. More information can be found at www.nelsoncountyemergencyservices.com.

CHAPTER 30

Survival

Elizabeth

This is one of the things I love most about Ben.

About ten miles from town stands the Majestic. At over fourteen thousand feet, it's the highest peak in the state, and the third highest on the continent. The climb takes two days for most people, and involves gaining seven thousand vertical feet.

It is not a walk in the park; it is a climb.

I'd wanted to scale the mountain since I first saw it. It pulled at me as I imagine Everest did to George Mallory. Because it was something that would push me to my very limits. Because it's only when I'm at those limits that I know I'm truly alive. Because I had some stupid notion that a missing piece of me could be found if I pushed myself to that place.

And, of course, because it was there. In fact, in Nelson, it is everywhere. It's the view on every postcard, a place others recognize even if they've never been here. It's the view from our kitchen window, the one I look at every morning, sipping my coffee till the mist burns away.

It claims lives every year. Usually more in winter, but every summer too. Unprepared tourists, usually, but more than once a local who was caught by a fast-moving thunderstorm, or lost their footing in the snow field, or twisted their ankle in the rocky debris at the bottom of the glacier. You get used to these kinds of deaths in Nelson. You just do.

The year I turned thirty-five, Ben agreed to climb it with me. He'd summited when he was eighteen with a group of friends. The way he always described the trip made it seem perfectly doable, and there are many for whom it is just that.

I was not one of those people.

Even though I've hiked my whole life, I'm afraid of certain kinds of heights. Everything else I'd climbed had involved a trail, no risk, no dangling off cliff faces. But the Majestic involved all of those things and more, and so while it drew me in, it terrified me too.

We spent what time we could that summer training. It was a light fire season, so I was often at home, and even when I was away, I could put in half days hiking or acquiring rope skills at a local gym. We decided to go at the end of August, if I could get away, since the snowpack would likely be gone by then. As I climbed up interior walls to try to get over my fears, I convinced myself I could do it.

We started out on a dry August day under an endless, empty sky. We had an arduous but breathtaking first day's hike up to the lower saddle, where we'd spend the night in a hut. Our packs were heavy but manageable. Eight hours after we'd set off, we were watching the sunset turning first one way, then another, snapping pictures, marveling at the two-state view. Somehow we managed to sleep in the hut, which was full of snoring men. Then we rose in the dark, dressed, and snapped our headlamps into place to take ourselves to the foot of the first wall we'd have to climb.

Our guide led the pitch and set up our ropes. I was to climb next, the rope trailing from him to me to keep me from falling. I was fine at first, but then the route veered off sharply to the side, right at the top of the fifty-foot pitch. The exposure made me nervous, and my foot started shaking. Then my leg. Then my entire body. My hands were so slick with sweat I started to lose my purchase. Everyone on the ground yelled encouragement, but nothing could calm me down.

I slipped. I lost my hold on the rock and fell sideways like a giant pendulum, crashing into the rock face with my shoulder before the rope could arrest my fall. It was all I could do to keep from sobbing. I had nothing left in reserve. I wanted to be lowered down and soothed and medevac'd off the mountain.

Then I heard Ben's voice.

"You got this, Beth. You're going to be okay."

He said it over and over again until my shakes went away, and my hands found the rock again, and I made it up to safety.

Three hours later, we celebrated on the summit, Ben kissing me with sun-chapped lips, and everyone slapping me on the back though we still had a long way down.

But it was Ben who got me up there.

Without him, I wouldn't have made it.

That, and a lot of other things.

I wake up on Saturday morning with one purpose: to tell Ben I'm pregnant. Come what may, whatever the consequence, he needs to know, and I need to tell him now. He'll be angry that I didn't say anything sooner. But I only really knew for sure last night before the town meeting, and with the chaos afterward, I didn't get home until late, and an emotional conversation at that moment wouldn't have helped either of us. So I climbed into bed and wrapped Ben's arm around me, like we used to sleep, like we used to be, and he snuggled into my back and his lips grazed my neck, and we fell asleep without any words passing between us, either of revelation or regret.

But even thinking about that is making excuses, so . . .

"Ben," I say, turning toward him.

An empty bed greets me. There's a Ben-shaped depression in the mattress, but no man to fill it. I glance at the clock. It's only a little after seven. He must be eating breakfast and letting me get some sleep.

I push myself up. I feel bone-weary tired. I can't remember the last time I felt like this. Is it the pregnancy, the exertion of the fire, or the fact that I haven't had a decent night's sleep in months?

Probably all three.

My phone shakes on the bedside table. An incoming e-mail alert. They're hourly now, the faint buzz of their arrival turning me over in my sleep. I know it will be bad without even reading it, but I read it anyway. Nothing's changed. More acres consumed, almost no containment, more personnel, more costs, more water drops coming throughout the day. I know that today will be the day that makes or breaks the fire, which seems fitting. It might also take my house. But perhaps I can salvage my marriage.

As if to confirm my gloomy thoughts, tendrils of smoke slip past the window like they're haunting me. I'm so used to being around smoke I didn't even notice the smell had seeped inside. I've caught the scent now, though. It's marking its territory. It wants me, this town, this idyll three miles away. It will not discriminate if it is not stopped.

Okay, Beth. Enough procrastinating.

I turn toward the edge of the bed, and the room spins. I place my feet on the floor and take a few deep breaths. I rest my hand on my stomach. It's warm to the touch. Is it possible I'm feeling the heat of the cocoon already forming inside me? How did I not notice it before? Given the state of my relationship with Ben, there's only one conception date that makes sense, and it's far enough back to make me embarrassed. Am I really so tone-deaf to my own body?

The nausea passes, and though I may still be a shade greener than my eyes, I pull a bathrobe over my pajamas and run a brush through my hair, and I will have to do.

I follow the smell of oven-baked croissants, suddenly ravenous, certain it will lead me to Ben. They're his favorite way to start the day, something his mother indulges him with whenever she can.

This feels like a good omen, that he must be in a happy mood. But as I near the kitchen, I hear raised voices. Ben's and—surprisingly, given the hour—his mother's. They stop talking when I enter. Ben's face is white as a sheet above his favorite sleeping T-shirt. Grace looks miserable, and I know what Ben is going to say before he does.

"Is it true?"

And though this is not how I imagined this would go, I lift my chin and put everything I have into a smile of good news, and say, "Yes, it is."

CHAPTER 31

Don't Fence Me In

Mindy

If Mindy had been allowed to sleep on the floor outside the cell where they were keeping Angus, she would have.

That's what she used to do when Carrie was in the hospital: sleep in her room, curled up on an uncomfortable chair. Sometimes she'd end up on the floor, resting on several crummy hospital pillows scavenged from various rooms to break the hardness beneath her, wrapped in a scratchy blanket to keep out the chill. There was a bed in the adjacent room—Peter sometimes slept there when one of their mothers could stay with Angus—but that seemed too far away to Mindy. She needed to be as close as possible to her daughter. She would have crawled right up into the crib with Carrie if she fit.

That's how she felt knowing Angus was locked behind bars, lying on some mattress on a metal bed, his personal effects confiscated. She hadn't been allowed to see the place where they put him yet, though she remembered from a conversation with Elizabeth that the cells were in the basement. Aboveground or belowground, just that word, *cell*, was awful, and she spent the night trying to prevent the images from every cop show she'd ever watched from racing through her mind. Just a few months before, she and Peter had binge-watched *Orange Is the New Black*, and she would've given anything to erase those scenes from her brain. The strip searches. The anonymous uniforms. The aching loneliness. The danger from the other prisoners. Surely Angus would be okay in the few hours she had to be separated from him?

And in the morning, they'd have to let her in. They must let her in. If only she and Elizabeth were talking, Elizabeth would know what to do.

And perhaps that was the solution now: Elizabeth.

Angus was the worst liar when he was a child. Not that he was bad at lying—goodness, no, Mindy would say whenever someone asked her about it. He was an excellent liar; it was almost something to be proud of, a prodigious skill.

He simply lied about everything—little things, big things, all the things in between. And not only when he was in trouble or wanted something. He seemed to delight in the act of fabrication, giving flight to his imagination, his apparent six-year-old dissatisfaction with the life he was surrounded by.

One time, when they were all flying to Florida for her father's seventy-fifth birthday, Mindy listened with fascination as Angus convincingly told the woman he was seated next to on the airplane about his conjoined twin sisters who had to be left at home because "they didn't fit properly into an airplane seat." They were joined "here," he said, pointing to his heart. "They share it, you see," he said with perfect solemnity. "It's awful dangerous."

Mindy admired his insight as she blushed at his falsehood. Mindy shared her heart with her children too, and it *was* awful dangerous.

A week with no television, that one had gotten him, and an admonishment given in the airplane bathroom to go back to his seat and apologize to the nice lady.

"But she *liked* hearing my sthrory," Angus said with the remnant of the lisp Mindy sometimes thought he played up when he was in trouble. But he couldn't be that calculating, could he? Not at *six*.

No TV wasn't a punishment that stuck, nor were any of the others. After one particularly bad lie about Carrie turning blue in her bedroom had brought a panicked Mindy and Peter scrambling up the stairs two at a time to find Carrie perfectly all right, quietly reading a junior ballet magazine, Peter had turned on his heel, picked Angus up, and administered a hard spanking, twice, to his eight-year-old bottom. Then Peter had thrust a crying Angus into Mindy's arms and gone to his study and closed the door. She knew Peter had fled in shame. His own father had been fond of the switch, and he'd vowed, they both had, never to spank their children no matter what.

When Peter emerged an hour later, his eyes still wet, they talked about taking Angus to a psychologist to see if something could be done. They got a referral from a friend, and a few anxious sessions later, they'd been reassured he'd grow out of it, that it was just a phase, perhaps longer than one might like, but a phase nonetheless. They weren't raising a sociopath, as they had both secretly feared. Angus was a caring and empathetic boy who simply didn't see the harm in telling people about the stories he made up in his head.

Angus had seen the psychologist for a year, and the lying had diminished, then disappeared. Or so they wanted to believe. Perhaps Peter did believe it, but Mindy was never sure. He stopped the overt lying, of course, the things he could be caught at. But whenever Mindy found him chatting amiably to a stranger when they were on vacation or somewhere else they were unlikely to return to, she always wondered.

"Your son is so *interesting*," she'd heard one too many times.

So Mindy knew that Angus was more than capable of spinning a tale. It was the rest of it that left her breathless, and doubting.

"I'm not sure I should be doing this," Deputy Clark told Mindy as he led her down the stairs to the holding cells as the sun was rising through the smoke-covered morning.

Mindy hadn't been able to get hold of Elizabeth. It took all her courage to call, but when the phone went right to voice mail, she hadn't bothered leaving a message. But that didn't mean she didn't have other tricks up her sleeve. Specifically, crying. She'd used the crying-mother routine to great effect in the past, and she wasn't above using it now. She was surprised, really, by how quickly the skill had come back to her.

It had been an effective tack to use on Deputy Clark, who was nearing the end of the graveyard shift and looking tired and annoyed. Mindy didn't want to wait until visiting hours; she wanted, no, she needed, to see Angus immediately. So she'd sat in the chair she'd hauled kitty-corner to his desk and asked to see Angus, and before he'd even gotten the "I'm going to have to check with the boss" out of his mouth, the tears were spilling from her. A second later, he was up and leading her down the stairs while making soothing sounds to calm her down.

The basement was dusky and stale. Two of the other cells were occupied by loudly snoring men who reeked of alcohol, sweating it through their pores.

It was still mostly dark out, and the half windows installed near the ceiling didn't let much light in. The bare lightbulbs hanging ten feet apart didn't do much to help. There was just enough light to ensure that Angus wouldn't have gotten a wink of sleep—even in the best of circumstances he always needed complete darkness—but not enough for her to really see things by. Like whether the mattress he was lying on was as thin as it looked. Or whether that was a cockroach scurrying across the floor. Or whether Angus could possibly have grown thinner overnight, or if that was simply another thing she hadn't noticed properly about him recently.

"Angus?" she said, her voice a wave.

"Mom?"

Mindy turned to Deputy Clark. "Thank you," she said, hoping he'd catch the hint and leave them alone for a while. Which he did, after warning her that they had ten minutes, or less if someone came in early. He wasn't going to get into trouble over this, no matter how heavy the tears.

When Mindy turned back to Angus, he was sitting on the edge of his cot with his feet planted on the floor. He was wearing his own running shoes, but the laces had been removed, as had his belt. His pants sagged at the back away from his black T-shirt.

He was staring straight ahead at the wall, and Mindy tried unsuccessfully to figure out what it was that held his attention. What happened to you when you spent the night in jail at sixteen? Did you just shake it off? And, oh my God, what if it wasn't only one night? What if it was months, years? What if—

"I didn't do it." Angus turned toward her, his skin pale in the low light. "But you don't believe me, do you?"

Mindy moved forward and gripped the cold bars that separated them. "I want to."

"Then why don't you?"

Mindy looked at her hands, the way her fingers circled the metal, how soft they looked compared to the rough environment. She wished she could small herself up, slip through the bars, take him in her arms the way she used to when he was little and skinned his knee or failed to make the hockey team. Back then, a kiss would make it all better.

But they were way past that now.

"I know you tried to change the alarm records. And that was you on the tape. So that's why I'm struggling."

Angus started. She didn't know what he was expecting, but it wasn't the unvarnished truth.

"No, Mom," he said, spinning his body so he was facing her and his legs splayed out in front of him on the bed. "You have it all wrong. I know it looks bad, I know that, but I swear to you, I didn't do anything. I didn't."

"Then tell me what happened."

"I can't."

"How am I supposed to believe you if you don't?"

Angus stood up and came toward her. He was so much taller than she was now, as tall as Peter. He was standing right in front of her, his hands covering hers through the bars, and she couldn't remember the last time they'd stood this close. He smelled of sweat and the same shampoo she used. So familiar, and yet alien, separated.

"When have I ever lied to you," Angus asked. "About something important?"

"Oh, Angus."

He gave her a sheepish smile. "But that was so long ago. I stopped all that."

"No, honey. You've been lying to us this whole time. This whole year, maybe longer. Haven't you?"

"Yeah."

"So, just tell me."

"I can't. I really can't. If it was just me . . . but it isn't."

"Those kids aren't your friends. Please don't tell me you're protecting them."

"I wouldn't do anything for those jerks."

"Is it something to do with Willow?"

He looked at Mindy, his face quieter than she'd ever seen it.

"How about if I ask you, just this one time, to believe me no matter what?" Angus said. "Could you do that? Could you do that for me?"

Angus's voice was quavering, and Mindy's whole body was shaking. She could feel them both trembling so hard she was sure they'd set the bars ringing.

She wanted to believe him. She wanted to make this right. She didn't know what to do.

"Time!" Deputy Clark called from the end of the hall, breaking them apart. "The sheriff's car just pulled into the lot. You need to scatter."

Angus's fingers were laced through hers the way they used to be when she breast-fed him late at night. His eyes were giving her that same direct-on stare too. A look of complete trust, like they were the only two people in the world, though Deputy Clark's boots were ringing ever closer on the concrete.

"Will you do it, Mom?" he asked.

"Yes," Mindy said. "Yes."

CHAPTER 32

Way Over Yonder in a Minor Key

Elizabeth

"Ben! Ben! Will you wait for me, please?"

He is rushing away from me, out of the kitchen, the back door, the house. I don't have time to stop to put on my shoes. I just tighten my robe around me and follow him out onto the gravel path. He's headed for his car, but he doesn't have the keys. He stands there, trying to figure out what to do, for long enough to let me catch up.

I stand next to him in the heated morning air. I'm out of breath, and there's a charred taste in my mouth.

"Please, Ben, can we talk?"

He slams his hand on the roof of the car. "Goddammit, Elizabeth. Can't you just let me be?"

I should let him alone, I should, but I can't.

"We have to discuss this."

He gives me an incredulous look and turns on his heel. He's not walking toward the house, but away from it, out onto the lawn. I stand there watching him, exhaling smoke like I've got a cigarette clamped in my teeth, the gravel digging into the soft pads of my feet.

Ben's already halfway to the long grass. If I keep standing here, I'm going to lose track of him entirely, and so I start to walk at first, and then in a moment, I'm running.

I'm on his heels when we reach where the field turns to woods, and now I have an idea where he might be going—his old hideout, his tree fort. Where he went his whole childhood when he wanted to escape his siblings, his friends, or think out what colors he should use in his next painting, what words he should use in his next story. He'd come out here, he told me, and lie on his back, staring through the Plexiglas ceiling at the trees or the stars. His place, he told me. One he'd managed to keep secret from his brother and sister, that he'd never showed to another soul. His place he shared only with me.

He'd discovered it when he was ten, built by the previous generation, and he'd scavenged nails and cast-off wood from one of the barns to rebuild it, make it safe. Patiently. Slowly. So no one would know what he was doing. So no one would discover him.

I push through the trees, and I can see him up ahead. He's standing at the base of the ladder now, his shoulders hunched forward inside his sweatshirt. He looks like a defeated man.

This is what I've done to my husband.

I have defeated him.

Perhaps I should turn around, give him the solitude he wants, set him free permanently. But for so many reasons, including the beginnings of the life inside me, I have to try to repair us, even if it's one board at a time.

"Ben."

He bows his head, resting the crown against the ladder. "Why can't you just leave me alone?"

"I can't. You know I can't."

This time he doesn't answer, just lifts his head and starts to climb, swiftly, with assurance.

I don't know if it's an invitation to follow him, but I take it as such anyway, my hands and feet less sure on the splintered rungs than his. He doesn't help me up the last bit like he usually does, and a piece of wood lodges itself in my thumb as I haul myself up and over onto my butt. This should be an easy task, but my arms are leaden from the work in the woods yesterday.

Ben's sitting with his back against the tree this house was built around. There's a worn place in the bark, a smoothed-down seat. I turn and scootch myself over until I'm facing him, cross-legged.

His eyes are closed. He looks as tired as I feel, worn out. Over.

"Ben?"

"Is it mine?"

"What?"

"The baby. Is it mine?"

The force of his doubt brings me up onto my knees. The wood is hard and uncomfortable, and I want to suck the splinter out of my thumb like a baby, but I have bigger hurts to mend.

"Oh, sweetheart. Of course it is."

"Not Andy's?"

"No, no, no. Nothing, nothing, *nothing* ever happened between us."

He opens his eyes. They're not full of trust. They are not full of relief. Only questions reside there, and anger.

"So that's what the other night was, then? Some last-ditch attempt to get what you wanted before you leave?"

"Of course not. It'd be too early to know if I was pregnant from the other night. To be honest, I don't know how far along I am, probably longer than I should be because I've been, we've been . . . Anyway, I'm pretty sure it was *that* night, you know?"

That night. Our last good night.

The Fourth of July.

We'd attended the annual outdoor concert on the lawn at the base of Nelson Peak. Augustana was playing—it always amazed me

that "big" bands come to our little town, but then again, sometimes it felt like the whole world passed through here. We're big
fans of theirs. I had their song "Boston" on repeat for what seemed
like months when it first came out. We'd crank it up in the kitchen
sometimes and sing it at the top of our lungs. About how we
wanted to start a new life and we were tired of the weather. We
sang that line with particular emphasis when the winter was at its
worst, snow upon snow, cold upon cold.

Anyway. Two months ago. July 4. A hot, hot night. I was wearing as few clothes as I felt comfortable in in public—my shortest
shorts (not that short) and a tank top. I was wearing an old baseball
hat of Ben's from when he played in high school, and my ponytail
poked out the back of it. He was dressed in cargo shorts and a
T-shirt. We both wore sandals. I felt like we looked very young. We
were certainly acting young. Like our younger selves. Yelling out
the lyrics. Drinking beers from Solo cups, me biting down on the
plastic rim so I could raise my arms up in the air.

They saved "Boston" for the encore. Our voices were hoarse
by that point, but we sang it out anyway, stealing glances at each
other, like this was our private song, our private moment. A more
thinking person might've wondered at a couple who'd adopt a song
about leaving, starting a new life in anonymity, as their own. But I
just felt happy for the first time in I-didn't-know-when, and when
the song was over we found a spot in the grass and lay on our backs
while the fireworks burst overhead, obscuring the stars.

When the last sparkler fizzled, Ben, drunk and frisky, chased me
up the hill to our house, grabbing my ass. I swatted his hand away,
saying the neighbors might see.

"Who cares about the neighbors, baby?" he said, pushing me up
against our front door.

What followed was rough and tender and frantic and slow. A
contradiction that was all us. Afterward, we didn't say much, just

stared up at the ceiling while Ben's hands wove through my hair. I went to sleep with a smile on my face and slept heavily through the night.

The next morning, as I picked up our clothes from where we'd left them on the living-room floor, I made a joke about the restorative powers of alcohol, which Ben took the wrong way, and instead of letting it lie, I picked up our last fight right where we'd left it off two days before, and we were back at square one.

And the morning after that, I called the divorce lawyer for the first time.

"That was a good night," Ben says.

"It was. The best."

"But that wasn't real life. Real life is what happened the next day."

I rock back on my heels. "You mean, the fight?"

"That fight. The fight the day before. All the fights. Aren't you sick of it?"

"I am. You know I am."

"Maybe it's better this way, then."

"You mean apart?"

"That's what you wanted, isn't it?"

"What I wanted was for things to change."

"Careful what you wish for."

"I know, right?"

He shakes his head. "Maybe we just should call it."

"But what about the baby?"

He can't help the smile that spreads across his face briefly at the thought of the baby—the baby we've tried so hard to make for so long—finally on its way.

"You're really pregnant?" he asks.

"I am."

"That's . . . I couldn't believe it when Mom told me." He shakes his head. "You know, I came into the kitchen this morning whistling, and she thought it was because you'd told me."

"I'm so sorry, Ben. I should have. I only found out for sure right before the town meeting, and then with everything that happened . . . I was looking for you to tell you this morning . . . I know that's probably hard to believe."

"It is."

"Does it change anything?"

"I don't know."

"I'm going to need more than that."

He looks up at the Plexiglas roof. It's covered in yellowed needles being shed by the aspens surrounding us. Wafts of smoke slip through the cracks in the joints, the door, everywhere. If there was magic here, the smoke would thicken and obscure us, and when it cleared we'd be in a new place, or maybe a different time. But the fire isn't magic. It's a threat, one that doesn't care what it takes, or from whom.

"Do you want to be one of those couples?" Ben asks.

"You mean the ones who stay together only for the sake of the kids?"

"Those are the ones."

"I never wanted to be one of those couples."

"I don't think anyone ever does."

"But we wouldn't be," I say, putting every ounce of certainty I have into the words.

"Beth, come on. We're *already* one of those couples."

This rocks me back onto the floor. Ben reaches for me a moment too late, and my head slams into the wooden wall behind me.

"Are you all right?"

I sit up, rubbing the spot that feels like it cracked.

"I think so. Clumsy me."

"You always were a disaster waiting to happen. It's amazing you came through all those fires all right."

"It is. Though I never seem to have an accident when I'm doing something like that. Only—"

"Only when you're with me?"

"I meant only when I'm in my real life."

"Is this your real life? I thought that was."

"Fighting fires?"

"Yes."

"Maybe it was. I don't want it to be anymore."

"What do you want, then, Beth?"

"I want to start a new life. With you. With us."

Ben works his jaw. He's trying not to break, not to let me see him cry. I thought I'd broken him before, but I was wrong. He's beaten down, but not finished yet. I could still do damage here if I'm not careful.

"If there wasn't a baby, would you still feel the same way?" Ben asks.

"I really hope I would."

"I think *I'm* going to need more than that."

"I could say yes, but I don't want to say anything I don't know for a certainty is true. That's what I meant by starting over. Cards on the table."

"Cards Against Humanity?"

"Ha. Ha."

That he could joke at a time like this . . .

That must be a good sign.

"For real?" he says.

"For real."

He looks me in the eye, green to green. "I hate what you do for a living."

"Working for Rich? I'm all too happy to quit."

"No. Firefighting. I hate it."

"But I quit that."

"Did you, now? That's why ForestFires.com is your home page, and you're constantly checking weather maps and following fires in progress? That's why you never gave in your badge?"

"And I was up on the ridge yesterday," I complete for him.

"Exactly. And in your condition too."

"It's a part of me, Ben. I don't know what to say. I'll probably never be able to completely let it go. But I'm ready to put it behind me."

"Why don't I believe that?"

"Because I've given you no reason to. But, listen. Yesterday, be-fore I . . . passed out, it was good at first being up there. Back in the old rhythm, doing something. Something important. But it struck me at some point that the whole reason I was doing it this time was because it was *our* house I was trying to save. I wanted to save *us*. I'm tired of always saving everyone else."

"I want to believe you."

"You can. You really can."

I think about taking his hand and bringing it to my belly. Use it like an ultrasound wand, hope it will pick up the faint strut of a tiny heart, even though I know all he'll feel is my own pulse. Because that smile from earlier, when he thought for a moment only about the baby, that smile is deep within him, waiting to break out, waiting to turn into the whoop for joy he would've made if we were having this conversation even a week ago.

But that would be manipulative, oh so very, and so instead I simply ask for what I want.

"I want this. You. Me. The baby. No baby. I want us to have a new beginning, maybe here, maybe somewhere else. Because I can't think of what my life would be like without you. So say yes. Please?"

CHAPTER 33

Outside Your Body

Mindy

Mindy wasn't sure when she first heard that saying about how having children is like volunteering to wear your heart outside your body for the rest of your life. She knew what it meant, of course. When Carrie was in the hospital, Mindy wished she could reach inside herself and replace Carrie's heart with her own. Even when Angus hurt himself in an ordinary way, Mindy often felt those hurts more than he did. And there wasn't a love like that, was there, the love one felt for one's children? Something more and different from what she felt for Peter, though she loved him every way she could.

And right at that moment, Mindy's heart was locked in a basement without adequate sunlight, two days from being hauled away to a juvenile-detention facility if the judge wasn't feeling of a mind to grant bail.

So Mindy knew why she got in her car after she left Angus and started driving toward Nelson Elementary.

She just didn't know what she'd say when she got there.

Mindy arrived at her destination as the volunteers were pulling into the parking lot to serve breakfast. A fleet of cars, driving in a caravan from a local caterer who'd agreed to provide sustenance to the displaced and figure out payment later. Mindy had received an e-mail asking her to participate. She'd been too preoccupied with everything to even respond. Now she was sure that even if she volunteered, they'd turn her away.

Mindy watched the beehive of activity as the volunteers exited their cars and popped open their trunks. There were some young women she didn't recognize, and in charge of it all was Honor. The younger women (well, maybe they weren't *so* young, early twenties) were tall and had those defined muscles in their legs Mindy could only dream of achieving. They were wearing shorts and T-shirts, almost like a uniform. It was still that hot, dry weather that was doing as much to fuel the fire as the wind and the lack of rain.

Her phone beeped with an incoming text. It was from Peter.

Where are you? it read.

She called him.

"I went to see Angus," she said in greeting.

"They let you in? I thought visiting hours didn't start until ten?"

"I'm his mother."

She heard Peter breathe deeply into the phone like he did when he was upset.

"You didn't even leave a note. We were worried."

"I've just got . . . everything on my mind right now."

"And I don't? Did you think that maybe I'd want to go with you?"

Mindy watched as one of the women lifted a heavy metal container from the trunk of her car, her arms straining under the weight. She stumbled and would have dropped it but for her friend's intervention.

"Mindy?"

"I'm here."

"Are you going to say anything?"

"What is there to say? Obviously, I didn't think."

"Is he okay?"

"He is not okay. How could he be okay?"

"Are you still there? Will they let me in to see him?"

"Ask for Deputy Clark. He seems like a good guy."

"Where are you?"

She got out of the car. The air struck her as if she'd opened her oven after baking a cake. The smoke was thicker than it had been, and she glanced over her shoulder at the Peak. From this distance, a couple of miles, it was a shadowy outline. Mindy shuddered. What had Angus done?

"Min?"

"There's something I need to try for Angus. Something I think might help."

"What are you talking about? The lawyer said—"

"I know what he said."

After they'd gotten home from the police station the night before, Mindy and Peter had called the best defense lawyer in town. He'd told them that he couldn't get Angus out before Monday and mentioned a terrifying amount of money as the bond the court was likely to set.

"Jim said he'd let us take a second mortgage on the house if we needed to," Peter said, referring to his boss.

Mindy looked at herself in the car window. Her hair was flat and her eyes were puffy and the T-shirt she was wearing was stretched out at the neck. There was a trace of Angus about the slope of her eyes, and they shared the same ears, but that was about it.

"Angus says he didn't do it," Mindy said.

"And you believe him?"

"I have to."

"Min."

"I know, Peter. To be honest, I've doubted him this week. But now . . . I think I believe him. I think we have to act on that basis."

"Did he explain why he was out of the house? What he was doing?"

"Not really, no, but—"

"Then how can you be so sure?"

"Why are you cross-examining me?"

"I'm sorry, Min. I don't mean to."

"I know. That's good of Mason. About the loan."

Peter sighed. He sounded close to his breaking point, and part of Mindy ached to get back in the car to go to him. But she had other priorities.

"Go see him, Peter. Go see him and listen to what he has to say. Can you do that for me?"

"Of course I can."

"Don't take Carrie. I don't want her there."

"Will you be home soon?"

"As soon as I can."

There were a lot more people inside the gym than the last time Mindy was there. So much had happened in the past week. So much had changed.

She wondered if it was too much to change back.

Mindy searched the crowded room. Most of the beds were full, and there was an oddly festive atmosphere about the place. Kids were running around between the cots, playing some made-up game, and the air was infused with the saltiness of mass-produced bacon and breakfast sausages. About twenty volunteers were manning the food station—those lithe, pretty girls Mindy had seen outside—with Honor watching over them all.

Tucker was sitting on a bench behind his mother, his eyes intent on his phone, his fingers moving nimbly over the screen. She felt a powerful animal instinct to go up to him right then and there and . . . No. She couldn't do that. Throttling the boy wasn't going to solve anything.

Mindy saw Honor's head move in her direction, and she ducked behind a group of people who were standing in the center aisle, gossiping about last night's town meeting. Mindy tried to block out their chatter as she looked for John Phillips.

"And that kid . . ."

"With the lighter? Spooky, right?"

"Parents ought to be . . ."

Mindy thought she saw the top of John Phillips's head poking out from beneath an army blanket. She was fairly certain it was the spot where he was sleeping last time. The room looked and felt so different, it was difficult to tell.

She walked toward his cot with no real idea of what she was going to say, only she knew she couldn't say it in this place, not under the scrutiny of this gang of gossips that was sure to grow if she sat there talking to John Phillips for any length of time.

"Mr. Phillips," she said when she got right up to him.

He was lying on his back, the blanket tucked up to his chin, like she used to do with Angus and Carrie when they were tiny to keep the monsters at bay. He seemed off in his own world, but answered on the second call. She asked if there was somewhere they could talk in private. He pushed the covers back slowly and sat up. He was sleeping in his clothes, and he didn't ask why Mindy wanted to speak to him as he pushed his feet into a pair of canvas shoes. Mindy felt a stab of guilt and asked him if he'd rather have breakfast first, but he waved her off. He wasn't hungry just then.

He walked toward the gym's back door with the assurance of someone who'd made this place his home. They wandered the halls until they found an empty classroom whose door wasn't locked.

John sat behind the teacher's desk. Mindy wasn't sure where she should go. Take a student's seat, or stand before him at the desk like she was awaiting punishment?

"Why are you here?" John asked. His voice had a rasp to it that hadn't been there before, like he hadn't been talking much or was fighting the edge of a cold.

Mindy still didn't know how to say what she wanted to, but she plunged ahead anyway.

"I'd like you to help my son."

"Who's that?"

"He's the one they're saying started the fire."

"Well, now, seems like there isn't much I could be doing to help him out. Besides, if'n he did it, he's the reason I lost everything."

"But he didn't do it. Angus is innocent."

"You're his mother. The way I reckon, you've got to feel that way."

"But I *didn't* feel that way. I'm ashamed to admit it, but I thought he had something to do with it at first. But I've talked to him, and he swears to me that he didn't, and I believe him."

"That's as may be. But I don't see what that has to do with me."

Mindy looked at the floor. It was twenty-year-old linoleum, scuffed and patterned with children's footfalls, scraping desks, the odd piece of hardened gum.

"You could take the blame," she said quietly.

"Beg your pardon?"

Mindy looked up. "You could say you realized that you did it by accident. I know they're saying that they'll prosecute regardless, but I'm sure that's not true. Not if we think of a plausible reason why it happened."

John watched her stumbling, blinking that slow blink of his.

"Maybe you left some glass by the fireplace and the sun caught it? Or, I don't know, you burned something, just quickly, not thinking because you were upset about the repossession. I mean, he's just a boy and he's got his whole life in front of him and . . ." Mindy trailed off helplessly, at a loss. She knew how stupid she sounded, how desperate. But that's what she was.

Stupid with desperation.

"I've still got life in me left, yet," John said warily.

"I didn't mean to imply otherwise. Oh, I don't know what I'm saying."

Mindy sat down in the chair behind her. She felt awkward and ungainly, not much different than she had when she was in elementary school herself.

"You love your son," John said.

"More than anything."

"I never felt love like that. We couldn't have children, and my wife wasn't the kind of person you could feel about like that, you see?"

"I'm sorry."

"I was for a long time too. But seeing you, well, that seems like a lot to carry around. Too much, maybe, for me."

"So you understand why I'm asking?"

"Sure I do, but—"

"Here you are at last," Kate Bourne said, standing in the doorway with her hands on her slim hips. She wore cropped khakis and ballet flats, her hair pulled back the way Carrie wore hers. "I've been looking all over for you."

"Do I know you?" John asked.

"We talked yesterday, remember? About the gala tonight. Oh, Mindy, I didn't notice you there."

Mindy wiped the tears from her face. "Why are you looking for Mr. Phillips?"

"I'm picking him up for the Fall Fling. It wasn't supposed to be my responsibility, as I'm sure you'll remember, but things being as they are, I thought it was best to take him in hand."

"But the Fling is hours from now."

"We've got a lot of work to do, haven't we? Finding him a suit and getting a haircut and, well, just generally getting him cleaned up."

"You don't need to talk about me like I'm not here," John said.

Kate's face flushed. "I apologize."

"It's fine."

"We should get going, though."

John looked at Mindy. "You coming with us?"

"I don't think so."

He stood up. "I don't hold with suits."

Kate's shoulders rose and fell. The Fall Fling was a black-tie af-fair. Always had been and always would be, Mindy had heard Kate say more than once. "How about some nice slacks and a shirt? You want to blend in a bit, don't you?"

"Hard to see how I'll be blending in."

"Yes, well, one can hope."

"Ayuh."

"Let's get moving, shall we?"

Mindy stood up as John moved from behind the desk. She wanted to reach out and stop him, but the force that had been pro-pelling her since the day before seemed to have evaporated through her skin.

"Thanks for speaking with me," she said.

"I'm sorry for your loss," John said, then followed Kate out the door.

CHAPTER 34

Surveillance

Elizabeth

Ben doesn't say yes, but he doesn't say no either. All he says is that he needs to think about it, and we should return to the house.

We split apart when we get back, me to the bedroom and Ben to the kitchen where his parents are anxiously awaiting the result of our fight. Dispute. Whatever's going on between us. There is no divorce in the Jansen household—they don't hold with it. Not that they know that this is where we were (are?) headed, but it must be obvious there's something wrong. Why else would I keep something we've both wanted so much from him, or been so insistent that Grace not tell Ben?

What's wrong with me, really?

What's wrong with us?

A wave of nausea sweeps through me, and I sit heavily on the bed. Maybe this will pass, or maybe I should be running to the bathroom in the manner of so many women I've seen over the years, on film, in life, in books.

A uniquely female gesture.

I'm part of that now. A pledge to this sorority.

I take a few deep breaths, and the feeling retreats. Sure to return, I know, but I'll take the momentary reprieve. My phone rattles and hums on the bedside table. Kara's calling.

"Are you okay?" she asks.

"How did you know?"

"I sent you three e-mails, and you didn't respond."

"Oh. Ha. Yes. Well. I have some news."

"You're pregnant."

"Yes. You knew?"

"I suspected."

"Why didn't you say anything?"

"It was not my business to."

I sigh. "Is that why you called?"

"No. I need you."

"What's going on?"

"You haven't looked at the reports this morning?"

"I've been . . . No. Things are worse?"

"We will face the crisis today. And my second has taken ill. I need your assistance."

I stare at the wall. James McMurtry stares back at me, an old favorite of Ben's that he'd taken the time to turn from poster to painting.

"I can't, Kara."

There's a long silence on the line. "Ah. It's like that, is it?"

"I need to make the right choice, for once."

"I understand."

Guilt tugs at me. "Is there really no one else? Because if there isn't, I'm sure he'll understand."

"No, that's fine. Andy will do it."

"Of course. But why didn't you ask him in the first place?"

"I think you know why."

In order to avoid going crazy waiting for Ben to give me his answer or constantly checking on the fire, I decide to follow up on a question that should be front and center: How did that video get out? See also: Why didn't I think to look for it myself?

I go to see Detective Donaldson first. He's sent me several apoplectic messages that he needs to speak to me ASAP.

When I get to his office, he's pacing with his cell phone held to his ear.

"Yup. Yup. I know. That's a short list, and you're on it. I'm just stating a fact. Yup. Will do."

He hangs up and runs his hand backward and forward over the top of his head.

"Who were you talking to?" I ask.

He turns around. "You been standing there long?"

"Only a couple of yups."

"This is not a time to joke. Have you spoken to Rich?"

"No, have you?"

He looks briefly at his phone, then puts it facedown on his desk.

"We have a situation on our hands," he says. "The leak of that video might cost me my job. So I want to know: How the fuck did that happen?"

"I have no idea. I didn't even know there was a video. Did you?"

He walks over to his computer and wakes it up. The video's frozen on his screen at the shot of the four boys and the girl in the square.

"I got it yesterday. I hadn't worked my way further than this when I interviewed Tucker and Angus."

"Was this the evidence you mentioned?"

"It was."

"Why didn't you show it to them yesterday?"

"I didn't have time to sit down with the timeline and examine the whole tape to match it up. Besides, that way I got them to commit to their stories. Angus obviously lied."

"So did Tucker."

Donaldson shoots me a look. "We don't know that he's one of the kids."

"I'll bet he is. Has Angus said anything since he was brought in?"

"Nope."

"What about identifying the others on the tape? They likely had something to do with it."

"We're working on that."

"Any leads?"

He clicked his browser closed. "Not any I'm sharing at the moment."

"So, what am I supposed to do?"

"How about doing your job while you still have it?"

The *Daily*'s offices are housed on the second floor of one of the older buildings on the town square. The paper does a truncated edition on Sundays, and the newsroom is only half-full. An eager intern points me to the desk I'm looking for.

Joshua Wicks's workspace is not what I expected. Rather than the sheaves of paper and mad conspiracy wall I'd imagined, there are only two large computer screens and clear surfaces that must be wiped down daily. A prominent bottle of hand sanitizer completes the picture. I watch his hands as they fly over the keys. They are chapped and rough, the hands of a man who washes way too frequently.

He must sense my presence, or perhaps he noticed my reflection in his screen. He turns around. He has a fresh-faced look for a man of thirty-five. In the right clothing, he could easily pass for a high school senior. His dark-brown hair is shaggy, and his matching eyes look tired. He's been working hard this week.

"Ms. Martin. A pleasure to see you," he says in his rumbling bass voice.

"I'm sure."

"You're here about the video?"

"I am."

"I'm not going to tell you how I got it."

"I'd expect nothing less."

"A phone call would have sufficed, then."

"I disagree," I say. "May I sit?"

He motions toward the edge of his desk, and I take a tenuous perch. He winces. I can only imagine the scrub-down it's going to receive after I leave.

"So?" he says.

"The town cameras all stream on the *Daily*'s website. Is it recorded here?"

"No. We just host the feed. They're not actually our cameras."

"Whose are they?"

"The town's."

"So the feed would be recorded on the town's servers?"

"That's right."

"Who has access to those?"

"I'm sure the police can get access. Or your office."

"Of course. But who usually has access?"

"Normally, that'd just be the town's IT department."

"Which is?"

"One guy. But not the droid you're looking for."

I shake my head. Men and their *Star Wars* references. Will they never end?

"Am I supposed to take your word on that?"

His eyes blink slowly. "Do what you want."

"Did you get the footage before it was e-mailed to the town?"

"Nope."

"Any idea what mailing list was used?"

"Isn't that something you should know already?"

I give him a look.

"Fine. Whatever. From what I can tell, they used part of the emergency services list."

"How'd they get that?"

"I can think of a few ways."

"Care to share?"

"I doubt they've got the best security on their servers. And any number of people use that list on a regular basis."

"So what's the motive behind sharing the video? Why not just take it to the police?"

He raises his shoulders toward his ears.

I try another tack. "You've been getting inside information all week. I know you can't tell me who it is, but perhaps you can tell me who it isn't?"

"That's asking me to do indirectly what I can't do directly."

I stand to go. "Had to try."

"Wouldn't respect you if you didn't."

"Thanks, I think."

He reached for the bottle of Purell. "I will tell you one thing. I heard your boss is mighty pissed about the release of that video."

"He hates leaks."

"Yes, I'm sure that's why."

CHAPTER 35

Mirror Ball

Elizabeth

The Fall Fling takes place where it does every year, in an enormous tent set up on a lawn maintained by Parks and Recreation at the foot of Nelson Peak. Nelson's Central Park, it's the setting for concerts, fireworks, Shakespeare on the Lawn, anything we can pack into an outdoor setting in the short months when things can be reliably planned in the open. Usually, it merely affords a beautiful view of the hill in its summer green splendor. Tonight, though, it might be a front-row seat to the end of, well, everything, really.

Before we got off the line, I asked Kara if the event should be cancelled. She sighed heavily and told me how she'd tried to convince the town to do that to no avail. The show will go on, only this time it will be guarded by fire trucks and the same spaghetti of yellow hoses that surround my house, valuable resources that should be deployed elsewhere but, in classic Nelson fashion, are being diverted from need to want.

But who am I to judge, here in my heavy ball gown, quickly let out to hide my expanding middle and my larger-than-usual breasts? The car I'm climbing out of cost more than most make in a year, me included. And the tickets for this event are something outside of any reasonable budget, paid for, like my dress, by Ben's parents.

"Are you feeling all right?" Ben asks, placing his hand on the small of my back. It's the same temperature as the smoky night, but my skin reacts through the silky fabric. A shiver. A flush. Ben still makes me feel this way.

"What are we doing here?"

Ben looks into the tent as his parents leave us to greet friends. He surveys the round tables covered in snow-white linen, the silver place settings glinting in the votive-infused light. There's a string quartet playing near the entrance and a DJ set up on the stage. Everyone is dressed in black tie and ball gowns, ignoring the haze that surrounds them. There are enough flowers in the room to nearly kill the smell of smoke. Suspended from the ceiling is something that looks very much like Chihuly's glass blossom sculpture that hangs in the Bellagio's lobby in Las Vegas. I know it can't be real, but it's a damn good facsimile.

"Because of the fire?" he says.

He's wearing a well-cut black suit and a silky black tie. It makes him look thinner, younger, almost movie-star good-looking, and several women have already thrown him appreciative glances. Ben gave me one himself when I came out of his room an hour ago. He'd tucked a loose strand of hair that was already escaping from my attempt at a chignon and said, "I'm glad we're doing this."

"Among other things," I say now.

Last time I checked, the satellite showed a few clouds looming on the horizon, though it's impossible to see them through the low-level fug that's hanging over us. I feel claustrophobic and nervous, a feeling that's not helped by the nearly constant roar of aircraft above us dumping their contents on the just-out-of-sight flames. The plume of smoke behind the Peak is still blazing straight up to the sky, but it's so much closer now. Based on what Kara told me, it must have reached the firebreak.

"We fiddle while Rome burns," I say. "Emperor Nero would approve."

"I think he was playing a lyre . . ."

I smack him in the arm. "Stop showing off."

He grins. "Our countrymen await."

He leads me into the tent, and we check out the board that contains the seating plan. We're at table three, in the first row to the right of the stage, in front of the plastic panoramic windows that provide a view of the Peak. They've turned on the night-skiing lights, and they glow dimly against the fading sky.

We stand in front of the window for a moment, looking out, looking up. If I close my eyes, I could be there with the crews. Manning a hose, raking the ground, lost in the smoke. Perhaps Ben senses this, and it's why he isn't saying anything. A test of my new resolve. I don't like to be tested, but if I want a future with him, I have to walk away from my past.

I turn my back on the fire and spend the next hour with Ben, weaving through the cocktail hour, brief traces of kisses being left on my cheek. There is much talk of what's happening on the Peak, of course, a few nervous glances toward the windows, but also of other, mundane things. We are invincible, of course, money being the ultimate shield against real harm.

About ten minutes before we'll be called to take our seats for dinner, Ben and I find ourselves on the outskirts of the dance floor caught by our own wedding song. "Us" by Regina Spektor. Someone looking for deeper meaning would read all kinds of things into that choice; we just liked the song. Monuments being built to love. Cities named after it. It seemed so big. So permanent. What we were hoping to create on a more modest scale.

I love this song. But it's not a song I would expect to hear here.

I turn to Ben, and he's standing there, looking shy, holding out his hand.

"Did you . . . ?"

He just waits, and I put my hand in his. He steps us into the slightly muddled crowd, his hand returning to the small of my back, the other gripping my left hand tightly, folded between us. We shuffle slowly in a circle.

"What does this mean?" I ask.

"Shhh," he says. "Let's be happy, tonight. We're going to have a baby."

His face breaks into that smile I've been waiting for, and I tuck my chin against his shoulder. We spin to the quick piano beat that's a bit too fast for a classic slow song. The music soars and crashes around us, and I have one of those movie moments, where scenes of my life flit through my brain like a highlight reel. Our first conversation. That tenuous moment on the Majestic. Our wedding day. The time we spent apart. The times we came back together. Our last good night. How broken Ben looked this morning.

"Ben?"

"Yes," his lips say into an escaped tendril of my hair, wafting it against my neck.

"I love you."

He holds me away from him, silent, still turning slowly.

I want him to say something. To say it back. To mean it. For it to be enough. And maybe he's about to, but it will have to wait until another time.

"Please take your seats, folks," Kate Bourne's voice crackles through the sound system as Regina's voice is cut off midverse.

Ben and I stand there, still in a dancing pose, looking at each other as the lights begin to flicker above our heads. *On/off. On/off.*

"We should probably sit," Ben says on the third flicker.

I nod, and we leave any progress on our détente for another time. I can't help but feel hopeful, though, as I take a seat on a fabric-covered chair that, though a rental, is nicer than anything we have in our own home.

Kate's voice booms through the speakers again, welcoming us. She's standing at the microphone in the middle of the stage. She's wearing a floor-length black dress made of silk chiffon. The material's gathered at the shoulders and has a plunging V neckline. Her collarbones stand out in sharp relief, almost like a coat hanger that the dress has been placed on for safekeeping. I guess she rethought her dress choice after seeing me at Caroline's. Given how my dress already feels like a weight around my neck, I'm wishing I'd done the same.

The fire rages behind me. Ben is seated to my left, and a business associate of his father's is on my right. His parents are across from us. I straighten out the silverware next to the bone-china salad plate and shift uncomfortably. I catch Grace watching me fidget. I give her a tentative smile, and she looks away.

Did she really tell Ben about the pregnancy by mistake? We haven't spoken today, other than a few polite words in the car. Her public face doesn't reveal anything, but after all these years of knowing her, I can't believe she acted maliciously.

"I need to go to the bathroom," I tell Ben.

"Everything okay?"

"I'm fine. I'll be back."

I rise and weave through the tables as Kate tells the crowd what it's been complaining about for the last couple of days—this night is in honor of John Phillips, all of the proceeds raised will be given to him so he can find a new home when this is all over, et cetera, et cetera.

I search the room for Mindy. She called me early this morning while I was sleeping, leaving only a missed call on my phone. I haven't called her back. In all the chaos, I forgot until now.

I don't see her anywhere, certainly not at Kate's table, where I would've expected her. But of course. Angus. There's no way she'd come to this event with him sitting in a cell. How could I have forgotten? And that's probably what she was calling me about this morning too. I should have called her back. A long time ago.

I reach deep into the pocket of my skirt and extract my phone. I can, at least, do one thing right tonight. I walk out of the tent, pull up Mindy's contact, and tap to dial her number. It rings so long I almost hang up, but then her voice mail clicks in.

"This is Mindy. Leave a message."

My voice catches at the familiarity of hers.

"It's Beth. Elizabeth Martin. Of course you know who it is. Sorry. Strange night. Strange week. I just wanted to say I'm so sorry about

Angus. And sorry also for not calling you back, earlier. If there's something you need, anything, please let me know. I'm thinking of you. I'm thinking of all of you."

I end the call. There's nothing more to say.

I slip the phone back into my pocket and start the semitreacherous walk across the lawn toward the public bathrooms. It's fully dark now, and although I have no trouble seeing between the lights on the hill and the phosphorescent glow of the tent, someone forgot to lay down a walkway between it and the cement slab five hundred yards away where the bathrooms are. I'm not quite sure how I'll manage with my dress once I get in there, but at least there are no Porta Pottys to deal with.

"Can I help you?" asks an older male voice. An arm slips through the crook I've created by holding my dress up off the moist lawn. When I turn to look, he has a face I recognize but can't place.

"Do I know you?"

"Graeme Fletcher. You missed an appointment with me earlier this week."

Graeme Fletcher? Graeme Fletch—oh, God. The lawyer. The divorce lawyer I was supposed to see earlier this week. I glance over my shoulder.

"No need to be nervous, young lady. I'm only escorting a woman to the bathrooms."

I smile at him. He's nearing sixty, with steel-gray hair and matching eyes. His tux fits him comfortably.

"Does that happen a lot?" I ask.

"People anxious about being seen with me in public? Frequently, I'm sad to say. Nature of the business."

"I've always wondered why anyone would choose to do what you do, to be honest."

"It can be steeped in misery, I'll admit. But only if you let it get to you."

"How do you *not* let it get to you? All the terrible things people who used to be in love do and say to each other."

He stops. We've arrived at the bathrooms. "Because I hope I make it easier for them. To move on. Get closure." He releases my arm. "But I'm guessing your missed appointment means you won't be needing my services?"

"No. I . . . I mean, I don't think so."

"I'm glad to hear it."

I thank him for the escort and enter the building. It all takes a bit of maneuvering. I make a mental note not to drink much of anything tonight so I won't have to repeat the process. Of course, I shouldn't be drinking alcohol at all. Because I'm pregnant. I'm pregnant. What will it take for me to really believe this? How can it be true after all this time? Now?

I struggle out of the stall. When I get back outside, Ben is there. Talking to Mr. Fletcher.

"What's going on?" I ask.

Ben turns toward me. "You were taking so long, I came looking for you."

My heart is beating like a drum. "Mr. Fletcher was kind enough to help me walk across the grass."

"He said."

"It was nice talking to you, Ben," Mr. Fletcher says, and walks away.

"Can you help me back?" I say to Ben.

I loop my harm through his, and we walk onto the grass. My heels dig into the soft grass, thoroughly moistened earlier today by the fire crews in case the worst happens.

"How do you know Mr. Fletcher?" I ask.

"He's an old friend of my folks. Have you . . ."

"Yes."

"What?" Ben drops my arm. A siren wails in the distance.

"I don't want to lie to you. So yes. I had an appointment with Mr. Fletcher. But I didn't go to it. And I told him I wouldn't be needing his services. Because I won't."

"You had an appointment."

"It was the only way I was going to bring myself to leave."

"And that was so important to you? Leaving?"

"It felt like it was."

"That's all you have to say?"

"Keep your voice down."

"I'll speak as loud as I goddamn want."

"I told you I wanted to split up. What did you think I was going to do?"

"I didn't think you really meant it."

"Well, I did."

We stand there, trapped by our anger and frustration. And then it hits me.

"You're never going to forgive me, are you?"

"I didn't say that."

"But it's the truth, right? You never forgave me for hiding those tests results from you, and now I've done something worse. You're not going to get past that. So what's the point?"

"What's the point? Are you seriously asking me that right now?"

"I'm not asking you anything! I'm telling you the truth."

"The truth. Ha! You don't even know what that word means."

"That's what you really think of me, isn't it? I'm just a lying, cheating mistake who abandoned you when things got too hard."

"Well, didn't you?"

This statement is such a mixture of truth and misconception that it stops me. Stops me cold.

"I can't believe this is happening," I say.

"You can't believe it? Jesus Christ, Elizabeth. You're the one who made it happen!"

"I made a mistake. One mistake. And you've been blaming me for it ever since. I don't deserve this. I don't."

I turn to leave, and Ben reaches out for my arm. I shrug it off.

"Let go of me."

"Everything okay here?" Andy asks. He's wearing his firefighter gear and is slightly out of breath.

"What the fuck is he doing here?" Ben asks.

"Stop it, just stop it. Andy's never done anything but be there for me."

"Oh, right. Because that's what I haven't done. I wasn't there for you. I'm not here for you now. I'm the bad guy."

"Will you two stop it!" Andy says. "We need to evac the tent."

My eyes go automatically to the mountain. Flames are dancing along the ridge, an orange flickering band that would be pretty if it wasn't a disaster. The sirens I heard in the background are now an approaching wail, and they match the panicked rhythm of my heart.

"When did it crest?" I ask Andy.

"About ten minutes ago. The wind swept it right past the firebreak. Two men down."

Two men. Two men I probably know. I push that thought aside.

"What do you want us to do?"

"We need to get everyone out of there without causing chaos."

The tent is the worst kind of place to evacuate, full to the brim with older people who've had a few drinks and with only one point of egress.

"Will you help?" I say to Ben.

"Yes, of course."

The three of us run across the lawn. I stumble over my shoes, and Ben arrests my fall. I kick them off, and we resume our sprint.

When we get there, Kate Bourne is still at the microphone, but now John Phillips is standing next to her. He's almost unrecognizable in a pair of dark pants and a dress shirt, and he's holding a massive check for $105,000. He looks petrified.

"It's superimportant that nobody say the word *fire*," I say to Ben quietly.

"What do we do?"

"We have to get up to the stage," Andy says examining the doorway we've just come through for a way to make it larger. "We'll say we need to evacuate the tent and ask people to disperse in an orderly fashion. It's the only way. Even then—"

"We can do it," I say. "You deal with the door, and I'll go up."

Andy and I make eye contact, agreeing on a course of action. He walks toward the bar to enlist the help of the waiters to open the doorway and stabilize it. If we don't handle this properly, the tent could easily collapse.

Ben and I walk briskly toward the stage. The uneven floor scratches at my bare feet, and the sirens' moan fills my ears. A few people give us curious glances, but most seem intent on the food in front of them.

We reach the stage and climb the stairs. Kate stops midsentence.

"What's going on?"

"I have to make an announcement." I place my hand over the microphone and speak quietly to Kate. "The fire's crested the ridge. We need to get everyone out of here."

Her hand flies to her mouth, and Ben steps in front of her, pushing her back, fencing her in so she doesn't cause a panic.

I take my hand off the microphone and speak in my most soothing voice.

"Ladies and gentlemen, I'm going to have to ask you to leave the tent in an orderly fashion. This is merely a safety precaution. Move rapidly but carefully. If you need assistance, please stay at your table and someone will be there to help you shortly."

"What's going on?" someone yells.

A plane rattles overhead, and now the crowd is muttering and looking around.

"Fire!" another voice yells. He stands and points toward the window. "I can see the fire!"

The room erupts in shouts and shrieks. Chairs scrape back. Several glasses are overturned, the red wine they contained staining the white linen beneath them.

"Please remain calm," I say loudly into the microphone. "Please listen to the instructions I'm about to give you . . ."

I stop because it's hopeless. My voice is being completely drowned out by the crowd. Three hundred people want out of here, stat, and they aren't going to wait patiently for instructions.

Everyone is standing now, jostling, pushing. I see an older man get knocked over. I look to our table but Ben's parents aren't there.

"Ben!" I shout, but it's Andy who comes to my side.

"People are getting hurt," he says, his eyes skimming the room, trying to find a solution.

"Do you have something to cut the tent?" I ask.

"Good idea."

"What?" Kate says, having escaped from Ben. "No, we'll lose our damage deposit and—"

"I don't think that's the most important thing right now."

Andy takes out his pocketknife and flips it open. He jumps down off the stage and walks to the window. He stabs a hole in the plastic and slides the knife down until it punctures the tent itself. He's able to cut through a couple of inches but then gets stuck.

I drop down next to him and take the other end of the fabric in my hands.

"Rip in the other direction."

We both start straining on the fabric. I lean back on the heels of my feet, putting my body weight into it.

The fabric lets go in one big roaring sound, and the release of tension tips me over onto the ground.

Ben is there to help me up.

"What are you doing?" he yells so I can hear him.

"We need to widen this. Can you help us?"

"Let me do it. You should get out of here."

"I'll never make it through the crowd. Where are your parents?"

"I can't find them."

"Let's open this," Andy says, "then you can look for them."

They work quickly together, pulling back the fabric and cutting the bottom so there's a second exit. Andy goes to the people nearest to us and directs them to turn around and follow him.

"Can you get them out of here?" Andy asks me, pointing to John Phillips and Kate, who are still standing on the stage, rooted to the spot.

"Where should we go?"

"Bring them to the arts building. We're sending buses there."

"Give me your knife for a sec."

He hands it over. I hold my skirt away from me and slash at the fabric near my knees. I put my hand into the hole and rip with the help of the knife until the bulk of the dress has tumbled to my feet. I kick it aside so no one trips on it. I give the knife back to Andy and turn to Ben.

"You need to find your parents and make sure they're okay."

"What are you going to do?"

"I'm going to stay here and make sure everyone gets out."

"That's not your responsibility."

"Of course it is. Please, Ben. I'll be fine. We'll meet up after, okay? Just be careful."

I hug him quickly as smoke flows through the opening in the tent like bellows are propelling it. I turn away from Ben and haul myself back onto the stage. I grab Kate with one hand and John Phillips with the other.

"We have to get out of here."

I tug, and they follow me down the stairs to the opening. Andy's standing to one side, holding onto the fabric, shouting at people where to go when they get outside.

Our eyes lock for a moment. "Be safe."

"I will. Go."

I pull Kate and John through the opening like toddlers. The flames are over the ridge now. I stop long enough to watch pink-colored water pouring from the belly of an aircraft. The smoke billows up from the doused flames. Then I turn my back to the Peak once more and give a tug in the right direction to my charges.

"Run!"

DAY SIX

CHAPTER 36

All Through the Night

Elizabeth

I leave Kate and John at the arts center, then turn and run back to the tent. There's a broken line of people hurrying across the lawn, and I stop to help an older couple. The man has a graze across his cheek. His wife's hands are shaking. When I get them back to the center, there are two EMTs doing triage and three big yellow school buses in the parking lot. An EMT wipes the blood off the man's face. He has only a small nick on his chin, so a quick bandage is applied and blankets are placed over both of their shoulders. Then I help them onto a school bus and into a seat.

"Where are you taking them?" I ask the driver.

"Mason," he says, giving the name of the next town over. "Everyone's being moved to the rec center."

I climb off the bus and hustle back to the arts center to see if I can help. Orderly lines have formed now, and I don't see anyone in need of immediate assistance. I lean against the side of the building to catch my breath. My ears are ringing from the howl of sirens and the near-constant air bombardments. The air around me seems tinged with the pink dye they put into the water drops to make it easier to see if they've hit their targets. There are small droplets of it staining what remains of my dress.

In all the chaos, I've lost track of Ben. His parents weren't in the arts center. I'm hoping they were near the entrance of the tent and took their car home with Ben in tow. I reach into my skirt for my phone, but I don't have a pocket anymore. The pocket of my skirt is somewhere in the tent.

The night air surrounds me like a furnace, my dress is in tatters, and my feet are swollen and bruised. But we got everyone out. We won't likely know till first light whether the fire's going to be held at the Peak. Everything that can be done is being done.

I try not to think about what that means for my house.

I look out across the field. A line of fire and smoke outlines the Peak against the night sky. The firefighters' headlamps wink like fireflies. The wind has picked up again, rattling the tent against its poles like it's sitting atop Everest. I tell one of the firemen I'm going to make a last check of the tent, and race away from the building before he can tell me no.

The tent looks like a speakeasy after Mardi Gras. Overturned tables, the air perfumed by spilled wine and burned-out votives. It's a miracle, really, that no one was seriously injured and the whole tent didn't go up in flames.

I walk tentatively through the space, sweeping for anyone missing, keeping my tender feet away from the broken china and glass. The rough edges of the tent flap behind me, snapping loudly.

I find the remains of my dress next to the side of the stage. I lift the skirt, but I know already from the weight that it's empty. I get down on my hands and knees to search. A large gust blows against the side of the tent, pressing the fabric to my face. I push it aside and peer under the stage. Something shiny is there. I lie flat on my stomach and reach as far as I can. My fingers brush the edge of what I'm certain is my phone.

As if brought alive by my touch, it begins to flash with an incoming call. I stretch farther, but I can't reach it. I flatten myself against the ground and inch under the stage. I can see the screen.

Ben's calling. I use my hands to inch myself forward as a large ripping sound fills the air. The wind shrieks, and I can feel the sides of the tent expand and contract like a set of lungs. My hand closes around the phone as my ears fill with sound. The stage buckles above me, thudding against my head, and I have just long enough to think about what a stupid idea this was before everything goes black.

"Ms. Martin?"

I blink awake, coughing, inhaling the smell of canvas and wine and smoke. It must've been a crazy night on the work site, celebrating the end of the fire. I can't even remember going to . . . Hold up.

Where the hell am I?

"Ms. Martin? Stay still while I move this."

I can't place the familiar voice, but I obey it.

I open my eyes. I can see, but I can't. Everything is black, and my eyes are stinging. Something also seems to be pinning my shoulders to the ground.

"Fire," I say. My voice sounds loud in my head and swallowed outside of it. "Fire," I say again.

"It's okay. There's no fire in here. You just stay still."

"Ben?"

"No, ma'am. I followed you over from the arts center. Seemed like this was a bad place for anyone to come by themselves. Good thing I did, leastaways."

I turn my head slightly to try to see who's speaking, and that's when the pain hits. My head is throbbing, my neck feels compressed, and a large cramp ripples through my abdomen.

Oh, God. Oh no.

"Need to get out."

"Yes, ma'am. It'll just be a minute."

"Get . . . help."

"I shouted, but everyone's taking care of the fire and loading the last group onto the buses. I don't have a phone."

Something clicks.

I squeeze my hand. I'm holding a phone. I slide my fingers over the screen.

9-1-1

"State the nature of your emergency."

"You saying something?" he asks.

"I . . ."

"Is anyone there? Do you need help?"

"You got a phone in there?"

"If you can't talk, please try to press one of the keys on your phone. Press it once for yes, twice for no. Do you understand me? Once for yes and twice for no."

I move a finger and press emphatically. *Yes.*

"Do you need help?"

A long beep.

"Is this Elizabeth Martin?"

Yes.

"Our system indicates you're near the base of Nelson Peak. Is that correct?"

I press a long note again, then say as loudly as I can, "Tent."

"You're in a tent?"

"Party. Tent. Collapsed."

"A tent collapsed near the base of the Peak?"

Yes.

"Are you injured?"

Another beep.

"How badly are you injured? On a scale of one to five. One being low, five being high. Give me a beep for each."

One. Two. Three. I pause. Four.

"Pregnant," I manage to gasp. "I'm pregnant."

"All right, ma'am. Assistance is on its way. Our emergency services are stretched tight this evening, but we'll get to you as quickly as possible. Please remain calm. Someone is coming."

The object pressing me into the ground digs into my back and then lifts before I can get the cry of pain out of my mouth.

I breathe in and out deeply, aware for the first time that I hadn't been able to take a deep breath before. My stomach cramps again. I try to reach down, but all I succeed in doing is losing my grasp on the phone.

I know where I am now. Trapped under the stage in the tent because I went looking for my stupid cell phone. Because of Ben. I needed to call Ben. At least I know he isn't in here. But if he got out, why didn't he come find me?

"Ms. Martin?"

"Mr. Phillips?"

"Ayuh."

"What are you doing here?"

"I followed you, as I said."

"I thought I put you on a bus?"

"Got off it, didn't I?"

"Why—"

"Let's get you out of there."

"Someone's coming."

"Maybe. You think you could push yourself on your stomach if I tug on your feet?"

I move my neck gingerly. Nothing seems out of place, though pain shoots down my back.

"Let's try."

He grunts and places his warms hands around my ankles. I push at the floor with the heels of my wrists. Pain shoots up the left side of my body, but I grit my teeth and ignore it. Push, tug, stop. Push, tug, stop. Nothing feels broken, just rattled, bruised. Push, tug, stop.

Time is a rubber band. I thought I knew what living in the moment was. All those forests. All those fires. Lost in the physicality of it.

But that was nothing. This is me being in my life. Right here. Right now. Inch by inch.

"That's it. Keep on going, you're almost out."

I push myself to the limit, and now John's hands are on my waist. After a couple more tugs, I am out from under the stage.

I roll onto my back and place my hands on my stomach. It's warm to the touch.

The power is out in the tent. Although my eyes have adjusted to the dark, I can only see shadows and outlines, a child's tracing of chaos.

"Can you sit up?"

I let him ease me up and against the edge of the stage. The tent has ripped completely open and is flapping out into the night. Two of the tent poles nearest the stage are lying on the ground, and the stage itself is tilted like a seesaw.

"We should get out of here," I say.

"You think you can walk?"

"Have to try."

I place my hands on his shoulders, and he levers me up. My legs feel shaky and my left arm doesn't seem to be working right, but we can't stay here.

I sling my right arm around his neck, and we shuffle out of the tent's makeshift opening. The wind gusts, and the canvas flies back and slaps at my face. Another cramp shoots through my stomach, doubling me over.

"I can't . . ."

"Just a bit farther."

"Bathroom. I need to get to a bathroom."

John Phillips nods toward the concrete bunker I used earlier. "That's the closest place.

I straighten up and take a few more steps.

"I'd carry you if I could."

"I can make it."

The wind is spiraling around us, and the sky is so dark. There's a thick band of smoke the wind can't disperse. The air is full of noise, louder than any concert I've ever been to. I've never felt this disoriented in my life. How do soldiers at war handle it? The noise? The pain? The fear?

We get to the bathrooms, and I shuffle into a stall, holding my hurt arm against my waist. As another cramp hits me, I sit there, too terrified to look. But when I finally bring myself to, there's nothing alarming. No blood. I need to get to a doctor, but I haven't lost this baby.

Not yet.

A siren is getting closer. I pull my dress down and limp outside.

"There she is," John Phillips says. "I'm not sure what's wrong with her. She got a good bump on the head when the tent collapsed."

"Ma'am," the EMT asks. "Can you tell me how you're feeling?"

I look into his shadowed face and voice my fears. "I think I might be having a miscarriage."

CHAPTER 37

Puddle of Grace

Mindy

Mindy and Peter went round and round in circles into Sunday morning.

Peter had seen Angus, who'd repeated what he told Mindy. He hadn't done anything, he couldn't explain what was going on, they should just believe him because he was asking them to. And Mindy had found it convincing, but to Peter it lacked conviction.

Maybe Angus was spent from his surroundings. Maybe Mindy had been too willing to accept something that wasn't true. Whatever the reason, she and Peter had switched places now. She was the believer, he the questioner. She was spoiling for a fight, casting around trying to find a new solution. Peter was trying to reconcile himself to a future he didn't think he could change. Both of them were filled with guilt and anguish and questions.

Whether Angus had done this or not, he'd been living a whole life they knew nothing about. Their own son. How did they let that happen? Why did he feel like he had to keep the darkest parts of his life from them? This wasn't just teenage autonomy. It felt like some fundamental mistrust or distance they couldn't explain or accept. They'd failed their son in some basic way, and now he might be lost to them forever. The idea that he might also be the cause of even greater losses was something that circled them like prey.

And even as they clung to each other, Mindy began to believe that, whatever the outcome, she and Peter might not survive.

When Carrie was sick, they were a united force. There was a common enemy to fight, and no doubt that they'd win was permitted between them. The unspeakable was not spoken. It was forbidden, banished, sent packing before it even arrived. While many of the couples around them, haunting the halls, cold cups of coffee clutched in their hands, were alone in their grief, Mindy and Peter drew together. The ties that bound them knotted them closer. Illness would not slip between them, they vowed. Only united could they cast the spell that would end up saving Carrie.

But now, there were two paths to choose. Even though the result would be the same if Angus was found responsible, regardless of his guilt or innocence, the fact that they were even on separate paths was like a slap in the face.

They were both stinging from the blow.

"Do we need to leave our house?" Carrie asked, jumping onto their bed with her usual grace.

Despite the fact that it was just past six, Carrie was dressed in what Mindy had come to think of as her uniform: a black leotard, pink tights, pointe shoes, and her hair tied back closely in a bun. A pink shrug covered her slender arms, and her face was flushed with exertion. Peter had installed a ballet barre in the garage a few years ago so she could practice whenever she wanted, and she rose early every morning to go through her series of pliés and relevés.

"Are you always up this early?" Mindy asked, saddened that she didn't know the answer. How many hours did her daughter put in at the barre every day, alone among the plastic boxes that contained her childhood toys and mementos? Mindy felt again that her watchfulness all these years had been for nothing. All it seemed to have done was keep her from seeing what was really in front of her.

Mindy sat up and rubbed her eyes. They were blurry from lack of sleep and the hours she'd spent in front of the computer when Peter finally drifted off. She'd alternated between watching the fire news, and googling the law about accidental fires and juvenile offenders. An evacuation order was issued, but they were outside its boundaries. The Fall Fling was in the fire's path, but there wasn't anything she could do about that. She'd sat there feeling helpless, refreshing her Facebook feed as people started posting photos of the melee and the injuries that resulted.

Another thing Kate would blame her for, surely.

Carrie hung her arms around Mindy's neck. She smelled like sweat and the slight mildew odor that clung to everything in the garage. Peter turned over and emitted a loud grunt.

"I couldn't sleep," Carrie said.

"Me neither."

Carrie climbed into her lap, folding her lithe limbs up to her chest and staring up at Mindy like she used to do when she was waiting for her next feeding. Carrie hadn't done anything like it in years, and Mindy felt herself break open. Life was so much simpler when cries could be soothed by a breast full of milk or a fresh diaper.

She wrapped her arms around Carrie's slim shoulders and spoke quietly so as not to wake Peter. "Are you sure you're eating enough?"

"I eat all the time."

"I know you do, honey, but . . ."

"I'm fine, Mom, I promise. I couldn't sleep because I'm worried about Angus."

"Me too."

"What was it like there?"

"At the police station? It's not too bad."

"How come I couldn't go, then?"

"They'd only let your father and me in." The lie sprang easily to Mindy's lips, but perhaps it was the truth.

"Angus must be going crazy in there."

"It won't be for long. We'll get him out tomorrow morning. But yes, I think he's scared. I'm scared for him. Your father and I both are."

"Maybe he could escape? He sneaks out of the house a lot."

"He does?"

Carrie unfolded her legs, holding them straight out from her body with her toes pointed. She'd always had a hard time sitting still, even before she started her dance training.

"I've caught him a few times. Am I in trouble because I didn't tell you?"

"I think we have bigger things to worry about right now. But . . . did you know he was out that night?"

"I thought I heard his window open, but I wasn't sure. No way I thought he was doing anything bad. I would've told you then, for sure."

"What did you think he was doing?"

"Seeing Willow? He really likes her, you know?"

"I do."

"But her parents? They are like superstrict. I mean, I know you're strict too, worried about me and everything, but she never lets Willow or Beech do anything. Not even in groups."

Beech was Willow's younger sister.

"How do you know Beech again?"

"She's in ballet with me, remember? Her mom comes to every class and just sits there, making sure she doesn't talk to the boys. As if. Who wants to talk to ballet boys?"

Carrie rolled her eyes. Mindy couldn't help but wish that she'd stay this innocent forever.

"Maybe she's there to watch her dance? Do you wish I did that more? Came to your classes?"

"God, no. All I do is make mistakes there."

"It's okay to make mistakes."

"Not all kinds of mistakes. Not mistakes like Angus."

Mindy stroked the top of Carrie's head. Her hair was so soft and slippery it was difficult for her to mold it into a bun, and yet she managed it. Every day she put her body into difficult positions and faced her limitations. *Where she did get the courage to do this?* Mindy wondered. Certainly not from her.

"Is it okay if I'm mad at Angus?" Carrie said.

"Of course it is. Whatever happened, Angus made some bad decisions. But he says he didn't start the fire, and we need to believe him, okay? We need to be strong for him as a family."

Carrie slipped to the floor, her pointe shoes making a hollow sound. She rose up on her toes and hovered there, her hands above her head in fifth position.

"Angus should stop thinking about Willow. He's being selfish."

"Do you know something you're not telling me, honey?"

Carrie descended gracefully into a demi-plié, her arms fluttering in front of her and out to finish the movement.

"It doesn't matter what I know."

"Of course it does. How can you say that?"

She shrugged and turned, then took a sudden leap into a grand jeté, landing soundlessly.

"It was something Beech said after class yesterday before her mom came up and dragged her back to her dungeon. Like how people should be talking to Willow. And that Willow was too scared of their parents to say anything."

Mindy felt a small beat of hope for the first time in days. She sprung up and swirled Carrie around in a circle, not caring if she woke Peter now.

"Put me down. Mom. Mom! What's gotten into you?"

Mindy wasn't sure, but it felt like something.

CHAPTER 38

Pieces of Me

Elizabeth

It's a slow ride in the ambulance to the hospital. The roads are clogged with people evacuating, and no one's pulling aside for the weeping siren above us. I would be panicking at how long it's taking if there wasn't a heart-rate monitor strapped to my belly picking up the rapid, steady thrum of the baby's heart. I watch it blip on the monitor as John Phillips holds my hand, murmuring soothing sounds and telling me we're almost there.

The hospital's no easier when we get there. Triage is full of those who got injured at the Fall Fling and in a pileup that occurred on the road out of town when a SUV flipped into a ditch. An exhausted-looking resident gives me a quick once-over. When I tell him my cramping seems to have stopped, a look of relief washes over his face, and he tucks me into a nook in the hall that affords a full view of the emergency room waiting area.

I ask John to call Ben's parents, Ben's cell phone. I even give him the number to our house, knowing there's no chance Ben's there but desperate for news of him. When John comes back, he's shaking his head and he doesn't have to speak to let me know he wasn't able to reach Ben. His parents are safe and sound at home, but they got there on their own. They've been trying to call both of us for hours with no success.

I turn my face to the wall and try to reach for something that will comfort me. "Try to stay calm," was the last thing the resident told me, and I know he's right, only how do you do that? I've never been able to, not when it came to me. I had ice in my veins when I was facing down a wall of flames. But in my own life, it's all turmoil and racing thoughts, and right now they're rushing head-on into the wall I'm staring at.

"At least you know he was all right a couple hours ago," John says.

He's got my blood on his shirt collar, and a streak of ash cuts his face in two. His new dress shirt, so white and crisp a few hours ago, is almost gray now, a match for his soot-covered black slacks.

"How do you know that?"

"Because he called, didn't he? When you was under the stage?"

Did Ben call me? Everything that happened before the stage collapsed is hazy.

"I think . . ."

John Phillips reaches into his pocket and emerges with my phone. He places it gently on my chest, faceup. I hit the power button, and a message flashes up, saying I've missed a call from Ben.

"Where did you find this?"

"When they's were putting you in the ambulance I checked in the bathroom, and you'd left it next to the sink. Seemed like it was the least I could do."

"Thank you."

He looks out into the waiting room, full of people huddled together.

"This is all because of the fire," he says.

"In one way or another."

"It's hard to imagine something that started so small causing all of this."

"Chaos theory."

"What's that?" John says.

"Oh, just this thing my dad used to say. About how if a butterfly flaps its wings in South America, it might cause a hurricane in the Atlantic . . ."

My dad was always saying things like that. And when I call and tell him I'm pregnant, I'm sure he'll say something about how there were six hundred unique spellings of Catherine registered in California last year, but of course, that's California. And I'll laugh and tell him he's kind of missing the point of my news.

"Do you think it's possible to have done something bad and not even know it?" John asks.

"Like an unintended consequence?"

"Yes, that's it exactly."

"I think that sort of thing happens all the time."

"Ayuh," he says and wanders away from me.

I pick up the phone. My battery's almost dead, and I don't have the energy for a call right now. I can barely keep my eyes open. I tap out a quick text.

At the hospital. We're fine. Please come.

I hit "Send." Then I close my eyes and drift into sleep.

I wake up alone in the hospital hall, the steady thump of the heart monitor pulling me back to reality. I can't tell what time it is. When I press my phone to check, it has no life left in it. My brain has that fuzzy feeling it gets after a couple hours of sleep, and the quality of light through the windows makes me guess it's about seven in the morning. Sunday, September 7, I'm going to assume.

I try to call for someone, but my mouth is dried out and my voice is a whisper. I prop myself up on my elbows, and when that feels all right, I sit up properly. And this, finally, brings someone to my side. The same young resident from last night, or today, or whenever I saw him.

"We feeling better?" he asks, his fingers pressed to my wrist to take my pulse.

I stifle the impulse to bite back at the "we." "We are."

"Good." He reads the output of the heart monitor. "Everything seems steady here. Any more cramping?"

"No. What caused it? Am I in danger of losing the baby?"

"As long as there's no bleeding, cramping in early pregnancy is quite normal. You've got a lot of hormonal changes going on. Your uterus and cervix are preparing themselves for the journey ahead. Just take it easy for a few days, and go see your obstetrician. You're healthy and strong. Everything should be fine."

"Thank you."

"You're welcome. Now, unfortunately, we're short on beds, so I'm going to have the nurse come relieve you of your IV, and then we'll discharge you."

I look down at the tube pushing fluids into my arm. I'm wearing only a hospital gown. I vaguely remember the tattered remnants of my dress being cut away from my body when I arrived.

"Is there some way . . . I'm alone and I don't have anything to wear."

His tired eyes crinkle. "I think we can find you something."

Half an hour later, I've had the IV pulled from my arm, and have been supplied with a pair of scrubs and the kind of paper slippers I used to get at my doctor's office in the winter as a kid. When I change in the bathroom, I can see the damage the night inflicted. I have deep-tissue bruising all along the left side of my body and across the back of shoulders. My legs are full of grazes and a few gashes that have already scabbed over. I wash the dirt off my face in the sink, the water turning almost black as I use too many paper towels making my face, neck, and arms recognizable. Then I climb into the blue pants and matching shirt the nurse gave me. Years of washing has made the fabric so soft I briefly consider giving all of my clothes the same treatment.

When I leave the bathroom, I find John Phillips waiting for me.

"Sorry for taking so long in there."

"You sure apologize a lot."

"Oh, that's a Canadian thing."

"How's that?"

"Saying 'sorry.' We use it like punctuation."

He nods but doesn't move.

"Did you need to use the bathroom?"

"No, I wanted—"

"Beth? Oh, thank God," Ben says, sweeping me into his arms and filling me with relief.

I pull back. He's wearing a firefighter's uniform. One breath of him tells me he's been fighting the fire. This is how I used to smell: smoke and sweat and chemicals. He smells like Ben and me made one. Ben and me made whole.

"Where have you been?" I ask.

"At our house."

"Is it gone?"

"No. It's safe. For now, it's okay."

"How did you get up there?"

"Andy brought me. Once we'd gotten everyone safely out of the tent, he told me he was going up there, and I asked to go with him."

"I wish you'd told me."

"I couldn't find you, and there wasn't any time. I tried to call you." He steps toward me again. "Is the baby okay?"

"Yes. It's fine. We're fine."

"I didn't even know you were in trouble. Not till I got your text. I should've stayed with you."

"No, you did the right thing. What's going on up there?"

He shakes his head. "It's touch and go, as far as I understand it. Holding for now."

And us? I want to say.

"Can you leave?" Ben asks.

"Yes. Where should we go?"

"I want to check in on my folks, if that's okay?"

"Of course. I—"

There's the muffled sound of a ringing phone in his pocket.

"Hold on," he says and takes it out. "Hello?"

He steps away from me. I listen to his side of the conversation. "Yes, she's with me. Right now? Yes, of course, of course, I understand. We'll be there in ten."

He turns off the phone. "Can you stand a slight side trip?"

"Where?"

"To the police station."

CHAPTER 39

Block Party

Mindy

Mindy approached Willow's house cautiously. It wasn't Willow who made her nervous, but Willow's mother, Cathy, who'd be a Coffee Booster if she didn't find that sort of thing beneath her. Part Kate Bourne, part barracuda, Cathy and her husband, Ed, had lived down the block from Mindy since they'd moved to Nelson, but Mindy could count the conversations they'd had on one hand.

Cathy and Ed's house was much like hers—a wood-sided split-level with a sharply peaked roof so the heavy snowfall that came every winter could slide easily to the ground.

Mindy stood at the end of their walkway trying to quiet her mind. But for the heavy tang of smoke, nothing looked amiss. It was inside that everything was in turmoil.

But Mindy was through with being nervous, she told herself, through with being the kind of woman who checked her friends' reactions before she'd show her own. That woman wasn't going to get Angus out of jail or figure out what had happened that night.

Mindy climbed the steps and pressed the doorbell firmly. It was only after she heard the chime sound loudly through the quiet house that she thought to check the time. It was only seven thirty in the morning, though it felt like it could've been anytime.

The middle of the night. The end of a long day. The smoke blotted out any difference in the light, and the number of hours she'd been awake made it moot anyway.

Mindy heard no footsteps and was about to ring again when Cathy opened the door, tightening her terry-cloth robe around her middle. She was a forty-five-year-old version of Willow: tall and firm-limbed with an aquiline nose. Like so many in Nelson, her hair was a frosty blonde, once naturally that shade, and her eyes an Icelandic blue. She looked at Mindy like she'd just let her child pull up all the tulips in her garden.

"Please leave."

"I only need a moment."

"If I didn't know for certain that they're all occupied with more important things, I'd call the police," Cathy said, her voice a steady metronome beat.

"Please, Cathy. Please let me in."

"Why, exactly? What do you want to talk to me about so urgently that you've come over at this time of the morning? Your reprobate son and how he tried to corrupt my daughter?"

"You've know Angus for years. He and Willow are friends. He wouldn't hurt her."

He loves her, Mindy thought but knew better than to say. Mindy didn't have to ask what had made Cathy so protective. She lived in that same space.

"Which you know how, exactly?" Cathy said. "Because *your son* told you so? Please leave."

"I'll leave just as soon as I talk to Willow."

"Even if Willow wasn't on an extended grounding, there is no way I would allow her to talk to you."

"But I think she knows something that will exonerate Angus."

Cathy's eyes narrowed. "Exonerate him for what, exactly?"

"For starting the fire. He didn't do it."

"Well, if that's true, and I'm not saying it is, the police will sort it out."

"I can't leave it at that. He's my son."

"I don't see how that's my concern."

"I think . . . I think Willow was with him that night. That was her in the video, I'm almost certain. And if the police think Angus is guilty, then they'll come after her too. As an accessory, at the very least."

Cathy's right eye twitched. "She had nothing to do with it."

"So she was out that night?"

"I didn't say that."

"What's the 'extended grounding' all about, then?"

"She doesn't know anything about what happened."

"I find that hard to believe. And I'm sure the police will too. I bet they'll be by sometime soon to talk to her. Or maybe they have been already?"

Mindy could tell she'd touched a nerve.

"I most certainly did not let the police talk to my daughter. And our lawyer has made it very clear that she won't be talking to them in the future."

"So, what then? Angus just takes the blame?"

"Everyone has to take responsibility for their actions."

"Why are you so sure he did anything? Maybe Willow's the one who started it."

Cathy crossed her arms over her chest in an effort, Mindy was fairly certain, to keep herself from slamming the door in Mindy's face.

"That's nonsense. Willow would never do such a thing."

"Not even by accident?"

"If she had, she would own up to her mistakes. We've taught her that much."

Mindy's mind raced. "You know what I see on that tape? I see a girl hanging out with a bunch of guys way past curfew. You know how people will talk once it gets out that it's her. You know what people are probably already saying."

"You're disgusting. If you were my child, I'd—"

"Wash my mouth out with soap? Come on. I'm simply trying to get you to see the other side of this. Everyone's so quick to jump to conclusions without any facts. That's all I'm trying to do. Get the facts."

"Oh, just let her in, Mom."

Cathy spun around. Willow was standing behind her, her eyes red from crying, her hair pulled back in a sloppy ponytail.

"What did I tell you about leaving your room?"

"You can't hide me up there forever. The truth will come out sometime."

Mindy took a step forward. Cathy resisted her advance for a moment, then backed away. Mindy approached Willow like she might startle at any minute.

"Do you know what happened that night, Willow?"

Willow nodded slowly. Pictures from her childhood hung framed on the walls around her, and in that moment, she didn't look that different from her eight-year-old self.

"Was it you in the video?"

"Yes."

"Did Angus start the fire?"

She shook her head. Some of the tension in Mindy's body fled.

"Do you know why he isn't talking to the police?"

"He's . . . protecting me."

Cathy frowned. "Protecting you? From what?"

Willow looked miserable.

"Can you prove he didn't start the fire, Willow?"

"I think so."

CHAPTER 40

I Know What You Did

Elizabeth

Our ride to the precinct is a silent one. Ben keeps glancing over at me from his side of his jeep without saying anything, and John Phillips seems to have retreated into himself.

He'd followed us to the car like a lost puppy. After everything that's happened to him, I thought we might as well bring him with us. We can take him back to the shelter afterward. And he has a vested interest in whatever we're going to do at the police station, which I assume has to do with who started the fire, though Ben didn't say much. He doesn't know much, really, only that Mindy called and asked us to be there.

I look down at my bruised and scraped hands. They feel useless, sitting atop my blue hospital scrubs. This was the same outfit John was wearing the first time I met him. He'd lost everything that day. Does that mean I have too?

At this point all I can do is sit back and wait to find out.

Mindy's car is there when we pull into the parking lot behind the precinct. I'd recognize it anywhere with its funny bumper sticker— WATCH OUT FOR THE IDIOT BEHIND ME. Peter stuck it on her car one year and waited till she noticed.

When we get closer, I can see that she's still sitting in the car, apparently having an argument with someone I vaguely recognize as one of her neighbors. There's also a girl about Angus's age sitting in the backseat. The girl climbs out and slams the car door behind her. She pulls the hood of her sweatshirt up over her head like she wants to disappear.

Oh God, I'm such an idiot. It's a wonder Rich ever hired me.

That's the girl in the video with Angus. Angus's girl.

Ben turns off the engine.

"Shall we get to it?"

All six of us walk into the station together. Mindy gives us the once-over—me in my hospital scrubs, Ben dressed up as a firefighter, and John the cleanest of the lot of us, but still looking like he's spent a night in a cave—and her eyes knit together in confusion.

"What's he doing here?" Mindy asks, her eyes resting on John.

"He was with me at the hospital. Long story. How's Angus? Have they let you see him?"

I can feel her resistance to talk to me like we're opposing magnets.

"Yesterday. I saw him yesterday."

"That must've been hard. Have you learned something? Is that why you called Ben?"

"You were at the hospital? Are you okay?"

"Yes," I say, my hand hovering above my stomach. "We are okay." Recognition floods her face. "Oh, Beth. That's wonderful."

"It is. Complicated, but wonderful."

"You were at the Fall Fling?"

"Yeah."

"And your house?" she asks. "Is your house okay?"

I put my hand on her arm. "Mindy, if you keep being nice to me, I'm going to break down right here."

"I'll stop, then."

"You'd better."

We give each other tired smiles.

"That Angus's girlfriend?" I ask.

"She is. And maybe his savior too."

"What does she know?"

Mindy shrugs, and we walk into the bullpen. Detective Donaldson is in his office. He looks haggard from being up all night helping to manage the evacuation. His desk is littered with Styrofoam cups, and the smell of stale coffee hangs in the air like a cloud.

We crowd around his doorway. He looks at us, a motley crew of trouble, and shakes his head.

"I'm sorry, folks, but we're closed for business. We've handed over control of the evac to the Staties, and I'm headed home to get some sleep. It's all-hands-on-deck, otherwise."

Mindy steps forward. "My son needs to be released."

"We've spoken about this, Mrs. Mitchell. His bail hearing is tomorrow morning. You show up there with your lawyer, and you'll probably be able to bond him out. No promises, though. He might be considered dangerous."

"Angus is not dangerous," I say. "That's ridiculous."

"We have information that will prove he's innocent," Mindy adds.

"What information is that?"

Mindy looks at Willow. Her mother takes a protective step in front of her.

"Do you have something to say, young lady?"

Willow shrinks under our collective gaze, but then her head turns toward the stairs, where Deputy Clark is leading Angus up from the basement. They haven't got him in a jumpsuit, thank God, but his clothes are rumpled and look slept in, if it's even possible to sleep in one of those cells.

"What's going on here?" he asks. His voice is hoarse, like he hasn't used it in a while.

"I could ask you the same thing," Detective Donaldson says.

"He needed to use the bathroom," Deputy Clark says.

"That's not what I meant. Young man, are you sure you don't want to talk to us, or are you going to let this young woman do the talking for you?"

Mindy makes a muted mewling sound and tenses like she wants to run to Angus. I hold on to her arm. "Steady. They aren't going to let you touch him," I say quietly.

Angus is staring at Willow, his face red, hollows under his eyes.

"Get out of here," he says.

"Yes," Cathy says. "I think that's an excellent idea."

She tugs on Willow's arm, but Willow won't budge.

"No, Mom. No. We have to tell, Angus. I have to tell."

Angus keeps shaking his head, but Willow has the sheriff's full attention now.

"If you know something, I'm going to have to insist you tell me. Your young man has been no help at all."

"He's not her young man," Cathy says.

"Yes, he is, Mom. I know I'll probably be grounded forever now or something, but Angus . . . He loves me, Mom. And I love him."

Mindy is shaking like a leaf next to me, and there are tears on her face. One glance at her tells me everything she's feeling: hope.

"Don't be ridiculous, you're only sixteen."

"What does that have to do with anything? What does that have to do with what happened that night?"

"Willow," Cathy and Angus say together.

"No, Angus. No. You can't protect me anymore. Not like this."

He flops down onto a bench and buries his face in his hands.

Willow walks past her mother and stands in front of Detective Donaldson. "Do you need to write what I say down or something?"

A few minutes later, Willow is sitting in front of Detective Donaldson. He's got a notebook open in front of him, and a mini-recorder's red

light is blinking next to her. Her mother is sitting in the other chair
in his office, while I'm standing in the doorway. Everyone else has
been banished to the bullpen.

"Go ahead, Willow."

"Tucker Wells and them, his gang, well, they've been picking on
Angus since last year."

"Why?"

"I think because . . . Tucker has a crush on me. But he's a creep.
He kept bugging me and bugging me, and one day I told him I
liked Angus. I figured that would make him go away."

"And did it?"

"For a bit. I mean, he started being nicer to me and to Angus.
We hung out together sometimes. But I knew he was still a jerk."

"Why hang out with him, then?"

She shrugs.

"What happened next?"

"One day, Tucker was teasing me, stupid stuff, I don't remember
exactly, and Angus stood up to him. Told him to leave me alone.
That made Tucker pretty mad."

"What did he do?"

"He was ragging on Angus all the time, you know? He was being
so stupid. And I knew Angus liked me then, so we started hanging
out. I didn't tell anyone because I'm not allowed to see boys."

"Did Tucker know you guys were hanging out?"

"Yeah. He figured it out eventually. That's when he got really
nasty."

"What was he doing?"

"Angus isn't going to get in trouble, right?"

"I think we're past that right now, Willow," I say. "Just tell
Detective Donaldson what you know."

"I'll ask the questions," Detective Donaldson says. "Go on,
Willow. Tell us what happened."

"Last year, Tucker wrote this story in English that got him into a bunch of trouble. About how he wanted to kill his sister? Anyway, his parents got him out of it, but he was pissed at the teacher for turning him in, so he had this cut-up ballet uniform put in his mail cubby."

"What does that have to do with Angus?"

"Angus put it in the mail cubby for him. It was one of his sister's. And he's good at getting into places. Like bypassing alarms and things like that? He figured out what the code was to the teacher's lounge and put it in there one day after school. That was when he thought he and Tucker were friends. I told him not to trust Tucker, but he didn't listen."

"I don't get the connection," Detective Donaldson said.

Willow shakes her head. "Tucker figured out Angus and I were still hanging out this summer, and he started to threaten to tell on Angus. About the ballet uniform."

"When was that?"

"A couple of weeks ago. I told Angus to tell him to get lost, but Angus was really worried about what would happen to him if the school found out. And I was pretty mad at him."

"Mad at Angus?"

"Yeah."

"Why?"

"I didn't know he'd done that with the leotard."

"Then what happened?"

"We got into this big fight last weekend. Then Tucker messaged me that a bunch of them were sneaking out that night, and I decided to go."

"To make Angus jealous?"

She nodded. "I forwarded the messages to Angus so he could see I was going out with them. He wrote me back saying it was a bad idea, but I didn't listen. I don't know why I did that."

"Did you sneak out of the house?"

"Yeah. I met up with them near the town square."

"Is that you on the video? You've seen it?"

"It's me. I thought there were going to be other girls too, but when I got there it was just Tucker and the guys he hangs around with. And Tucker was acting like he'd won some bet or something when I showed up, so I texted Angus. I told him we were going to John Phillips's house."

"Why did you go there?"

"Tucker has this weird obsession with him. I think those guys have been playing pranks on him for a while. They're such a bunch of jerks."

"What happened when you got to his house?"

"We just sat around the fire pit. Tucker brought beers with him—I think he stole them from his dad—and he was drinking them real fast. He wanted me to drink too, but I said I wouldn't. Then he tried to kiss me." She looks down at her shoes. "I pushed him off me, and then Angus was there and he kind of jumped on Tucker. Those other guys were about to beat Angus up, but I said I'd start screaming, so Angus and Tucker kind of tumbled around on the ground for a bit, and then Angus punched Tucker in the side real hard, and Tucker rolled into the bushes and puked."

"What happened next, Willow?"

Willow wipes the tears from her cheeks.

"Tucker and them took off, and Angus walked me home."

"There must be more to this," Detective Donaldson says. "There's no reason you couldn't have told us all this a long time ago."

"We couldn't. Tucker was kind of . . . um, blackmailing us."

"What was Tucker blackmailing you with?"

Willow stays silent for what seems like a very long time as her face turns red. She's avoiding making eye contact with her mother, who has shoved her hand in her mouth in horror. Then she says, "Pictures."

"What kind of pictures?"

"Some . . . some private pictures I took for Angus. All the girls do it," she said, equally defensive and embarrassed.

"Did Angus ask you to take these pictures?"

"No! I just wanted him to know how much I liked him. But it was really stupid. And I'm never going to do it again, okay, Mom. I'm not."

"How did Tucker get these pictures?"

"I forgot to erase them from my phone. He was bugging me one day at my locker, and he took my phone when I wasn't looking, and he found them. I guess he e-mailed them to himself. I didn't even know he had them until this week."

"What was he going to do with them?"

"Send them to everyone in school."

"But why?"

"Because Angus said he'd tell everyone Tucker started the fire to get back at him for trying to kiss me. He wasn't trying to get Tucker in real trouble. But when Tucker said he had those pictures, Angus told him he'd talk to the police unless he gave the pictures back. But Tucker wouldn't give them back, so we didn't know what to do."

"So, it *was* Tucker who started the fire?"

"No. I mean, he did make a fire in the fire pit, but it was small and it was almost out, and then after those guys left, Angus and I poured the rest of the beer on it and we made sure it was out."

"That's a bit hard to believe given what's happened."

"But we know who started it. Angus and me. We saw."

"What did you see?"

Willow turns and points at someone who's visible through the glass wall of Detective Donaldson's office. John Phillips. "We saw him start the fire."

CHAPTER 41

Flaws in the System

John

John woke that night from a fitful sleep.

In fact, he'd never fallen asleep, not really, just skimmed along the surface of it like trailing your fingers in the water over the edge of a sailboat.

It was those damn papers. That thick buff envelope sitting in the middle of the dining-room table where he'd left it after finding it on his front step when he returned from the grocery store.

He didn't think you could just leave envelopes like that on someone's front stoop. Not when the papers inside said you were going to lose your house and everything in it if you didn't come up with more money than you'd ever had in your whole sixty-seven years. Seemed to John like you'd have to hand those kinds of papers to a person directly. Give them a chance to know there was terrible news inside before they opened it. Give them time to work up to the moment.

But maybe that's just how it went on the TV. He didn't know. All he knew was that's what the papers said, far as he could understand them through all the *whereas*es and *aforesaid*s.

Why couldn't people just write what they mean, anyhow?

"You have not paid your mortgage in six months, and so now we are going to take your house away from you." This John could understand. This John knew was coming. Sometime. Just not that day, in a thick manila envelope waiting innocently for him after he'd spent all the money he had to spend that week on nearly expired tuna fish and reduced-price bread.

He turned on the lumpy mattress, trying to find a more comfortable position. The bed creaked loudly, and he was completely awake now. Awake and unsure of how he was ever going to get to sleep again. Not with that . . . that intruder in the house, yes, that's what the envelope was, an intruder in his life. Well, he'd dealt with intruders before, hadn't he?

He swung his legs over the side of the bed, a plan forming. He slung on the worn bathrobe Kristy bought him for their last Christmas together, three years ago that had been. He liked to think she'd be sympathetic about his current situation, but something told him she'd just shake her head in that way she had, taking a deep drag on her perpetual cigarette.

"You never could plan worth a damn," Kristy would say in a voice that'd grown raspy and hard. John remembered how beautiful and soft her voice had been when he'd met her in the church choir, but that was a long time ago.

"Ayuh," John said into the stillness, like Kristy might be able to hear his laconic agreement with the words he imagined she would say if he were talking out his plan with her, seeking her approval or amendment.

But silence was his answer, just as it had been every day since she'd died.

"Ayuh," he said again, like a bullfrog greeting the night. He was comforted by the sound of someone talking, even if it was only himself. "That ought to do the trick."

Plan at the ready, he belted his robe against the chill and crept down the stairs. Silence was a key part of the operation. You had to be careful not to startle an intruder. You never knew how they were going to react when caught. That was the way people got killed. Like that eighteen-year-old Mexican kid who almost died right down the street about a year ago, when he was found creeping around Rayland Irving's living room. Rayland didn't give him a chance to explain. He'd just pumped off both barrels of his shotgun, *blam! blam!*, and that was that.

'Course, the envelope couldn't hear him coming. It didn't know he'd picked up a package of cheap diner matches from the bowl full of them in the hallway, left over from when he used to bring them home for Kristy so she'd never want for a light. And it surely wasn't aware of the fire pit at the back of his property or his intentions in that regard.

John slid his feet quietly against the cold floor. In the living room, he stared at the package, watched the way it reflected the moonlight that streamed through the windows he'd washed only the other day. He could hear his own breathing in the gravelike house. Silent like the grave. *Where did that expression come from?* he wondered before telling himself to focus.

He scooped up the envelope. Working quickly now, he held it against his chest and rammed his feet into the gum boots he always kept by the back door. The porch door swung behind him, oiled silent, and now he was outside. It was actually warmer outside than in, the leftovers of the warm breeze that had been blowing all summer, drying out the air, the trees, the grass, still lingering despite the hour. As he walked across his property, the ground crunched underneath him like it was covered in frost. John wondered where he'd be when the snow came. He always loved the first snow, and all the ones that followed, how it made the world go hush, how you could feel alone inside it without feeling lonely.

He reached the fire pit. Some half-charred wood lay in it, just visible in the moonlight he was navigating by. A couple crushed beer cans twinkled up at him. Those damn kids had been here again, drinking on his property. He'd heard them a few nights ago but hadn't had the gumption to confront them.

No gumption. That was Kristy's voice again. Well, he was showing her, wasn't he? He'd show everyone.

He placed the envelope on top of the logs and flipped open the book of matches. They were old, having sat in the bowl for years collecting dust, and it took him several tries to light one. When the fourth one finally caught, he bent his stiff knees and held the yellow flame to the envelope's corner. It had some kind of coating on it, and it took a moment to catch. The flame licked John's fingers, and he dropped the match, cursing. He put his thumb in his mouth, sucking it, while he watched the thick legal papers slowly burn.

When he was sure it was well and lit, that there wasn't any undoing what he'd done, he turned back toward his house.

So as the fire receded behind him, he didn't see the charred corner of the envelope detach, glowing, as it rose into the air and came to rest at the edge of the longer wheat-colored grass that surrounded his property.

Instead, all he thought as he sucked his still-stinging thumb and slopped back to his house in his crunching gum boots was: *Maybe now I can sleep.*

CHAPTER 42

Corralled

Mindy

When Mindy got home with Angus hours later, Peter and Carrie were waiting for them on the front stoop.

It had been a slow drive through eerily quiet streets. The smoke was pea-soup thick. When Mindy turned on her fog lights briefly, the world disappeared, like they were inside a snow globe.

It was just the four of them in the car. Mindy, Angus, Willow, Cathy. Cathy was a tight ball of anger and kept pulling at her seatbelt like Carrie used to do when she was little, claiming it was strangling her. Angus and Willow were mirrors of each other in the backseat. Each in their separate corner, but with a hand laid flat on the seat between them, the edges of their fingers touching.

Was this something lasting between them? Mindy wondered. Would this experience bring them closer together, or would Willow's sacrifice of her privacy be too much for Angus? Their combined explanation for why they didn't tell about John Phillips's involvement sooner was that they didn't think anyone would believe them, that they didn't want to get him in trouble, and that they'd get into so much trouble themselves for being out that night in the first place.

When Detective Donaldson pointed out that this didn't explain Angus's silence once the video came out, Angus said Tucker had threatened him again, saying that if he said anything, he'd send out the pictures. Tucker *had* started a fire that night, and he didn't know they'd seen John Phillips start one later. For all Tucker knew, he was the source of the fire. And Angus didn't see how there was any way he could explain everything without it all coming out. The pictures. The blackmail. He couldn't take the risk. Besides, it was his fault Willow was in trouble. He'd made some joke once about pictures—it was just a joke, he swore—but she'd taken them anyway and look what happened. He deserved to be punished for that, didn't he?

Mindy was stunned by both the insight and naïveté of his thinking. He hadn't thought there'd be any long-term consequences, she realized. Like a teenage smoker who casts off the possibility of lung cancer. Not because he didn't accept that the risks were real, but because he believed his youth provided some kind of cloak of invincibility. His future wasn't set, it was something malleable, avoidable.

When they reached Cathy's house, Cathy nearly dragged Willow from the backseat before the car came to a full stop. But Willow broke free from her mother's grasp to come around to Angus's side of the car. He had his window down and she leaned in and kissed him, so briefly it was almost nothing. Then she turned and ran up her front steps and into her house.

A silent moment later they were at their own house. Peter and Carrie were right inside the door as if they'd been waiting for them at the window. For the first time in a year, Angus let himself be hugged by his father, his sister. He hugged them back too, hard and long like he used to do when he returned from a month away at summer camp and his friends weren't around to hoot and holler at the sissiness of it.

When he finally let go, he headed straight for the shower, throwing promises over his shoulder that he'd tell Peter everything as soon as he'd washed away the jail smell and burned the clothes he was wearing. Carrie screamed with laughter at his awkward choice of words, and he flashed a smile, so good to see.

Whether he, or any of them, would be able to lather off the memories, doubt, and tension this week created was something Mindy was already worried about, until she reminded herself she wasn't going to worry anymore. She was going to hold on to this new state inside her. She felt like an old motor that had turned over after one last try, the try made just to be sure. Her resolve kept threatening to stall out, but she was keeping a steady foot on the accelerator. She felt both exhilarated and exhausted all at once.

This reprieve was short-lived. When Carrie retreated to the garage "because all this drama is seriously interfering with my training," Peter put the kettle on for tea and told her they had a decision to make. The fire still wasn't under control, and the evacuation order had been extended on a voluntary basis to the whole town.

"I think we should go," Peter said.

"But Angus just got home."

"I know. But I don't want to get caught in the chaos. I've been talking to people about what happened at the Fall Fling. Did you know that twenty-five people ended up in the hospital?"

"Elizabeth."

"What about her?"

"She was in the hospital."

"You've been in touch with her?"

"She was at the police station. I asked Ben to bring her in case I couldn't get Detective Donaldson to listen to Willow."

"You can fill me in on everything in the car."

"Where will we go? The elementary school?"

"I was thinking somewhere further. What about Zion National Park? We've always talked of going."

"You want to go camping in the middle of all this? What about school? What about work?"

"I called Jim, and he's okay with giving me a couple weeks off. And I called ahead—there's a hotel, well, really a motel, that's having a special right outside the park. I think it would be good. For Angus. For us."

Mindy's brain was spinning. These last few days, she'd thought of nothing but getting Angus out of trouble. What would happen afterward wasn't something she'd let filter into her thoughts. But now, they were there. At the end of this. And what was there to do? How were they supposed to mend and move life forward? Was Angus supposed to go back to school when it resumed, assuming there was a school to go back to, and pick up teenagehood where he'd left off? And what about her and Peter? What about the life she'd been living a week ago? Spin class and errands and nothing, really, that was connected to the person she thought she'd end up being?

"Yes. Okay. Let's go."

She leaned into Peter and kissed him hard, like she did at the party the night they met, surprising both of them.

"Thank you," she said. "Thank you for thinking of this."

"It's our family, Min."

"It is. A good family."

"I'm going to start packing the car. Can you get Carrie out of the garage?"

"This motel doesn't happen to have a ballet barre somewhere, does it?"

He smiled. "No place is perfect."

"This place has been. Pretty close to."

"We don't need perfect," Peter said. "Let's just go for ordinary."

Mindy got Carrie out of the garage easily. The words *road trip* were barely out of her mouth before Carrie was sprinting, tap, tap, tap, toward the house asking whether there was a pool where they were going to stay. Mindy told her to ask her father, but she wasn't sure Carrie had heard her. As someone whose happiness often came from others, Mindy felt Carrie's joy shoot through her. This would be good. This would be what they needed.

Mindy walked toward the garage door and clicked it open. She took their daypacks and water bottles from the container where they kept them and brought them to Peter's car, leaning them up against the side. Just to be able to breathe clean air would do them all wonders, she thought, her eyes itching. To see the sky, clear of smoke. Or were those clouds? Who could tell anymore.

She went back into the garage and looked around for something else that needed to be moved, or put in place, but there was nothing. She ran her hand along Carrie's barre—smooth, polished wood that was slightly shinier at the place where Carrie normally stood. She put her own hand in that spot, her feet slipping into first position for the first time since she'd shown the basic positions to Carrie when she was four. Her right knee protested at the turnout, but she dipped into a plié anyway, first demi, then full. Maybe when they got back, she should take that adult ballet class they were holding at Carrie's studio. And find some work. Something more than the volunteering she'd been doing and hating. She had the beginning of an idea of what that might be, but she didn't want to fully voice the thought, not even to herself. Not yet.

"Carrie looks just like you," Elizabeth said.

Mindy turned around, less gracefully than she would have liked. "I must look funny standing here."

"Not at all," Beth said. She was still dressed in her hospital scrubs. *Because she didn't have a home to go back to,* Mindy thought. *Not right now. Maybe not ever.* "I always wished I could do that."

"You could. Anyone can."

She shrugged. "Soon I'll be too big to do anything."

"That is such great news, though."

"It is."

They stood there, staring at each other. Mindy couldn't remember a silence like this between them. From the beginning, they'd always been so easy together, filling the air with idle chatter, gossip, and the deeper stuff too. For the last year, Mindy had been living with all of that in her head, along with a fistful of regrets.

"Why are you here, Elizabeth? Do you need something?"

"Ben brought me."

"Oh, I see," Mindy turned away, tears forming. "Well, we're about to leave so, if there wasn't anything . . ."

"Min, come on. Of course there's something."

"Something Ben thinks you should say?"

"Yes, but that doesn't mean I don't mean it too."

"Mean what?"

"I'm sorry. I'm really sorry. I was cruel. I froze you out. I pushed you away because I needed to push everyone away. I did it to you. I did it to Ben. And I've nearly lost everything because of it."

"From where I'm standing, you seem to be getting everything you've always wanted."

Elizabeth laughed then, a full belly laugh that left her clutching her side with a frown of worry.

"Everything okay?"

"I've been cramping, but the doctors say it's nothing."

"I bet it doesn't feel like nothing."

"No. It really doesn't."

"What was so funny, then?"

"If you knew what a complete disaster my life has been recently . . ."

"So tell me about it."

"Now?"

"No, we're going out of town for a while. But maybe, when I get back?"

"I'd like that. I really would."

"I would too," Mindy said. "And I'm sorry too. Those things I said, about it being your fault you couldn't get pregnant. That was so awful. You can't imagine how bad I've felt."

"Oh, I can imagine."

Elizabeth took a step toward her and folded her into a hug.

"I've really missed you, you know?"

"I've missed you too."

CHAPTER 43

The Smell of Rain

Elizabeth

When I climb back into our car after I say good-bye to Mindy, I'm not sure where we should go. I suggest we go to Ben's parents, like he mentioned earlier, but he's talked to them and they're resting, and in the end, he says, he doesn't want to go there. He feels too restless, and maybe we should just check into a hotel or something.

"Everything's booked," I say. I'd checked at some point earlier this week, when I thought I might have to find somewhere other than Ben's parents to stay for a while. The only places left were places we could only afford if Ben's parents were paying, or if I only intended to stay there for an hour or two to turn a trick.

"What do you suggest?" Ben asks. His leg is bobbing up and down.

"You seem really jumpy."

"Yeah. I . . . I don't know what to do with myself."

I have the odd urge to start singing Dusty Springfield's "I Just Don't Know What to Do With Myself," only the White Stripes version. But I'm a terrible singer, and that would be a really weird thing to do, wouldn't it?

"How about we go to my office?" I say. "I have a change of clothes in my desk. And then we'll figure it out from there?"

He agrees. Is that a good sign, or only a sign that he's being kind to his pregnant, likely homeless, soon-to-be-ex-wife? Or maybe it simply hasn't occurred to him that we could go our separate ways today. That he doesn't need to be chauffeuring me about town or anywhere. That he could cut whatever ties still bind us, and sail away. But that's me forgetting about the baby again, and now I get it. He's worried about him or her. He's still here because of the part of him inside me. And sometime today he's going to tell me that. When his mind settles down. When I've stopped doubling over with cramps.

When I tell him it's okay for him to go.

Ben drops me off at the office and says he's going to see if he can rustle us up some sandwiches.

"If Sandwich Time hasn't been abandoned," he says with a smirk, but there's a good chance it has been. Driving over here from Mindy's was like driving through a stage lot—the buildings all look fake-fronted, cardboard cutouts of some real, lived-in place, somewhere else.

I find the clothes I remembered in my desk drawer—black yoga pants and a long sweatshirt. There's even fresh underwear, socks, and a bra. I had some notion, when I started working here, that I might have the need to change my clothes after combing through a dumpster or chasing down a witness who didn't want to talk to me. Really, I was imagining myself as Laura Holt from *Remington Steele*, all tousled in the dirt while Rich stood by watching. Only Rich is no Remington Steele, far from it.

I find Rich sitting at his desk, a bottle of whiskey open before him. It's the first time I've ever seen Rich in jeans or a T-shirt. He looks far from himself, the only connection being his ever-present cowboy boots.

He's staring out the window at his regular view: the Peak, the fire, the abandoned town. I try to remember if I know where he lives in all this mess, but I come up empty. Probably somewhere safe, like Ben's parents, or his sister. I scan his office, looking for an image I remember. I find it on his ego wall—a picture of him and Honor and Tucker. His hand is on Tucker's shoulder.

"You've heard?" I say. "About John Phillips?"

"I just came from speaking to Detective Donaldson."

"I guess I was wrong, after all."

"Seems like."

I sit in the chair in front of him, wondering if I should say what's on my mind. He could fire me on the spot. And really, I have no evidence but my suspicions, which haven't proven to be the most reliable of late.

But, what the hell? Might as well get as many answers as I can today.

"You're the one who leaked it, right?"

His gaze shifts away from the window. "What's that?"

"The surveillance video. You knew Tucker was involved somehow, and you knew if that video came out, the police would be more likely to believe Tucker's story. Blame Angus."

"That's ridiculous."

"You've been steering me away from him from the beginning. You didn't want me to go ask questions at the school. You didn't want me looking into anyone but John Phillips."

"And John Phillips was responsible."

"But you didn't know that. You thought Tucker started it. What happened? Did Honor tell you something? Maybe that Tucker had been out that night?"

His eyelids flicker.

"That's it, isn't it? After John Phillips pointed the finger at a group of kids, before he knew who Tucker was. Honor came to you, didn't she? She knew he'd been out that night. Thought he'd started the fire. That's why she's been volunteering at the school so much."

"I'd tread lightly, Elizabeth. Very, very lightly."

"You were taking an awful risk. Putting your job on the line like that. You must love Tucker very much. He's like a son to you, isn't he?"

"We never had any children," he says, after a moment, twisting his wedding ring around his finger.

"But what about Angus? What about John Phillips? Didn't they deserve your protection?"

"No one could've predicted that kid would allow the blame to be placed on his shoulders. Why would anyone do such a thing?"

"Because your nephew was bullying him and his girlfriend."

He shudders and takes another drink. "John Phillips did it. I said that from the beginning."

"John Phillips did it," I agree, "but that isn't what matters."

"I think you should go."

I stand. "I'll be back for my things."

"We got the right man," Rich says as if he hasn't heard me. "It's the result that matters."

"I used to believe that. Now I'm not so sure."

I find Ben in the car outside, a bag of sandwiches on my seat, two cans of soda resting in the drink holders. He asks me where to, and part of me wants to say, let's get out here, let's do what Mindy and Peter are doing and just pick up and leave. But I've been do- ing that my whole life, moving on, never staying in one place for long. I called it my job, but that's what I was doing. Never sticking anywhere. Putting my life at risk. Cloaking everything I was doing in the sanctity of saving others.

I've got to learn to stick. Stay. Root myself. Whether Ben's a part of that or not. I owe it to the child we're going to have.

I owe it to myself.

"Wanna go watch the fire?" I ask.

He doesn't say anything, just puts the car in gear and drives to the arts center—as close as we'll be able to get without being in anyone's way.

He parks the car, and we get out. Something feels like it's shifted in the air. Underneath the smoke there's another smell I can't quite identify. But standing out here long enough to figure it out isn't an option. Ash is falling around us, and it's difficult to breathe. I follow Ben inside. Last night it was full of people. Now it's deserted like the rest of the town. A fireman's radio crackles from where it was forgotten on a table. I pick it up and listen.

I hear Kara's voice and hit the "Transmit" key.

"IC Panjabi, this is Martin," I say. "Is a status update possible?"

"Good to hear your voice, Martin," she says after a moment. "We're kind of busy here."

"Understood."

"I just posted an update."

"Hand me your phone?" I say to Ben.

I go to ForestFires.com and load up the latest report. A hint of good news. They've held the fire at the ridge, pushed it back, and contained it from spreading down the slope to our house.

"We going to need a new house?" Ben asks.

"Looks like maybe not."

"I've always liked that house."

"I love that house."

The radio crackles again. "You still there, Martin?" Andy says.

"Here, Thomas. You all right?"

"Affirmative. You?"

I meet Ben's eyes. "Affirmative."

"You take care," he says, and all that's left is static.

I put the radio down, waiting for Ben to say something.

"He's a good guy, Andy," he says.

"He is."

"And I get it, now, sort of."

"Get what?"

"This," he says, turning to take the Peak into the sweep of his arm. "Fighting against it. What you've been doing all these years. When I was helping Andy last night, I felt kind of . . . alive in a way I haven't before. Useful."

"It's the adrenaline."

"Sure, maybe. But we were really doing something. Making a difference. I don't want you to give it up."

"Really? You were saying just the other day how you hated my job."

"I hate how it takes you away from me. But you haven't been happy since you quit. And I feel guilty about that."

"You didn't ask me to quit. In fact, if I remember right, you told me I shouldn't."

"But I didn't insist. I should have. I should've seen how important it was to you."

"What you do is important too. Think of all of those kids you help."

"You mean like Tucker?"

"Okay, maybe not him. But you never know, this might be a turning point for him."

"Maybe. And for us?"

My mouth goes dry. *Don't screw this up, Elizabeth. Don't you dare.*

"I want that more than anything, but only if—"

"If we really forgive each other?"

"Yes. Can you?"

"I want to. You?"

"I want to too. I want to forgive myself."

"How do we do that?"

"You're asking me? I'm the idiot who thought getting divorced would solve things."

He laughs at that. Kind of like how I laughed with Mindy earlier today. Free. Open. Like happiness was possible.

"That maybe wasn't your brightest moment."

"Well, you did agree with me."

"I did."

"And it did get us here."

"It did."

"So maybe it wasn't such a bad thing," we say together. Then smile the smile we always smile when we say something at the same time. Like we did early Tuesday morning, only this time it's a reminder of good things to come, not good things gone away.

Ben reaches out his hand, and I take it. His fingers squeeze mine almost too tightly. I close my eyes for a moment, trying to control the emotions that feel like they might take me over at any moment. There's a loud clap in the distance, and I realize what it was I smelled outside.

"Rain," I say, opening my eyes.

"What?"

We look out the window. The wind has picked up again and seems to be coming from a new direction. We can see the Peak for the first time today. The ridge of flames is no longer visible, though the smoke plume is just as black and ominous. But there's another force at work up there. A cumulonimbus cloud is towering behind it. As we watch, it advances and swallows up the smoke, the Peak, the flames, like it wants to swallow up the town. It's black and angry, and I feel like I'm watching a swarm of Dementors advance on a fresh crop of wizards.

The sky flashes with lightning, and thunder booms again, so close it sets my ears ringing. The cloud sweeps around the building, and now it's raining. A few drops at first, and then it's like a shower someone's turned on full blast.

Rain, rain, *rain*.

"Wanna go outside?" I ask.

"Seriously?"

"Why not?"

I tug on his hand, and we push open the doors and walk into the sheets of water. We do it like I used to walk into the ocean, without hesitation, becoming one with the storm, breathing in the cleansing downpour. We are soaked to the skin in moments, but the rain is so warm that its temperature is almost indistinguishable from our own.

And though it's hard to see anything, Ben's grip is tight in mine, and I know in my bones that everything's going to be okay.

Acknowledgments

You'd think, after five books and one novella (!) that these things would get easier, and yet, no.

That being said, I must give thanks to:

Cam, Therese, Kathleen, and Lisa for reading early drafts and telling me this book didn't suck. And to Allie for insisting I write the book in the first place.

My mom for the constant typo checking and smiley faces in the margins.

Therese, Therese, and Kathryn for an awesome writers' retreat where a section of this book was written. My hand is raised to tell the next story.

My friends for having my back and making me laugh and supporting this weird adventure I go on every year or so.

Ditto to David, who bears the brunt of the clattering of my laptop when we're supposed to be watching TV together.

My four nephews (Owen, Liam, William, and Anders) for making my life more full.

My editor, Tara Parsons, for her unbridled enthusiasm, and the whole team at Lake Union for their amazing work on this book, and *Hidden* before it.

My agent, Abigail Koons, who's always in my corner and makes it possible for me to keep doing this.

My writing partners, Adrian Wills and Martin Michaud, for collaborating on other projects that will hopefully see the light of day eventually.

To each and every one of my readers who continue to let me dream for a living.

To the members of the Fiction Writers Co-op for support, laughs, and wisdom.

And to Shawn Klomparens, for introducing me to Jackson Hole.

Reading Group Guide for *Smoke*

1. When the book begins, Elizabeth and Ben's marriage is on the verge of breaking up, but their personal crisis is overshadowed by a forest fire that is threatening their town and their home. Can natural disasters have a positive side, in that they help us reprioritize our lives? Or are the same problems that we had before going to resurface once the crisis is over?

2. Some of the couple's issues had to do with all the things Elizabeth hid from Ben in their marriage. Why do you think she kept so much from him? What does hiding things from a spouse do to a marriage?

3. Elizabeth felt that she needed to choose her husband and the hope of having a child over her career. Do you feel that this was a fair sacrifice for her to make? How did this contribute to the problems in her marriage?

4. When we first meet Mindy, she's friends with a group of catty women whom she doesn't seem to like. Why do you think she stayed friends with them? Does this contribute to her unhappiness? Have you ever been friends with people you didn't like out of expediency or for other reasons?

5. What are the similarities and differences between Mindy and Elizabeth?

6. At first, we don't know who set the fire that's threatening Nelson, Ben, and Elizabeth's house. What does this mystery reveal about the characters?

7. Mindy evolves in this story from a shrinking violet to a strong character intent on defending her children. She also might have caused some issues in her own marriage in the process. What do you think the future holds for her?

8. Elizabeth never had a sexual affair with her coworker Andy, but they did seem to have a deep emotional connection. Do you think someone can have an emotional affair? If so, is this as bad, or worse, than a physical one?

9. As you were reading the novel, did you hope that Ben and Elizabeth would reconcile by the end? Why or why not?